The Sexton Blake Library

Published 2020 by Rebellion Publishing Ltd,
Riverside House, Osney Mead, Oxford, OX2 0ES, UK

ISBN: 978 1 78108 782 4

10 9 8 7 6 5 4 3 2 1

A CIP catalogue record for this book is available
from the British Library.

Designed & typeset by Rebellion Publishing Ltd

Cover art by Crush Creative

Printed in Denmark

The Sexton Blake Library

ANTHOLOGY I: SEXTON BLAKE
AND THE GREAT WAR

Selected, edited and discussed by Mark Hodder and Sexton Blake

BAKER STREET, LONDON

STEPPING INTO HIS room was like stepping back through time. The decor and furniture were Edwardian, the atmosphere was hazy with blue tobacco smoke, and logs were crackling behind an antique fireguard.

He gestured me into a scuffed leather armchair and settled in the one opposite.

I stretched out my legs to allow my rain-soaked trouser bottoms to dry and I stared at him.

He exactly resembled the portraits by the best of his illustrators, Eric Parker. If you were to merge a photograph of a young George Sanders with one of a young Boris Karloff, you'd get the picture. There was a well-contoured brutality about the face. Handsome, cultured, charismatic, but very, very dangerous. I could well understand how Mademoiselle Yvonne Cartier and all those other remarkable women had fallen under his spell. It was in his eyes, especially. They were a strange, gleaming blueish grey, like quicksilver, and missed nothing. I felt them rapidly assessing every detail of me, leaving me, in less than a minute, with the disconcerting notion that he already knew me better than I knew myself.

Thunder rumbled and rain pattered against the windowpane.

"Cigarette?" he asked, proffering a silver case.

I waved it away. "Those things will kill you."

He gave a wry smile.

I had, with that comment, acknowledged and accepted the limitations placed on this interview; the questions—specifically those pertaining to his longevity—that I was not permitted to ask.

"Well then," he said, leaning back and striking a match. "Where would you like to begin?"

Audio recording had been prohibited, so I opened my notepad and clicked my ballpoint. We were going to do this the old-fashioned way. "How about with the author who invented you?"

Again, a slight upward curving of the lips.

He put a hand to a decanter on the table beside him. I nodded. He poured two large measures of brandy and passed one to me.

"Harry Blyth," he said.

"Or Hal Meredith," I said. "His pen name."

"I chose him because he'd done me some small favour."

"This was back in 1893?" I said, conscious of how absurd it sounded.

He steered around that particular query. "Harry was a jobbing writer. He'd done some newspaper work and had a few yarns published in the penny dreadfuls. I was in with Viscount Northcliffe—"

"Alfred Harmsworth," I put in. "Chief of Amalgamated Press."

He grunted an affirmation, drew on his cigarette, and puffed out a cloud of blue smoke. "Harmsworth was keen to jump aboard the Sherlock Holmes bandwagon. Detectives were the big thing. The public was clamouring for more. So I encouraged him to ask Harry to create a new one. Harry came up with Gideon Barr."

"Who?"

"Exactly. I had to put him right. Paid him a visit. 'Harry,' I said to him. 'My name is not Gideon Barr, my name is Sexton Blake, and this is what you're going to write.' Then I outlined my scheme."

"Which was?"

"Try the brandy," he said. "It's really very good."

I did and it was.

Blake drew on his cigarette again and watched its smoke billow toward the high ceiling.

"Mainly," he murmured. "I wanted my abilities exaggerated in order to disconcert my enemies."

"In essence, propaganda."

"Yes. I made a science of it. I was the first to do so."

"If you'll forgive the observation, that first story, which appeared in the Halfpenny Marvel story paper, was pretty dreadful."

He quirked an eyebrow. "Bluntly said, but I don't disagree. The early tales were silly melodramas replete with mustachio-twirling villains and utterly implausible coincidences. It was the style of the time. Nevertheless, they were inspired by real cases and they served their purpose."

I resisted the temptation to gulp at the brandy. I felt nervous but I wanted a clear head.

I said, "Why did Mr Blyth sell the rights to the character to Harmsworth?"

"Because I told him to do so. Even in those early days of my career, I was dealing with too many cases for a single writer to document. Also—" He paused, reached for his glass, took a sip, put it down, and examined the tip of his cigarette. "Also, I was a qualified doctor with a sharp eye. Harry had a weak constitution and pushed himself too hard. I knew he wasn't going to be around for much longer."

"He died of typhoid fever in 1898."

"He did, poor fellow. By that point, Harmsworth was already distributing my case notes to other writers. In their hands, the Blake character gradually gained popularity."

"But—" I hesitated and cleared my throat. "But why that popularity? I mean, if you'll forgive the observation, the character was little different to all the other detectives crowding the pages of the story papers."

He smiled again.

They came to him quickly and easily, those smiles. They were fleeting but warm and authentic.

Another pause, another taste of tobacco, another sip of brandy; a man at ease with himself, in no hurry, commanding and entirely in control.

He said, "The fictional Blake survived for the simple reason that there was a real Blake financing him. As for his lack of distinguishing features, that, I fear, was simply a reflection of the truth. I was still a novice, despite the dramatic nature of my various early adventures. I wasn't, in those days, fully formed. I was trying things out. Different techniques of detection."

"Different assistants," I observed.

"Indeed."

"Even a trained ape, at one point."

"The less said about Griff, the better."

"And then along came Tinker."

He gave a little snort of amusement. "If you meet him, you'd best employ his proper name. Edward Carter is rather embarrassed by his old moniker. Few of us get away with using it nowadays."

"I'll be careful," I said. "The author W. J. Lomax introduced him into the stories in 1904. Was that actually when you met him?"

"Yes. That year and the following were significant ones. Everything pretty much fell into place. Firstly, I happened upon the Baker Street house, which Mrs Bardell had just opened up to lodgers. It so suited my requirements that I rented it complete and became its sole occupant aside from Tinker and the good lady herself. I was thus able to use a room for consultations, another as a laboratory, a third as a photographic dark room, and so forth. Secondly, I was given Pedro the bloodhound by a grateful client. A truly extraordinary dog. And thirdly, I began to build a more functional relationship with Scotland Yard thanks to the grudging support of Detective-Inspector Spearing."

"The house, landlady and dog being added to the stories by William Murray Graydon," I noted.

"One of the greatest of my earlier authors. A tremendously prolific writer."

"And Spearing by Norman Goddard. By the way, did he really speak like that? Spearing? Those short, jerky, incomplete sentences?"

"Yes, as a matter of fact, he did. The mannerism developed after he received one too many blows to the head."

I took another sip of brandy and recalled that a younger Spearing had been the principal protagonist in many "non-Sexton Blake" stories and had seemed quite different in them. Now I had an explanation.

Blake flicked his half-smoked cigarette into the fireplace.

In a contemplative tone, he murmured, "Tinker, Pedro and I getting together changed everything. We were, from the outset, an efficient team."

"Unquestionably," I agreed. "And as soon as the trio was complete, the nature of your cases changed. For the next five years or so, you appeared to throw yourself into investigations that involved adopting roles in many different fields of industry. In 1905, for example, there were accounts entitled—" I consulted my notes. "The Warder Detective, The Army Detective, The Railway Detective, The Navy Detective, The

Fireman Detective, The Cab Driver Detective, The Mechanic Detective, The Post Office Detective, and The River Police Detective. In 1906, you became the reporter detective, the beefeater, the gamekeeper, the diver, the—"

He raised a hand to stop me. "No need to list them all. It was intentional. To be an efficient criminologist, I required knowledge. I wanted to know what people did and how they did it. Therefore, I made myself an expert in as many fields of endeavour as possible."

I shook my head in amazement. "This astonishing drive of yours, it's incredible. Do you attribute it to some particular childhood exp—"

"Off limits!" he snapped.

I stopped and blinked. "I'm—my apologies. I didn't mean to—"

He waggled his fingers dismissively and adopted a gentler tone. "Let's not stray beyond the bounds, hey? I believe we've reached the point of decision. You stated in your letter that you intend the first collection of my old cases to be drawn from those that occurred in the lead up to, and during, the Great War."

I uttered a sound of agreement, reached down to my briefcase beside the chair, and pulled from it a plastic binder. "From the perspective of a reader, it feels like that's when you, at least as a fictional character, really came into your own."

"Blessed be the authors," he responded. He took the proffered binder and put it on his lap. "Yarns from the old Union Jack story paper, I presume. Which have you chosen?"

He opened the binder and looked down at the illustrated cover inside.

"Ah," he said softly. "Ah, yes."

"It can hardly said to have been well-written," I observed, "but it's full of exuberance, which I feel exemplifies the tales of the period."

THE CASE OF THE
NAVAL MANOEUVRES

"WE'RE GOING TO have to talk about political correctness in these stories," I said. "Times have changed. Ethnic slurs aren't acceptable. Should I excise them?"

Blake frowned and I detected a hot spark in his eyes, though it was most likely a flash of lightning reflecting from the window.

"The censoring of history is a characteristic of fascism," he said. "Would it not be preferable to provide context? To mention, perhaps, the truth of empires and how they are maintained?"

I reached for my glass and gulped at the brandy.

For seventy years, Sexton Blake had been an icon of the British Empire—its ambassador to the reading public—and now he wanted me to discuss the truth of what he'd represented?

All right, in for a penny, in for a pound.

I took a breath and said, "Empires invade other countries, exploit their resources, and suppress the native populations. To justify this and to obscure the greed and violence, such expansionism is dressed up as 'extending civilisation,' as 'raising primitives to our exalted level,' as 'helping.' It is loathsome nonsense."

"Quite so," he responded. "And back then, when it became

apparent that a rival empire, in this case a German one, might emerge, the notion that 'British is best' and 'foreigners can't be trusted' became a central theme in popular fiction, perhaps nowhere more so than in the Sexton Blake yarns. The authors were simply being patriotic. Were they able to step outside of their age and regard it with an impartial eye, I daresay the anti-German sentiment would have felt as unpleasant to them as it now does to us."

I said, "And the role you played in demeaning the subjected and demonising the enemy, how do you feel about that?"

"Steady now," he admonished. "I didn't write the stories."

"Nevertheless, the language attributed to you was remarkably jingoistic at times."

He gave an almost imperceptible shrug. "We are children of the time in which we are immersed, all borne high—and low—by the zeitgeist. It's important that our mistakes and misjudgements remain on record. We can measure our progress—or lack thereof—by them." He sighed. "Our attitude toward foreigners was despicable back then. I don't deny it. Thank goodness we are more self-aware now."

"Are we, though?"

"I think we better know that we are being bad when we are being bad."

I indicated the binder on his lap. "The insults aimed at Germans are perfectly understandable within the context of war. I won't remove them. However, antisemitism and racism directed at non-whites has not yet, regrettably, been completely relegated to the past. Where I encounter instances of them, I'm going to have to hit select-delete."

He gave a jerk of his chin. "With my full approval. Perhaps footnotes to mark the excisions? Allow readers the opportunity to see how much or how little political incorrectness there was on a story-by-story, author-by-author basis?"

I nodded my agreement.

THE CASE OF THE NAVAL MANOEUVRES

by Norman Goddard
UNION JACK issue 253 (1908).

THE FIRST CHAPTER

The Kaiser's Speech—The Base in the North Sea—
What did he mean?—Sexton Blake to decide.

"THESE MANOEUVRES—WHAT will they show?" Colonel von Harmann asked in a rather sneering tone of the junior officer who sat next to him.

"Why, many things," Lieutenant Krantz answered doubtfully. "There is the test of seamanship, the—er—"

"Seamanship!" the colonel growled. "Himmel! What does seamanship count for in a modern sea battle? It would just be hammering away with the great guns, and the one that got the right shot in first would win. A game of chance—like all these affairs of war!"

This conversation was taking place at the mess of the First Regiment of the Kaiser's Pink Dragoons, and, as usual, the conversation after dinner had turned upon the subject of arms, for your German soldier is a man who makes more than a light study of his profession. He loves it until he believes that nothing could stand against his army and its organisation. And on this particular night there were the coming British naval manoeuvres to discuss, the meeting of more than three hundred war vessels in the North Sea. Not for years had such

15

a huge naval demonstration taken place, scarcely ever before had strict secrecy with regard to them been kept to the extent of not allowing even distinguished spectators aboard the ships while the mimic fighting, the attacking and repelling, was in progress.

It was this secrecy most probably that had attracted to the eyes of all countries to the North Sea. Previously Great Britain, proud in her great naval strength, had not hesitated to make quite public all her manoeuvres by sea, yet this time—

Other nations, including some who could scarcely be said to love the little island, were asking each other what it meant.

Colonel von Harmann lit a large cigar, and puffed away jerkily. He felt in the mood for argument, and the young lieutenant was likely to prove rather an easy victim.

"And why," he asked, "has the North Sea been chosen for the scene of this affair?"

Lieutenant Krantz twisted his wineglass between his fingers, and his high German forehead, crowned by bristling hair, puckered thoughtfully. He parted his lips to give an answer, but before he could do so one came right from behind the colonel's chair.

"But I can tell you, friends," it said. "Britain has just awakened to the fact that it is from the North Sea that she is most open to attack."

Colonel von Harmann turned sharply, then sprang to his feet, his hand going up to the salute.

"The Kaiser!" someone else ejaculated; and, with a clattering of chairs, every officer was on his feet.

Wilhelm II, Emperor of Germany, flung off his long military cloak, revealing the fact that he was wearing the uniform of a colonel of the regiment; and certainly, with his upturned moustache, and rather grim expression, he looked a soldier to the life.

"Be seated, comrades," he said quietly. "There is no need for officers to stand to welcome a brother officer."

In obedience to this permission the officers, who numbered rather more than a score, dropped back into their chairs again, and the Kaiser seated himself beside Colonel von Harmann.

"A cigar, your Highness?" the latter suggested, pushing a box forward.

"No, colonel," the Kaiser answered, with rather a wry smile. "The throat is still troublesome. But you were discussing when I came in?"

"The value of these British naval manoeuvres in the North Sea," the colonel answered promptly.

The Kaiser laughed softly and sipped the glass of wine that the colonel had poured out for him.

"Their value?" he echoed.

"Yes, sire," Colonel von Harmann glanced keenly at the upright figure beside him. He knew, as many another powerful man in Germany did, that the Kaiser was perhaps the best informed man in the country, and that his opinion was one to be relied upon.

"So." The Kaiser sipped at his wine again, then the smile died from his lips, and he rose to his feet. Instantly every eye was turned upon him. There was something curiously strong about the rather spare, upright figure.

Memories of other speeches that had stirred the political world, of letters written in hot haste and afterwards repented, entered the minds of the officers present, and some of the older ones regretted that a few civilians were present. Through them things might leap out—things that were better left—

"Comrades"—the Kaiser's voice rang out strongly, though with just the touch of hoarseness that told of a throat liable to give trouble at times—"some of you were discussing why these manoeuvres are to take place in the North Sea.

The explanation is not hard. For years and years the British have thought only of the south as the point where they would be attacked in case of war, and there they have built their great forts, and sunk their mines, and held their ships in readiness, making their position so strong that it would have taken more than an ordinary foe to go against them with a chance of success. But now"—the Kaiser threw out his right arm with a dramatic gesture—"they have looked towards the north, and into their brains has come a certain thought."

There was a pause, so silent that it seemed as if every man in the room was holding his breath.

"In the North lie the Shetland Islands"—the Kaiser spoke slowly and distinctly, as if he did not wish a word to be lost—"unprotected, yet the finest base a force attacking Great Britain could possibly possess."

"Why have we not examined them?" Colonel von Harmann muttered excitedly, but not in so low a tone that the Kaiser failed to hear him.

"But we have!" The Kaiser's voice rang enthusiastically, and there was a grim little smile on his lips. "We have no enmity with England now, but even then we do not blind our eyes to the future. Some day the quarrel may arise—which Heaven forbid—and then it will be remembered that more than once our fleet has cruised there, even anchoring in Lerwick Harbour, and taking soundings of every fathom of the waterway, until our officers know it better than the men of the British navy. So, we have not been idle, and even now that these manoeuvres are to be secret, are there not ways—"

The Kaiser stopped abruptly, and pulled at his moustache. A sudden doubtful light had come into his eyes, and he stood like a man who fears that he has committed himself. Then he sat down, leaving his sentence unfinished, and began to discuss the affairs of the regiment with Colonel von Harmann.

*　　*　　*

"Kaiser's Strange Speech!" Everywhere in London the newsboys were shouting it out, and Londoners, with memories of other speeches, were buying the papers eagerly.

Somehow, most of the details of the German Emperor's speech had leaked out, and for the first time Britishers were realising why the manoeuvres were to take place in the North. Some, strong in geography, were pointing out how easily a hostile fleet could pass from the Shetlands to the Atlantic, and so to the unguarded Western coast.

"Why don't the Admiralty think of these things?" men asked each other.

As a matter of fact, the report of the speech had sent ugly thoughts into the brain of more than one man responsible for the safeguarding of Great Britain, and into none more than that of the Prime Minister himself. He had already taken action, and now he was pacing his study in Downing Street, waiting for the arrival of Mr. Henry Kennard, Chief Lord of the Admiralty.

Time after time he paced the room, a look of worry on his face—the face which, save for the white hair above it, was that of practically a young man. And from time to time he paused by a great map of England that had evidently just been hung on one of the walls, and his white, rather nervous finger traced a track from the Shetlands round to the western coast.

"Mr. Kennard!" a footman announced, and a man of medium height, with a thin, keen face, walked briskly into the room. He was in evening-dress, and the black clothes made him look slimmer and younger than he really was.

"I am glad you have come," the Prime Minister said eagerly.

"This speech?" Mr. Kennard queried, as he coolly seated himself and took a cigar from the open box on the table.

"Yes." The Prime Minister had ceased to pace the room, but

he did not seat himself. "Since the report of that speech came through I have learnt some unpleasant things. It is only too true that the Germans know the Shetlands and Lerwick better than we do, that both by land and sea they have made a most thorough examination of the part."

"You believe in the speech, then?" Mr. Kennard asked quietly.

"Yes." The Prime Minister spoke as a man who is utterly and entirely convinced. "That there is actual danger from Germany just now I do not fear. The countries are friendly, and even if they were not the business that they do with us is too important to be shattered by a war. So far peace pays them, but we must not forget that some day it may cease to do so, and then—"

"And then?" Mr. Kennard echoed.

The Prime Minister was standing in front of the map again.

"We shall know what fools we have been unless we act quickly," he answered.

Mr. Kennard started, and removed the cigar from between his lips. The line that was cut between his eyes had suddenly become deep and black, and the well-marked eyebrows nearly met above it.

"You have a plan," he said shortly, stating a fact, not asking a question.

"Yes."

"What is it?"

Before the Prime Minister could answer, the footman had entered again.

"Mr. Sexton Blake to see you, sir," he announced.

Mr. Kennard rose sharply from his chair, took the Prime Minister by the arm, and led him to the window.

"This is the famous detective?" he asked, in a whisper.

"Yes."

"But surely you are not going to allow him to dabble in affairs of State?" Mr. Kennard objected.

The Prime Minister shrugged his shoulders a trifle wearily, and his eyes roamed back to the map.

"Who else is there?" he answered.

"The secret service agents," Mr. Kennard said sharply.

The Prime Minister turned sharply, and there was that in the expression of his face which showed that his mind was fully made up. Men who knew him well, colleagues in the Cabinet, were aware that when that look came into his eyes that there was no turning him from his purpose.

"This is no case for them," he said, in a low voice. "They are clever men, some of the best in England, but for this task we must have the best, and this Sexton Blake is acknowledged to be that."

"And suppose I refuse to let him dabble with my department?" Mr. Kennard queried a trifle sharply.

"Then I shall act on my own account," the Prime Minister assured him. "You cannot prevent an agent of mine going to the Shetlands." He turned to the waiting footman. "Show Mr. Blake in here," he ordered.

A few seconds later Sexton Blake entered the room. Over his evening-clothes he wore a heavy motor-coat.

"I am sorry I am late," he said quietly; "but I was engaged in a case at Somerset when your message came. My assistant 'phoned me, and I motored up."

"It was very good of you to come so promptly," the Prime Minister said. "Perhaps you can guess what the trouble is?"

Sexton Blake smiled, nodded at Mr. Kennard, and then crossed to the map on the wall.

"There is the trace of where a finger has passed more than once from the Shetlands to the Western coast," he said quietly. "Adding that to the fact that Mr. Kennard is here, I can surely suggest that I am wanted with regard to this speech of the Kaiser's."

"Yes," the Prime Minister assented eagerly. "Do you think there is anything in it?"

"Yes."

Mr. Kennard smiled cynically, and put down the butt of his cigar.

"Surely—you will pardon the seeming rudeness—there is no reason why you should be the judge of that?" he said.

"I fancy there is," Sexton Blake answered coolly. "I have the pleasure of knowing the Kaiser—having worked both for and against him—and I can assure you that even his wildest speeches have truth in them—a good foundation of truth."

He turned to the Prime Minister.

"There is no need to beat about the bush," he said. "You wish me to find out how far the Germans have gone, and whether they are even watching these manoeuvres?"

Just for a second the Prime Minister hesitated; then he nodded.

"If you are willing," he agreed.

"I can start tonight," the great detective said simply.

"And we have your word that everything you discover, or see, you will keep secret?" Mr. Kennard put in sharply.

Sexton Blake drew himself up with a touch of haughtiness.

"You are at liberty to send someone else!" he answered.

"Tush, man! We mustn't quibble over a word," Mr. Kennard said quickly. "You would go alone?"

"No!" Sexton Blake answered. "I shall take one man with me, and my young assistant."

"They are to be trusted?"

"As myself," Sexton Blake said quietly. "I will be going. There is no time to be lost."

"And as regards fee," the Prime Minister put in, "why—"

Sexton Blake raised a hand sharply.

"I do not think there is any need to discuss that," he said, with a touch of pride. "I would willingly undertake this task for nothing—I am patriotic enough for that. Anyway, there will be time enough when I have finished to settle such matters."

By the door the great detective paused.

"You will hear from me day by day," he said quietly—"unless matters prove so serious that I dare not trust them to the wires. Good-night!"

The door closed behind Sexton Blake, and Mr. Kennard picked up a fresh cigar and lit it.

"A self-reliant man," he remarked.

"The only man in Britain for this task!" the Prime Minister answered, with conviction.

Sexton Blake stepped into his waiting motor, and as it drove away he lit up a cigar. There was nothing in the expression of his face to show that he was returning home to make preparations for commencing on one of the biggest cases of his life—a case that involved the security of a great nation.

THE SECOND CHAPTER

In the Shetlands—The whirr from above—
The trailing rope—Aboard the Airship.

THE WIND CAME strongly from the sea, so that the two men and the boy who stood looking out across the water had to bend forward to keep their balance. They were standing on a rocky promontory, of which there are many in the Shetland Islands. To their right, the lights of the town of Lerwick lay, but beyond that everything was dark.

From below, came the snapping of the waves as they spent themselves against the rocks.

"Don't believe Fleet here at all," Inspector Spearing, of Scotland Yard, who was the shorter and broader of the two men, jerked impatiently. "No lights, no whistles, no anything!"

Sexton Blake laughed, and turned his back to the wind while he lit his pipe. He had lost no time in setting out on his mission; and Spearing, after some difficulty in the way of obtaining leave without giving the exact reason for it, had come with him.

Sexton Blake had thought of him the moment the Prime Minister had asked him to undertake the work, for he knew well the splendid qualities of dogged pluck that the worthy official of Scotland Yard possessed. True, such qualities might not be required; yet Sexton Blake had a strong impression that they would be.

For years it had been common knowledge with him—there were few things escaped him—that the Germans had more than once cast eyes upon the Shetlands, and he did not think it probable that these manoeuvres would be allowed to take place without them knowing as much as possible about them.

"What's that, sir?" Tinker asked sharply, pointing seawards.

Sexton Blake shaded his eyes with his hand, and stared out into the darkness. There was not a star in the sky, and beyond the rocks on which the men stood everything was dark as a pit. Only the breaking waves told how near the water was.

A speck of light shone out—but how far away it was impossible to tell—winked, and vanished. Then a second one—away to the left—leapt into existence, and began to flash and blink at a tremendous rate.

"Warships—signalling, my lad," Sexton Blake said quietly. "If it's a general order from the flagship, you'll see more lights in a minute. Ah, there they go!"

Suddenly, right out in the darkness, fully a hundred bright, blinking lights had leapt into life, evidently answering the first one that had appeared, and the sea that had been so dark seemed to be illuminated by powerful stars.

"Is the Fleet there?" Sexton Blake queried, turning to Spearing, with a laugh.

"Don't know!" the worthy official growled, not willing to admit himself wrong. "Fool's game, anyway! Don't believe understand each other's signals!"

The lights went out as quickly as they had come, but only for a second did the sea slip back into darkness. Then, from a hundred different places, great flashlights glared out, dazzlingly white, and played upon the rocky coast.

A few fell upon the harbour itself, revealing the masses of

shipping lying there—the hundreds of drifters and trawlers that make Lerwick one of the most important fishing centres of the world. But most of the lights played upon the barren rocks, and one, flashing a trifle upwards, shone full upon the detectives as they stood on the rocks. They were compelled to turn their heads, the light was so dazzling.

"Give in!" Spearing snapped. "Fleet there, sure enough!"

Now the lights swung away from the shore, and flashed around the sea in great circles. From place to place they slipped, and every time they moved their rays were broken by the great turrets of battleships, by the four straight funnels of the first-class cruisers, by the low-lying, waspish looking torpedo craft that seemed to fairly swarm round the larger vessels.

Sexton Blake drew his breath in sharply.

"A sight like that makes you believe that we do really boss the sea," he said, in a low tone.

For more than half an hour the lights swung round slowly, then rapidly, resting on certain places on the land, as if trying to wrest the very secrets of Nature from the rocks.

And they went out, leaving the night darker than before, and not even the twinkling of a riding light showed where the great Fleet lay. Possibly they had steamed away; maybe they still lay at anchor. There was nothing to give an answer.

"Getting hungry!" Spearing growled, rubbing his eyes to get the departed glare out of them. "Time for supper. Hungry—very!"

"All right; you get along with Tinker," Sexton Blake answered. "I shall stop here and finish my pipe."

"Can't I stay, too, sir?" the boy asked eagerly.

"No. There is nothing to stay for."

Sexton Blake was left alone on the rocks, and he seated himself—knees drawn up, elbows on them, pipe between his teeth—and stared out to sea. He was trying to think in what manner the Germans could—

The detective sniffed sharply, tapped the ashes from his pipe, put his foot on them—and sniffed again.

"Petrol!" he muttered, and stood staring round. "Yet there can't be a car round here. No roads worth speaking about."

But the smell of petrol, faint but pungent, was in the air right enough, and as the seconds passed it seemed to be growing stronger. For a moment the detective thought of motor-boats, but quickly put that idea away from him. He knew that the Fleet did not carry them, and that the searchlights would quickly have picked out anything of that kind had it been on the water.

Whi-r-r-r!

It was a curious sound—not unlike that made by a revolving air fan—and Sexton Blake looked round sharply as it reached his ears. The wind was light and variable now, so that it was difficult to judge from what direction it came.

Whi-r-r-r! The sound came nearer, and was followed by a small but distinct explosion.

"The exhaust of a motor!" Sexton Blake muttered; and again his eyes searched the darkness.

He remembered that there had apparently been nothing but a very rocky footpath up to the spot on which he was standing, so how was it possible for a motor-car to be coming in that direction? Yet, unless his usually keen ears were playing him false, one was certainly approaching.

A rope struck sharply across his face, and mechanically he gripped it. It swung him off his feet, clear of the rocks, and so out over the breaking waves. Then, for the first time, he knew that the whirring noise came from something dark and huge that hovered above him in the air. From there also came the faint smell of petrol.

With the instinct of self-preservation, Sexton Blake pulled up the slack of the rope that hung beneath him, and hitched it around his chest, so that the strain of holding it was no longer on his hands. It was the work of a few seconds only; then he turned his eyes upwards.

In the darkness of the night it was possible to see nothing more than a patch that loomed darker than the sky, and to hear very faintly the thudding of a motor. This last noise was so slight that another hundred yards would have made it inaudible.

Sexton Blake knew, as he swung out over the waves, that he was hanging on to the trail-rope of an airship or dirigible balloon, which had come from somewhere inland, and was now stealing out to where the Fleet lay, if it had not sailed to execute some manoeuvre.

Was it a hostile craft? Sexton Blake caught his breath sharply as the thought occurred to him. It might be one of the British airships from Aldershot; but it might just as easily be one of the foreign ones that had lately met with much success. If the tales about their flights were true, they might easily have flown a long way on a dark night like this—secretly and unobserved.

And for what purpose?

Until now the sound of breaking waves had come clearly to Sexton Blake's ears; but they began to die away, and he knew that the airship, whatever her nationality, was rising rapidly. This certainly looked as if she wished to escape observation, and to be out of the range of the searchlights should they flash out again.

A dash of sand, ballast from the strange craft above him, struck the detective's face, and as it did so a terrible thought came into his mind.

Suppose some hostile power had been waiting for such time as this, a moment when most of Great Britain's magnificent Fleet lay within a small space, to drop deadly melinite bombs, or some equally death–dealing and destructive explosive among them?

Sexton Blake felt as if his heart had stopped beating, and for the briefest fraction of a second the trail-rope nearly slipped from him. Then his grip tightened, and he resolved that whatever the risk to himself he had got to discover what nationality the men were who were controlling the airship that swayed along above his head.

No sooner was Sexton Blake's mind made up than he was ready to act. By keeping the rope hitched under his arms, and holding it in place with his teeth, he contrived to get his hands free, and set to work to drag off his boots and socks, which he let fall into the sea. That accomplished, the really arduous part of his task commenced.

Hand over hand, using his bare feet to grip with, so as to take some of the strain off his arms, Sexton Blake clambered upwards. He knew that the climb before him was most probably one of three hundred feet or more, enough to make the strongest and most determined man hesitate; but he reckoned that by resting frequently he would be able to accomplish it.

Sixty feet he covered, until he was panting for breath. A hitch of the rope under his arms and across his chest, and he hung resting in a natural swing. Only a minute, then on again, upwards over another sixty feet of swaying rope.

All the time he kept his eyes turned upwards, and with every foot he covered he began to see more plainly the airship that lay above him. At first it had been nothing but a darker blotch in a dark night, but now it was beginning to take shape and form. He could see the long balloon, narrow at one end, broadening out at the other—much the shape of a bottle-nosed shark.

From the narrower end something like a tail protruded, and there were projections, not unlike fins, half-way along the body. Below the body lay a long canvas car, capable of holding at least a dozen men, and it seemed to Sexton Blake that the airship was large enough to be capable of lifting that number.

Up again, another rest, on once more, until every line of the airship was visible to the detective's eyes. He recognised the pattern then. It was like the Zeppellin, so recently purchased by

Germany, but built on a much larger scale. Only a short time back he had made a journey abroad specially to see the airship about which so much had been written, and so he could make no mistake now, even though this craft of the air was fully twice as large as the one he had previously seen.

Ay, Sexton Blake knew now that this ship was no Nulli Secundus[1], but the airship of a rival—if not mildly hostile—country, and he hesitated as to whether he should continue his climb, or slide down the rope and hang there until a chance of escaping either by sea or land presented itself to him.

He looked down, and as he did so the flashlights of the ships of war stretched out their great arms of light again, and he realised what a distance he was up, that no one aboard the ships could possibly catch so much as a glimpse of the airship.

His mind was made up. He would learn more fully what the men above him were doing. Probably he would be captured, but there were ways of escape, and—

Sexton Blake started to climb upwards again, resting as before, until his fingers gripped the thin aluminium rails that formed the bottom of the car of the airship. He raised himself still higher, gripped the edge of the car, and pulled himself upwards.

A startled, angry cry in German reached his ears, powerful hands gripped him, and he was dragged into the car.

The car swayed violently as the detective was hoisted into it, and a voice from the forward end of it, a voice that Sexton Blake seemed to recognise, called out for them to be more careful.

Ten men were in the car, not counting the one who was steering and the one who was controlling the engines.

They came crowding forward now, all save one, who remained in the front of the car, a military cloak drawn tightly round him.

"Who is the spy?" this man demanded, in German.

And again Sexton Blake fancied that he had heard the sharp,

commanding tones of the voice before.

A big man, with a certain tone of authority, faced the detective, as the latter clambered to his feet.

"How did you get here?" he growled.

Sexton Blake smiled coolly, and waved a hand to where the guide-rope trailed down.

"By that," he answered.

"Yes," the German agreed, thrusting his face closer. "But why did you do it?"

"Not for fun, I can assure you," Sexton Blake replied, holding up his hands to show how the climb had torn the skin on them. "I was standing on the edge of the cliffs when your rope struck me. I had to grip it to save myself from being flung over into the sea. And then—why, what else could I do but clamber up?"

"So?" the German growled doubtfully.

"That is the truth?" the man in the bows demanded.

"Why, yes, your Majesty!" Sexton Blake answered.

A sharp cry broke from the man in the bows, and he flung his cloak from him with an impatient gesture.

"How do you know me?" he asked sharply.

"Yours is a voice to remember, sire!" the detective answered coolly.

The man in the bows rose and came forward along the swinging car, and even in the darkness it was possible to make out the martial visage and upturned moustache of one of the greatest rulers that Germany has ever known—Wilhelm II.

"Who are you?" he asked sternly.

Sexton Blake bowed, and there was a hard little smile on his lips.

"Once I worked for your Majesty," he answered, "twice— the regret is mine—against you."[2]

"Sexton Blake!" the Kaiser ejaculated.

"Precisely," the detective agreed; "and I am sorry that I cannot add, at your service!"

THE THIRD CHAPTER

The Escape—The Airship Makes a Search—
Inland before the Dawn—The Hiding Place Among the Rocks.

ONE OF THE greatest manoeuvres that the British Fleet had ever made was in progress, the utmost secrecy being kept with regard to it, not a single man, save the officers and crews, being allowed aboard the ships of war, though previously guests had been permitted to be aboard.

Yet over the Fleet, though hidden by the night, hung the airship of a great foreign Power that for years had been building a navy that was to rival the one that lay off the Shetlands—a Power that by land had for many years been Great Britain's superior, and which now was doing its utmost to add to that its superiority by sea as well.

And on board this airship was none other than the ruler of this nation—the Kaiser Wilhelm himself.

As the latter stood pulling at his moustache, his keen eyes on Sexton Blake, he had much the look of a naughty boy caught robbing an orchard. His blue eyes held a doubting look, and more than once he stopped when about to speak.

"It is well it is you, Mr. Blake!" he said at last. "If it had been another man—" He shrugged his shoulders, and explained no further. "I admire such men as yourself—men who have in their time even dared to thwart my will."

Sexton Blake smiled. He knew, as well as anyone living, that the Kaiser's great fault was his entire belief in his divine rights as a ruler.

"I consider myself honoured, sire," he answered.

The Kaiser hesitated, then took the detective by the arm and led him to the forward end of the cage, where no one would be able to overhear them if they spoke in a subdued tone. He took a stool, and motioned the detective to take another.

There was silence for some minutes, during which time Sexton Blake saw that the great airship was hovering almost motionless over the Fleet, and it was the Kaiser who broke it.

"You wonder why I am here?" he said abruptly.

"No," Sexton Blake answered, with a smile; "I know!"

"You think it is to spy upon these manoeuvres?" the Kaiser continued sharply.

"The word spy is a hard one to apply to your Majesty," Sexton Blake objected.

"But the right one—so?" the Kaiser persisted, tugging at his moustache. "This is no time to mince words, herr, but to make terms. For the first, let me explain why I am really here."

Sexton Blake bowed, and his face became positively wooden in expression. He did not know what the Kaiser was going to tell him, but he did know that it would be wise to appear not to doubt it.

"I am here"—the Kaiser spoke slowly, and his eyes met the detective's unflinchingly—"more by chance than anything else. For nearly a year back this airship has been building secretly, and as soon she was completed, nothing could satisfy me but that I myself test her merits. So I embarked on her. That we headed here was natural."

Sexton Blake bowed, but made no answer. Inwardly he thought that some of the explanation was true—some.

"For the rest"—the Kaiser spoke with a lightness that he obviously did not feel—"there is the question of your silence."

"Yes?" the detective murmured.

The Kaiser was tugging at his moustache again, for he knew that in Sexton Blake he was dealing with no ordinary man.

"It will be awkward, cause bad feeling, if it is known what has happened," the Kaiser went on. "You can see that I have done no harm; but even then I would like to show my high esteem for you by offering some little present."

"Your Majesty was always a diplomat," Sexton Blake murmured. "I have never had a bribe offered me in such nice terms!"

"Bribe?" The Kaiser's face flushed. "I am offering you a present!"

"I apologise, sire," Sexton Blake answered; "but I never accept presents from rulers of foreign nations in cases like this!"

The Kaiser sat silently twisting his moustache, and from time to time glancing inquiringly at the detective.

"Very well," he said at last; "there are other ways of getting your silence—without buying it!"

The Kaiser moved back to where the man sat working the petrol-engine, and Sexton Blake was alone. He sat still in the bows of the car, trying to see down to the ships that lay below, but only an occasional flashing signal told him where they were. All the time, too, he listened for anything that the Germans might let drop, but heard nothing of importance.

The airship hung almost motionless, and it was not until one in the morning that she began to move back towards the shore, Sexton Blake judging the direction she was taking from the wind.

Then he looked down, and saw lights moving out to sea. The warships were outward bound on some manoeuvre. But he had more than that to occupy his brain, for he wanted to know what had really brought the Kaiser to the Shetlands, how they had managed to keep the presence of the great airship secret, and just how much had already been done to make the islands a naval base for the German Fleet should it ever be required.

Of one thing Sexton Blake was certain, and that was that at the first moment he would have to escape. What he would do after that there was plenty of time to decide.

Back towards the land the great airship was travelling at a steady pace, her screw hardly turning, the wind carrying her along; and as she drew nearer she sank lower, the men in charge evidently wishing to be able to sight some particular spot.

This gave Sexton Blake hope, and from time to time he glanced over the side of the car to see how far she hovered above the water.

A hundred feet below the water showed darkly, and as that height was reached two of the Germans came towards Sexton Blake, a coil of stout cord in their hands. As they approached, Sexton Blake rose to his feet. He knew what the rope was for— to make him a prisoner—and he was not taking anything of that kind just yet.

"You will make no resistance," the nearest of the Germans growled. "Even a brave man knows when defeat is his."

Then once again Sexton Blake glanced over the side of the car, and this time he saw that the water was no more than eighty feet below him. Without hesitation he gripped a rope, and leapt to the side of the car. On the rail he balanced himself, and, with sharp cries, the Germans rushed at him.

Too late! Cleanly, as dexterously as if there had been no hurry whatever, Sexton Blake dived, and went flashing down towards the water. It was an ugly job, but he was an accomplished diver, and had no fear of it. Besides, he was not a man accustomed to worrying about his own safety when the well-being of Great Britain was at stake.

Almost without a splash he struck the water, and a few seconds later was on the surface. That the airship carried a searchlight he had no doubt; but he also knew that they dared not use it for fear of attracting attention. A bullet might bring them down, then it would mean the discovery of the Kaiser aboard.

A cause for war almost, and that before Germany had built the Navy that she was planning.

As Sexton Blake merely kept himself afloat, he looked upwards, and saw the airship coming down towards the surface; also he could hear excited orders being given in the Kaiser's voice, and he knew that he was not to be allowed to get away so easily.

Within a couple of feet of the water the car of the airship descended, and with the screw going slowly she began to make a search of the waves. Twice she passed close to the detective, but each time he dived, and kept below the water as long as his lungs would permit him.

Round and round went the airship in narrowing circles, and it seemed to Sexton Blake that his recapture could only be a matter of time. The diving below the water was tiring him, too, and he knew that he could not do it many times more.

Again the airship swung her blunt nose round towards him, and in the darkness he saw her coming. Below the surface he dived, and stopped there until his chest felt like bursting.

With a spring he came to the surface, and caught his breath hard as he shook the water from his eyes, and found the car of the airship right above him. Then his hand shot out, and he gripped the aluminium rods.

"Throw out ballast; she dips too low!" he heard a voice cry as his weight bore the car down lower towards the waves, until his head went beneath them, in fact, and then the car shot higher, dragging him with it.

Gently, inch by inch, Sexton Blake dragged himself up and wriggled his body between the lower supports of the car, which were about a foot below the ones on which the car actually rested, and lay there at full length.

Then he smiled, for he reckoned that he was going to learn many things. First he would discover where the airship had been hiding inland; secondly, he would know for what purpose the airship was visiting the shipments, but of the extent of that knowledge there was no guessing.

The airship still continued to hover round, sweeping the sea in search of the man who had leapt overboard; and little did the men aboard of her imagine that he was lying more or less comfortably under the car itself.

"Must be drowned, the dog!" a guttural voice said from above. "We must get inland before the dawn."

"No brave man is a dog!" the voice of the Kaiser answered, a touch of anger in it. "I tell you, I would have given much, Harmann, for a few men like Sexton Blake in Germany."

Ballast splashed into the water, and the airship rose rapidly and shot away towards the land, her propeller doing well over a thousand revolutions a minute.

There was certainly not much time to lose if the airship had to go far inland before the dawn. Sexton Blake endeavoured to turn round to see where they were going, but found it impossible, the space in which he lay being too small to move in.

Soon, however, he knew that the land had been reached, for the sound of the waves no longer came from below.

"Stop! We are there!"

As the order rang out, Sexton Blake wriggled his legs down from his perch, and his feet grated along a rough surface. Without hesitation he let go, and fell flat onto his face. Glancing upwards, he saw the great airship looming up only a few yards away, and heard the clank of a grapnel as it struck the ground.

Noiselessly he crawled along the rocky ground, round behind a boulder, and lay still. There would soon be something startling to report to the men who had feared, after reading the Kaiser's speech, for the safety of the Shetlands.

THE FOURTH CHAPTER

A Change of Identity—The Cave by the Shore—
What is inside?—The Truth.

LYING BEHIND THE boulder, Sexton Blake heard the Germans embark, while Colonel von Harmann gave orders in his deep, decisive voice. He appeared to be in supreme command of the great ship and the detective remembered the many rumours he had heard with regard to the control this officer exercised over his Royal master.

At present the detective could not make the slightest guess at where he was, and even by daylight it would be difficult for him to place the spot where the airship lay, for he knew little or nothing of the Shetlands.

It seemed to him, however, that probably they were on one of the smaller islands, which are nothing more than masses of rocks, and which year in and year out are only visited by sea-birds, save when some good ship, driven there by the storm, flings onto the merciless rocks the bodies of brave men. A few of these survive—very few.

By now the grey in the sky had spread, and over to the eastward it held the look of morning. A faint pink hue had joined the grey, and for a time Sexton Blake wondered why the bottom of the sheet of colour was cut off so abruptly. Later he learnt the truth.

An hour passed, and during that time the Germans had worked on without pause. Then all movement ceased, and the men seemed to have retired. A smell of gas reached the detective's nose, and he wondered where it came from, unless the balloon was being emptied. Later, by the aid of chemicals, it would not be difficult to refill it.

So day dawned, and as Sexton Blake's eyes grew accustomed to the dim light he saw much to marvel at, and also much that he had already surmised.

All around him rose high rocks, and he saw that the spot where the airship had landed was entirely surrounded by these, so that she lay in a kind of pit. Not that she would have been noticed much by anyone passing, for the great gasbag had been emptied and stowed somewhere, though the detective could not see where.

The car, with all its complicated machinery, had been pushed on a trolley into a long wooden barn, the sides and walls of which were literally covered by boulders. Beside this building was a smaller one.

All these things Sexton Blake saw, and wondered at the laxity of a Government that had allowed a rival nation to explore these wild islands, and to leave them so unguarded that they had practically already taken possession of one of them.

He smiled as he thought of the surprise that his report would cause, and he meant to take steps to nullify these preparations that must have been going on for years.

While these thoughts were in Sexton Blake's head, the Germans came out of the shed in which they had packed the car. First came the Kaiser, more unmistakable than ever in the light of day, talking eagerly to Colonel von Harmann. Behind him followed the rest of the men, and Sexton Blake started and peered forward eagerly as he caught sight of one of them.

The man was his own height, the rather pale, clean-shaven face, adorned only by a small moustache, was not unlike his own.

"If he is here till the night, I fancy we shall change places," the detective muttered.

The sight of this man had put an idea into his head. It was a daring one, but he was used to such things. Capture might mean anything, even death, if the Kaiser were not there to interfere.

As soon as the Germans had entered the building, which was obviously a kind of living place, Sexton Blake drew a small tin box from his pocket, produced a mirror from it, and propped it up against a stone. Then, by the aid of an eyebrow pencil, he altered his eyes the veriest trifle, and cut a small but beautifully made false moustache into the shape worn by the German officer. This he fastened, then looked closely at himself in the glass.

"As far as I can see, there is no difference," he mused, "and to-night I may have a chance of comparing it with the original."

That the Kaiser would not attempt to leave save by night Sexton Blake had no fear, for there would be too much chance of him being recognised, especially as a keen but quiet watch was being kept in all the towns for foreigners while the secret manoeuvres were on.

During the next hour Sexton Blake lay behind the boulder, fervently hoping that no one would come in that direction and discover him, and at the end of that time a stroke of luck came his way that helped him considerably.

The German he had marked out emerged from the smaller of the buildings, stood uncertainly with a pair of heavy field-glasses in his hands, then started off briskly across the rocks. Within six yards of Sexton Blake he passed, but the boulder held its secret.

The detective had thought to have to wait for the night before putting his daring plan into execution, but his chance had come much earlier.

He glanced at the building where the officers were, and saw that the door was tight closed. True, someone might be watching from a loophole, but he risked that. Turning, he crawled along in the direction that the German had taken, moving from boulder to boulder, only raising his head from time to time to make sure of the direction his quarry had taken. This was not difficult, for the man was making for one of the highest points of the rock, and so was easy to keep in sight.

Higher and higher the detective climbed, glancing back to make sure that he could not be seen from the hut, and at last stopped, lying flat on the rocks, with the sea stretching out in front of him. Nowhere could he see the German, and he had time to glance round and take his bearings.

Where he lay he could command practically the whole of the little island—for that it was—and he saw that it lacked absolutely any sign of life or vegetation. It was just a clump of rocks that looked as if they had been piled unceremoniously upon each other; and not three miles away lay Lerwick, the roofs plainly discernible in the sunshine.

Now came the most dangerous part of Sexton Blake's mission— the finding of the German whom he meant to impersonate.

He looked round searchingly, without daring to raise himself from the ground, and his keen eyes soon caught sight of a boot sticking out from behind a rock that lay a matter of thirty yards distant.

More cautiously than ever, and with all the cunning of an Indian, the detective crawled in that direction, and reached the rock. Within a yard of him the boot stuck out, and from the way it occasionally moved the detective could see that the German was shifting his position, so as to get a better view of the sea.

Sexton Blake shifted a few inches nearer, and hesitated. A new plan had suggested itself to him, and though it was risky, it promised well of success. He stretched out his hand until the fingers hovered over the boot, then they clutched it, and he heaved at it with all his strength.

A smothered oath came from behind the boulder, but before it could be repeated in a louder tone Sexton Blake had darted round the rock, and was kneeling on the German. The latter, taken by surprise, made no effort to keep the detective's grip from his throat, but once the fingers had closed on it, he struggled wildly.

Right on the edge of the rocks, with a drop of fully a hundred feet to the jagged stones below in front of them, the two men fought; but Sexton Blake had started with an advantage, and he kept it. Gradually he wore his enemy's strength down, half-choking him, until he lay still. Then, using only his left hand, keeping the other on the German's throat, he released the belt from his waist, and managed to jerk it tight round the other's wrists.

The rest was easy, and within five minutes the German lay bound and gagged, his own belt fastening his ankles.

Sexton Blake stood looking down at the helpless man, and a little smile played around his lips.

"I fancy you will be safe," he said in German. "I must apologise for treating you in this manner, but must point out to you that trespassers are always liable to little troubles like this."

The German, who was rapidly recovering, turned purple with his efforts to free himself or speak, both of which were in vain.

Looking round, Sexton Blake discovered a nook between two boulders, and into this he carried the man. Then he rolled other boulders up—heavy ones that he was only just able to move—so that the man lay in a pit from which, in his helpless state, it would be quite impossible for him to escape.

By the aid of his pocket-mirror Sexton Blake compared his make-up with the face of the German, and slightly altered his moustache. Next, he turned his attention to the clothes, and saw that the man was wearing a blue lounge-suit, which might have been a brother of his own. Only the collar and tie were different, and these he quickly appropriated and donned.

"Again I must ask you to pardon a liberty," he said pleasantly; and thrust a hand into the man's pocket, and pulled out some letters.

All of them were addressed to Lieutenant Bergern, and the detective returned them after noting that fact. Then, with the man's field-glasses swinging from his hand, he calmly turned and strode down the rocks.

His heart was beating a trifle faster than usual. Perhaps it was because of the struggle that he had just had. Perhaps because he was about to walk calmly into the hands of the Kaiser and his officers, trusting to pass as Lieutenant Bergern.

Down over the rocks he went, and there was not even the slightest sign of hesitation in his manner when he caught sight of the Germans gathered outside the hut.

"Hurry!" Colonel von Harmann cried sharply.

Sexton Blake quickened his pace, and saluted in true German fashion as he joined the group.

Not one of the party looked at him suspiciously.

"There is nothing in sight, Lieutenant?" the Kaiser demanded. "No boats coming towards here?"

"Nothing, your Majesty," the detective answered.

"Himmel!" the Kaiser said, ejaculating angrily. "Please to remember that I am now Colonel Kelner!"

"Nothing, Colonel!" Sexton Blake said, thankful that his slip had aroused no suspicion. Of his German he had no fear, for he spoke the language like a native.

The Kaiser turned to Colonel von Harmann a trifle impatiently.

"We will see this cave!" he ordered.

"I am ready!" Colonel von Harmann answered; and turned and gave instructions to six of the others, stationing them at various points along the rocks.

As each one started off to his allotted place, Sexton Blake's heart seemed to stand still for a second, for if one was sent to where the real Lieutenant Bergern lay a prisoner, all would be over. But the six left, not one going to that spot, and the detective breathed freely again.

"Surely there is no need for all this?" the Kaiser said a trifle irritably.

"There is every need," Colonel von Harmann answered respectfully. "It matters nothing to me if I be captured, all my comrades in arms; but think what it would mean if those Britishers laid hands on you. You would be the laughing-stock of the world—"

"They would not dare!" the Kaiser muttered fiercely.

"Or Britain might take your actions as a cause for war," the colonel continued impressively.

The anger died out of the Kaiser's eyes, and he looked round uneasily.

"Yes, yes!" he agreed. "We must not give them excuse. So far there need be no war or rumour of war. I am not here to force trouble and expense of fighting on my country, but to make sure of victory should such an occasion arise."

"Let us go to the cave."

Sexton Blake knew now practically all that he desired to know, and he had information enough to startle even the Prime Minister. Nevertheless, he had no intention of getting back to London yet, even if he could escape, for there was more for him to learn. He already knew that the Germans had made their preparations for turning the Shetlands into a naval base should the time for war with Great Britain ever arise, and he meant to discover just what those preparations were, so that they could be made valueless.

Colonel von Harmann turned and led the way from the spot, Sexton Blake and the Germans not on guard going with him. The detective was more than a little relieved to find that no one suspected him in the slightest. In fact he had only one fear now, and that was that Spearing and Tinker would roam around the islands in search of him, strike this one, and be captured.

For three or four hundred yards the little party walked briskly over the rocky ground, and entered a narrow defile. Down this they went, stopping eventually right on the edge of the water, the waves breaking ten or fifteen feet below them. From here Lerwick, and much of the surrounding sea, could be plainly seen.

"A good spot to watch from," the Kaiser said thoughtfully. "It is well chosen."

Colonel von Harmann smiled, and tugged at a boulder that lay on his right. It came away with surprising ease, revealing an opening four feet high and three broad. To some extent this was obviously natural, but chisel-marks showed where it had been enlarged.

"You will go in?" the colonel queried.

For answer the Kaiser stooped, and entered the cave, the colonel close behind him.

Sexton Blake calmly made a move to follow, but a German gripped him by the arm and held him back.

"You forget that it is not permitted, comrade!" he said sharply. "The secret of the cave is for the colonel only—and the Kaiser!"

Sexton Blake muttered something unintelligible, and drew back, realising that he had very nearly made a fatal mistake.

Twenty minutes passed, and when the Kaiser emerged there was a smile of satisfaction on his face.

"It is good—very good!" Sexton Blake heard him say to Colonel von Harmann.

"What lay within the cave?" the detective asked himself.

THE RAIN CAME down steadily, and save for the noise of the heavy drops splashing on the rocks, and the faint rumble of the sea, there was no sound on the little island of which the Germans had taken such complete possession, yet Sexton Blake paused every few feet as he moved along in the darkness. An hour back he had taken his turn at watching from the rocks, and that had given him his opportunity of coming down to the cave that held the German's secret.

There was little risk that he would be discovered, but, nevertheless, he was taking the most minute precautions. When possible, he hid in the shadow of rocks, and every time he moved a foot he took care not to displace so much as a pebble. He was bound upon the accomplishment of a task that would probably mean much to Great Britain, and at such a time it was wise to avoid the smallest risk.

Down into the cutting between the rocks he made his way, peering along it to make sure that the cave was not guarded. There was no one there, and he moved cautiously forward.

Outside the cave at last. With quick fingers Sexton Blake gripped the boulder as he had seen Colonel von Harmann do it, and it came away in his hands, evidently fixed on some cunningly concealed swivel, and before him lay the narrow, black entrance.

He stooped, his back bent nearly double, and passed in. Inch by inch he moved forward in the darkness, feeling his way with his hands, and before he had gone ten yards he found that the passage broadened out, and that the rock roof was high enough for him to stand upright. Then he drew from his pocket an electric-lamp, and switched it on.

For a moment the bright rays dazzled him, but as his eyes became accustomed to it he looked eagerly around.

Certainly there was not much to be seen.

The cave was fully forty feet square, and was fitted all around with shelves, on which stood dozens upon dozens of electric-accumulators. At the far end of the place stood a petrol-driven engine, obviously meant to generate the electricity with which the batteries were stored. In the centre of the cave was a table, and it was to this that Sexton Blake crossed.

Then the detective caught his breath sharply, for at the edge of the table a row of electric buttons protruded, each one bearing a number. The rest of the table was covered by a chart each part of which was marked by a number corresponding with one of the buttons.

What did it mean? Had the Germans laid mines all around the Shetlands? Could they, if they so willed it, blow the great fleet that was manoeuvring to pieces? What other explanation was there?

Carefully avoiding contact with the buttons, Sexton Blake seated himself in the chair that stood before the table, and examined the chart more closely. He looked for Lerwick Harbour, to see how that was marked, and saw to his amazement that there was no mark at all. He sought for other well-known channels and moorings, but in each case there were no numbers there. Then he turned to the parts that were numbered, and saw that they were places in the Shetlands which had certainly never been regarded as landing places or harbours.

Puzzled, unable to understand the meaning of it, Sexton Blake rose from the chair and commenced to make a closer examination of the cave. At first he could discover nothing more; but at last, right in the darkest corner, he found an opening concealed by some planks. Pulling these aside, he stepped boldly through, and found himself in a smaller cave, which had evidently been used as a store-house.

Lengths of rope, coils of cable, lay everywhere, but it was a pile of stuff in a corner that attracted Sexton Blake's attention, and he crossed to it. As he examined it a smile curled his lips, for at last he understood the use that the Germans had put the island to.

The thing that he examined was a length of cable, but the curious part was that at every twenty feet along it a powerful electric-bulb was fixed, this being shaded so that the light could only shine upwards.

It was a piece of cable such as had been designed by a certain Leon Dion for lighting ships into port. Instead of the old buoys, this cable with lights attached was sunk to the bottom, and laid along the navigable channel, then, when the lights were switched on from the shore, the lamps threw a bright glow up onto the surface of the water, and by following this, a ship was able to make port without the slightest trouble.

So far as Sexton Blake knew, this system had as yet not been adopted by any country, but it was obvious that the Germans had seen the advantage of it, and put it to a practical use.

How long they had been at work in the Shetlands the detective had no idea, but he did know that they had discovered fresh landing places, each of which had been marked on the chart fastened to the table, the entrance to them being marked by the sunken lights.

Yes; Germany had made her preparations well. She had ignored the regular ports, knowing how closely they would be guarded once there was a rumour of war in the air, and had found and marked fresh ports for herself.

Sexton Blake hesitated. Should he destroy these preparations? For five minutes he stood undecided, then a solution came to him. He would leave things as they were, and prove at the first opportunity, by a practical demonstration, the danger in which the Shetlands lay.

From his pocket Sexton Blake drew a sheet of paper and a pencil, and for the next hour he sat at the table and worked. When he at last rose and left the cabin, his pocket held a complete copy of the chart of the Germans.

THE FIFTH CHAPTER

Away from the Island—Pursued—Spearing arrives in time.

CONFIDENT NOW IN his disguise, which at present no one had suspected, Sexton Blake calmly made his way back to the centre of the island, the faint light that came from the living-hut being guide enough. He entered the place without hesitation, and stood in the presence of the Kaiser and Colonel von Harmann who were poring over papers. Both looked up as the detective entered.

"You are back early, lieutenant," the Kaiser said shortly.

"The night is dark," Sexton Blake answered, "and to look out to sea is to fix the eyes on a blank wall."

The detective crossed to the further end of the room, where a number of sleeping-bunks had been fixed up, and threw himself into one. Never in his life had he been in such an extraordinary position, and he meant to make the most of it. True, he had already learnt many things, but there were still others to learn.

Above all, did the Germans contemplate an attack on Great Britain, or were all these preparations merely—

"Five years, not a day less," the Kaiser said irritably, with the air of a man who has finally come to a conclusion that he did not wish to reach.

"I should say four—not a day more," Colonel von Harmann corrected. "You say, wait for these battleships that are building; but I say that there is no need. Has not our fleet been here before, so why should it not come again?"

The Kaiser rose from his seat and paced up and down the floor. When he stopped at the table again the moody expression had left his face, and he laughed.

"Why, so, Harmann," he said, "we speak as if we meant to attack Great Britain, while in reality all this is merely a precaution, a way of making our power felt should the occasion ever arise. I hope to heaven it never may!"

Sexton Blake's face was towards the wall, or the men must have seen the expression of relief that crossed it. At last he had heard what he had been so anxious to hear—that there was no real danger from Germany—for the present, at least.

Over by the table the Kaiser and Colonel von Harmann were examining their papers, and Sexton Blake, tired with all that he had been through, dropped off into a doze.

He awoke with angry cries in his ears, and he sat up sharply in his bunk, his hand dropping to the pocket in which his revolver lay. He looked out into the room, but for the present only the colonel and the Kaiser were there, and they had sprung to their feet, their eyes towards the door, from the other side of which the sounds came.

"We can't have been discovered?" the Kaiser asked, in an agitated voice. "I was a fool ever to come here."

"It is our own men—there is something wrong!" the colonel growled in answer. "They make noise enough to be heard in Lerwick."

Before more could be said the door was flung open, and two of the Germans, a third man between them, whom they were supporting by the arms, came into the room. This third man, who appeared to be suffering from exhaustion and excitement, was the real Lieutenant Bergern.

Looks of amazement were on the faces of the Kaiser and Harmann.

"What is this?" the latter gasped. "Who is this man?"

"I am Lieutenant Bergern," the rescued man answered, in a weak voice, throwing himself free of the others, and standing upright, though he swayed slightly on his feet.

"This morning some man leapt upon me, half stunned me, then bound me, and left me a prisoner. Only now have my comrades found and liberated me."

With a cry, the colonel swung round and faced Sexton Blake, who, seated on the edge of his bunk, was smiling blandly. But behind his smile his brain was working rapidly. At all costs he had to get away. He knew that, and he meant to do it.

"There is the traitor!" Bergern screamed, pointing a shaking hand at the detective.

The latter slid down from his bunk, and stood with his hands in his pockets. The likeness between him and the real man was simply remarkable. They were alike as two peas.

"I think this man must be mad," he said quietly to the staring Germans.

Lieutenant Bergern made a fierce rush forward, but Sexton Blake gripped him by the arms and flung him back. At the same time he moved nearer to the door, though no one seemed to notice it.

With a half mad gesture, as if he wished to convince even himself of his identity, Lieutenant Bergern snatched papers from his pocket and flung them onto the table.

"Does that prove who I am?" he cried.

The Kaiser glanced down at the letters, Colonel Van Harmann looking over his shoulder; then both swung round upon Sexton Blake, who stood within ten feet of the door.

"Who are you?" he demanded.

Quite calmly Sexton Blake peeled the moustache from his upper lip, his expression changed, and he stood revealed.

"I am really sorry that you do not remember me, sire," he said, in a tone of regret, "even if not as a friend, as a worthy foe."

"Sexton Blake!" the Kaiser gasped, and his face went white.

Cries of rage broke from the other Germans, and one snatched at a revolver that lay on a shelf.

"Stop!" Sexton Blake thundered, and there was something in the tone that sent the man's hand dropping hastily to his side.

Sexton Blake still stood smiling against the wall, but now there was a revolver in his hand, and its barrel covered the Kaiser.

As the Germans saw this, and realised that their ruler was in danger of his life, they stood spellbound and speechless. Any one of them would have willingly given up his life for the Kaiser, but how—

"You see, it would be foolish to get excited," Sexton Blake remarked in an even tone. "Excitement makes the hand unsteady, and this is a hair-pull trigger."

The Kaiser straightened himself, and there was no fear in his eyes.

"You forget who I am!" he said fiercely. "I am the Kaiser!"

Sexton Blake bowed, but his eyes never left the other's face, and his hand did not remove the fraction of an inch.

"I think you are forgetting that you have already told me that you are Colonel Kelner," he said, very slowly and distinctly. "I must also add, Colonel, that where I should hesitate to shoot the Kaiser, I shall have no such qualms with regard to you."

The German who had tried to snatch the revolver from the shelf was eyeing the weapon again.

"One more thing!" the detective said sharply. "You are the leader here, so if one of your men makes a move against me, I shoot!"

There was a dead silence. From the expression of the Kaiser's face, it could plainly be seen that unpleasant thoughts were passing through his brain. Not that he feared death—he was too much of a man for that—but he was wondering what would happen when it was discovered that he was no longer in Germany. How would his death be explained?

"And to come down to my own position—which, I admit, is awkward," Sexton Blake continued calmly, "I must ask you to obey my orders."

"Never!" Colonel von Harmann growled.

"It must be!" the Kaiser said bitterly. "I am thinking of my country, not of myself!"

"It is a wise man who knows when he is defeated," Sexton Blake remarked. "All move over to the bunks."

At first the Germans hesitated, but a word from the Kaiser, who had already moved, sent them to the position ordered by Sexton Blake. There they stood glaring, and the detective quietly backed to the door.

He opened it, and stood in the doorway, a little smile on his lips—a smile that spoke of quiet determination rather than mirth.

"Gentlemen," he said coolly, "I have been through some exciting experiences in my time, but I really think that this one caps all. Good night!"

With a sudden jerk the detective had swung round and raced away across the uneven ground. His only chance was to get clear of the island by swimming, and that was what he intended to do.

From behind came wild cries of rage, and before Sexton Blake had run a hundred yards, making for the cleft in the rocks where the secret cave lay, two rifle bullets whizzed unpleasantly close to him. One struck the rock, splintering a small piece against his face.

"Whew!" he ejaculated. "I did not think they would dare to fire!"

There was no mistake about them daring to do so, for a perfect volley of shots pursued the running man; but now boulders lay in between him and his pursuers, so that there was little danger of being hit.

The firing ceased, the Germans evidently realising the uselessness of it, but the sound of men scrambling along behind him told Sexton Blake that he was not to be let off so easily. Down the cutting he ran, pulling up where it dropped sheer down to the rocks.

In the darkness he peered over, and just made out the rocks some fifteen feet below him; then a bullet hummed by, and he dropped down. His feet slipped on the slimy rocks, and he fell forward, missed his grip of the stone, and plunged into the sea.

Luckily the waves were slight, or they must have dashed him back against the rocks, and so beaten the life out of him. As it was, he was well able to fight against them, and a few strong strokes took him out into practically clear water.

Would he still be followed, that was the question?

Twenty yards from the shore Sexton Blake turned and looked back. He saw the dark outline of the rocks of the little island, and as he scanned them closely a figure showed darkly on the summit, paused there a second, and came hurtling down into the sea, diving straight past the rocks.

The diving man was an enemy, yet Sexton Blake could not help catching his breath as he realised the risk that he was taking of hitting the rocks, and a sigh of relief escaped as he saw the man rise to the surface and strike out towards him.

No longer could Sexton Blake hesitate, and he swirled around in the water and swam straight for the open sea. As he did so, he caught a glimpse of another man diving from the rocks, while at the same moment a rifle cracked, the bullet splashing into the water close to his head.

The Kaiser and his men knew what would happen if he

escaped, that the plans that had taken them years to formulate and carry out would all be knocked on the head, and they were doing their best to prevent him getting clear.

With a steady over-arm stroke Sexton Blake swam through the smooth water, meaning to get well out from the land, then turn and make for Lerwick. This would mean a three-mile swim; but he had accomplished that distance many a time before, and had no fear of failure now.

A hundred yards, two hundred, he covered, and turned to see where his pursuers were. To his amazement, he saw that the nearest was within ten yards of him, and swimming with a powerful over-arm stroke that was sending him through the water like a fish. Sexton Blake was no mean swimmer, but he realised that this man was quite as good as himself, and that a hard race lay before him, with for a prize—his life. Not that he thought of the latter. His one idea was to get away, so that the plans of the Germans, their years of subtle scheming and working, should be made useless.

Sexton Blake swam hard now, altering his stroke to a racing one, but when he looked back, after going a quarter of a mile, he saw that he had gained scarcely a foot on his pursuer. Probably the man had thrown most of his clothes off, so as to swim better, but the detective did not pause long enough to follow his example.

Low in the water, striking out straight ahead, Sexton Blake swum for dear life. A current caught him and whirled him in the direction of Lerwick, but that gave him no hope, for it would help his pursuer just as much. More than once he thought of stopping and fighting it out with the man, but each time put the idea from him. He knew what a fight in the water meant—probably the death of both. Life was precious to him just now—Great Britain had to be warned of its danger.

A splash behind Sexton Blake caused him to turn. The

German was so close behind that he could almost have reached out a hand and touched him, and between his teeth was an ugly-looking knife.

The man took the knife from between his teeth, and sprinted with it ready in his hand. Sexton Blake tried to do the same, but his sodden clothes held him back, and he could not increase his pace.

Something ripped down the back of his coat, and he knew that it was the knife, which had just missed cutting into his flesh. Desperately he swung round to face the attack.

Then a strange thing happened. The German let go his knife, which sunk in the water, and turned and raced for the shore.

What did it mean? Why had he given up his task when it seemed so easy of accomplishment? Sexton Blake watched the man racing away, and was filled with amazement.

Chug, chug, chug!

The sound of a propeller reached the detective's ears, and as he turned in that direction he could faintly make out the outline of a small craft coming towards him.

"Help!" he shouted, and swam slowly in its direction, his strength failing him now that the worst of his task was over. That the boat was an English one he had no doubt, for he was certain that the Germans dared not approach with the Fleet so near.

A few minutes later a warship's steam pinnace swirled alongside the detective, and he was hauled into it.

"What been doing?" the voice of Spearing jerked. "Couldn't find you anywhere. Got permission to search islands. Beast of a job. Admiral so high and mighty."

"Leave him alone," the voice of Tinker put in. "Can't you see that he's done right up?"

"I'm all right." Sexton Blake managed to sit up, gasping for breath, and turned to the young officer in charge of the pinnace. "Kindly make for the flagship at once," he said.

The officer looked doubtful, though he knew who the rescued man was.

"Sorry, sir," he answered, "but I have orders to return to my own ship if you are found."

"As you will." Sexton Blake was quickly recovering, and his voice was quite steady. "I can only tell you that if you do not obey me now you may have no ship to return to to-morrow."

The officer bent forward from the tiller, a questioning expression on his face.

"What do you mean?" he demanded.

"Possibly the admiral will tell you when I have explained to him," Sexton Blake answered coldly.

The officer hesitated, annoyed at the way he was being treated, yet impressed by the detective's voice and manner.

He put the tiller over until the pinnace headed for Lerwick and the flagship.

THE SIXTH CHAPTER

The Admiral surprised—A Night Landing—
The Airship pursued—The Kaiser in trouble.

THE LITTLE PINNACE ploughed its way through the smooth sea at a good pace, Sexton Blake sitting in the stern, entirely recovered from his exertions. But even now he was not out of his difficulties. He had decided to see Sir Henry Farrar, the admiral in command, and to show him all that was on the little island.

But the Kaiser? That was the trouble. Sexton Blake knew the type of man that the admiral was, and that he would make the Kaiser a prisoner as readily as he would punish one of his own men, and that was just what the detective did not want. He wanted to get the Kaiser away, to make terms with him.

Well, there was no time to think about it now, for the pinnace grated against the gangway of the flagship. The young officer led the way up onto the deck.

"How is that?" a gruff voice demanded angrily. "Lieutenant Anderson, I thought you knew that no one was to be allowed aboard a ship of the Fleet during the manoeuvres?"

Lieutenant Anderson saluted a trifle nervously. It was the admiral who was speaking, and most of the officers went more or less in dread of him, though he was a kind enough man at heart.

"I know, sir," he answered; "but this is Mr. Sexton Blake, the man who was missing. His friends are with him."

"But, hang it all, why bring 'em here?" the Admiral snorted. "Think I run this ship as a home for lost civilians, or what?"

Sexton Blake stepped forward and bowed stiffly.

"I am pleased to meet you, Sir Henry," he said.

The admiral glared, especially when he saw that the young lieutenant evidently wanted to laugh.

"Sorry can't return the compliment, sir," he said shortly. "I must ask you to leave at once. No one allowed aboard now. There are important manoeuvres to be carried out to-night. Good evening!"

But Sexton Blake held his ground, though he would have liked to have turned and taken the man at his word. But he remembered what his discovery meant to Great Britain, and he thought of the country, not of the man before him.

"You know why I am here?" he asked shortly.

"Heard something about it," the admiral admitted grudgingly. "Lords of the Admiralty!"

"Precisely, Sir Henry," Sexton Blake agreed. "They sent me up here to find out things, and I have succeeded."

"What are they?" the admiral growled suspiciously.

Sexton Blake shrugged his shoulders.

"Surely there is some better place than this to discuss important affairs," he answered.

The admiral frowned; he was not used to being dictated to at any time, and especially on his own ship. But something in the detective's quiet bearing, a certain dignity which even his sodden clothes could not rob him of, impressed him.

"Come to my cabin," he said shortly.

Along the deck the men went, and into the admiral's state-room. It was a plainly furnished apartment, with none of the fancy articles that many an officer ashore regards as essential to his comfort. It was the room of a man.

"Sit down!" Sir Henry said; and Sexton Blake took a chair by the table. "Now tell me what all this mystery means," the admiral continued. He glanced at the clock on the wall, and frowned impatiently. "In ten minutes I must sail."

"As you will," the detective answered boldly, "but I should advise you to postpone the manoeuvre, however important it may be."

The admiral's face went positively blank with amazement, and an angry flush showed under the tan.

"Don't fool!" he snapped. "Not used to it."

"Neither am I," Sexton Blake assured him. "I have come here to avert one of the biggest dangers that ever threatened Great Britain."

"Go on!" the admiral ordered, and again the quiet force of the detective was dominating him.

"You know that on more than one occasion the Germans have explored these islands," Sexton Blake commenced, "also that they have taken soundings all around them."

"Yes."

"But you do not know," the detective continued, speaking slowly and impressively, "that they have made charts showing a clear dozen landing places of which we have no knowledge, and that, what is more, they could steam up to them without danger."

"Impossible!" the admiral said shortly, though it was obvious that he was impressed. "It would mean taking soundings all the way."

Sexton Blake shrugged his shoulders, as a man weary of trying to convince another against his will.

"You have heard of the Dion system of undersea lights showing the way down a channel?" he queried.

The admiral started badly, and leant forward eagerly over the table.

"Yes," he said sharply.

"The Germans have laid such a system in each of the harbours they have discovered," Sexton Blake said calmly. "Should they at any time wish to attack Great Britain, making the Shetlands their naval base, they have made every preparation to do so."

The admiral sprang to his feet, all his calm leaving him. Then he stopped before the detective.

"You can prove that?"

Sexton Blake drew the chart that he had made, sodden with sea-water, from his pocket, and laid it on the table.

"That is a copy of their chart," he said.

For several minutes the admiral pored over it, and his face was set grimly.

"How and where did you come by this?" he demanded; and there was no longer doubt in his eyes.

In as few words as possible Sexton Blake described all that happened, omitting only one fact—the presence of the Kaiser. He knew that the Admiral would not hesitate to make that august person a prisoner, and he was perfectly certain that that was about the last thing that the Government would want.

At the end of the recital Sir Henry paced up and down the cabin, but quickly came to a decision. He touched a bell, and an officer entered.

"Signal that the ships will remain at anchor tonight," he ordered. "Then get thirteen men and man the largest steam-pinnace. I will take command."

The officer looked astounded, but touched his cap and hurried out to obey.

"We will teach these Germans whether they can play games like that with us," the admiral said, as the door closed.

"And what will you do with the Germans if you capture them?" Sexton Blake queried.

"Hold 'em as prisoners until I get instructions to let them go."

"And the airship and the cave?" Sexton Blake continued.

"Blow 'em up!" the admiral growled.

In an almost incredibly short space of time the officer returned to say that all was ready, and the admiral, followed by Sexton Blake, went up onto the deck. As they reached it, Spearing and Tinker stepped forward.

"They will remain aboard here until we return," Sir Henry ordered.

"I think not, sir," Sexton Blake answered. "They are in this game with me, and they see it through, or I abandon it."

Once more the admiral's temper nearly got the better of him, but he remembered in time that the detective was the only man who could guide him to the little island without delay, so he nodded his assent, and they all clambered down into the pinnace. Thirty sailors were there already, their rifles between their knees, looks of excitement on their faces. That they were engaged on some expedition out of the ordinary, they could guess, and were fairly dying to know what it was.

"Cast off!" the admiral ordered, and Sexton Blake quietly took his place at the tiller. The night was dark as pitch, and as the vessels of the Fleet lay without lights, it was going to be no easy task to steer among them.

Away went the pinnace, a keen look-out being kept in the bows, Sexton Blake heading her away for the little island where he had so nearly lost his life. Beside him sat the admiral, who was fidgeting with the hilt of his sword.

"It is not possible for them to have filled their balloon and got away?" he whispered.

"There is no telling," Sexton Blake answered, "as I do not know what apparatus they have got there. Probably it is good, for they must have known that at any time they might have to make a bolt for it.

"Half speed!"

Right ahead loomed the little island, as the detective steered with the greatest caution. In the great darkness it was impossible for him to make out the cutting where he intended to land, and there was nothing for it but to steer close to the shore until they reached it. He, too, thought it possible that the Germans might be able to get their airship ready in time to escape, and he sincerely hoped that that would prove to be the case.

Chug, chug, chug!

The sound of a motor reached the ears of the men in the boat, and as they peered forward, they saw the great bulk of an airship come slowly from the little island. She was low down, so much so, in fact, that her car only just cleared the rocks.

The admiral levelled his glasses, and now that the time for action had come, his hands were steady as steel.

"She's only half filled," he said, in a low voice, "and they don't seem to be able to lift her."

Over went the helm, and the pinnace steamed straight towards the airship, which was only moving very slowly out to sea.

"Full speed ahead!" Sexton Blake shouted.

Hand over hand the pinnace overhauled the airship, the screws of which only turned slowly, as if there had been no proper time to adjust them.

"Unless she can lift out of our reach, we've got her!" the admiral growled.

The sailors were gripping their rifles hard, every one of them staring towards the airship, and they were whispering excitedly together.

A petty officer came aft and saluted the admiral.

"We could put some shots through her from here, sir," he said.

"Then do it; but tell the men to shoot at the balloon, not at the car," the admiral ordered.

A series of sharp clicks told that the sailors were getting ready.

"Aim high, at the balloon two hundred yards!" rang out the order of the officer.

"Fire!"

A sharp, cracking volley broke the stillness of the night.

"Fire!" rang out again, and a second volley whistled through the air.

Through his glasses the admiral watched the airship, and a smile curled his firm lips.

"They've gone home!" he ejaculated. "See, they're running for the shore!"

He was right enough; the airship, which seemed to be sinking lower towards the waves, was swinging round.

"Push those engines!" the admiral shouted. "We've got to get there first!"

The screw revolved faster, and, taking the risk of going ashore, the pinnace raced for the spot for which the airship was making. It would be a near thing—a very near thing—which won.

Straight at the shore the airship drove, and two dark figures dropped from her cage. A couple of men had leapt overboard to lighten her weight, and she rose perceptibly. But the pinnace was close on her, and it was plain that she would reach the shore almost at the same time.

Over the edge of the rocks the airship swayed slowly and sluggishly, and at the same moment Sexton Blake put the helm hard over, and the pinnace grounded against the rocks just below the cutting where the cave lay.

There was no need for the admiral to give an order. Out of the pinnace the sailors swarmed, and, clambering on to each other's backs, swarmed up the wall of rock. The admiral was helped up, swiftly and roughly as any of the ordinary seaman, and so were Sexton Blake, Spearing, and Tinker.

Right above them, only a few feet away, the cage of the airship swung.

"Here's a rope!" a man yelled, and a dozen of his comrades leapt to it and bore the airship down.

A German leant over the car to cut the rope free, but he was too late. Already the car had grounded, and men were slashing at the ropes that held it to the balloon.

Out of the car the Germans came tumbling, and revolvers began to spit viciously.

In the darkness it was hard to tell friend from foe.

It had been no idle wish that had made Sexton Blake insist on coming to the island with the sailors, no desire even to be in at the death of the Germans' plans. He had come there because, if possible, he meant to get the Kaiser away. He realised fully what trouble his capture would mean—possibly it would even lead to war. Besides, he had already formed a plan that would secure Great Britain against a possible war with Germany, and which would also save the building of the warships that were to be laid down to keep pace with the rival Fleet.

Out of the car the Germans tumbled, firing wildly, and Sexton Blake was in the midst of it. A glance showed him where the Kaiser was, at present unattacked, and the detective leapt straight at him.

The Kaiser threw up his right hand, a revolver gripped in it, but before he could use it, Sexton Blake had wrested it from him and thrown him to the ground.

"Keep still," he panted, "and I will get you away!"

In the confusion of the fight, each man was for himself, and no one took note of Sexton Blake as he lifted the Kaiser and carried him bodily away to behind a ridge of rocks, where he put him down.

"Stay there!" he commanded sternly. "I will see you safe, and do my best to avert a great scandal!"

The Kaiser folded his arms, and on his strong face was the expression of a man who knows himself to be absolutely beaten.

"I am in your hands," he said, in a voice that shook ever so slightly. "I was a fool to come. I bow to Fate."

"You are safe, I tell you, sire," Sexton Blake answered sternly, "if you obey me. Stay here, and I will get the sailors away with their prisoners. I will return later. In the meantime"—he drew a small pair of scissors from his pocket—"I am afraid that your moustache will have to come off. I shall have to take you to Lerwick, and the loss of it will be disguise enough."

The Kaiser started back, his fingers touching the moustache which had always been such a distinguishing mark on his face.

"I refuse!" he said sharply.

"As you will," Sexton Blake agreed. "If a little personal vanity is to stand in the way of your safety, sire, I will say no more."

The Kaiser's face worked, then he shrugged his shoulders resignedly.

"Very well," he agreed.

A few snips of the scissors, and the moustache was gone. That the disguise was good, there could be no doubt, and few people would have recognised in this clean-shaven man the fiercely-moustached Emperor of Germany.

"Stay here," the detective ordered, "and I will return as soon as possible. It may be hours, even a day; but you can trust me."

"So," the Kaiser answered simply, realising how much he must put his trust in this man.

Back to the fight went Sexton Blake, to find it all over, nine prisoners lying on the ground.

"Wondered where you had got to," the admiral said sharply.

"I went in pursuit of another of the men, sir," the detective answered quietly; "but he took to the sea. The tides are strong here—he is probably drowned."

In the darkness the admiral held out his hand to Sexton Blake, who took it at once.

"Britain owes you a great debt, Mr. Blake," he said earnestly.

"As a Britisher, I am proud to be of service to my country," the detective answered simply. He could have added that he expected to be of even greater service before this case came to an end.

"What next, sir?"

The admiral pointed to the wreck of the airship.

"All this must be blown up," he said, with determination. "The rest will lie with the Government. If I had my way"—he glared fiercely at the prisoners who lay bound on the ground—"Germany would hear of this underhand work with a vengeance."

Quick orders were given, and the wreck was piled into a heap. Then Sexton Blake piloted the admiral and an engineer officer, who carried dynamite cartridges and a coil of wire, to the cave in which the chart and the electric apparatus lay. For five minutes they were in it, and when they emerged, the engineer unwound, as he walked, a coil of wire.

Two hundred yards from the shore the little pinnace lay, and a thin line of wire, invisible in the darkness, ran from her to the rocks. On the deck it was connected with a button.

"Mr. Blake," Sir Henry said quietly, "you have so far been the leader in this great work. Will you finish it?"

Sexton Blake nodded, stepped forward, and knelt beside the bottom.

"Now," the admiral ordered.

The detective's finger pressed the button. A second passed, then on the little island two sheets of flame leapt upwards.

Germany's plans and her great airship had been scattered by dynamite cartridges.

With a smile, the admiral seated himself in the bows, and glanced at the prisoners who lay on the deck.

"Back to the ship," he ordered, adding, in a lower voice to the detective, "I think that finishes your work, and finishes it well."

The detective bowed in acknowledgement, but inwardly he knew that his work had scarcely started, and that much more had to be accomplished before he would be satisfied.

THE SEVENTH CHAPTER

The Kaiser brought to Lerwick—
Sexton Blake springs a surprise—Bound for England.

"I OWE YOU a debt that I shall never be able to repay, Mr. Blake," the Kaiser said gratefully, holding out his hand to the detective. Strangely enough, however, the latter did not seem to notice it.

"There is time enough for that when you are safely back in your own country, sire," he answered.

The Kaiser turned sharply and looked at his companion, but could read nothing in the expression of the calm face.

"What do you mean?" he asked.

"Many things may happen before then," Sexton Blake answered.

The Kaiser shrugged his shoulders sharply, and felt for the moustache that was no longer there.

"What can happen?" he demanded. "I am disguised, and I can soon get a vessel back. Once I am across the frontier I can keep all this dark, and can feign illness until—" he paused, feeling at his bare upper lip again, thus explaining the unfinished sentence.

The two men were seated in a small sailing vessel, which was now creeping into Lerwick Harbour. There was nothing suspicious in this, for no order to exclude all vessels while the Fleet was manoeuvring had been given, and this craft might well be one of those filled with curious sightseers who kept on going out to the Fleet.

Without hindrance the men landed, none of the loafers on the quay imagining that the man who walked with such martial tread was none other than the Emperor of Germany.

"We will go to my hotel," Sexton Blake said.

"As you will," the Kaiser agreed. "I can trust you to make all arrangements."

"You can, sire," the detective agreed; and there was a curious little smile on his lips.

Straight to his private room in the hotel Sexton Blake led the way. Spearing and Tinker were both there, and they rose respectfully as the Kaiser entered.

"Be seated, my friends," the detective said quietly. "For the time being his Majesty is plain Mr. Smith. It is wiser, I think."

"So," the Kaiser agreed, with a smile. "And I can assure you that Mr. Smith is hungry. It is late for dinner, but we can have something to eat. After that we will discuss the best plan for getting me back to Germany."

Sexton Blake had been lighting a cigar, but now he turned to the Kaiser with uplifted eyebrows.

"I beg your pardon?" he queried, as if in surprise.

"We can then make plans to get me back to my own country," the Kaiser repeated.

"But there is plenty of time for that." Sexton Blake flung the used match into the grate, and smiled. "Our more pressing need is a plan to get you to London."

"London!" the Kaiser gasped.

"Precisely, Mr. Smith." Sexton Blake examined his cigar to make sure that it was burning to his satisfaction, and dropped into a chair.

The Kaiser dropped his fist angrily onto the table.

"Enough of this fooling, my friend!" he said fiercely. "You know that I must return to Germany at once if suspicions are not to be aroused."

"My dear Mr. Smith," Sexton Blake protested amiably, "you are surely not going to be so ungrateful as to tear yourself away so soon?"

"I tell you I must get back!" the Kaiser thundered.

Sexton Blake fixed the ash from his cigar, and his smile was that of a man whose mind is made up, and whom nothing will turn from his purpose.

"Do you imagine," he said slowly, "that this escapade of yours is to pass so lightly? Can you, as a sane man, think that Britain is going to demand nothing of you in return?"

"What can they demand?" the Kaiser asked, in a shaking voice.

"That is not for me to say," the detective answered; "but there are those in London who will decide."

"You dare not take me there!"

Sexton Blake rang the bell, and a servant entered.

"Bring anything you have to eat," he ordered; "then find out how soon there is a boat sailing round the coast to Liverpool."

As the door closed behind the man the Kaiser turned angrily upon the detective.

"This is too much!" he cried angrily. "I have only to announce who I am to be treated with proper respect."

"Or disbelieved and be treated as a spy!" Sexton Blake answered.

The meal was served quickly, Sexton Blake whispering a few instructions to Tinker before it arrived, and the boy at once left. It was eaten practically in silence, and at the finish the Kaiser stood staring out into the street. Presently he started, and dragged a handkerchief from his pocket.

"Recognise friends, sire?" the detective queried pleasantly.

"Why?" the Kaiser snapped.

"I fancied you were waving to them."

"What friends should I have in this place?" the Kaiser answered hastily. "I am tired. Show me my room, and I will get to sleep."

Sexton Blake led the way to a room at the back, which overlooked the gardens of the hotel.

"Pleasant dreams, sire," he said, as he retired. "You will, of course, have no objection to a watch being kept outside your door? I am very anxious about your safety, as you know."

"As you will," the Kaiser answered shortly; and there was a little smile on his lips.

OUT IN THE garden Sexton Blake crouched behind a clump of bushes, and beside him were Spearing and Tinker.

"You are sure of what you have said, my lad?" the detective whispered.

"Yes," the boy answered confidently. "Two Germans passed the hotel, and that was when I saw the Kaiser raise his handkerchief."

"How know he is here, though?" Spearing jerked doubtfully, nodding towards the window of the Kaiser's bed-room, which was quite dark.

"Riddles are not in my line, my friend," Sexton Blake answered, his eyes in the same direction; "but I should say that—Ah! Look!"

A light had appeared in the window, evidently that of a candle, and three times it moved from side to side before disappearing.

"Looks uncommonly like a signal," Sexton Blake remarked.

"Sorry for the men who obey it—very!" Spearing jerked, feeling the great muscles of his arms.

Half an hour passed, and there was not a sound in the

garden, and the light appeared no more in the window. From the harbour came the occasional hooting of sirens.

What was that?

Something very like a soft thud reached the ears of the waiting men, then they caught sight of two dark figures, bearing something between them, coming across the grounds.

"Ladder!" Tinker whispered.

Spearing moved, ready to get into the fight at once, but Sexton Blake held him back with a touch on the arm.

Cautiously the two men moved across the grounds, reached the wall of the hotel, and raised the ladder beneath the window.

"Now!" Sexton Blake whispered, and moved forward. Only a dozen yards or so separated them from the window.

One man was already climbing the ladder, the other holding it at the foot, when the detectives made their leap. There was the click of handcuffs, and the man at the bottom was as neatly manacled as Spearing had ever done a job of the same kind in his life. The one above looked down quickly, and reached for his pocket, but before he could draw weapon Sexton Blake had snatched the ladder from under him, and he fell sprawling to the ground.

Click! The second man was handcuffed.

"What does this mean?" he blustered, in German.

Sexton Blake drew a cigar from his pocket, and lit it.

"That is just what you will shortly have to explain to the police, my friend," he answered.

"Tinker." He turned to the boy, and handed him a whistle. "Just go and call the police. You will guard these men, Spearing, and charge them as a suspected characters. Remember that we were taking a stroll in the grounds when we discovered them."

"Right!" The worthy official jerked. "What about you?"

Sexton Blake reared the ladder against the window again.

"Oh, I have a little call to make!" he answered, with a smile.

Up the ladder he went, and tapped at the window. It was instantly opened.

"It is you, Fritz?" the agitated voice of the Kaiser asked.

Sexton Blake clambered into the room, dropped the window, and switched on the electric light. A cry of anger broke from the Kaiser as he saw who it was in the room with him.

"What—what are you doing here?" he asked, in a shaking voice.

"I am guarding you, sire," Sexton Blake answered coolly. "There are a terrible lot of suspicious characters about, you know; in fact, we have just arrested two in the garden of the hotel."

"Who—who were they?" the Kaiser asked, trying to speak indifferently, but with poor success.

"I really did not have time to question them," Sexton Blake replied lightly; "but I certainly fancy that they were Germans."

THE EIGHTH CHAPTER

*The Terms That Were Not Accepted—Spearing in Error—
Where is the Kaiser?—On the Roof—Arrested.*

THE TRAIN WHIRLED along from Liverpool, carrying its usual load of passengers to London. The majority of the compartments were well filled, but a first class one, right in the centre of the train, on the window of which had been stuck a "reserved" label, held only three men and a boy—the Kaiser, Sexton Blake, Mr. Spearing, and Tinker. Pedro was back in the guard's van.

The detective smoked away placidly, and on his face was the expression of a man who is quite satisfied with life. Spearing, sleeping in a corner, also looked as if there was nothing much to trouble him just now, while Tinker busied himself with writing a chronicle of the events of the past few days.

Only the Kaiser, sitting moodily in a corner, his fine eyes staring out through the window into the night, looked discontented. His face was pale, unnaturally so, and the fingers that felt his upper lip trembled suggestively. No difficulty had been experienced in getting him away from Lerwick, and now they were speeding on towards London. That was what probably worried the Kaiser. He knew that he was in no personal danger, also that it would be possible for him to explain his absence from his own country, but he did not know the exact reason why his captors insisted upon taking him to London.

Maybe it was to exact a price from him. But why could they not have arranged that already, and let him go? Surely his word was enough to ensure payment of any sum, however large?

"It is permitted that a prisoner smoke, Mr. Blake?" he asked.

"I apologise, sire," Sexton Blake answered, pulling out his case and offering the Kaiser a cigar. "I think you will like these."

The Kaiser bit off the end with his strong teeth, and lit up. For a minute he smoked steadily, but it was obvious from the way that he continually glanced at the detective that he had something to say.

"What do you gain by all this?" he asked abruptly, when he did break the silence.

"Why, little enough," Sexton Blake answered. "A little honour, perhaps, and that is not a very substantial thing."

"It would be secret, too," the Kaiser continued. "Whatever you are taking me to London for it will be impossible to hold me there."

Sexton Blake flicked the ash of his cigar through the open window.

"As to that, sire," he answered, "the length of your stay will depend upon yourself."

"Then it will not be long!" the Kaiser growled.

"The moment our terms are accepted, and your word given to keep them, I shall see that you reach your own country in safety," Sexton Blake assured him.

The Kaiser gnawed at his upper lip. There was an angry look in his eyes, and it was plain that he only controlled his temper by an effort of will.

"What will the terms be?" he demanded.

Sexton Blake shook his head protestingly.

"Perhaps I can guess," he said, "but guessing is an

unsatisfactory thing."

The Kaiser chewed at the end of his cigar until it was of no further use as a smoke, and flung it impatiently away. Sexton Blake offered him a fresh one, but he refused.

"Mr. Blake," he said in a low tone, after glancing across at Spearing to make certain that he was really asleep, "let me suggest the terms. I have been beaten over the Shetlands, and I admit it. Your report will permit the authorities to take precautions to prevent such a thing happening again, and that is all you want. It would be easy for me to escape if this train slackens; my English is good, and I would find my way back to my own country."

"You will not find it easy to escape, sire," Sexton Blake corrected.

"But why not?" The Kaiser was bending forward eagerly, and his strong face was working. "You have but to fall asleep—in an instant I have thrown open that door and dropped out onto the line. You awake and rush after me with your companions—but you go the wrong way. It is all so simple! I return to Germany, and you receive—what is your price?"

"It is all so simple, as you say, sire," the detective agreed; "but one thing you have erred."

"So?" the Kaiser queried.

"I should rush after you the right way," Sexton Blake explained. "It is a habit of mine that I have often found useful."

The Kaiser's hands clenched as if he would have loved to strike the smiling detective in the face.

"You are a hard man!" he said bitterly. "But the price must be fixed soon, if I am to escape before London is reached! A hundred thousand marks—what of that?"

Sexton Blake shook his head, and his eyelids drooped as if the conversation bored him.

"You shall be head of my secret police," the Kaiser went on

eagerly. "I would give much to have such a man as you in my service!"

"A man who has sold his own country?" Sexton Blake asked meaningly. "You must have strange tastes, sire!"

"Then, Himmel, name your own price!" the Kaiser growled.

Sexton Blake lit a fresh cigar, and through the blue smoke he looked his distinguished prisoner full in the face.

"My price is beyond your compassing," he said sternly, "for your escape will only be purchased by my death." His face set hard, and there was an angry light in his eyes. "Had any other man asked me to sell my honour—my country—I would have thrashed him as one beats a faithless dog! In your country such things may be easy—the buying and dealing in men's consciences—but here a man puts his conscience before his fortune; his country before everything!"

"All men?" the Kaiser sneered.

"There is no country that has not got its black sheep," Sexton Blake answered, with a shrug of his shoulders; "but thank Heaven ours is a small flock!"

The Kaiser opened his lips to speak again, but the detective held a hand up sharply to silence him.

"I have given you my answer," he said quietly.

The brakes grated on the wheels, the lights of a station showed ahead, and the train drew up in it.

"My chance!" the Kaiser said sharply. "Two hundred thousand marks!"

For answer, Sexton Blake leant forward and roused Spearing.

"Got there?" the latter jerked, reaching for his hat.

"No," Sexton Blake answered. "I am going to the bar to get fresh cigars. You will guard our—er—guest until I return."

"May I come with you, sir?" Tinker asked eagerly. "I'm as stiff as a board."

Sexton Blake nodded, and he and his young assistant stepped

out onto the platform, leaving only Spearing and the Kaiser in the compartment. The detective did not hurry, for the train waited ten minutes, and he and Tinker lingered in the bar drinking coffee.

"Time to go, my lad," Sexton Blake said, putting his cup down.

As he turned towards the door Spearing, his usually ruddy face pale, came rushing through the crowd. Sexton Blake caught his breath sharply, knowing that the worst had happened.

"Gone!" Spearing gasped.

But before he could say any more, for his wild look was already attracting attention, Sexton Blake gripped him by the arm and led him outside, where there were fewer people.

"Quick!" he ordered. And even his usually steady voice shook a trifle. "Tell me what has happened!"

"Someone came to window!" Spearing jerked. "Looked like German! Got up to tell him compartment was reserved! A door banged behind me—looked round—Kaiser gone!"

Sexton Blake had expected this the moment he caught sight of the Scotland Yard official, but now that the truth was put into words it nevertheless staggered him. After all the trouble— after all the danger that he had gone through—that the Kaiser should escape in this simple manner!

Then his jaw set hard. He was not beaten yet; he would prevent the Kaiser leaving the country.

At a run, he went down the platform, followed by Spearing and Tinker; for the guards were already bustling people into the train. He seized an official by the arm.

"Could anyone have left the down side without a ticket— someone who had arrived by this train?" he asked sharply.

"No fear, sir!" the man answered, with a confident grin. "We've got used to people trying to bilk us in that way, and that there is no earthly chance of anyone getting through on either side without a ticket!"

Sexton Blake slipped a sovereign into the man's hand, and the latter at once became all attention.

"Try the gates," the detective ordered. "Find out if anyone without a ticket has paid to go through."

"Right you are, sir!" the man answered, and hurried away at a trot. He wondered what all the excitement could be about, but the sovereign was in his pocket, and that was good enough for him.

That the Kaiser had no money on him Sexton Blake knew, but the man who had tapped at the window might have joined him and paid.

The official came hurrying back.

"No, sir," he announced. Then a brilliant idea struck him. "Detectives?" he queried. "Prisoner got away?"

"Yes," Sexton Blake admitted, not seeing what else he could do.

"Then I'll tell you what the man has done, sir," the official continued. "He's slipped into another carriage, and means to try and get away when the train slackens down somewhere."

A whistle blew, and there was no time for the detectives to hesitate.

"He may be right," he said sharply. "We must take the train and watch." In a lower voice he added: "if he has escaped I'll follow him to Germany if necessary—the matter shall not rest here!"

Sexton Blake was not the type of man to give in easily, and he had no intention of being beaten now.

As the train was on the move, the detectives and the boy scrambled into their reserved compartment and dropped into their seats. The door on the opposite side still swung open, showing how their prisoner had escaped, and Spearing, growling with anger, closed it. Just then he would have fought an army singlehanded, if it would have given him the chance of getting the Kaiser back. Never before had he made such a bloomer; though, like every other man, including Sexton Blake, he had made mistakes in his time.

"Being a fool!" he jerked disgustedly. "If I were you, never let me work with you again!"

A wry smile crossed Sexton Blake's lips, but he held out his hand to the crestfallen official.

"It was not your fault," he said simply. "I never ought to have left you alone. I should have remembered that he was no ordinary prisoner, and that some steps were bound to be taken to free him."

"But all the men who were with him on the airship were captured, sir," Tinker put in.

"Yes, but you can be sure that there were others in Lerwick," Sexton Blake answered bitterly; "men who had been working at the cables showing the new harbours. It is one of them who has got him away."

"And do you think that he is on the train, sir?"

Sexton Blake shrugged his shoulders, with the manner of a man who admits himself baffled.

"We shall know soon, lad," he replied.

But he was to know sooner than he expected—very much sooner. From above, on the roof of the carriage, sounded a sharp blow, such as might have been made by a man's boot, and Sexton Blake, his eyes sparkling, leapt to his feet.

"That's it!" he cried. "Why didn't I think of it? In the dark station, no one would have noticed him crouching on the roof!"

To the door Sexton Blake sprang, and flung it open. He saw that his compartment was the last one of the coach, so that it would be easy enough for a man to slip to the back of it and mount the iron steps that led to the roof.

Sexton Blake went in this direction now, moving confidently despite the speed of the train, and reached the back of the compartment; Spearing and Tinker behind him. Up the steps he went, and peered over the roof.

On it lay a man at full length, his fingers gripping the electric light fitting, and at a glance it was possible to see that it was the Kaiser.

"Hardly a comfortable way of travelling, sire!" Sexton Blake called out; having to raise his voice to make himself heard above the wind.

With a jerk that nearly threw him from the roof the Kaiser swung round, and a revolver gleamed in his hand.

"Go back!" he cried fiercely. "I have the means of protecting myself now, and I shall use it!"

With a sharp jerk Sexton Blake drew himself on to the roof, and a bullet whistled by his head. The next second he was on the Kaiser, gripping his revolver-wrist and holding him down. But even then the Kaiser was not giving in easily. His blood was up. Freedom had been so near to him, and he was going to struggle to retain it.

Now Spearing and Tinker were on the roof, too, crawling along to help their chief.

With a mighty show of strength, for which few would have given his slender physique credit, the Kaiser raised himself to his knees, his arms locked round the detective, and the two swayed backwards and forwards, the revolver going off again in the scuffle, the bullet cutting through Spearing's felt hat.

It looked as if the Kaiser was never destined to return to Germany, but was to be picked up—a corpse—from the line. A fall from the train, at the pace at which she was travelling, would mean certain death.

Sexton Blake was struggling to get his man in a grip that could not be shaken, and the others were unable to help him on the sloping roof.

"The train's stopping!" Spearing shouted.

It was right enough. Evidently someone had heard the struggle on the roof—possibly the revolver-shot—and had pulled the alarm-bell.

Sexton Blake redoubled his efforts, hoping to be able to get the Kaiser back into the compartment before the train actually stopped; but the latter struggled like a madman, and twice nearly flung himself and Sexton Blake from the roof. With a jerk the train stopped, and excited voices shouted out, directing the guards to the scene of the struggle; but still the Kaiser fought on, not reckoning what the consequences might be.

A guard came clambering on to the roof, another following him.

"Here, what does this mean?" The first shouted.

At last, realising his position, the Kaiser stopped struggling, and a guard seized him and dragged him down to the line. Sexton Blake and Spearing followed, and were instantly surrounded by excited passengers; but Tinker managed to slip down in the darkness and clamber into an empty compartment. Not that he minded being captured with his master, but he felt that his freedom might mean much later on.

"What does this mean?" one of the guards demanded, addressing Sexton Blake.

"This man was our prisoner," the detective answered promptly, "and he tried to escape."

The guard eyed Sexton Blake up and down suspiciously.

"I reckon you'll have to prove that," he said. "Will some of you gentlemen help me to take these men to the van, and stop there until we reach the next station?"

Very crestfallen, his face working with emotion, the Kaiser allowed himself to be bundled into the guard's van with the others. A good dozen of the passengers—all young men—followed, so that there was no chance of escape.

"This is terrible!" the Kaiser whispered, in a shaking voice.

"It is your own fault," Sexton Blake answered bitterly. "You will now learn what the inside of a police cell is like."

A mile further on the train pulled up at a station where it was not marked to stop, and a few words to the stationmaster explained the state of affairs. Five minutes later the train moved on, engine-driver and stoker working hard to make up the time they had lost.

The Kaiser, Sexton Blake, and Spearing were being marched under strong escort to the police station of Atborough.

This did not particularly worry Sexton Blake. On the morrow he knew that Spearing would be able to clear up matters without revealing the Kaiser's identity.

Little did he know the developments matters were to take, or he would not have been so easy in his mind.

THE NINTH CHAPTER

Bad News—Tinker Knows Something—What Next?

AT THE POLICE-STATION no time was wasted, and the three men were formally charged before the inspector. The Kaiser boldly gave his name as Smith, and related how the others had attacked him, evidently meaning to rob him, and to prevent this he had escaped from the compartment and clambered onto the roof. They had followed him, that was all.

"What is your name, my man?" the inspector demanded haughtily, addressing Spearing.

"William Spearing!" that worthy snapped.

"Occupation?" the inspector asked mechanically.

"Detective, Scotland Yard!" the famous official growled.

The inspector dropped his pen and stared; then he laughed.

"I suppose you'll be telling me next that this man"—he indicated the Kaiser—"was your prisoner?"

"Should if I liked talking to fools!" Spearing snapped, his temper getting the better of him.

The inspector in charge kept perfectly cool. He was sure that this man was an impostor, and was only too glad to make him commit himself. It would be all the hotter for him when he went before the magistrate on the morrow.

"You have your warrant?" he suggested cunningly.

Spearing started, and ran his fingers savagely through his bristling hair.

"No," he admitted lamely. And the inspector turned to Sexton Blake.

"You?" he said.

"Sexton Blake, sometimes called a detective."

"What, another!" The inspector threw up his hands in mock awe. "You can, of course, prove that?"

"Certainly!" Sexton Blake answered. "Mr. Hardy, the mayor, will do that."

The inspector looked doubtful, and lost some of his bullying manner. Perhaps, after all, these men were genuine, and should that prove to be the case things might be very awkward.

"Very well," he said shortly, "if you wish it I will send for Mr. Hardy in the morning."

Without further commitment, the three men were marched away to separate cells. This did not worry Sexton Blake, as he was so tired that he would be glad to sleep even in a cell, and Spearing was almost pleased at having a chance of making the officious inspector look cheap the next morning. Only the Kaiser, his shoulders very square, looked savagely at the policeman who conducted him to the cell where he was to spend the night.

Early the next morning Sexton Blake requested his gaoler to send for Mr. Hardy, the mayor, but it was not until nearly eleven that he arrived at the police-station. He was a little, fussy man, whom Sexton Blake had once helped out of a trifling difficulty.

"Why, Mr. Blake!" he cried, seizing both the detective's hands. "What are you in here for?"

"You had better ask the inspector," Sexton Blake answered, nodding at the man, who was standing rather sheepishly by the door. "I told him who I was, and that Mr. Spearing and myself were merely endeavouring to prevent a prisoner, an important one, escaping."

"But he was brought here, too—the prisoner?" the mayor asked eagerly.

"Yes," Sexton Blake admitted.

"Ah, then not so much harm is done, after all!" the mayor said, in tones of evident relief. "On behalf of the authorities, I apologise for the mistake that has been made. Your prisoner is safe, and—"

"But he isn't," the inspector put in, in a shaking voice.

A dead silence fell over the men in the cell; then Sexton Blake darted forward, and gripped the inspector by the arm.

"What do you mean?" he cried, shaking the man backwards and forwards.

The inspector wriggled free, and made a frantic effort to look dignified.

"Why—why, an hour ago a Mr. Leiberbaum came here"— the inspector licked his lips as if they had gone very dry—"and offered to go bail for Mr. Smith, saying that he had known him well in Germany."

"And you let him go?" Sexton Blake cried.

"What else could I do?" the inspector asked angrily, recovering his nerve. "Mr. Leiberbaum is one of our oldest and richest inhabitants."

"A naturalised Englishman?"

"Why, I don't know," the inspector admitted. And again there was a silence. It was Mr. Hardy, the mayor, who spoke first.

"He could really do nothing else, Mr. Blake," he said apologetically. "This Leiberbaum is a substantial house-holder and therefore a fit and proper bail."

Sexton Blake seemed to rouse himself from a reverie, and his thin lips were set hard.

"May I go now?" he asked shortly. "Mr. Spearing, too, of course?"

"Certainly, sir," the inspector said eagerly, positively anxious to see the last of his prisoners. "I can only say again, sir, that I am sorry that—"

"And where does this Leiberbaum live?" Sexton Blake interrupted sharply.

"The Oaks, Merivale Road, sir," the inspector answered.

Without another word, the mayor, trotting excitedly after him, Sexton Blake stepped from the cell into the office, and a few seconds later Spearing, looking very angry indeed, joined him.

"Hear of this!" he snapped at the inspector. "Have you at Yard and teach you your business!"

How much more Spearing would have poured out it is hard to say, but he had no chance to say more, Sexton Blake gripping him by the arm and leading him from the police-station. A cab was passing, and he hailed it, and bundled the surprised official in.

"The Oaks, Merivale Road!" he ordered.

The cab drove away, and Spearing turned in amazement to his companion.

"What meaning of this?" he demanded.

Sexton Blake related what had happened, and Spearing's face fell as he learnt of the Kaiser's escape.

"What doing now?" he jerked.

"I am going to bluff this Leiberbaum," Sexton Blake answered.

Through the town the cab drove, and turned into a road which was evidently occupied by people of means. The houses were large, standing in their own grounds, and most of them boasted stables. The Oaks, before which the cab stopped, was perhaps the biggest and most imposing-looking of them all.

Sexton Blake and Spearing stepped out, and as they did so

a boy, who had been lounging on the other side of the road, strolled up. His clothes were muddy, but not particularly old, and, though his face was grimed over, Sexton Blake had no difficulty in recognising his young assistant.

"Spare a copper, guv'nor!" the boy whined.

Sexton Blake made a pretence of feeling in his pockets, and that gave Tinker time to speak.

"Hung about outside the police-station, sir," he whispered; "saw a big, fat man—didn't look like English—go in. When he came out the Kaiser was with him. I followed them here."

"Good lad!" his master answered, in a low tone. "Go round to the back; make sure that he does not leave that way."

Tinker darted off, and Sexton Blake moved towards the gate. There he stopped thoughtfully.

"You had better wait here, my friend," he said, "in case they are bold enough to try and get him away openly."

"Right!" Spearing grunted. And his fingers jingled the handcuffs in his pocket. He was not likely to make a mistake again.

Quite in the manner of a casual visitor, Sexton Blake strolled up the well-kept drive, even stopping once or twice to admire the roses that bloomed in profusion on either side of it. But not once did he really remove his eyes from the windows of the large house. He expected to see people watching, but if they were doing so they managed to hide themselves very successfully. He knocked boldly at the door, and a maidservant answered it.

"Mr. Leiberbaum at home is?" Sexton Blake asked, with a strong German accent.

"I think so, sir," the girl answered. "What name shall I say?"

"Colonel von Harmann," Sexton Blake told her, speaking very distinctly so that no mistake should be made.

The girl departed, leaving the detective standing in the hall, but she quickly returned.

"You are to come in, sir," she announced.

Down the broad hall she led the way, and flung open the door on the left.

"Colonel one Hyman!" she announced, remembering the name as nearly as she could. And Sexton Blake walked quietly in.

A tall, very fat German, aged about sixty, rose eagerly as the detective entered, but as he caught sight of his visitor his heavy jaw dropped.

"There some mistake is," he said, in a guttural tone. "I was a friend expecting."

"I am afraid you will expect him a long time, Herr Leiberbaum!" Sexton Blake remarked, suddenly flinging open the door to make certain the servant was not listening outside.

"And for why?" the German asked, his great round face curiously pasty and flabby-looking.

"Because he is a prisoner onboard one of our battleships," the detective informed him. "You see, the colonel came to see the manoeuvres, and what more could he want than to be actually aboard one of the battleships?"

Herr Leiberbaum sank heavily into a chair, and his fat, white fingers beat nervously on the desk before him.

"But for why have you come here?" he asked slowly. "And who are you?"

"I am Sexton Blake," the detective answered quietly.

"The man who—" The German broke off abruptly, and added, in a shaking voice: "Of you I have heard."

"And I am here," Sexton Blake continued, taking a chair, "to assure myself that his Majesty suffered no harm last night."

The German's chair went back sharply, the legs grating on the polished floor, and he glanced sharply over his shoulder at a closed door.

"What do you mean?" he growled.

The lids had been lowered languidly over the detective's eyes, now they were raised, showing how keen and searching the grey eyes were.

"Don't fool!" he said shortly. "It was you who bailed the man Smith out, the man whom you knew to be the Kaiser—my prisoner. You were followed here, and entered with him."

A curious look of dignity had come into Herr Leiberbaum's manner, and the colour was creeping back to his flabby cheeks.

"So," he admitted calmly.

"And where is he now?" Sexton Blake snapped out the words, hoping to bustle the man into an admission, but for once he was not successful.

The fat German shook his head slowly, and there was a grin on his lips.

"As a detective, it is that you are good, perhaps," he answered, "but as a diplomatist—nein."

Sexton Blake thought rapidly, turning over in his mind, and quickly came to a decision.

"Listen to me, Herr Leiberbaum!" he said earnestly.

"My ears are at your service—so," the German answered placidly.

"I know that it is you who have helped the Kaiser," he continued sternly, "meaning to help him to get back to his own country. Well, suppose you succeed?"

The German shrugged his shoulders. He evidently did not intend to commit himself.

"Do you think that that will end this matter?" Sexton Blake went on. "No; I tell you it will make it worse. Then there will be no treating first hand with the Kaiser, and there will be only one answer to his movements—war."

"Germany has an army!" Herr Leiberbaum sneered.

"Great Britain has a navy!" Sexton Blake rejoined. "Your country is endeavouring to make hers as powerful, but at present she has not succeeded. A great army is no use unless you can land it."

Herr Leiberbaum rose impatiently, and paced up and down the room. He stopped before Sexton Blake, and there was a fighting look in his eyes.

"It is that I have admitted what I have done," he said firmly. "I am a German, even if to England I have come, and the Kaiser is my ruler. He has been here, and I am proud to make owning of it. What can you do? You can search this place—to find him gone."

Sexton Blake looked keenly into the German's face, knowing that he lied, but it told him nothing.

"What can you do?" the German continued. "You can have me arrested—so. And with what would you charge me? You could not the accusation make that I had saved the Kaiser, for that would mean war, and your country is no readier for that than mine."

Sexton Blake rose and took up his hat.

"I admire your pluck," he said.

"I am a German—the Kaiser is my ruler," Herr Leiberbaum answered quietly.

Without further words, the detective left the house, admitting inwardly that he had entirely failed to bluff the stolid German. But of one thing he was certain, and that was that the Kaiser was still in the house. But how to get him out? Herr Leiberbaum had spoken the truth when he had told Sexton Blake that he dared not act openly, but, on the other hand, the detective had not the slightest intention of being beaten. What could he do?

Outside he found Spearing pacing up and down like a sentry.

"What news?" the worthy official jerked eagerly.

"The Kaiser is there right enough," Sexton Blake answered shortly.

"Good!" Spearing started towards the house, his fingers on the handcuffs in his pocket, but Sexton Blake gripped him by the arm and held him back.

"No, not that!" he said sternly. "We have got to get him away, but there must be no publicity."

THE TENTH CHAPTER

The Kaiser Leaves—The Carriage Accident—
The Cab that was Not Empty.

HERR LEIBERBAUM STROLLED down the drive before his house, a fat cigar between his teeth, a perfectly placid look on his heavy-featured face. Apparently, he had not a care in the world, and, as he stopped and examined his roses, blowing a little cigar-smoke over the ones that showed signs of blight, there was nothing about him to suggest that his mind was in the least perturbed. He was just the prosperous merchant taking an interest in his garden during his spare time.

In this manner Herr Leiberbaum strolled down to the front gate, and stood leaning with his elbows on the top of it. It was early evening, dusk was just commencing to fall, and in this aristocratic part people were mostly dining. Anyway, the broad road was empty save for a tradesman's cart that stood right at the further end.

A smile of satisfaction broke through the German's stolid expression, and he turned and walked briskly up the drive. As he reached the front door it opened, and the Kaiser's white face looked out.

"All is well?" he asked eagerly.

"Your Majesty need have no fear," Herr Leiberbaum answered reassuringly.

"Fear?" The Kaiser's eyebrows contracted angrily, and his fingers fidgeted with his bare upper lip. "It is not that I have fear, but I am thinking of what may happen if I do not return to Germany soon."

"There is nothing to stop you now, sire!" Herr Leiberbaum said hopefully. "It is plain that they believe that you have already left here, and by now the boats for the Continent are being watched. But you have nothing to do but go north. I have given you the names of a dozen men who will help you in coast towns, for they are all loyal Germans, even if they do live in England. Your yacht is cruising in the north, so what will be easier than to send a code message to her. She will come to any part of the coast, and a boat will fetch you off.

"What could be easier?"

The Kaiser gnawed his upper lip doubtfully.

"Just because it all sounds too easy do I doubt its success," he answered. "I know this Sexton Blake, and twice has he thwarted even me. It is not like him to give up a case so easily, especially when such great issues are at stake."

Herr Leiberbaum shrugged his shoulders a trifle impatiently. He had risked a lot to help the ruler of his native land, and this hesitation annoyed him.

"Very well, sire," he said; "we will think of another plan!"

"No, no!" the Kaiser cried hastily. "Order the carriage round at once!"

Leiberbaum touched a bell, and less than a minute later a closed carriage drove round to the front door.

"This man could not possibly have been bribed?" the Kaiser whispered anxiously, peering out at the solid face of the coachman.

"He, too, is of our country, sire," Leiberbaum answered. "There is no time to lose. I have already told the man to drive to Bellborough, ten miles from here. That place will not be watched. He will time his arrival so that you only just have time to catch your train. Here is your ticket."

Just for a moment more the Kaiser hesitated, then he stepped into the carriage. He held out his hand to Herr Leiberbaum.

"I shall not forget," he said gratefully.

"Nor I, sire," Leiberbaum answered, bending ponderously over the outstretched hand.

The carriage drove away, and the Kaiser, leaning back in a corner, felt that his troubles were over at last. Once he was clear of the town he would make for someplace right up in the north, after sending instructions to the commander of the Hohenzollern to proceed there. Possibly, Blake was keeping an eye on the Royal yacht, but the Kaiser knew that he dared not do anything once he was on board.

The carriage proceeded rapidly, the broad roads of the residential part were left behind, and the busier thoroughfares entered. The Kaiser leant back further in his corner, fearing that he might be recognised, forgetting that the loss of his moustache was about the finest disguise that he could possibly have had. And with each yard that he covered, he began to feel more and more relieved, and to believe that Sexton Blake had at last been baffled.

"Illness o' the German Hemperor!" a newsboy yelled, and the Kaiser, glancing out of the carriage, saw those words on the poster. He bit his lip savagely, realising that his absence from public life had already been noticed, and that some excuse had had to be made to account for it.

A little further on another boy was displaying a placard, and the words on it brought a growl of anger from the Kaiser.

"Where is the German Emperor?" the bill ran.

The Kaiser pulled the check-cord, and the coachman pulled up. Out of the carriage the Emperor leant, forgetting all about secrecy now, and bought a paper. Little did the grimy-faced urchin who sold it imagine that the scare-line on the placard that he held in front of him referred to this angry-looking man to whom he sold the paper, and who gave him a piece of silver, and drove on without waiting for the change. It was only when the carriage had gone a couple of hundred yards that he discovered that the silver coin was not a shilling, but a piece of foreign money.

"No wonder 'e was in sich a 'urry!" he growled. "S'pose I'll be able ter pass it somewhere!"

Leaning back in the carriage, the Kaiser unfolded the paper with fingers that trembled rather badly, and he had no difficulty in finding the part of the contents that referred to himself. The headings were heavily leaded, and ran as follows:

"WHERE IS THE KAISER?"

Is He Watching The Manoeuvres?

"Our Berlin correspondent telegraphs us that for more than a week the Kaiser has been invisible, and that several state functions at which he was to have been present have been postponed. The reason given for this is illness, but it is hard to believe that that is true, for not one of the court physicians have been to the palace. Naturally, there arises the question as to where the Kaiser really is. To answer it is impossible, but, perhaps, it is easy to guess.

"WHERE IS THE HOHENZOLLERN?"

"The Imperial yacht is somewhere in the North Sea, and we need scarcely remind our readers that that is where the great secret manoeuvres are taking place. Already the yacht has been close to the war vessels, and it is reported that the Kaiser has been seen on board. This seems to be probable, yet, if it is the case, it is surely remarkable that his Majesty paid no visit to the admiral in charge, despite the fact that a salute of guns was fired as soon as the Royal yacht approached.

"Surely, considering that even British vessels are forbidden to follow the manoeuvres with sightseers on board, something should be done to check this German spying. True, the spying is being done by no less a man than the Kaiser, but that only makes it more significant.

"Is it not quite time that this kind of thing was put a stop to?"

The Kaiser crumpled the paper up and threw it away.

"The fools!" he muttered.

The carriage was passing along a busy thoroughfare now, and the traffic was at times congested.

Suddenly, a heavy cart swung out of a side turning, tried to cut in front of the Kaiser's brougham, swung round to avoid a collision, but was too late. The heavy wheel of the cart caught the rear wheel of the brougham and fairly ripped it off.

In an instant all was excitement. The shock of the impact had thrown the brougham horse, which was now doing its best to kick the carriage to pieces, and the coachman hastily jerked the door open.

"Afraid you were hurt, sir," he whispered, as he helped the Kaiser out.

Already a crowd had sprung up, apparently from nowhere, and a policeman was forcing his way through. The Kaiser went white, fearing recognition.

"Now then, what's all this?" the constable demanded importantly.

The Kaiser looked round quickly, his one idea being to get away from the crowd.

"Cab, sir?" a man shouted, drawing his cab up beside the crowd.

Without hesitation, the Kaiser pushed his way through the crowd.

"Bellborough station!" he ordered, and stepped into the cab.

With a cry he started back, but a hand gripped his wrist. The cab was already occupied—by Sexton Blake!

"What does this mean?" the Kaiser demanded in a shaking voice.

"Merely that I am not beaten so easily as you imagine, sire," the detective answered blandly.

"Then you—"

"Precisely," Sexton Blake explained. "The accident was arranged by me. Of course, I could have followed you to Bellborough, but I was not anxious to make a scene there—for your sake—and it is so much easier to explain in this cab."

The Kaiser moved nearer to the window.

"I shall order the man to stop!" he said fiercely.

"I should not, if I were you, sire," Sexton Blake protested. "You see, the man happens to be Mr. Spearing, and I doubt whether he would take orders from you."

The Kaiser leant back in his seat, the look of a man who knows that he is beaten in his eyes.

"Where are we going!?" he asked at last.

"We are carrying out my original intention, sire," Sexton Blake answered. "We are going to London."

"I refuse!" the Kaiser snapped.

Sexton Blake shook his head playfully, and called to Spearing to drive faster.

"You really should not joke, sire!" he protested.

THE ELEVENTH CHAPTER

In London—By Way of the Embankment—
The Call for Help—The Kaiser Captured.

SEXTON BLAKE HELPED the Kaiser to alight from a cab, and dismissed it.

"Where are we?" the latter asked sharply, looking round at the practically deserted streets.

"Why, by St. Paul's Station, close to the Embankment, sire," the detective answered readily.

On the other side of the road a cab pulled up, and four men clambered out. They walked briskly across to the station and entered the booking-office. If anyone had followed them, however, he would have seen that they did not take tickets, but stood close to the door, one of them peering out, as if waiting for someone.

"But why here?" The Kaiser protested. "Were you not taking me to this Prime Minister of yours?"

"Precisely," Sexton Blake agreed. "It is quite time that you made the terms that will purchase your liberty, and I mean that you shall do so to-night."

"Bah, you mean great things!" the Kaiser sneered, but there was an uneasy look in his eyes. "Others know that I am here, and I tell you that if I do not go free soon it will mean war."

Sexton Blake bowed coolly, and lit a cigar.

"I am aware of that," he admitted—"quite aware that men of your own country know that you are here. You think it possible that I can have passed all the years that I have at detective work without knowing that there is quite a small army of Germans in England? Ay, I know that, and that practically every town, every defence in Great Britain is as well known to your officers as to ours—more shame to us! Your spies have worked well for years, unhampered by our authorities, though the truth has been pointed out to them!"

"They have laughed—saying they were too strong for us," the Kaiser sneered.

"And at present we are," Sexton Blake said quietly; "for your plans are not mature, especially now that you have had that little upset in the Shetlands."

The Kaiser glared as he thought of the work of years being done by a few dynamite cartridges.

"Let us go to this minister of yours!" he snapped. "Perhaps he will see reason."

Sexton Blake nodded, and slipped his arm through the Kaiser's. The latter tried to free himself, but found it impossible.

"Am I to be treated as a criminal?" he demanded haughtily.

"Why, no, sire," Sexton Blake answered, "but as a precious possession that must on no account be lost. Besides, it has been raining, and the pavements are slippery. What more natural than I should try and prevent you falling?"

The two crossed the road, and entered the Embankment. It was ten o'clock, an hour at which there is very little traffic about, for it is too early for the theatre traffic to be swarming down onto the Embankment. Here and there a couple of ragged men lounged on the seats, but a penetrating drizzle was falling, and that had driven most of the outcasts to the shelter of arches and doorways, where they would crouch until the police should turn them out.

On the river the lights of an occasional barge or tug glimmered, but even they were made dim by the rain.

If Sexton Blake had looked behind him he would have seen that the four men who had entered St. Paul's Station were following. True, if he had looked back, he still would have thought nothing of it, for what was there remarkable in four men walking westwards along the Embankment at that hour of the night?

Past the Temple Sexton Blake and the Kaiser walked, stepping out briskly, and it was then that the four men following separated, and one hurried on ahead of the rest, and passed the detective and his companion. He was a ragged-looking fellow, and he walked with the shuffle peculiar to the outcast, vagrant class. His companions had quickened their pace, too, but slackened it again when within twenty yards of the detective.

Something about the furtive manner of the man who had shuffled past attracted Sexton Blake's attention, and he followed him with his eyes. He saw him hesitate, glance round once or twice, then turn towards the steps leading from Cleopatra's Needle to the river.

A queer feeling gripped at the detective's heart. No man in London knew better than he what a favourite place for suicides this was, and he quickened his footsteps.

"Help!" The cry rang out shrilly from the direction of the steps, breaking off as if choked back by the water.

Jerking the Kaiser with him, Sexton Blake started forward at a run. He guessed that the outcast had flung himself in, meaning to take his life, but had learnt to fear death as soon as he had struck the water. There are many would-be suicides like that, men who do not realise really what they are doing until the bony hand of Death is really at their throats.

In the ordinary way, Sexton Blake would not have hesitated to dive in after the man, but things were different now. He was linked to the Kaiser, and not for so much as a second dared to release him.

Straight to the steps he ran, still dragging the Kaiser with him, and stood peering down at the swiftly-running river. He could see no trace of the vagrant, and decided that the tide must have already—

Someone leapt from the shadow of the wall, and Sexton Blake, seeing him coming, tried to dodge aside. In this manner he half avoided the blow aimed at him with a heavy cudgel, but even then it struck him down the side of the head and glanced off on to his shoulder, causing him to stagger back.

Before he could recover himself a pair of powerful hands had gripped him, and he was being forced down the steps towards the water. The danger of his position roused him, and in the darkness he stared into his assailant's face.

It was a face to remember, too. Livid white, adorned—if the word may be used—by a straggling, red beard. But the one thing that the detective noted more than all else was a scar that had severed the upper lip at some time or another, healing so that it was all puckered and drawn up.

All this Sexton Blake saw, but the blow on the side of the head had temporarily weakened him, and he struggled but feebly as he felt himself being forced down the steps.

Then he was heaved backwards, the evil face with the red beard was no longer near to his own, and he struck the cold waters of the Thames and sank beneath the surface.

The shock of the cold water revived him, taking away the dazing effects of the blow that he had received, and he struck out strongly to get his head above the surface. Then he shook the water from his eyes, and found that the tide was fast carrying him past the steps, with a strength that there would be no fighting against.

He cursed himself for a fool, telling himself that he ought to have known that another attempt would be made to rescue the Kaiser. He looked to where he had left his distinguished prisoner, and a gasp of amazement broke from him.

By the light of a lamp on the Embankment Sexton Blake saw four men struggling, and the man in the midst of them was the Kaiser. Then the tide carried him on, and he could see no more.

Sexton Blake's brain fairly swam, partly with the blow that he had received, partly with what he had just seen. Why was the struggle going on if these men were rescuing the Kaiser? For what other reason could they have thrown the detective into the Thames?

A sharp splash caused Sexton Blake to turn, and he caught a glimpse of a man struggling in the river. In a glance he saw that he could not swim, and, without hesitation, he turned and swam back towards him. The tide prevented him making much progress, but it also bought the struggling man towards him.

Just as the man was about to sink, Sexton Blake contrived to grip him.

"Keep still," he panted, "and I will save you!"

The man made no answer, he had fainted, and Sexton Blake, swimming on his back, the man's head supported on his chest, struck out down stream, working close to the wall so that he might strike the next lot of steps.

The tide was running with a vengeance, and it was less than five minutes when he was able to scramble on to the steps and drag the unconscious man after him. Up the steps he went with him, and laid him down, thankful to see that there was no one about, for he was not anxious to have to answer a lot of questions just then.

He looked keenly along to where he had seen the struggle going on, but the place was deserted.

A cab came crawling by, and the detective hailed it. The man at once drew up to the kerb, but made a move to go away again as soon as he caught sight of the condition of the detective's companion.

"No inquests fer me," he growled.

Sexton Blake seized the reins, and the horse stopped.

"Here, leggo!" the cabby cried angrily, flourishing his whip.

"A sovereign to take us to Baker Street," the detective said shortly.

"He ain't corpsed?" the cabby asked, nodding at the insensible man.

"No."

"Then I'll do it for two quid," the cabby said. "It's worth that fer messin' the cushions up."

Without comment Sexton Blake carried the man into the cab, and it drove away. Then he turned his attention to the man, starting as he recognised in him Herr Leiberbaum's coachman. He tried to bring him to, and had just succeeded when Baker Street was reached. Tinker opened the door, and his face was blank with amazement when he saw that it was not the Kaiser who was with his master.

"What's wrong, sir?" he asked quickly.

"Get brandy at once, my lad," Sexton Blake answered shortly, "then 'phone Spearing to come here; I think there will be work for him."

A stiff dose of brandy quickly brought the young German to his senses, and he staggered from the couch on which the detective had laid him.

"Where is he?" he cried, in a shaking voice.

"The Kaiser?" Sexton Blake queried.

"Yes, yes," the German agreed, a terrible look of fright in his eyes. "What have they done with him?"

Sexton Blake gripped the man by the shoulders and forced

106

him back onto the couch.

"That is just what I want you to tell me," he said sternly.

For a moment the man lay staring up at the detective, then he dragged himself to a sitting position, and gripped him by the arm.

"You are Sexton Blake," he asked hoarsely—"the man who captured the Kaiser?"

"Yes."

The young German looked quickly round the room, as if to make sure that no one else was there.

"Then you must save him!" he cried. "Within an hour he may be dead!"

Cool man though Sexton Blake was he staggered back, and his face went pale. The man on the couch was not bluffing, for his eyes were wild with fear. He spoke the truth.

"What do you mean?" Sexton Blake held more brandy to the man's lips and made him drink it.

By an effort the German controlled himself, and began to speak hurriedly.

"After the smash I guessed something was wrong," he said, "for I knew who did it and I was driving. I have served his Majesty, and I did not hesitate. I slipped from the crowd, leaving the carriage to take its chance, and followed you to the station. I heard you take tickets for London, and I took one, too, but not before I had telegraphed a friend of mine to meet me and bring others, men to be relied upon, with him. I used a code that he and I had made for fun years before, and so I could tell him what he had to do—to rescue the Kaiser."

The man groaned, and buried his face in his hands.

"Little did I think that he had turned Anarchist, that such a chance as this—"

"Ah!" the detective ejaculated. "Quick, go on; there is no time to be lost."

"He met me," the German continued, in a shaking voice; "and three friends were with him. I did not like the look of them, but he told me that they were to be trusted. There was no time to doubt him, for we had to follow you. When you went along the Embankment we made our plans, and one of them then hurried on and gave the cry that took you to the steps. You were flung over, and then—I saw something was wrong.

"My companions flung themselves at the Kaiser. I rushed to his rescue, but was thrown into the river."

The man stopped, and hid his face in his hands again, but Sexton Blake gripped him by the shoulders and dragged him to his feet.

"Where did this friend of yours come from?" he demanded.

"Great Adam Street, Soho," the man answered.

Sexton Blake's brows contracted sharply, for the man had named one of the most notorious Anarchist roads in that district. What should he do? Little had he thought that his endeavours to help his country would end by placing the Kaiser's life in imminent peril.

If he were killed by these men, what would follow? Sexton Blake dared not think. He must act at once, without a second's delay.

There was a thundering knock on the door, and Spearing entered.

"Came at once!" he jerked. "What's wrong?"

"Everything," Sexton Blake answered huskily.

"Kaiser escaped!" Spearing grasped.

"Worse," Sexton Blake replied, and his voice was shaking. "He has been rescued from me by Anarchists!"

Spearing's red face went pale, for he needed no further explanation. He knew that the Kaiser was a doomed man unless he could be rescued at once.

"Any clue?" he jerked. "Make the raid at once—only chance!

What mean if never goes back to Germany?"

"Don't talk of it," Sexton Blake said, in a low voice. "I dare not think."

"Then what do?"

"You must get a dozen men at once," Sexton Blake answered, "and we must raid the house in Great Adam Street. They may not have taken him there, but they probably have, believing this man"—he nodded to the German—"to be dead."

Spearing hurried to the 'phone, and for five minutes he spoke rapidly into it.

"Take cab," he said. "They'll be there soon as we shall."

Tinker hurried off to fetch a taxi-cab, and while he was away Sexton Blake hurriedly changed his clothes.

"Help yourself to fresh things while we are gone," he said to the German, who had quite recovered by now.

"I am coming with you," the man said quietly. "My emperor is in danger. I can do no less."

Sexton Blake paced up and down the room, his face deadly pale. When he had started for the Shetlands, at the request of the Government, he had little thought that his investigations would end like this. Now his brain was filled with one thought only; everything else was banished from it. The Kaiser was in danger, and must be rescued. Nothing else mattered.

"The cab, sir!" Tinker announced.

Out into the street went the three men and Tinker, and clambered into the cab.

"Great Adam Street, Soho!" Sexton Blake ordered huskily; "and drive—drive like blazes!"

"Can't exceed the limit, sir," the man said civilly. "If I get my licence endorsed there'll be trouble."

Sexton Blake drew a couple of sovereigns from his pocket, and thrust them into the man's hand.

"Get on!" he said sternly.

With a bound the motor started forward, and whirled at top speed down the street, the driver getting every ounce out of her. But that was not fast enough for the men in her, for they knew that the life of a great emperor was at stake.

THE TWELFTH CHAPTER

Terrible News—The Burning House in Soho—A Daring Rescue.

THE DRIVE TO Soho was not a long one, but it was all too far for the men in the cab. Their faces were deadly white, and they did not speak a word. They were men facing a desperate hope—men who knew how desperate a chance it was—and they could not speak.

Only Sexton Blake broke the silence by thrusting his head out of the window, and shouting to the driver to go faster. Twice policemen had tried to stop them, but the man had contrived to escape by dodging down side turnings. All this meant a loss of time, and every second was precious.

Sexton Blake was sure that if the Kaiser really was in the hands of Anarchists that they would not hesitate for long. They would know the dangers they were running—that the whole country would be turned upside-down to find their prisoner—and so they would settle with him promptly, and clear out of the way. The detective could fancy them chuckling at the chance that had fairly been thrust upon them, and he ground his teeth.

Yet, if the worst happened, who could be blamed but the Kaiser himself? What other ruler would have risked what he had risked; have come across the sea in—

With a jerk the cab stopped in Shaftesbury Avenue, and the men in the cab saw that a cordon of police was stretched across the road. A fire engine—the horses at full stretch—swayed by, the police moving aside to admit it.

"Can't get through here, sir," a policeman said civilly to Sexton Blake.

The detective and the others clambered out.

"Where is this fire?" the young German cried hoarsely.

"Great Adam Street," the constable answered. "Seems to have started all of a sudden, and was fairly roaring when the engines arrived."

"Adam Street?" the German gasped. "Ach Himmell! If they have—"

Sexton Blake gripped the man by the shoulder.

"Be quiet!" he whispered fiercely. "There is no reason it should be the house."

But in his heart he thought it likely. What easier and safer way could the Anarchists have found of disposing of their noble prisoner than to bind him and fire the house? From what the policeman had said, the fire had been well started.

Spearing touched the constable on the arm.

"Must get through with my friends," he said sharply.

"Impossible,"—the constable answered, thrusting the worthy official back—"unless you are the owner of the house!"

"I'm Spearing—Scotland Yard!" the official jerked.

The constable hastily peered forward, recognised his chief, and drew aside.

"Very sorry, sir!" he said apologetically.

But Spearing heard nothing of it, for he had hurried on with the others towards the scene of the blaze.

Guided by the steady thud of the engines and the glare in the sky, the detectives went up a road on the left. Instantly the whole scene burst upon them.

The fourth house on the right was burning furiously, flames issuing from all the lower windows, despite the streams of water that a dozen engines were pouring onto them. Firemen were working strenuously to save the adjoining property, but it seemed more than probable that half the street would be involved.

"It is the house!" the German gasped.

The firemen were too busy to take any notice of the newcomers, and they forced their way forward until a policeman barred their way.

"Not safe!" he said sternly.

"Are all the inmates saved?" Sexton Blake asked quickly.

The policeman nodded to a group of five men, obviously foreigners, who stood on the pavement a score of yards away.

"Yes, sir," he answered. "There they are. Take it cool, don't they?"

The men certainly did appear to do so. They stood there, their hands in the pockets of their ragged trousers, staring at the fire, as if it fascinated them. One had a cigarette between his teeth.

The young German coachman stared hard at the group for a second, then a fierce cry broke from him.

"It is the men—the murderers!" he whispered hoarsely.

Sexton Blake needed no further bidding, but crossed the road in the direction of the little group. They saw him coming, started back when they recognised him, and looked for a way of escape. There was none, for in one direction was the flames, in the other the detectives.

The young German coachman darted forward, and flung his arms round one of the men; and at the same instant Sexton

Blake recognised him as the man with the red beard and the scarred lip who had thrown him into the river.

"Where is he?" the German demanded, in a hissing whisper.

The red-bearded man tried to shake himself free, but the other held on with grim strength.

"What is it that you mean?" the bearded man asked, with a great show of surprise.

His companions were stealthily edging away, and the detectives made no effort to stop them. Already the house was burning so furiously that it seemed impossible that anyone could be alive in it; and all that they wanted to know was whether the Kaiser really was there.

"You know!" the young German snarled, and bent his lips close to the man's ear. "I mean the Kaiser!"

The bearded man flung himself free, and laughed harshly.

"Look!" he cried, a kind of madness taking possession of him. "Look how the flames lick up towards him!"

A gasp of anguish broke from the young German as he realised that the Kaiser was in the burning building, and he turned and ran towards the flames. But, quick though he was, Sexton Blake was quicker, and he had already rushed up to the men in charge of the escape.

"To the top window!" he ordered hoarsely.

The escape officer turned towards the flames, and shook his head at them.

"The house is empty!" he said gruffly. "Anyway, it is impossible to enter."

"The house is not empty!" The words broke from Sexton Blake like shots. "On the top floor there is a man who cannot get away, because—"

The sentence broke off short in the detective's mouth. He realised that, even now, he dared not give away the real state of affairs.

"Sure?" the officer asked shortly, his square jaw becoming more prominent.

"Yes."

A quick order was given, and willing hands seized the escape, and ran it towards the flames. The crowd, which had been noisy hitherto, suddenly dropped into a strange silence. They knew, as they saw the escape moved, that the burning building was still occupied; and they fairly held their breath as they thought of the nerve that a man would have to attempt a rescue.

The flames were darting out from the lower windows in something like a sheet now, and the moment the escape was placed against the wall the fire was licking at the paint of it.

The heat was so great that the men who had placed it in position rushed back hurriedly.

"Impossible!" one of them gasped, putting out with his fingers his smouldering beard.

Sexton Blake looked at the darting flames, at the red-bearded Anarchist, whose scarred lips were distorted by a fiendish grin, and he did not hesitate. It was indirectly through him that the Kaiser was in danger, and it was, therefore, his duty to get him to a place of safety—if it was not already too late.

Too late! As that terrible thought flashed into the detective's brain, he buttoned his coat tightly, and darted for the escape. A policeman threw out his arms to stop him, but he dodged him, and reached the foot of the ladder.

The heat and glare of the fire was so great that he was compelled to close his eyes, and so he felt blindly for the first rung of the ladder.

"Come back!" a hoarse voice yelled, in a frantic command.

But Sexton Blake took no heed of the order. He knew, as the others did not, that the man who lay in the doomed building was Wilhelm the Second, Emperor of Germany. The papers were full of rumours concerning him, his health, his doings, his interest in the manoeuvres; but none of them could say that he was in London, and just now in grave peril of his life.

Up the escape went Sexton Blake, and a jet of water, striking him in the back and playing over him, refreshed him, so that he mounted quickly. He managed to open his eyes, and so was able to fairly jump past the rungs of the ladder, round which the flames were licking. He reached the window-sill, and it was so hot that he could scarcely put his fingers on it.

From below came a hoarse cheer, and as Sexton Blake glanced down for the briefest second he saw the young German close behind him.

"Go on!" the man gasped, in a voice choking and cracked by the heat. "They need help—my duty!"

Already the smoke and heat were making Sexton Blake's head swim, and he realised that he had got to be quick if he was to come out of the building alive. The hose was still playing on him, and he drew a handkerchief from his pocket, held it in the water, then tied it hastily round his mouth and nose.

The smoke was coming out of the window in volumes, but Sexton Blake plunged through it, the German close behind him, and they found themselves in a small room. Through the cracks of the boards smoke was rising steadily, evil, pungent smoke that meant death to those who breathed it. Round the room the two men went, dropping on their knees, searching the hot floor with their hands, but there was no one there. Then they sought for a fresh room, and it was the German who found the door.

A cry, like a gasp, broke from him, and he summoned up all his strength, and flung himself against the woodwork. It gave under the blow, and he was flung through into the room beyond, closely followed by Sexton Blake.

Here there was not so much smoke. The window of the room was open, and through it came the glare of the fire below. It revealed a body, still and inert, lying just beneath it.

Staggering, half-choked, Sexton Blake reached it, and his shaking fingers felt the rope that bound the man's lips, and the scarf that gagged his mouth. From his pocket he dragged out a knife, and slashed through the cords.

"Quick!" he panted. "Help me with him! The window!"

But no answer came, and when Sexton Blake turned he saw that the young German lay insensible on the floor, overcome by the smoke and heat.

There was nothing for it but for Sexton Blake to make the rescue single-handed. He lifted the still body of the Kaiser in his arms, wondering as he did so whether there was life still in it, and half dragged, half carried it to the window in the next room.

A great cheer rose from below as Sexton Blake appeared at the window.

"Jump!" Came faintly from below, and the detective saw that the escape had been moved, and that down in the street stood men, apparently right in the flames, holding a tarpaulin.

He raised the still form of the Kaiser, balanced it, and let it drop. He saw it land fairly in the tarpaulin, then turned and staggered back into the room to fetch the young German. He could see nothing now, for the smoke had made him quite blind, and a great red pillow seemed to be forcing itself down on the top of his brain. But even then he remembered the man lying still on the floor, and groped his way to him. His knees gave way, and he continued on all-fours until he touched the body.

Now came the greatest struggle of all, and it was only the detective's marvellous nerve that pulled him through. He gripped the man by the collar, and inch by inch dragged him to the window. There he tried to raise him, but four times his strength failed him. Again he made the effort, and this time got the body to the sill.

With his arms around the young German, seeing and knowing practically nothing, Sexton Blake toppled from the window, and went whirling down towards the street. In a state of semi-consciousness, he felt himself strike the tarpaulin; then a great explosion shook the air, and he lapsed into unconsciousness.

The Anarchists had laid their plans well, and had made sure of the house and its contents being destroyed by placing bombs there. But Sexton Blake's pluck had made their efforts futile.

SEXTON BLAKE OPENED his eyes, and dimly saw that he was in his own bed-room in Baker Street. His head still ached terribly, but even then he remembered all that had happened. The kidnapping of the Kaiser, the fire, the rescue.

"The Kaiser," he asked, in a weak voice. "What of him? Is he alive?"

"Very much, thanks to you," a quiet voice said; and the Kaiser himself moved from a chair by the window and bent over the detective.

"You owe me no thanks, sire," Sexton Blake said, with a wry smile. "It was my fault that your life was put in danger."

The Kaiser shrugged his shoulders, and a moody expression crossed his face. He could not help thinking of the defeat of all his plans for forming a naval base in the North Sea.

"No, the fault was mine," he said slowly. "I have been too ambitious, and I have paid the price."

Sexton Blake dimly wondered why the Kaiser had not escaped, and he glanced towards the door, instinctively looking to see if it were guarded. The Kaiser saw the look, and smiled.

"I have never taken advantage of a disabled enemy," he said quietly. Then added, with a rueful smile: "Besides, I rather fancy that your large and muscular friend, Mr. Spearing, is in the passage."

THE THIRTEENTH CHAPTER

Downing Street—The Ministers have a Surprise—Terms Arranged.

THE STUDY OF the Prime Minister's house in Downing Street looked exactly as it had done when Sexton Blake was first summoned to it, to be sent from there to the Shetlands. The map of Great Britain still hung on the wall, a number of little flags, evidently indicating the position of the vessels of the manoeuvring fleet, being stuck in it. That was the only change.

And the Prime Minister himself, his clever face wearing a worried look, was again pacing up and down the room. Also, as before, he stopped from time to time and studied the map, his finger tracing the way from the Shetlands to the western coast.

Then, just as before, the door opened, and a manservant announced:

"Mr. Kennard."

The young-looking Lord of the Admiralty came in briskly, and shut the door behind him. He was older-looking, and the dark marks under his eyes suggested that he was suffering from want of sleep. In his right hand he carried a bundle of papers.

"Still studying roads for enemies," he remarked, with a laugh that was distinctly forced.

"Precisely," the Prime Minister agreed. "You know what Mr. Sexton Blake said: 'if you do not hear from me you will know that I have learnt things that I dare not trust to the wires.' Now I am worrying my brain as to what he has discovered. Can you guess, Kennard?"

Mr. Kennard seated himself with an air of carelessness, but the twitching of his mouth showed that he was not so much at his ease as he wished to appear.

"Will you give me a cigar?" he asked. "It steadies my nerves."

The Prime Minister pushed a box over, and Mr. Kennard lit up. It might have been noticed that his strong, capable fingers were shaking a trifle. The Prime Minister did notice it, and wondered what was the matter.

"Can you guess what Sexton Blake has discovered?" he repeated.

Mr. Kennard flung the used match into the grate, and twisted his cigar nervously between his fingers.

"I know," he answered, with a quick glance towards the door.

"You have heard from him?" the Prime Minister asked eagerly.

"No, from Ferrar," Mr. Kennard corrected. "I have the message here—sent by wireless via Dover. Obviously he is afraid of saying too much."

"The message!" the Prime Minister cried eagerly. "In the half an hour I must be in the House, and it may be something to speak about."

"I fancy not," Mr. Kennard answered; and there was a savage note in his voice. "Listen! This is the message:

"'Germans have marked special harbours. Shetlands to have been base for operations. Nine prisoners. Sexton Blake will explain.'"

Mr. Kennard looked up, the paper shaking between his fingers.

"Nine prisoners!" the Prime Minister echoed in amazement. "What does he mean?"

Mr. Kennard flung his half-smoked cigar into the grate, and his brow was furrowed across and across.

"They can't have got as far as that," he muttered.

"Don't talk in riddles! As what?" the Prime Minister demanded.

"Of garrisoning the place!" Mr. Kennard explained desperately. "Yet how otherwise could there be prisoners?"

There was silence for fully a minute; then the Prime Minister spoke.

"You have seen Sexton Blake?"

"No," Mr. Kennard admitted. "I sent to his house yesterday evening, but he had not returned. I then left a message that he was to come here as soon as he was back in London."

The Prime Minister shrugged his shoulders wearily, and suddenly looked like a man who wondered whether the weight of the office he had voluntarily taken upon himself was worth supporting.

"I have always known that Germany was making preparations in case of war with us," he muttered, evidently speaking his thoughts aloud, "but to have gone so far as this—no."

"This mimic naval war may turn into grim earnest," Mr. Kennard said; and his jaw bent forward, and his eyes sparkled.

He was a peaceable man, some said too much so for his post; but now that danger loomed so close ahead the fighting blood of the Britisher was showing. Even his slim body seemed to expand, and he squared the shoulders made rounded by much study.

"Hardly that—" the Prime Minister began, but stopped as a knock came at the door.

"Mr. Sexton Blake, sir," the servant announced.

The two Ministers looked at each other, their eyes sparkling.

"Show him in at once!" the Prime Minister ordered sharply.

The man departed, but a few seconds later the door re-opened, and Sexton Blake entered. He came in slowly and heavily, like a man who is tired. His face was pale, and he carried his right hand in a sling.

"You are hurt!" the Prime Minister ejaculated, pushing a chair forward for the detective.

"Why, yes," the latter admitted, in a voice not quite so strong as usual. "Our profession is like that, you know; there are dangers."

He seated himself, and leant back wearily, but there was a sparkle in his eyes, and a faint smile came to his lips as he thought of what he had come to tell.

"We have had a message from Admiral Ferrar," Mr. Kennard said sharply, impatient to come to the point, "but it tells little."

"I may see it?" Sexton Blake held out his uninjured hand, and the message was handed to him without hesitation. He smiled as he read it, and tossed it on to the table.

"It certainly tells little," he admitted.

"But why?" Mr. Kennard demanded.

"Because the admiral only knew a little," the detective explained. "There were certain things that it was well not to tell even him. The existence of the German airship he was bound to know, and—"

"Airship at the Shetlands?" the Prime Minister gasped.

"Precisely," Sexton Blake assured him. "An airship carrying twelve men—Germans."

The Prime Minister rose excitedly from his chair, unable to keep still.

"What were they doing there?" he cried.

Sexton Blake shrugged his shoulders, and his eyes glittered.

"What have the men been doing there for months past?" he answered.

Mr. Kennard held up a hand as the Prime Minister was about to speak.

"Let us get the matter straight," he said, in a voice made hard by his efforts to keep it under iron control. "Kindly tell us all that has happened, Mr. Blake—all."

Then Sexton Blake told everything, leaving out the identity of the Kaiser, and the two Ministers sat and stared at him in astonishment. They were drinking to the dregs a very bitter cup, for they knew that long since the North should have been guarded.

The Prime Minister crossed the room, and traced his fingers along the great map. Unconsciously he drew out the flags, and jabbed him them into places right inland. Certainly he was very upset by the news that he had just received, and not without reason.

"Who was the man behind all this?" he asked suddenly, facing the detective.

"The Kaiser," the latter answered.

"No, no; I mean the man at the Shetlands," the Prime Minister explained.

"The Kaiser," Sexton Blake said again.

There was a dead silence, during which the two Ministers stared at the detective with startled eyes.

"You don't mean," Mr. Kennard said at last, in a low voice, "that the Kaiser was on the airship, that he himself was directing operations?"

"You have seen the reports in the papers," Sexton Blake answered, "the rumours as to where the Kaiser really was? Well, I could clear them up. The Kaiser was in the Shetlands, and is now in London."

"In London?" Mr. Kennard repeated the words like a man in a dream.

"As a matter of fact"—a faint smile played round the detective's lips—"he is waiting in the next room."

The Prime Minister stared at the detective.

"He must be mad!" he muttered.

"No; I can fetch him in," Sexton Blake assured. "If you think, you will understand that I could do nothing else. I dared not let him fall into the admiral's hands. It would have meant war."

"But what does it mean now?" the Prime Minister asked, like a man in a dream.

"Why, just what you like to make it," the detective answered; "but one thing I will tell you. The Kaiser realises the awkward position that he is in, and that at all costs he must get back to his own country without delay. He is ready to make practically any terms to accomplish that."

The Ministers looked keenly at each other. At last they saw how the detective had placed the game in their hands.

"You have done more than well, Mr. Blake," the Prime Minister said earnestly, "so well that I am going to ask you to do one thing more."

The detective bowed, his eyebrows raised inquiringly.

"Suggest our terms," the Minister explained.

"That is simple," Sexton Blake answered. "It is rumoured, not without good foundation, I believe, that five millions must be spent on warships at once."

Mr. Kennard nodded, and looked eager.

"This is necessitated almost entirely by the action of Germany," the detective continued. "If we can induce them to swear not to increase their naval strength, not to go on with this mad competition in naval expenditure, the five millions need not be spent."

The Prime Minister rose to his feet, and held out his hand.

"Mr. Blake," he said, "you and I ought to change places."

Sexton Blake rose, and moved towards the door.

"I will bring his Majesty in," he said quietly.

The two Ministers stood staring at the open doorway, and they stared even harder when Sexton Blake returned with a clean-shaven man. Then an angry laugh broke from the Prime Minister.

"This is no time to joke, Mr. Blake," he protested. "This is not the Kaiser."

The clean-shaven man drew his heels together, bowed, and stared at the Ministers haughtily.

"Unfortunately it is, gentlemen," he said quietly, "though the last few days I have almost doubted my identity."

Then the Ministers realised that Sexton Blake had spoken the truth, and they bowed respectfully.

"Let us get to work, gentlemen," the Kaiser said abruptly. "I admit myself in your hands. Your terms are bound to be mine."

"You will not find them so very hard, your Majesty," the Prime Minister murmured.

"In five years things would have been different," the Kaiser continued, with a burst of anger. "There would have been no talk of terms then."

"I am glad that it is not five years hence, then, your Majesty," the Prime Minister said, "just as I hope that trouble between our two nations may always be five years ahead."

For half an hour the Ministers and the Kaiser spoke in low tones.

"I have your permission to announce this in the House?" the Prime Minister said at the end of that time.

"So!" the Kaiser admitted. "In fact, with your permission—" he lowered his voice, as if someone outside the room might hear.

"Why, certainly, sire," the Prime Minister agreed; and there was a little smile on his lips.

ALL THROUGH THE afternoon the House had been engaged in a debate on Irish Small Holdings, and, despite a few heated speeches by the Labour members, it had developed into such a heavy business that the benches had practically emptied. But with the evening they began to fill, and by eight o'clock a strong muster of the members had assembled.

A rumour had gone round the House that the Prime Minister had an important announcement to make, and it had been added, apparently on good authority, that it was with regard to the naval manoeuvres now in progress. That was enough to bring the usually lagging members to their places, especially when they heard that it was the attitude of Germany towards Great Britain that was to be discussed.

Every member knew that the proposed expenditure of at least five millions of increasing the Navy was entirely due to the fact that Germany was laying down huge ships as fast as possible, and they wondered whether it could be possible that even a larger sum would have to be voted if Great Britain was to still command the ocean. Labour members sat and blandly smiled, thinking that here was a chance to pour out heated words in favour of the scheme, for new ships would mean work for hundreds of men.

At five minutes to nine the Prime Minister entered, Mr. Kennard with him. The former looked a trifle pale, but his eyes were those of a man who has gained a great triumph, and who sees the realisation of one of his fondest dreams within reach. Mr. Kennard held his head high, but his thin face showed no sign of anything.

As the Ministers entered, two visitors were ushered into the Distinguished Strangers' Gallery. The pale man, whose right hand was in a sling, a few of the Members might have recognised as Sexton Blake, the famous detective, but it is safe to say that in the clean-shaven man with the haughty expression not a single one of them recognised the fiercely-moustached Emperor of Germany.

A few more remarks concerning the Irish Small Holdings

were made, then Mr. Kennard rose to his feet. Instantly a great hush fell over the House.

"Gentlemen," he said, and in his voice there was just the suggestion of a tremor, "I have a statement to make to-night which I believe will meet with general satisfaction—even from the Opposition. For some time past the action of certain foreign nations has led us to consider whether we ought not to considerably add to the numerical strength of our fleet."

"Germany!" a Labour member cried.

"As my honourable friend has remarked," Mr. Kennard continued, "Germany is the nation to which I chiefly refer. For years she has been endeavouring to make our supremacy on the sea a thing of the past, until we have been driven into a corner, forced to spend millions of money. Well, we have thought over the situation, diplomacy has not been idle, and at last I am able to announce that an arrangement with Germany is about to be entered into which will render the expenditure of this vast sum on ships of war unnecessary. In short, Germany will not increase its navy, and so we, too, may call a halt."

As the Chief Lord of the Admiralty paused, Mr. Alexander Brown, Labour member for North Buswell, rose excitedly to his feet.

"And may I ask whose word we have for that?" he demanded.

"The word of the Kaiser himself!" Mr. Kennard answered, with dignity; and for a moment his eyes were turned towards the Strangers' Gallery, to where a clean-shaven man of haughty aspect sat nervously feeling at his upper lip. "I may also add"—Mr. Kennard spoke slowly and impressively— "that it is quite likely that, as a mark of confidence, his Majesty will be permitted to witness the end of the present naval manoeuvres."

The excitable member for North Buswell was on his feet in an instant.

"May I ask whether his Majesty will witness them under an oath of secrecy?" he demanded.

But Mr. Kennard sat down without answering, and up in the gallery the Kaiser laughed softly.

"After all, my friend," he whispered to Sexton Blake, "there are more boring entertainments than this Parliament of yours. So?"

THE FOURTEENTH CHAPTER

The Attack on the Thames—Repelled—The Kaiser Leaves for Germany—The Imperial Explanation—The End.

IN THE BROAD mouth of the river all was dark as pitch, and the wind that blew in sharply from the sea raised waves that would not have discredited an ocean. Here and there sailing barges beat their way out, the water washing over their scuppers, but most of the smaller vessels were content to lie in safety further up the river. A day or two made no real difference, and a fair wind and sea is worth waiting for.

Through the choppy waves a vessel came ploughing its way, its white hulk looking ghostly in the darkness, and swung round right beside a huge battleship which was steaming just strongly enough to hold her own against the tide.

The white boat was the Hohenzollern, the Kaiser's yacht, and the German Emperor himself stood on the bridge. Once more a fiercely-upturned moustache adorned his lip, and only the man who stood beside him, who was none other than Sexton Blake, could have said that it was one of the finest imitations that had ever been worn.

By an act of diplomacy the famous detective had got the Kaiser aboard his yacht at Dover without attracting attention, and now, as had been extensively published in the papers, he was to watch the final stages of the manoeuvres—the attack on the Thames and attempted capture of London.

Away to right and left of the Hohenzollern great battleships, not a light aboard of them, loomed up, and it was only the occasional rattle of a chain, or the snap of an order, that made one sure that they were real, and not things of the imagination. Other craft; cruisers, destroyers, torpedo-boats, lay rocking in the waves, but their low-lying hulks were invisible in the darkness.

Now and again there was a sharp swish of water, a quick panting of machinery, and one of the torpedo-boats would dash by, the water coming back in a sheet over her bows, her crew in oilskins, bound on a scouting expedition.

All this seemed to fascinate the Kaiser, for he stood on the bridge of his yacht and watched every movement with his eyes in absolute silence.

"They are well handled, these boats," he said at last, a trifle grudgingly.

"Their officers come of a seafaring race, sire," the detective answered quietly.

The Kaiser lapsed into silence again, and pulled carefully at his moustache. And all the time warships were creeping up, stealthily and surely, taking up their positions for resisting an attack.

Then, right ahead, at a distance it was difficult to judge, a light flashed sharply—once, twice.

From all sides came the ringing of bells in engine-rooms, and the air was filled by the great white arms of the Fleet's searchlights. From side to side they swept, circling, making sudden plunges, hunting out the enemy. For the moment the night had vanished, and a day of dazzling brightness had taken its place.

Right ahead lay the attacking fleet, which one of the torpedo-boats had discovered creeping up, and now she lay— battleships, cruisers, and seemingly numberless smaller craft—

exposed to the defending fleet. Technically she was beaten, but the discovery did not complete the manoeuvres that the Kaiser was to witness.

Again engine-bells rang, and with surprising swiftness the great war vessels of the defending force darted forward in pursuit of the attacking force. First went the torpedo-boats, fairly leaping into their strides like whippets, and the destroyers and the cruisers were not far behind them. Last came the mighty battleships, gathering way until behind them rolled out a swell heavy enough to sink a barge.

"Very pretty, my friend," the Kaiser sneered, "but it is not war."

"No, thank Heaven!" Sexton Blake answered fervently, watching one of the sinister-looking cruisers pass.

The Kaiser paced restlessly up and down the bridge as his yacht followed in the wake of the battleships.

"But why?" he demanded. "War is a good thing for a nation. It makes her men self-reliant, it keeps her on her guard, so that she does not get slack, it gives the ambitious—"

"In the first two things you are right, sire," Sexton Blake interrupted coolly, "but you spoilt yourself when you spoke of the good that war does to the ambitious. It is those men who make war, confident in the strength of arms behind them, really not needing more land and possessions, but only wresting them from their neighbours because of—ambition. They forget the men who have got to die to gratify that ambition, the mothers and sweethearts who must weep, the toilers who go more heavily to their tasks because they are so taxed—to pay for this same ambition—that they scarce seem to touch the money that they earn so hardly. Ambition is a terrible thing when it leads a man to throw a nation into bloody strife."

"A ruler—" the Kaiser began; but again Sexton Blake interrupted him.

"I know what you would say, sire," he said, "that a ruler

is not as other men, and you are right, for his actions can do much for his people. A word from him means happiness or pain, not to his own family, but to millions. Yet, through it all, he should remember that it is only accident of birth that has made him the ruler of a nation, should not forget that but for that he might not be the man with the ambition for conquest, but the struggling man forced to pay the price for it."

The Kaiser was silent for a minute, a moody look on his face, then he turned to the officer on the bridge and gave him an order that made Sexton Blake eyebrows go up in surprise.

"Then you will follow the manoeuvres no further, sire?" he asked.

"No," the Kaiser answered, with determination. "I am tired of all this playing at battle, and I am going straight home."

"You will have good news for your people?" Sexton Blake suggested.

The Kaiser shook his head, and a rueful expression crossed his face.

"Ah, but you do not know my people!" he said quickly. "They would coin their very blood into money to pay for arms—if I told them to."

"But you have lost ambition in that direction, sire," Sexton Blake said.

"Why, yes, my friend," the Kaiser answered slowly. "I fancy that I have only two ambitions left."

"I may ask what they are?"

"An ambition to go home," the Kaiser answered, a dreamy look in his eyes, "and to have you at the head of my secret service." He swung round upon the detective, and his face was very eager, but Sexton Blake spoke before he could say more.

"Remember, sire," he said earnestly, "that Britishers are patriotic, too, and that I am one of them."

"No offer would tempt you?" the Kaiser persisted.

"None while Great Britain belongs to the Britishers," Sexton Blake assured him.

The Hohenzollern, gathering way with every yard she covered, swept out of the Thames, taking the Kaiser back to his people.

TINKER CAME HURRYING into the breakfast-room at Baker Street, a broad grin on his face, a newspaper in his hand.

"Anything about the Kaiser's plans yet?" Sexton Blake asked, looking up from his breakfast.

"I should jolly well think so, sir!" the boy answered. "Oh, he's got out of it beautifully! Just read it, sir!"

The boy thrust the paper excitedly under his master's nose, pointing to a column that was headed:

"NO DANGER FROM GERMANY.

Five Millions Saved.

The Kaiser's Reason.

(From our special correspondent in Berlin).

"The Kaiser has reappeared again, and it is now known that his disappearance was owing to his presence at the British naval manoeuvres, and not, as it was feared, to illness. It is quite evident that his Majesty is much impressed by what he has witnessed, although his statements are evidently intended to give quite an opposite impression.

"Last night, in a semi-official speech, he announced that Germany would not continue building ships of war, that, in fact, no more would be laid down for years, as

"Germany Is Already the Superior of Great Britain."

Sexton Blake dropped the paper, and laughed. Certainly the Kaiser had wriggled out of his difficulty very neatly. But what did that matter?

133

"There is another piece you ought to read, sir," Tinker said, pointing to another paragraph, which was headed:

"RUMOURED NEW PEER

It is rumoured on good authority that Mr. Sexton Blake, the famous detective, whose name has been before the public for so many years, is to be offered a peerage in return for his services to the State. It appears that for some time he has been the government's principal secret agent, and that even during these manoeuvres he was not idle."

Sexton Blake crumpled the paper up in his hands.

"Get the car round after breakfast, my lad," he answered shortly.

"Anything important, sir?" Tinker asked eagerly.

"Yes," Sexton Blake answered. "I've got to stop this nonsense by telling the Prime Minister that the name of Sexton Blake is all that I want."

THE END

Notes

1. *Nulli Secundus* ("Second to none") was Britain's first powered military airship. Officially British Army Dirigible No 1, she was launched on 10 September 1907. A month later, while she was moored, high winds posed such a danger that she was dismantled and later rebuilt as *Nulli Secundus II*.

2. This is a reference to earlier *Union Jack* stories.

ON WAR SERVICE; OR, SEXTON BLAKE'S SECRET MISSION

THE RAIN BEAT with greater force against the windowpane. The thunderstorm was directly overhead.

I'd sat in silence, watching wisps of steam rise from my drying trouser legs while Sexton Blake read through the record of his tussle with Kaiser Wilhelm II. It hadn't taken him long. His reading speed was at least twice as fast as my own.

When he finished, he sighed and murmured, "Dear old Goddard. His writing style was erratic but he was consistently entertaining. A great loss."

"Killed on the French front," I said.

"During the Battle of Vimy Ridge. He was just thirty-six years old."

After a moment of silence, I changed the subject. "You met the Kaiser on a number of occasions."

"We had a complicated relationship," Blake murmured. He shook his head in what I took to be an expression of regret. "A strange man. Narcissistic, bellicose and impetuous. Very bombastic. He had a tendency to speak before thinking. Ultimately, it was his undoing, but not, unfortunately, before he'd ignited a world war. Can I refill your glass?"

I declined the offer.

Blake turned to the next issue in the binder.

The Union Jack story paper launched in 1894. By 1905, it had become "Sexton Blake's own paper," featuring a Blake tale every week through to 1933, when, after issue number 1,531, it had been transformed into the larger format, and ultimately far less popular, Detective Weekly. Until 1929, all the Union Jack stories were published anonymously. Blake, however, appeared to have no problem in recollecting who wrote the one he was looking at.

"Cecil Hayter."

"Best known for recounting the earlier of your various adventures in Africa," I observed. "Though in this case, it's a war story. I think it gives a good indication of the rather flexible role you adopted during the conflict."

His right eyebrow went up. "Flexible role?"

"Well, you didn't, as far as I can ascertain from the published material, serve in any official capacity in the armed forces, but you certainly visited the front lines on more than one occasion—even went behind them—and, at home, you hunted spies and defeated many plots that would have otherwise damaged British interests."

He raised his right hand and tapped its knuckles against his chin. "Hmm. I had intended to join up, of course, but before I could do so, the prime minister approached me."

"Asquith?"

"A ring of the doorbell, a shriek from Mrs Bardell, and up the stairs he came. He can't have been in my consulting room for more than five minutes, and when he was gone, I was left with documents giving me special dispensation to serve my country at home and abroad in whatever capacity I felt would do the most good. Occasionally, I was commissioned to undertake particular missions." He tapped a forefinger on the Union Jack in the binder. "This was one of them."

ON WAR SERVICE;
OR, SEXTON BLAKE'S
SECRET MISSION

by Cecil Hayter
UNION JACK issue 645 (1916)

SEXTON BLAKE SAT back in the depths of a great, green leather-covered armchair, watching his man in a sleepy sort of way from beneath half-closed lids. His hands were folded lightly on his knees, and by special permission he was allowed to smoke a cigarette. The fact that that permission had been given freely, without his even asking for it, told him that his help was very badly needed indeed, and he smiled inwardly, for, as he was well aware, smoking in any form was not allowed, as a rule, in that big, gloomy room just off Whitehall.

It was a huge place, over forty feet long, with two fine Adam fireplaces, and the walls were lined with bookshelves and maps on rollers. A very large and rather ornate desk strewn with papers stood within a few feet of him. The only light, saving that from the fires, came from a low, green-shaded electric table lamp, and on the far side of the desk sat a smartly-dressed elderly man with grey hair and moustaches. Keen-eyed in spite of his gold-rimmed pince-nez, with a flower in his buttonhole. But his face was haggard and worn, deeply seamed with worry and anxiety as he sat in the little oasis of light and peered at a pile of papers.

"And so you want me, Sir James, for—what?" said Blake at last, after some five minutes' silence, broken only by the scratching of a pen and the occasional tinkle of a cinder in the grate.

"Just a moment, please, Mr. Blake," replied Sir James, and gave an apprehensive glance backwards over his shoulder towards his secretary's table, which stood empty.

Blake noticed the glance and the apprehension, took a final puff or two at his cigarette, and flung the end into the grate.

"I'm in no hurry," he said lazily. "Please don't mind me. But by the signs of things I shall be in a deuce of a hurry when things start moving," he added to himself under his breath.

The parchment-like paper crackled, and Sir James laid his pen neatly in the rack with a sigh of relief.

"I beg your pardon, Mr. Blake," he said, blinking over his glasses, "but we're hard put to it these days. You've done us many services in the past, hard services, and—er—dangerous. I sent for you here to ask you to do us another. It will be— ahem!—risky, but it will be well rewarded, and we may be able to prove our gratitude in other ways. There is a C.B., for instance, at my disposal, which I am free to—"

Blake rose to his feet.

"Is this war service, Sir James?"

"In a way, yes."

"Then if I can be of use I want neither C.B.s nor rewards. In short, I want my instructions as briefly as you can give them to me."

"Thank you, Mr. Blake; but it was my duty to make the offer to you, as I should have made it to anyone else, and it is a very special and difficult mission."

"Then the sooner you give me the details the better."

Sir James unlocked a drawer of the desk and drew out a long, official-looking envelope. From this in turn he took a big, folded sheet of stamped paper, which he passed across.

"You can read it, if you like. In fact, you had better read it. I know that its contents will be perfectly safe with you."

"H'm!" said Blake. "There's nothing wrong with my memory. Couldn't I give this message or whatever it is verbally? Frankly, Sir James, I distrust papers of any kind on this kind of job. They can be stolen, photographed; a hundred-and-one different things may happen to them, and they increase the risk tenfold. Now, if I were to carry the contents of this, here, in my head, the message could certainly be neither stolen nor photographed, and the only way they could be lost would be by someone succeeding in putting a knife or a bullet into me, in which case they would be none the wiser, and you could send another man."

"Quite so!" said Sir James drily. "If you could carry the contents in your head. But, unfortunately, long though your head is, and remarkably capable as your brains are, as I am the first to acknowledge, neither head nor brains are capable of reproducing signatures, and if you will glance at that paper you will see that the signatures of the—er—shall we say 'personages' attached are the most important part really of the whole document. They guarantee the matter, they are men whose names are known throughout the world, and if that scrap of paper were to be found by the agents of either of the Central Powers there would be such a 'flare-up,' to use a vulgar expression, that I doubt whether we could put the flames out in time to save the building."

He took off his glasses and polished them thoughtfully on the corner of his handkerchief.

Blake nodded and opened the paper handed to him. As he

read it his face grew grave, and he gave vent to a low whistle of astonishment.

"This is a pretty tall order, Sir James," he said, as he refolded the paper.

Sir James drew imaginary plans on the desk with an ivory paper-knife.

"It is," he assented. "That is why I sent for you. Any lesser job I might have given to a lesser man. In this case, having a free hand, I chose you. Our own agents are too well known; and though they mean all right, between you and me, they are apt to be a trifle clumsy in their methods. Oh, they're plucky enough, but they lack discretion!"

Blake nodded.

"And my instructions?"

Sir James scribbled a name and an address on a piece of paper and passed it across. It read:

"Adolph Schmidt, Rue le Heron, No. 19, Antwerp."

"You are to deliver that paper to that address and bring me back a receipt, which I alone shall be able to identify by certain marks." He glanced round anxiously again, though there was nobody in the room except themselves—a sure sign that his nerves were overstrained. He dropped his voice almost to a whisper. "The receipt will be written on a small square of tracing paper, the left-hand bottom corner of which will be torn off as though by accident. Here is the man's photograph. Look at it closely, so that you are positive that you can identify him and not get taken in by a man dressed up to resemble him."

Blake studied the photograph carefully, and then turned to the back, on which was written in Sir James' own neat handwriting a terse description of the colouring of eyes and hair and a note of a missing canine tooth and a slight scar on the left temple.

"This is," said he, "to be brief, a guarantee for a consignment of two hundred thousand rifles and a thousand rounds of ammunition per rifle, to be delivered at some port unnamed before Christmas of this year, and, as you say, the names of the guarantors place the matter beyond all doubt."

"Quite so," said Sir James. "The destination of the consignment is purposely omitted for additional safety, but it is known to the man who calls himself Schmidt and to the others concerned. The port was fixed on and the arrangements made six weeks ago. The importance of this lies entirely on the quantity stated as having been secured, and the signatures. The German agents would stick at nothing to lay their hands on that paper. It would prove a formidable weapon, and might involve the Powers of a country which up to now has remained neutral."

"They know of the existence of this paper, then?"

"Unfortunately, yes."

"And it is essential that it should be delivered to this Antwerp address, to a town overrun with German troops and spies?"

"It is too late to alter that plan now. Even this building has been carefully watched, as I have good reason for knowing. My private telephone has been tapped on several occasions before now. They may even have overheard my message to you and followed you on here, though I think that that is unlikely."

Blake nodded, and strolled over to the heavily-curtained windows overlooking the street.

"Be kind enough to switch off that light, Sir James," he said.

Sir James reached out his hand, and the room was at once plunged into darkness. Then, and not till then, Blake cautiously parted the curtains and peered down into the street below. For a full two minutes he stood there quite motionless. Then he let the curtains drop back into place.

"You can light up again now, Sir James," he said across the darkness. "There are two of them right enough, and I fancy there is a third somewhere further down the street, for I saw something like a signal pass. Isn't there some back way out of here—a lower window, or something—by which I could reach that maze of mews which lies beyond?"

"There is a way," said Sir James doubtfully. "It leads through what used to be the cellars of the house. They are used now for storing old documents chiefly."

"Capital! The very thing! And now, with your permission, I'll ring for a messenger I left below."

He touched the bell, and a grizzled commissionaire with half a dozen medals glistening on his breast answered it.

"You will find a messenger-boy waiting in the hall," Blake said. "Bring him up, please."

"Yes, sir," said the man.

Blake bent over the desk, took up a telegraph-form, and wrote a message. It was addressed to himself, making an urgent appointment for the afternoon of the next day, and the signature appended was that of Sir James.

He chuckled as he wrote it.

"That'll puzzle 'em if they read it," he said. "They'll probably detach one man to follow the messenger to the nearest post-office and look over his shoulder as he sends the message off."

"But this messenger-boy—" began Sir James.

"Oh, that's all right! He's my assistant—Tinker. I thought he might come in handy, so I told him to get into a messenger-boy's uniform and follow me here after a ten-minutes' interval, and to wait in the hall till he heard from me. Even if they saw him come in they won't connect him with me, and there are dozens of messenger-boys always coming and going here."

There was a tap at the door, and Tinker entered, holding his cap in his hand. His uniform, truth to tell, was a trifle tight for him.

Blake nodded.

"Off with that coat!" he said. "Now open your shirt."

Tinker did as he was told.

Blake took the envelope containing the precious message and slid it inside the shirt.

"No one must catch sight of that on any account; and you will be followed and watched, at any rate, as far as the nearest post-office, where you will send off this telegram, addressed to myself. If anyone tries to look over your shoulder as you do so give him every chance; but after that you must give him the slip, and cut back home and change into country kit for travelling.

"You will be at the station in plenty of time for the Queenborough-Flushing boat-train. Take a third-class smoker —corridor for preference—and collar two seats. After that wait till I come. If I'm not followed I shall get into the same compartment; if I am I shall choose another close by. But on no account must you recognise me until I speak to you. Wear that envelope next to your skin, and have an automatic in your pocket. You'll find plenty of money in the desk. Bring it; we shall need a lot. Also bring the two bags that are ready packed, and a spare ulster and cap for me. Now clear out, and carry that telegraph-form openly in your hand. We leave for Holland to-night. Mrs. Bardell must look after Pedro. I don't know when we shall be back."

"Very good, sir!" said Tinker.

"Now, Sir James," said Blake quickly, "I'll trouble you for a dummy duplicate of that envelope and its contents—blank paper, of course, and a big official seal on the outside. After which, if you'll show me the way to the cellars, I'll be off."

Sir James looked puzzled. He never did quite understand Blake's methods, but he was far too wise to question them.

He took the big sheet of officially headed foolscap, folded it with care, and, having placed it in an envelope of similar size, made a huge blob of red sealing-wax on the flap, the size of a half-crown piece, and sealed it with an important-looking seal. As he did so a whimsical smile flickered across his tired, worn face.

"I don't know what on earth you want this for," he said, "or why you want it so blatantly sealed; but I don't mind telling you in confidence that the seal itself is merely an old Egyptian curio I picked up a for a few shillings in a pawn-broker's the other day as I was walking to the office, and the hieroglyphics mean 'all men are frauds,' or something to that effect."

Blake also smiled as he picked up the envelope and put it in his pocket.

"Most appropriate," he said. "Here are you, a person of importance in the State affairs, placidly preparing an entirely fraudulent document for your own ends, myself aiding and abetting in the scheme; and those fellows outside ready to stick at nothing—even murder—to lay hands on it, because their Government will pay them highly to do so. Pretty gang of scoundrels we are all round—eh?"

Sir James rose and held out his hand.

"Goodbye, and good luck!" he said. "It's on my conscience that I'm asking you to run an unfair risk. But what can I do? It's risking the life of one man against the lives of perhaps hundreds and thousands of others. That's the literal truth, and you are the one man I can entrust with the task.

"I leave all details to you. I ask no questions as to your ways and means and methods. But, my dear fellow, that paper—the real paper, I mean—must not be found or read, except by those for whom it is intended. The risk is enormous. If I don't see or hear from you in ten days—say, a fortnight's time—I shall take it for granted that you will have destroyed either the paper or yourself, or both. And, mind you, if you are not killed, but merely taken prisoner with that paper on you, it will be my bounden duty to disavow you—to be like a Trojan, in fact—

swear that you were not acting under my instructions, and that I have no interest in you or your movements whatever. I shouldn't dare lift a finger or bring the slightest diplomatic pressure to bear to save you. You clearly understand?"

Blake lit another cigarette and laughed.

"It certainly isn't your fault if I don't. You know, Sir James, you really have a positive gift for elucidating uncomfortable possibilities. I assure you that I haven't the slightest intention of being caught if I can help it; and the bare idea of a German fortress makes me shudder. The feeding, especially just now, is abominable, they tell me. I'll tell you a secret. At heart I am a positive epicure, and I adore a really decent and well-cooked meal. Now, if I may ring for the commissionaire again and get him to show me the way through the cellars, I'll be off. I shan't have a whole heap of time to spare as it is, and I've a lot to do."

Blake rang again, and the commissionaire came back, expressionless as some wooden automaton.

"Hawkins," said Sir James, and gave a little deprecatory cough behind his hand, "you know the cellars where those old documents and things are stored. I want you to take this gentleman down there and help him to get out through the window and grating at the far end. You have the keys of the padlocks, I believe. There are some suspicious-looking men hanging about the street outside in front of there, and Mr. Blake doesn't wish to be seen. You will not mention this to anyone either now or later. You understand me?"

"Perfectly, Sir James. Would you please follow me, sir?" he added, turning to Blake.

"I'm quite ready," said Blake. "Goodbye again, Sir James! It is just half-past five, I see. If I am not back here in this room with what you require by, say, six o'clock on this day fortnight, you had better send another man at once, for I shall have come to grief. There is one point, however, on which you can set your mind at ease. They may bag me, but they won't bag the paper, even if I have to eat it under their very noses."

The two men shook hands again, and Blake followed Hawkins out of the room and down the stairs.

They descended to the basement, and so into the cellars beyond—a dingy, musty-smelling place with festoons of cobwebs hanging from the ceilings.

Hawkins paused a moment to light a candle in a rickety old iron candlestick, and they made their way gingerly along by its flickering light until they came to a much-begrimed window showing faintly lighter against the general gloom.

Blake reached out a hand and brought the open palm of it down on the candle-flame, leaving them in darkness.

"Can't be too careful. Might have been seen from the outside," he said. "Get to work with those keys, and give me a leg-up."

The ex-sergeant obeyed stolidly, fumbling with the rusty latch and bars of the window, which he at last managed to open, giving admission to a little well-like area some five feet square, with a padlocked grating above of rather smaller dimensions.

This grating was within easy reach as they stood in the well.

Hawkins unlocked the two padlocks fastening it down, gave Blake the help of his broad back to clamber on to and raise the grating, and accepted two half-crowns thrust through the bars after the grating was closed again; and Blake, with a brief "good-night!" and a word of thanks, went padding softly and swiftly down the alleyway leading to the regular Hampton-Court-maze-like tangle of mews which lay beyond.

Ninety-nine Londoners out of a hundred may have passed daily within a respectable stone's-throw of those mews without ever being aware of their existence. Private motors are housed there cheek by jowl with old, emblazoned family coaches in the next stable—coaches that are only used at great State functions, such as a gala night at the opera or a coronation.

Ostensibly there is no more respectable labyrinth of by-streets in London, and its inhabitants are ultra-respectable, upper-class servants, earning big wages and deserving them. But at the same time, to a man in Blake's position, they were very likely to prove a veritable death-trap. He knew every turn and twist of them as he knew the inside of his own pocket, and he knew very clearly their possibilities if a few paid agents of the great German spy system had been warned to lie in wait for him there, on the bare chance that he would choose that way. So he walked swiftly, keeping well in the centre of the cobbled roadway, and even hummed a snatch of a tune as he walked; but his eyes searched out all the darker corners on either hand as he did so, and his ears were alert to catch the slightest unaccustomed sound.

Yet even so, as he rounded a sharp angle, three men sprang at him from behind the shelter of a doorway in a bunch.

The light was bad and tricky, owing to the new war regulations, but he had almost what is called "cat's sight," and suffered less from the darkness probably than they did. Also, he had been expecting trouble, and was prepared.

He sprang aside to get his back protected by a solid wall, and, with a sudden lunge of his stick, caught the leading man full in the mouth with the ferrule end. The man dropped with a muttered, guttural curse, and lay on the stones, spitting out loosened and broken teeth.

Almost at the same instant the second made a savage blow at him with a sandbag—that silent, deadly weapon of the East American crook. Blake dodged in the nick of time, and so saved his skull; but the blow caught him on the shoulder, momentarily paralysing his right arm, and causing him to drop his stick with a clatter.

The man raised his sandbag again, and Blake caught him a swift left-hander on the point as he did so.

There were no complaints.

"Two!" said Blake cheerfully. "Now, then, Hans, or Fritz, or whatever your beautiful name may be, it's your turn to join the dance. Come along; only be quick, as this is my busy day!"

The man feinted, and Blake glimpsed the sheen of steel in his right hand.

The fellow wanted to use his knife, that was clear enough, but he wasn't whole-hearted about it. The sight of his two companions lying on the stones, much the worse for wear, had taken the grit out of him, and he hesitated. That was his mistake, because Blake didn't. He brought round his stick, which he had hurriedly picked up, with a whistling, back-handed cut, which caught the fellow stingingly across the ear, half dazing him with the sudden pain, and throwing him off his balance.

Blake dropped the broken stick, caught the man's knife hand by the wrist, and again above the elbow. There was a twist, a jerk, a quick upthrust of Blake's bent knee, and a sound like the sound of a snapping hurdle, followed by a perfect bellow of pain and the tinkle of steel on stone.

The man's forearm had been broken at the elbow joint, and he dropped like a log, whimpering and cursing.

A window somewhere up above was flung open, and a groom's voice was heard complaining petulantly, and asking: "What the, which the, how the blank something or another couldn't a poor beggar have his tea in peace?"

Blake chuckled, and hurried away, keeping close to the wall this time.

"I will say one thing for old Sir James," he said to himself. "When he does give you a job, it's never what you might call really dull. Things happen. I wonder what the next item on the programme will be?"

He emerged from the labyrinth of the mews at the upper end without further mishap, took several sharp turns, and then a step or two backwards, to make sure that he wasn't being followed; and, having satisfied himself on this point, he headed straight for the Cafe Royale, in Regent Street—a favourite restaurant of his in emergencies, because of its different entrances and its giving on to different streets—a very useful thing from his point of view, as he had found on more than one occasion.

He passed straight to the grill-room, casting quick, keen glances at the various occupants, for the crowd is generally one of many nationalities, and it was quite possible that Hans or Fritz, at present nursing a broken arm in the mews, might have confederates there.

He saw nothing suspicious, however, in his brief survey, and ordered himself a dinner with the care of a man who knows that he may not have a chance to taste food again for the next twenty-four hours or more.

After his dinner he had coffee and a cigarette, and, contrary to his usual custom, ordered a small jug of milk with his coffee.

His next proceedings were, to say the least of it, a trifle unusual. He had purposely chosen a small table in a corner, so that no one could get behind him or look over his shoulder, whilst he himself could command a clear view of the entire length of the room.

He drew the big official envelope out of his pocket, slit open the bottom end neatly with a knife, and, under cover of the tablecloth, withdrew the blank sheet which it contained.

This he placed on the table before him, and, taking a folding pen with a clean nib in it from his waistcoat pocket, he dipped the nib in the milk, and wrote something in a bold hand across the centre of the page. The writing was, of course, invisible, and as soon as the milk had thoroughly dried he refolded the paper, replaced it in the envelope, paid his bill, and strolled out by the door at the opposite end to that by which he had entered—after which he made his way leisurely to Victoria Station on foot.

He had plenty of time in hand, and had no wish to appear on the platform a second earlier than was absolutely necessary. He was not hankering after publicity in his movements.

He took his ticket, booking straight through to Flushing, and noticed that passengers were being stopped at the barrier and taken aside to be searched. Holland is a neutral country, but experience has taught the authorities that many very unneutral things and people, especially people, have been smuggled through it since the war.

He glanced at the big clock. The train was due to start in under a couple of minutes, so he went up to the barrier to show his tickets. The collector glanced at them, and nodded, and immediately another official stepped up to him.

"This way, sir! We shall have to go through you as a matter of form. I'm afraid you've cut it rather fine. You'll have to go by the next boat. Orders, sir! All intending passengers are warned to be on the platform at least half an hour before the train starts. If they aren't, it's their fault, not ours."

Blake nodded, and slightly turned up the lapel of his coat, giving the man a glimpse of a small silver badge which had been concealed beneath it.

The man looked, stepped back, and touched his cap.

"Beg pardon, sir. I didn't know, of course. You'd better hurry; she'll be off in a minute!"

Blake nodded once more, and hurried along the platform. He had barely gone twenty paces when he heard the sound of a violent altercation going on behind him.

He glanced backwards over his shoulder, and saw the man whom he had hit on the "point" in the mews struggling frantically with two burly but quite placid officials.

"Search me on der train!" he cried excitedly. "I tell you I haf nothings! Search me on der train! That I catch the boat is imberative!"

"Can't be done, sir; it's against orders. You can cross to-morrow morning. It will only make a few hours' difference. Only my advice is, turn up in plenty of time!"

Just then the man caught sight of Blake; their eyes met, and he began to rage again.

"I haf to go!" he yelled, struggling.

"Yes, you will certainly 'haf' ter go—to the lock-up, if there's any more fuss!" was the imperturbable answer.

"Take him away, Jarvis. You know what to do with him if he becomes troublesome! Bloomin' German thug, that's what he is!" he added to himself.

Blake chuckled, and raced down the platform. He glimpsed Tinker waving to him, the carriage door swung open, and Blake leapt in as the train began to gather speed.

They had their compartment of the corridor carriage all to themselves.

"Who was your friend with the beautiful voice at the barrier?" asked Tinker.

"Hump! We'll call him an acquaintance!" said Blake. "I met him for the first time just after leaving Sir James, and had to knock him down to avoid being sandbagged. There were three of the beauties waiting for me in the mews at the back there. It's awkward, for, of course, he'll wire to his people out there to look out for us on the frontier. Everything all right?"

"Yes, all serene. Pedro hasn't eaten Mrs. Bardell yet—at least, he hadn't when I left. They didn't search me, because I said I was travelling for Sir James, and gave them one of his cards, which I annexed while I was waiting in the hall this afternoon. I photographed the paper you gave me, and made two film transparencies. They are quite good, and will easily enlarge to twice the size of the original. The films themselves are two and a quarter by one and a quarter. I thought they might come in handy if we are obliged to destroy the original. One film is stitched into the lining of my hat. The other is in the handle of that toothbrush of yours—you know the hollow-handled one with the screw end to it. Here's your automatic, by the way, and I've a dozen full cartridge slips stowed away in the bags."

"Good!" said Blake. "Now I'd better change out of this kit as soon as I can. Pull those blinds down on the corridor side; I don't want an audience."

Ten minutes later Blake was rigged out like a typical American commercial traveller, and Tinker had stowed his other things into a spare gladstone he had brought for the purpose.

"We'll leave that in the cloak-room at Queensboro'," he said, as he slipped into a big travelling ulster.

A few deft touches of grease-paint here and there altered him in a way that was little short of miraculous; yet it could not strictly have been called a disguise, and would have defied detection in the strongest light.

Tinker sat in the corner and gnawed sandwiches, and, after a quick run, the train pulled into Queenborough Station.

Before it came to a standstill Blake said quickly:

"You look after the baggage, and that gladstone for the cloak-room. You'll find me somewhere on board. I want to catch every face that passes up that gangway, and to do that I must get there first. I want to see if I can spot anyone who looks as if he might be a friend of Hans, Fritz & Co. Be as quick as you can to join me." And with that he was off like a flash.

Unhampered by any luggage except his ulster and the automatic in the right-hand pocket, he was well ahead of all the other passengers, and long before the first of them came blundering up the gang-plank Blake was leaning over the steamer's rail smoking a cigarette, and scanning the faces each in turn as they passed under the glare of the sizzling arc-lights overhead. As a matter of fact, there were only a couple of score or so of them all told, mostly businessmen, whose love of money was greater than their fear of lurking submarines. Tinker was amongst the last of the crowd.

"Anything doing?" he asked Blake, as he dumped down the bags on the deck beside them and joined Blake at the rail. "I've stuck the other bag in the cloak-room and given the ticket into the stationmaster's charge in case of accidents."

"Nothing so far," said Blake, in an undertone; "mostly drummers of the ordinary type. Two women—obviously English—but not a soul who looks like a German."[3]

Warps were cast adrift, engine-room bells clanged imperatively, and the steamer slid silently away into the darkness. There was quite a big lop of sea on outside, and soon Blake and Tinker had the deck to themselves.

"Well, we are all right so far," said Blake, at last throwing away the end of his cigarette. "We may as well turn in and get some sleep while we can. I don't suppose we shall get much chance the other side. By Jove, look there, they are dry-nursing us with a vengeance!"

On either quarter there had come stealing up out of the darkness the long, lean hulls of destroyers, swirling along without lights, and visible mainly by their white bow waves.

"They need to take care of us evidently," said Tinker. "I've never had an escort of the British Navy before; makes one feel stuck-up and important, doesn't it?"

Signals were interchanged between the mail-boat and the destroyers, and in obedience to these the mail-boat swung onto a new course.

They were evidently being piloted through a mine-field, for after a little while the course was abruptly changed again, and in this way they zigzagged about for a considerable time. How the destroyers managed to pick up their marks on such a pitch-black night was a sheer mystery to Tinker; yet there was never a second's pause or hesitation. They seemed to pick their way as easily as anyone could have made their way down Regent's Street or the Strand in the good old days when those thoroughfares were ablaze with light.

Blake and Tinker turned in at last, and when they woke the destroyers had vanished, and the Dutch coast lay ahead of them, a thin grey line in the chill dawn.

Blake had already made up his mind as to the most practical route, and that was to take the train to the little frontier station of Rosendaal, and try and slip across the border from there; to go up the river or take the more ordinary route he considered impossible. For the man whom they had left struggling on the station in the grasp of the ticket-collector would have been certain to wire to his confederates as soon as ever he was at liberty, and they would be watching the main routes; but it was just possible that they would overlook the more roundabout way via Rosendaal.

At any rate, it was a chance that had to be run. As soon as the steamer was alongside the quay they made their way to the station and ate a hearty breakfast, and by the time they had finished, the train was ready to start. They secured a compartment to themselves, for there were few passengers, and the train went trundling through the lowlands of Holland.

They were safe enough so far, the frontier was the critical point, and even Blake's pulses beat a bit faster as they drew near.

The train slowed down, and suddenly came to a stop just short of the station. Whistles tooted wildly, and then the train backed away a little. A fat Dutch guard came along the footboard.

"There will be a quarter of an hour's delay!" he called out. "All passengers are to remain in their carriages. Passengers and their luggage will be searched before crossing the frontier!"

Blake and Tinker looked at one another blankly. They had a pretty shrewd idea of what the search would be for. Their friend of the station had evidently not overlooked the possibilities of the Rosendaal route.

They looked out of the window, and saw that the platform was crowded with German uniforms. It was evident that the search would be a thorough one.

Blake thought for a moment. There was no time to be lost.

"It's a chance, but we must risk it," he said. "Give me the paper quickly."

Tinker fumbled in his shirt and pulled it out.

Blake tore off the envelope and unfolded the paper. Then he pulled down the spring blind of the nearest window and pinned the paper to it by the corners, after which he let the blind roll up again with a snap.

"Settle yourself down again in the corner," he said. "Pretend to read—anything—and look as unconcerned as you can."

Tinker nodded, and Blake tore the envelope to shreds and let the pieces flutter out of the window, then he lit a cigarette with care, and settled himself in the opposite corner.

He had barely done so when the train moved slowly forward again and drew up level with the platform. Instantly four or five German officials appeared at the door of each carriage. Blake shot a keen glance at those crowding round their door. There were four agents, two of them non-commissioned officers under the command of a stolid-looking lieutenant. The latter had evidently been furnished with a description of them, for the moment he caught sight of them he pointed excitedly, and called out in German:

"There they are. Search them well!"

The door was flung open, and Blake sprang to his feet in well-simulated surprise.

"What's wrong, Herr Lieutenant?" he asked, in German.

The latter growled out a vague answer, and his men pounced on their bags, which they opened and rummaged without ceremony. Blake had already deposited the dummy envelope with the big seal there, and a sergeant snatched it up with an exclamation of triumph. The lieutenant seized it, and slit open the flap. But his face fell when he discovered only a blank sheet of paper inside.

He turned it this way and that, and tried it upside-down for all the world like a monkey at the Zoo who had got hold of a piece of looking-glass. Finally, he replaced it in the envelope and thrust it into his tunic.

"Search their bodies!" he ordered harshly. "Off with their coats, waistcoats, and boots!"

"Gently, gently!" said Blake, in German. "We are quite willing to be searched if necessary, Herr Lieutenant, but we will hand you our things one by one. Here is my coat. Take care, there is an automatic in the pocket."

"To carry arms is forbidden."

"In Belgium possibly, but we are still in Holland. Here is my letter-case; it contains a fair sum in notes. With your permission I will give our value, a hundred marks, to be divided amongst your men if you will kindly ask them to get over this job as soon as possible. Here are my waistcoat and boots, and for the rest your men can search for themselves. I assure you that they will find nothing on me but some loose change.

"As for that envelope and sheet of paper you have there, you can see for yourself, and I give you my word that it hasn't the slightest political significance."

The lieutenant grunted, and the men searched both Blake and Tinker to the skin. They searched the cushions, the floor, everything in fact but the one place they should have searched— the carriage window-blinds.

At last they swung off in disgust, leaving the two to dress themselves and collect their scattered belongings as best they could.

"Phew!" said Blake. "That was a near shave. I kept my eyes skinned ready to make a grab for the automatic if that fat-headed lieutenant had tried the blinds. They would have bagged us in the end, of course, but we should have had time to destroy the paper first, with luck. I suppose they'll let us go on now. Hallo! What the deuce are they up to?"

"Keep your places!" rang out a harsh order. "No trains can cross the frontier to-day. You will be sent back to the next station till further orders, and you will remain under guard. Anyone attempting to leave the train without permission will be shot!"

"Cheerful animal, isn't he?" said Tinker, grinning.

"I wish that on the whole I'd put a bullet through him," said Blake, as the train backed slowly out of the station to Tollen, a little one-horse place a few miles down the line.

Here, though quite irregularly, they were searched again, by the Dutch guards this time, and they performed their duties good-naturedly enough. It was a mere farce of a search, and the corporal in charge offered them a particularly vile brand of cigar apiece. Blake lit his, with the resigned air of a stoic philosopher—Tinker, not feeling equal to the task, surreptitiously dropped his out of the window, and gave a sigh of relief.

At the next station they were told they would be free to get out and do what they pleased—or words to that effect.

"So far, so good—no damage done," said Blake, and, unpinning the paper from the blind, he handed it to Tinker to hide away.

"I don't want to swank," he said, "but it's me they're after, not you but me, mark you! They know me by description perfectly. I very much doubt if they have had more than a casual sort of catalogue of your personal beauty, and, therefore, the paper will be safer with you. If they collar me, you know exactly what to do with it. Anyway, they shall have a run for their money. By hook or by crook we've got to get that paper to Rue le Heron, in Antwerp, between us, and we've never failed yet. I reckoned on getting through by this route. It's panned out a blank, so we must try another.

"The first thing for us to do is to get back to Flushing. I know an old pilot skipper there whom I was able to do a good turn to once. He'll help us if he can."

After a dismal two-hour wait in the little wayside station, and a cold, drizzling rain, they took a train back to Flushing, crossed the footbridge over the lock, and made their way to a small inn on the far quayside.

Here Blake left Tinker alone whilst he conversed with the host, a burly Dutchman, in his private sanctum. The upshot of the interview was that within an hour they were both provided with typical Dutch shoregoing outfits—baggy trousers, short jackets, sabots, and all complete. Their faces were stained with walnut-juice, their hands reddened with ochre, and their luggage placed in safe keeping. All they carried with them were their automatics with spare clips, their money—changed into Dutch currency, and equally divided between them in case of emergencies, and, of course, the all-important paper sewn into Tinker's vest.

Just as they had finished their change of kit, Blake burst out chuckling.

"What's the joke?" asked Tinker gloomily

"That fat pig of a moon-headed lieutenant—who collared the dummy paper—didn't you hear what he said?"

"I only understood about one word in ten," grumbled Tinker. "You know German isn't my strong point."

"Well, what he said was that he was going to take the paper to the police bureau, to have it tested for invisible ink. He'll get a surprise when he does."

"Why? There wasn't a line on it."

"Not a visible line, certainly; but I scrawled a word or two in milk on it, and when they come to hold it up to the fire—a dodge they are certain to try—they'll see clearly written large and plain, 'You condemned fools!' Only I expressed it a little more bluntly than that, in low-down German slang, which will bite home. I should like to see that fat lieutenant's face when he reads it! Got your automatic handy, so that you can grab it in a hurry? Good! We'd better be getting down to the quay. Old Bogo, our host, will be ready by now."

They went out across the flagged pavement-way to the waterside, and there found their host busy on board one of the many hogaast lying by the landing-stages. She had a single-pole mast, light spas, and her hull and leeboards were rich with Stockholm tar. Her draught was roughly two feet with her leeboards up. She was anywhere between twenty-five and thirty ton, and she could have outpointed and outsailed any ordinary racing-cutter of her own size. Ostensibly she was carrying a cargo of potatoes and other vegetables to sell in Antwerp—in reality she was carrying Tinker and Blake, who had chartered her as the easiest way of getting into Antwerp, since the railways were closed to them.

Bogo, in the midst of splicing a badly-frayed length of main-sheet, caught sight of them, and bellowed a welcome as they came on board.

"De tide him goot," he explained, "and de windt, once we get clear the lock, we go like—what you say?—blazes, smoke!"

From Flushing to Antwerp is, roughly speaking, ninety miles, and the first thirty is mostly a steeplechase across iron-hard and ever-changing sandbanks; but that is just where a boat of the hogaast type comes in. She can haul up her leeboards, and skim over stretches of water that would tear the bottom out of any deeper draught vessel.

They made good time, carrying a fair wind with them nearly all the way, and, as Blake had calculated, it was just dark when they finally moored up alongside the fish-market quay. They said goodbye to their host, and clambered up the steep, slippery steps.

"Wait for us till dawn," Blake said. "If we are not back by then you'd better clear out, in case of trouble."

"No matter, my friend," called the cheery Dutchman, "I my vegetable have to sell. I cannot leave till the market be open."

"All right, then," said Blake, "we shall know where to find you in case of need."

He and Tinker turned away and walked swiftly across the open yards, amongst all sorts of litter, and so through the dock gates. Outside was a German sentry, with fixed bayonet; but seeing them dressed as ordinary Scheldt boatmen he paid no attention to them. He had seen hundreds of the same type pass within the last hour.

Once clear of the docks and the sentry, Blake paused a moment to take his bearings by the tall spire of the cathedral, and swung away to the left.

They wound their way through many crooked, old-fashioned streets, and finally turned sharply to the right.

"The Rue le Heron," said Blake, and scanned the numbers carefully, many of them half obliterated, till he came to nineteen.

Once the Rue le Heron had been a prosperous residential quarter of the Antwerp merchants, but now it had fallen on evil days, and the big, stately houses of old-time were let out in tenements, and stuffy, ill-conditioned flats.

Number nineteen was dated back to the seventeenth century. It was of greystone, with mullioned windows. The heavy iron-studded door had been battered in, in the early days of the siege, and now hung wide listlessly on one hinge, all awry.

The place seemed absolutely deserted, but far away up on the

160

third floor Blake's keen eyes had discovered the faint glimmer of a candle through the crack of a curtain.

"That will be our destination, I expect," said Blake. "Anyway, we'll go and see. Come on!"

They made their way cautiously up the rickety stairs, for it was pitch dark inside the building, and they had to grope their way foot by foot. Someone passed them on the stairs when they were half-way up. They felt rather than saw that it was a man. He was either very reckless, or very familiar with the building, for he was coming down at breakneck speed, and would have dashed into them if they had not stood aside, close up against the wall, to let him pass. As it was, he was blundering on without even seeing them. His breath was coming in little whistling gasps, as though he were half-scared out of his wits by something, and presently they heard him running over the flagstones in the street below.

"Well, he was in a deuce of a hurry, anyhow," said Tinker, in an undertone. "I suppose he couldn't have been our man by any chance."

Blake shook his head.

"Schmidt was described to me as a man well past middle age; that being so, he'd never have been able to get along at that pace—in the darkness, too. That was a much younger man altogether. He may, of course, have been one of Schmidt's agents, an understrapper, or he may—" Blake broke off suddenly, with an exclamation.

"Great heavens!" he cried. "He's more likely to have been an agent for the other side! The hurry he was in, and his hard breathing struck me as vaguely suspicious at the moment. Come on, quick!"

He struck a match, and then another. There was blood on the stairs—fresh blood, which glistened in the flickering light. He pointed to it, and dashed blindly up the stairs two at a time.

A faint bar of yellow light showed ahead of them, filtering through the crack under the door. The latter stood partly ajar, and they burst in.

Blake's surmise proved only too true. Adolph Schmidt lay half-across the bed with two gaping wounds in his chest. He was in his shirtsleeves, having discarded his coat and waistcoat, and had apparently been busy writing when he was attacked. For the lamp stood on a table in the centre of the room, which was littered with papers. There was an overturned ink bottle, a broken pen, and a splintered chair—evidence of the brief struggle which had taken place.

Blake took in the whole scene at a glance, and sprang for the lamp. As he did so he took a brief look at the scattered papers. They were mostly short paragraphs for the local news-sheets. He recalled the fact that Sir James had told him Schmidt ostensibly made a living by newspaper writing. It was a mere farce, a cloak beneath which to hide his real profession; but so far it had served its turn. Blake snatched up the lamp, and carried it to where the man lay half on half off the bed.

He was breathing and still conscious, as Blake could see by the intelligent gleam in his eyes, though his face was drawn with pain.

Blake's first action was to try and stop the bleeding, but the briefest inspection showed him that the wounds were fatal. A small carafe of cognac stood on a cupboard near by. He dashed some into a glass, added water, and held it to the man's lips. The man—he was a grizzled little imp of a fellow, with a face normally shrewd and clever—drank greedily.

"So," he said faintly, in fair English, "you haf come too late! The paper?"

Blake signed to Tinker, and the latter unfolded it, and held it up.

"I cannot see! I must trust!" gasped Schmidt. "In the inside pocket of the coat you will find receipt."

Tinker fumbled in the coat, and drew out a small square of tracing-paper with one corner roughly torn off.

On this was scrawled:

"Goods arrived safely.—ADOLPH SCHMIDT."

At a gesture from the injured man Tinker transferred it to his own pocket.

"You will go on!" he gasped. "The paper—it must be delivered! It must! You understand?"

Blake nodded.

"I understand. We will go on. I pledge you my word to that. If it is humanly possible, the paper shall be delivered. But who to, and where? I understand that you and the man you were to take this to know the port hinted at. Who is the man, and what is the port?"

Schmidt fought for breath and strength, and Blake gave him another sip of the brandy-and-water—for he was nearly gone, and it was essential that he should rally enough to speak again.

"Captain van Zyl," he panted—"Captain van Zyl, at the Lion D'or Cabaret, on the 'quai' at Stiltz. He will give you receipt same as mine. Give him that, and it is finish. He know all the rest, and he arrange everythings. He is not suspect as I—not yet, anyways. But you must be hurried. No; do not wait for me. I am nearly finished, too."

"I'm hanged if I'll leave you like this!" said Blake.

"But yes. Go—go quick! I know—I know those German pigs. Soon they will be back; they do not leave any dead or dying in the houses—they fear it make too much talk. Soon they come to take me away. That man who killed me, he tell them. I am too old to serve my country in the field, yes; but I have done the best I can—the best I can! An' it grow dark an' cold! I—"

His head fell back suddenly, and became a dead weight on Blake's arm.

Tinker looked askance, and Blake nodded.

"He was right," he said, in a low voice. "It is finished."

He slipped his hand inside the man's shirt. There was no responsive beat of the heart, but his fingers encountered a small metal object, hung by a slender gold chain. It was a locket of plain gold, set with a single diamond of no great value.

There was an inscription on it, and Blake held it up to the light to read it. Translated, it ran:

"To my dear Armand—Le Duc de St. Pol et Anmere."

Blake replaced it gently without opening it. Whatever it may have contained was the dead man's business, and no one else's. And the Duke of St. Pol and Anmere wore one of the highest titles in Belgium, and had owned some of the greatest estates, though he had died in a garret under an assassin's knife, and made a pretence of eking out a precarious livelihood by scribbling paragraphs.

In his own words, he had served his country to the best of his ability, cheerfully running risks day by day, knowing full well that, sooner or later, the German spies were bound to find him out.

"There lies a very brave gentleman," said Blake, taking off his cap, "and you and I, old man, must fulfil our promise to him if we can."

Tinker had already restored the paper to its hiding-place under his shirt, when he suddenly darted to the door, and listened.

"There's someone coming up the stairs," he whispered. "Germans—half a dozen or more of them, by the sound! We must get out of this!"

Quick as thought Blake had extinguished the lamp.

"Upstairs with you!" he said, under his breath. "Don't make a sound. We must chance the attics."

Swiftly and noiselessly they made their way to the top floor. It was hard to find their way in the dark, but a faint moonlight was beginning to filter through the windows of the various rooms, and when Tinker stumbled once the noise was smothered by the tramp, tramp of the approaching Germans.

They made a dive into one of the attics at the back, and crouched there, listening intently.

The Germans poured into the room below, and at once it was obvious that their suspicions were aroused. Either one of them, sharper than the rest, had spotted a glimmer of light in the room when they first came opposite the house, or their agent, the murderer, had explained the position of the body, and that he had left the lamp burning when he left the house. Be that as it may, hoarse orders were at once given to search the house from top to bottom, cellar to attic, and electric-torches and lights began flashing in all directions.

Sexton Blake leaned out, and touched Tinker on the arm.

"We must take to the roof, old man!" he whispered. "They are after us, right enough. I caught a sentence just then. They have had word that two Englishmen who were on that tin-pot Dutch train, got away, after being searched at the frontier, and have been traced as far as Flushing, suspected of secreting a paper of vital importance. That paper, they know, was intended for St. Pol, here. They murdered him on the chance of getting it, having missed us. But, of course, they were premature. They may quite possibly have had the house watched by a man stationed in the cafe on the far side of the street in front. Anyway, it's us for the roof, and Heaven send that the tiles aren't loose—it's an eighty-foot drop!"

They crawled through the little dormer-window onto a roof, the slope of which was considerably over one in three, with a rickety-looking gutter at the edge of it, which sagged badly, and promised little or no dependable handhold.

Tinker flung himself flat on the tiles, and clung to a piece of iron upright, whilst Blake, hanging on by one hand, managed to refasten the window from the outside more or less securely. He was barely in time, for once more they heard hoarse shouts and the trampling of heavy-booted feet, and lights began to flicker across the window-panes.

Blake swung himself onto the top of the gable of the dormer, and crouched astride. Without actually clambering through the window it was impossible for anyone to see, because he was directly over their heads. Tinker, for his part, clawed his way up to another iron stanchion, and lay flat alongside the gable. He was painfully conscious that his boots might be visible if anyone craned out very far, however tightly he tucked his legs up under him. The Germans, however, contented themselves with much more practical measures.

The officer in charge gave the order:

"Fire-pastilles in every room, and a dozen tins of kerosene and a bundle of straw on the ground floor, will burn the rats out if we can't get them any other way! It'll make a fine blaze, and if the next houses catch, so much the better. There'll be another Belgian or two gone to glory. Half a dozen men posted in the street below, and if anyone comes out after we've started the fire, let him have it—ball-cartridge first, and then the bayonet!"

"Pleasant sort of brute, isn't he?" said Blake, under his breath. "And we seem to be 'it,' as the Americans say. Hang on a bit whilst I go and explore. I'm not going to be roasted like a pheasant if there's a way out anywhere. If the worst comes to the worst, we must destroy that infernal paper, and make a charge down the stairs. It's a tight corner, old chap, and I've dragged you into it. But don't you worry; we'll pull through somehow."

There came a scraping of tiles and a shuffling of feet, clawing, slipping, and sliding, as Blake made his way up to the ridge of the roof, and vanished on the far side.

It was three or four minutes before he returned, breathing quickly.

"I think we can manage," he said. "It isn't a nice job, and I don't pretend that it is. But there is a big beam running across an alley-way at the back which leads to the houses on the far side, where the roofs are guarded by a parapet, and are flatter than here. If we can cross that beam, we shall be all right. I'll go first and test it. If I fall, you must do the best you can. Phew! There goes the smoke. They don't seem to be losing much time."

"Right-ho!" said Tinker. "I'd rather break my neck than be cooked alive, any old day! But I'm lighter—why not let me go first?"

"Because you've got the paper, old man. If the beam will bear me, it will bear you. If I come to grief, you and the paper must find another way. The longer we talk about it the less we shall like it. Come on, and let's get it over. This place will be a sizzling furnace inside the next ten minutes. The tiles on this side are getting hot already, and there's a crowd collecting in the street below."

Blake led the way up the slippery, sloping tiles, and Tinker followed him. Once across the roof ridge, they dropped into shadow out of the fierce glare of the flames, which were spreading rapidly, for the fire-pastilles were getting in their fine work.

They lay on their backs, and slid slowly down, gripping at every roughness in the surface that they could.

The beam which Blake had spoken of was a solid affair a foot square, and had evidently been fixed there at some time to act as a support for the old bulging walls. It ran right across the alley from side to side, and was roughly fifteen feet long. On the nearside where they were it was fixed fully five feet below the level of the guttering; on the other, it was almost flush with the parapet.

"Well, here goes!" said Blake. "We shall do no good by waiting. Look! the flames are already coming through the windows on this side. Wait till I call, and then lower yourself down as I do. I shall be there to steady you, and mind, whatever you do, don't look down; if you do, you're bound to get giddy!"

Very cautiously Blake let himself down the slope of the roof, hung for a moment from the gutter, until he could feel the beam with his feet, and then gradually lowered himself till he sat astride. Luckily an old and solid lightning-conductor ran down the side of the house close to the beam, and he was able to steady himself by it in lowering himself down. This was the most ticklish part of the operation.

As soon as he was firmly astride the beam, he called out to Tinker:

"Ready! Take it easy. I'll steady you!"

Tinker gave a gulp. He had a good head for heights in the ordinary mountain climbing, but this, with a sheer drop to the paving-stones below, was a different affair altogether. He set his teeth. He knew that he was shivering like a leaf, and when he reached the guttering he had a frightful sinking sensation at the pit of his stomach.

Then he heard Blake's voice saying quietly:

"All right, I've got you!" And he felt Blake's hands catch him round the waist, and his feet touched the beam. "There's a lightning-conductor on your right!" Blake went on. "Steady yourself by that. Gently does it. Now lower away slowly!"

Almost before Tinker realised it, he was sitting beside Blake astride the beam, still feeling sick, but comparatively secure.

The worst part was to come, however. They were both facing the burning house, and it was imperative that they should turn round and face the other way before attempting the crossing. Blake had nerves of steel. He swung both legs over to the same side of the beam as nonchalantly as if he had been sitting on a country stile, and in a trice he was sitting facing in the direction they had to go.

"Your turn now, young 'un!" he said cheerfully. "It's as easy as pie. Take hold of my shoulders to steady yourself as you turn, and then keep your eyes glued on the small of my back, and don't think of anything else."

How Tinker did it he never knew; but he did do it, and then, with both hands free to grip the woodwork in front of him, it became easier.

He could hear the cries of the people far away below as they watched the fire; but he kept his eyes rigidly fixed on Blake's back, and, using hands and knees to grip with, they made their way across bit by bit.

The distance was really quite short, and almost before Tinker was aware of it, they were on the other side.

"Here we are," said Blake cheerily, and, swinging himself over the low parapet, he turned and gave Tinker a hand.

Once in comparative safety, Tinker had to lie still, panting for a minute or two, so great was the reaction, whilst Blake worked at a small window he had spotted from the far side. It was a rickety affair of leaded glass, and he had it open in no time.

In a couple of minutes they were both inside, standing in a sort of garrett.

There was no difficulty about light. The whole place was as light as day from the glare of the burning house they had just left, and even as they looked the flames began to curl round the beam by which they had crossed a few moments before.

"Sold again, Bosches!" chuckled Blake. "You didn't get us that time, after all! Now let's go and explore. I hope there are no beastly Germans billeted here. If there are, you must leave me to talk to them."

They made their way down the rickety staircase, the upper part of the house, though furnished, seemed unused, and they descended to the lower floors.

They were going along a passage, treading gingerly, when suddenly a door on their left opened, and a man appeared, holding a lamp.

He gave a startled exclamation on catching sight of them. Then, seeing, as he thought, two Belgians of the working-class, he recovered himself.

"What are you doing here?" he called sharply. "If you have come to rob, you might have spared yourself the pain. I have nothing left. The Bosches have taken everything!"

"You have your life, monsieur," said Blake. "The Bosches have done their best to deprive us of ours. Have no fear, we are British. We have just come from that house across the way, which is on fire. We escaped by means of the big beam which connects that house and yours. We are sorry to intrude, but there was no other way."

The man stared, and beckoned them into the room he had just left.

"You came by that beam?" he said incredulously. "Truly you British are remarkable people! Never has that been done before, though once a man from a circus tried it for a wager. His nerve failed him half-way across, and—Pauf! It was all over!"

"You say the Bosches are after you?[4] I will help you if I can. But why are they after you? There are many British in the town still."

"Do you happen to know who lived in that burning house, monsieur?"

The man looked at them searchingly.

"A very great person," he said, "whom I have the honour to serve."

Blake nodded.

"The Duc de St. Pol lived there," he said, "under a name not his own. We were the bearers of a message to him. The

Germans had mortally wounded him before we got there. He died in my arms. Somehow they got news that we were in the house, so they came back and fired it."

"Monsieur de St. Pol dead!" exclaimed the man.

Blake nodded.

"He shall be avenged!" said the man savagely. "I was in his counsel. Is it by any chance you were to bring a certain paper? A Britisher was to come, and—"

"It was we who brought the paper—too late! We were stopped on the frontier, and had to go back and get here by another way."

"The paper—you have it safe?"

"Yes."

"Heaven be praised for that! But you must not be found here. They will make a house to house search. I know them. They will ransack the whole quarter. Perhaps they have begun already. Wait; I will go and see!"

He set down the lamp on the table, and made his way cautiously to the street door, and peered out. In a minute he was back again, and had slammed the bolts behind him.

"Quick! You must be quick!" he said nervously. "Already they are searching the house only two doors away!"

Blake gave a whistle of surprise.

"I should have thought they would have taken it for granted that we were roasted to cinders by now."

"They take nothing for granted. Someone may have caught sight of you high up on the beam. They may have seen the open window above. A hundred things may have happened, but they will be here in a minute!"

"Phew! Is there no back way out?"

"Yes. Follow me. I will show you!" He seized and lighted a candle, blew out the light after a last look round, and led the way down a passage. The old quarters of Antwerp are veritable rabbit warrens. Many of the houses are connected by passages and secret doors which lead into other houses facing on a different street altogether, a street which to reach in the ordinary way might involve a walk of a quarter of a mile and more.

At the end of the passage they came to a small room plainly furnished as a bed-room, though it had no window.

"Help me move the bed," he panted.

Blake pushed it aside. The man dragged away a mat from where the bedstead had stood, and laid it down in another part of the room.

There was a trapdoor on hinges, which he jerked open.

"Go down. There are steps," he said. "You, monsieur," he added to Blake, "are strong. You come last, and perhaps you can contrive to pull the bedstead back over the trap. It is not heavy."

Blake nodded, and when his turn came, standing on one of the lower steps, and supporting the half-open trap on his shoulders, he seized the bedstead by the legs, and dragged it back into its original position. As he did so he distinctly heard hoarse voices challenging from the street beyond, and there came the crash of blows on the door.

"You see?" whispered their host significantly.

"I certainly hear," said Blake drily, and let the trap back into place as he descended.

"We were only just in time," said the man. "They will have the door down in a few minutes. It is old and rotten. Follow me. This way!"

By the guttering candle-light they found that they were in some spacious cellars which wound this way and that in a perfect maze of passages.

"At one time, long years ago," explained their host hurriedly, "the house was a fashionable inn, famous for its wines. That was before the quarter fell into disrepute. Now all is gone long ago."

They hurried along through the dust and the cobwebs, now branching off at right angles, now apparently doubling on their tracks, till even Blake lost all sense of direction. Their guide, however, never hesitated for an instant, and in the end brought them to another rugged set of ladder-like steps similar to those by which they had descended.

He went up these, beckoning to the others to follow, and pushed open the trap. On emerging, they found themselves in what was really no more than a large cupboard built into the thickness of the wall, apparently.

The man passed the candle to Blake, and whispered to him to hold it, while he himself, after a little fumbling, slipped back a small slide in the door, revealing a peephole, to which he placed his eye. Blake noticed a glimmer of light coming through the aperture and shine on the man's cheekbone as he did so.

Evidently there was some sort of living-room beyond.

A brief scrutiny seemed to satisfy the man, for he rapped three times with his knuckles on the panels, and then slipped a spring lower down and swung the door open.

The room beyond was a small one, panelled in old Flemish oak, though the rest of the appointments were meagre enough in all conscience—a bare deal table covered with a coarse cloth, a cheap, shaded lamp, and a few wooden chairs. On the table stood a flask of rough country wine, half a loaf of black bread and some onions, and an earthenware pot of some kind of vegetable soup. As the door opened, a man who had been seated at the table sprang to his feet, with an exclamation of surprise not unmingled with alarm.

Their guide stepped forward, his finger pressed to his lips.

"Hist! Caillaux, it is I!" he whispered. "There are the two Britishers who brought the papers you know of. We expected only one, but two were thought safer. And"—his voice broke—"Monseigneure is dead. The Bosches killed him to-night."

The man Caillaux rapped out a savage oath. He was a dark, swarthy, powerfully-built man, and Blake saw his grip tightened on the knife he was holding till the skin over the knuckles showed white.

"Monseigneure!" he gasped, and the other nodded. "His house is burning to the ground-even now. These British escaped across the beam to my house. But there is a search being made all down the street, so we were forced to come here through the cellars. Get us food and wine, for there is much to be done, and we are hungry. Here is money."

Caillaux nodded and went out.

"Now, messieurs," he said to the other two, "you have the paper. Do you know where to take it, and how?"

"The duke spoke before he died," said Blake gravely. "If I mention the one word 'Stiltz' it should be sufficient to show you that we know where. The question of how is another matter. But I think I have a way."

Their guide nodded.

"If so, good! If not, or you are in trouble, you can rely on Caillaux. He is rough, but he is trustworthy."

Just then Caillaux returned with a basket of wine and provisions of the poorer kind, including some cheese, and dumped them on the table.

"You will look after these brave British," said the elder man, "and help them in every way you can. They have to go to a house in Stiltz. If they need you you must. Now I must go quickly. No, not that way. By the street. If I do not return home at once I shall be suspected—if I am not suspect already. I shall go straight to the German commandant and make a complaint. It is the wisest course. I have dined at a restaurant with a friend. When I come back I find my house broken into and ransacked—by German soldiers, so they tell me—and I am come to ask why.

"That will be my story, but it must be told quickly, so now adieu!"

He shook hands with Blake and Tinker, and vanished into the darkness.

They, for their part, set to ravenously on the coarse fare, for it was long since they had broken their fast. Then they determined to set out for the docks and find their old friend Bogo. He would not be able to sail until after the markets opened, but they hoped to be able to find a hiding-place on the hogaast, and persuade him, by the offer of a good round sum, to take them up to Stiltz through the canals.

They found the boat easily enough lying at her old berth alongside the quay, and dropped noiselessly on board.

Bogo was sound asleep on his bunk in the cabin. As soon they had roused him he put a piece of heavy sailcloth over the skylight of the cabin as a matter of precaution, and lighted the swinging lamp.

Blake explained the position briefly, whilst Bogo nodded gravely and smoked.

"The markets open at five," he said at last. "If I do not take my goods for sale it would be suspicious. At six I shall be back. Then we will make sail as you say, and as soon as—"

He broke off suddenly, for there was a trampling of feet on the quay overhead, and a hoarse shout of command in German.

"Name of a dog!" he said in a whisper. "Hear that? It is an order to search all vessels lying alongside! You will be found! Quick! Into the sail-locker you goes! It is the one chance! These German pigs know little about boats. They may not find you."

Blake and Tinker slipped into the big sail-locker forward right up in the bows under the deck, and hid beneath some piles of old worn sails and musty canvas. Bogo slipped the sliding panels to, and they could hear him industriously rolling casks of apples in front of it and piling up crates of vegetables.

Then he went back to the cabin, put out the swinging lamp, and, flinging himself on his bunk, snored lustily. For such a stolid-looking man, his acting was a fine piece of work.

Heavy boots resounded on the deck above, and the clang of grounded rifles. A voice bellowed an imperious summons down the open companion-way, but Bobo snored peacefully on. There came more heavy footsteps and the clank of a Sabre, and an officer and two men entered the cabin with lanterns.

"Hi, you!" bawled the officer, shaking him roughly. "Wake up, you drunken pig!"

Bogo condescended to wake.

"Name of a dog!" he said, blinking in the lantern-light. "Can't a man have a bit of sleep after supper—and I, who have to be up at four in the morning, as I'm a Dutchman? It's barely time for a man to sleep off his liqueur!"

"Dutch are you?" said the officer doubtfully.

He had strict orders to behave in as friendly a manner as he could to all Dutchmen.

"Of course I'm Dutch, and full of good Dutch brandy at that!" He essayed a hiccup. "Try a spoon for yourself, captain, to keep the cold out. The bottle's there beside you."

The office looked longingly, but shook his head.

"My orders are to search the ship, captain," he said, a trifle more civilly.

Bogo poured himself out a good stiff peg and drank it down.

"Search away," he said, yawning. "You'll find plenty of cockroaches. What on earth do you want to search for at this time of night?"

"Two Britishers, captain."

Bogo grunted.

"What do I want with verdamned Britishers? You can't eat 'em, you can't drink 'em, and you can't sell 'em!"

He poured himself out another glass, and this time the officer accepted the offer, whilst his men made a lumbering search in, to them, unfamiliar regions. Needless to say, they found nothing, not knowing where to look, and came in to make their report, looking rather crestfallen.

The officer drained his glass and signed to them to go on ahead.

"No boat is to leave her moorings till further orders," he said, with a tinge of his former truculence. "To-morrow the search will be resumed. Also, no boat may ascend the river beyond this point. They are at liberty to ply between here and Flushing after the search has been completed. The penalty for disobedience will be a fine and the destruction of the boat."

With that he clanked off, and Bogo heard him and his men go clattering along the quay.

He gave a sigh of relief, and mopped the sweat from his forehead.

Then he closed the hatch, relit the lamp, and hurried forward to roll aside the barrels and crates.

"You heard?" he asked anxiously, as he opened the locker door.

"Partly," said Blake. "We must be off. They'll make a thorough search by daylight, and as you can't go up-river you'll only be running risks for nothing. The sooner we are off the better. We must go at once."

Bogo nodded.

"Over the dock wall," he said. "They will have left sentries at the gates. Good luck go with you!" He shook them both by the hand and watched them till they were out of sight.

"We must get back to Caillaux, and by another way," said Blake, as they hurried along the dark streets, "although for the life of me I can't think of a plan, the net seems to be drawing tighter."

They made their way to Caillaux, and gave a prearranged knock—a short, two long, and a short.

Caillaux was apparently half expecting them, for he was still fully dressed, and opened the door immediately.

Blake explained matters, and Caillaux nodded.

"I feared as much," he said. "A man came here half an hour ago and said that the boats were being searched, so I waited up for more news. This is a bad business. Wait you here. I will see what can be done."

In a little under twenty minutes he was back.

"I have a plan," he said slowly; "not a great plan, but the best I can think of. My cousin has a cart—one of the little country carts—and two dogs. Also he has a pedlar's licence countersigned by the commandant, which allows him to sell his things in the villages round about.

"At five in the morning he will be here with his cart and the dogs, also rough clothes like his own. You will go with him. You are to be a travelling tinsmith, with black smudges on your face and hands. The young British must walk with a limp and a crutch, as though lame. If you once pass the barrier I think that all will be well. The lame boy will pass as my cousin's nephew, who helps him, and who is really lame. They have often been seen travelling about together, and the young Britisher can be made to look like him. Also the Bosches will be looking out for a party, not of three, but of two. Now you had better rest while you may, for you will have to start early and you will have far to walk, for you must travel by a roundabout way little frequented."

"It's a good plan," said Blake. "Risky, of course, but the best we can do. I'll take your advice and turn in."

"At five," said Caillaux, "I will call you. Have no fear."

A little after that hour next morning they set out. There was a cold drizzle of rain, and except in the vicinity of the market-places there was hardly a soul stirring. Even the German sentries were more than half asleep, and huddled, sheltering in the doorways.

Caillaux's cousin was called Jean, a keen-eyed, shrewd-looking man of about forty, with a pronounced hump, in spite of which he had the reputation for being enormously strong.

Blake wore a rough peasant smock, a peaked cap drawn well down over his eyes, and his face and hands were liberally blackened with soot. He had a three days' growth of beard, and smoked a big Belgian pipe full of coarse tobacco.

Tinker, as the lame boy, also wore the rough clothes of the country, and was about as tousled and disreputable an object as could be well imagined.

At the barrier Jean produced his pass. It was for two, but Blake had skilfully altered the two into a three and added a hieroglyphical sort of signature.

The sentry at the barrier glanced at it casually, nodded, and knocked it contemptuously aside, and the next moment they were in the open country, trudging through the rain and mud, with the dogs straining at their harness.

Blake heaved a sigh of relief, and as soon as they were well out of sight he tucked away the big, foul-smelling pipe under his blouse and lit a cigarette.

The most dangerous and difficult part of their journey was, as he believed, past.

They straggled through one or two villages, and came out on a bare, open plain, with nothing to be seen but endless rows of poplars.

Suddenly from behind a copse a party of three Uhlans[5] came swirling down on them, with a brief command to halt. There was nothing for it but to obey, so they halted in the middle of the road. Blake's hand slipped unobserved beneath his blouse, and he gripped his automatic. Even then all might have been well, but one of the men with a particularly brutal face spurred his horse up against Tinker, with the idea of baiting a cripple, as he supposed, and making him hop aside.

Tinker, taken by surprise, cried out angrily in English without thinking, and, as bad luck would have it, the trooper understood English well.

"Ach!" he cried. "An infernal British spy!" And, stooping in the saddle, he snatched off Tinker's cap. The next instant he had drawn his revolver and aimed it straight at Tinker's head.

There was no time to hesitate, and Blake's automatic rang out first. The man reeled and dropped, and the other two men charged with drawn swords.

Again Blake's pistol snapped, and Tinker fired at the same time. To miss at that range was impossible, and both saddles were emptied. Jean, with great presence of mind, caught the horses before they could escape and held them.

"Here's a pig's mess," said Blake. "It was them or us, though. Jean, you'd better leave us. If you're seen with us after this you will be shot for certain; alone you will be safe enough."

"Three Bosches!" said Jean, without a trace of compunction. "Lay them in the ditch there and cover them with brambles and branches whilst I see to the horses."

Blake looked round anxiously. In all the broad stretch of plain there was nothing to be seen but the spire of a village church three miles off.

"We'd better carry them to that thicket there and hide them as best we can. It will be safer than the ditch, and you can tether the horses there as well. With any luck we ought to be miles away before they are discovered."

Jean nodded. It was a gruesome task, but finally they got the bodies sackwise onto the horses. Jean whistled to the dogs to follow him with the cart, and they made for the copse fifty yards away.

Here they hastily made three rough graves and laid their burdens in them. The horses they tethered amongst the trees some little distance away. Had they let them loose they would have gone careering back to the stables, and an outcry would have been raised at once.

The great thing to do now was to put as much distance between them and the scene of the tragedy as possible. They would have avoided the village if they could, but there was no other road available, and the dogs couldn't drag their cart across country. So they were compelled to go on and risk it. They would have passed straight through if they could, but bad luck seemed to dog their steps.

Just as they were passing the principal inn two men who knew Jean well called out to him to come and have a glass of wine. To have refused would have seemed unnatural, so there was no help for it.

Some Uhlans were standing near the door of the inn, to make matters worse, drinking out of great tankards, and could hear every word that was said clearly.

Jean went forward, inwardly cursing his friends. Tinker and Blake remained by the cart, pretending to rearrange the things on it.

"Hallo!" cried one of the men. "Who have you got there? That's not your nephew. And who is the other, with the black smudge on his face?"

"Acquaintances," said Jean gruffly. "Surely a man may have acquaintances if he likes! We travel the same road, and we have a permit to travel together."

At the word "permit" a sergeant of Uhlans pricked up his ear.

"So, then," he said harshly, "let us this permit of yours examine. There are too many of your sort travelling with these permits, and half of you are spies. If I had my way I'd soon make an example of one or two of your sort, I can tell you. A tree and a bit of rope would be my permit, and you wouldn't want it renewed, either."

He guffawed hoarsely at his own wit, and held out his hand for the paper.

"So," he said, "you come from the city, from Antwerp? Did you meet any of our men on the way? There was a patrol of three. They should have been back a long time ago. Did you see them?"

Jean scratched his head perplexedly and spat thoughtfully.

"Hi, Pierre," he called to Blake, "did we see any Bosches on the road?"

The sergeant scowled at the name and strode up to Blake.

"Did you see any? Answer sharp!" he ordered.

Blake, who had relighted his foul-smelling pipe before entering the village, also spat thoughtfully. It is a natural custom of the Belgian peasant classes.

"Yes, Herr," he said slowly, in broad patois; "we saw three, I think it was."

"Which way were they going?"

"Towards the city, Herr."

"How far away?"

"It maybe an hour or an hour and a half's journey," replied Blake, using the usual method of the country in reckoning distances by time instead of miles.

"Teufel!" said the man. "They were ordered not to go beyond the wood. And you"—he turned suddenly on Tinker—"how far do you say it was?"

For Tinker to have attempted to answer would have been fatal. The man would have detected his English accent at once.

Blake intervened hastily. He pointed to his ears, and then nodded at Tinker.

"He is wrong here, Herr," he explained. "And here also," he added, pointing to his throat.

Tinker, taking his cue, made a sort of gurgling noise like a dumb man trying to speak, whereupon the sergeant dealt him a savage kick.

"Guard, turn out!" roared the sergeant. "Seven men to patrol

182

the road at once. Orders have come in to have it carefully watched. Two English spies are supposed to be trying to escape that way. The telephone came in an hour ago."

Everything was instantly bustle and confusion as men buckled on sword-belts and ran for their horses.

Suddenly the sergeant turned on Blake.

"You saw nothing of them, I suppose?" he asked, in perfect English, eyeing him keenly the while.

It was a neat trap, and it took all Blake's self-control to preserve his air of stolid unconcern. Had he not been well prepared for such a contingency, he might have been surprised into answering. As it was, not a muscle of his face moved. He merely sucked at his big pipe, as though quite unconscious that he was being spoken to.

The sergeant gave a grunt of disgust, and turned abruptly away.

The next moment he and his men were cantering down the road.

"Phew! That was a near thing, young 'un!" said Blake, under his breath. "When he tackled you, I thought the game was up. That man is not such a fool as he looks, by any means. The sooner we are out of here the better I shall be pleased."

Jean evidently thought so, too, for no sooner had the last trooper clattered out of sight than he sprang to the dogs, got them on their feet, and urged them forward at the best pace they could manage, his own face wet with perspiration. Nor did any of them stop until they had left the village far behind.

"They are bound to find the horses," Jean panted at last. "When they come up to the wood, the beasts will neigh to the others, and then, if they hunt about, the fat will be in the fire, and we shall have the whole lot after us helter-skelter. There is blood on the saddles, too."

Blake nodded.

"We'd best part company here," he said. "By yourself, you may be fairly safe, but that sergeant more than half suspected us. We had better chance our luck, and cut across country."

"There is the passport made out for three," replied Jean. "If I were to show that, they would ask me where are my companions. No; we must go on as we are. Further on there is a bridle road which we might take, and so avoid the next two or three villages. If we can do that, we may throw them off the scent, for we shall be in a wooded country then."

Blake nodded, and took out a handful of money.

"What's your cart and stock worth? Will this cover its value?"

"Twice over, and more," was the simple answer.

"Then this is my plan. The next time we come to a deep pond or ditch we weight that cart with stones—anything you like—cut the dogs loose, and in it goes. You can fetch it later or not, as you please. And in the meantime you can explain that it has broken down, and that you've left it to be repaired on the road, if anyone asks. We can get along three times as fast without it, and we can cut across country."

This was accordingly done. Cart, stock, and all was run into a deep, overflowing sluice, where it sank at once, and they headed direct for the woods, the two dogs following obediently to heel.

Jean knew the country like the back of his hand, and led them by many a cunning short cut. Twice they saw Uhlans patrolling in the distance and once they nearly blundered into a lot who were bivouacking in a small thicket; but they drew back in the nick of time, and, after all, there was nothing very suspicious about three bedraggled, mud-stained peasants tramping through the country with a couple of dogs at their heels, even if they had been seen—provided, of course, that news of them had not been sent on ahead.

They had had to make wide detours, however, and darkness

was coming on; so, reluctantly enough, they made their way to a small farm Jean knew of, where he went forward alone to buy food and wine, the idea being that they should pass the night in the hayloft of one of the outbuildings.

He was back in no time with the provisions and an old stable lantern.

"They have seen no Uhlans so far," he reported. "This lies far off the regular roads. There is only a farm-track, so we can eat and rest safely."

They made their way into the loft, and rested luxuriously on the hay as they ate. After that Blake lit a cigarette, and Jean puffed stolidly at his pipe. They were just congratulating themselves on their quarters, when Tinker suddenly sat up and listened.

"What was that?" he said.

They could hear the pattering of the rain and the moan of the wind; and then, borne on a sudden gust, came the squelch and clatter of horses' hoofs. A small party of cavalry had evidently swung up the accommodation road of the farm.

Instantly Blake put out the lantern and extinguished his cigarette. Jean did the same to his pipe.

"There are seven or eight of them by the sound," whispered Blake. "Here give me a hand with these hay bales."

Groping in the darkness they dragged a couple of bales over the trap by which they had entered the loft; a third they took to the window of the loft, through which the hay was raised to be stored, by means of a rope and pulley, and tossed it bodily over, to break their fall in case they had to jump for it.

They had barely finished when the troopers came clattering up. The farm people had already taken the alarm.

The order to dismount was given, and the horses were led into the barn below their hiding-place. Blake, peering through a crack between two boards, could see them plainly, for one of the troopers had found a couple of lanterns and lighted them.

There were, as Blake had surmised, eight in all. They were hitched by their bridles to hooks round the wall, and the men, leaving the doors open, were battering at the entrance to the farm itself, demanding food and drink.

The farmer himself came and opened the door to them, and lights, hurriedly made, shone from the windows. Resistance on the part of the old couple would have been worse than futile; so, unwillingly enough, they set out what provisions they had got.

From the loft window it was possible to see right into the room of the farm and watch the men lounging around the table, whilst the man and his wife waited on them.

Blake watched for a while in silence.

"I am going down," he said at last. "I must try and hear what news those fellows have got. Our future movements may depend on my knowing all I can."

Without another word, he clambered through the opening, let himself hang by his hands, and dropped lightly on to the bale of hay beneath.

He stepped cautiously across the yard to the window of the sitting-room, and with his knife prised it slightly open.

The Germans were too busy eating and drinking to pay any heed. In fact, some of them were already partly fuddled, and had evidently done themselves over-well before they rode up. Nearly all of them had big flasks, mostly empty by now, in their pockets.

"I tell you, it was two condemned Englishmen that did it," a man at the head of the table was saying, thumping on the table with his clenched fist. "They and a dog of a Belgian! But we shall get them—we shall get them all right. They were seen in the village three miles away, and interrogated. They had a little country cart with them, and they had the effrontery to own up that they had seen our men heading towards the city.

"A patrol was sent out, and when they came to a little patch of wood one of our horses threw up his head and whinnied. He was answered by another horse, and a search was made.

"Three were found, and identified as belonging to our troop—they were tethered to some trees in the heart of the wood—and three hastily-dug graves were found, too. The sub-officer in charge had already questioned the men in the village, and could give a description of them. One is an ordinary beast of a Belgian; the other two, though dressed as peasants, are British spies. One is tall and thin, with a grimy face—he speaks German well; the other is smaller, and pretends to limp, walking with the aid of a stick.

"We got onto the field-telephone to the town at once. The smaller of the two, I should tell you, can speak little or no German, and pretended to be deaf and dumb. And what do you think we found out?

"They are British Secret Service agents carrying papers of vital importance. They were known to have been in Antwerp last night, and the whole town has been turned topsy-turvy to find them. They even searched the boats along the quayside, but they were artful enough to get away somehow. Later it was discovered that a party of three answering to their description managed to pass the barrier after five this morning. The commandant is furious, and has offered a reward of five thousand marks for them, dead or alive, so long as the paper they carry is found on them. They were known to have been heading this way when last heard of."

"We could do with five thousand marks—eh, comrades? Fritz, pass that wine. Pah! The sour stuff! Haven't they any brandy in the place? We must be off in an hour—we're to strike back into the main road and examine all farms to the westward."

Blake waited to hear no more, but stole round to the back door, where the old man and woman were hastily packing their valuables. He placed his finger to his lips warningly, and passed the woman a handful of gold.

"Go, and go quickly, before they do you harm," he whispered. "If they burn the house you shall be repaid in full. You have quarter of an hour clear in which to get away. Don't be frightened. They will not catch you, for they will be on foot, and already their legs are drunk. Now hurry!"

He darted away back to the barn, and was half-way across the yard, when suddenly the house door was flung open, and a man came reeling unsteadily out. A flood of lamplight streamed from the door across the cobbles, and for Blake to gain the shelter of the shadows was impossible.

He simply "froze," as the big-game shooters phrase it. In other words he stood perfectly rigid and stockstill.

The man almost blundered up against him before he saw him.

"Hallo!" he said thickly, with dull surprise.

Blake said precisely nothing at all, but he struck swiftly at the side of the fellow's heavy jaw with all his force, and the man collapsed with a grunt, and lay still.

"Good for twenty minutes," said Blake to himself, as he bent over him, "and he'll be a pretty sick man then." He picked him up as though he had been a sack of coal and carried him to the barn, where he dumped him down in a corner. Then he went round to the loft window and called softly:

"Come on down, quick!" he said. "No time to spare. Drop on to the hay, and I'll steady you!"

Jean and Tinker dropped as they had seen Blake drop, and he grabbed at them each in turn.

"The old people have gone," he whispered. "They've taken your dogs with them, Jean, to a safe place nearby."

And he gave them a brief account of what had happened.

"Tighten up the girths on those horses, quick!" he ordered. "We shall have to make a dash for it when the time comes."

"Fritz," bellowed a voice from the house—"Fritz, confound you! Have you watered the horses and given them a feed?"

Blake growled out an unintelligible answer in low German, and drew back into the shadow of the barn doorway.

"Hurry," he whispered—"sharp as you can!"

"Fritz," came the voice again, "why the blazes don't you answer?"

A second figure came lurching out into the stream of lamplight, and from inside the room came a raucous chorus.

The new-comer was a lieutenant rather more sober than the rest, a big hulk of a man, and for some reason he seemed vaguely suspicious.

Blake let him reach the threshold of the barn, and then he caught him a swinging below behind the ear, and the man went down like a pole-axed ox. The crash of his fall and the clatter of his sword must have been heard inside the room, for the chorus stopped suddenly, and there was a sudden angry uproar as it dawned on them that something must be amiss.

Any attempt at further concealment was useless.

"The horses!" cried Blake.

Jean and Tinker dashed out, managing three apiece. Blake caught the other two.

They swung themselves into the saddle, and made a dash for it, straight at the group, which was now racing out into the yard, Blake leading, his automatic in his spare hand. A man grabbed at the bridle of the led horse, and was ridden down. Two more sprang forward, and Blake's automatic flashed twice. The troopers had left their carbines in the room, lances were piled in the barn, only an erratic fire from hastily-snatched weapons followed the small party of three, all high and badly aimed, and before they could fire again the three and the horses were out of sight.

"So far so good," said Blake. "There is no worse hand at

189

walking than your German cavalryman, and by my reckoning it must be a good eight miles to the nearest village, through slippery mud all the way at that, too. In the darkness, and their heavy boots, it will take them nearer four hours than three. I don't think we are likely to see or hear of them again unless they fall in with one of their own patrols."

The three rode quietly across a field and dropped into a lane.

"Two miles along this," said Jean, "we come to the main road again leading westward towards Stiltz."

Blake nodded in the darkness, and felt about to see what the contents of the saddle-bags might be. There were two canvas sacks slung crosswise, containing fodder. A canvas haversack containing a couple of bottles of some sort of wine, a loaf, some cheese, and a lump of what, by the smell of it, was hare. There was a carbine in the bucket, and a nondescript bundle of loot—mostly rubbish, to judge by the weight and feel of it. A long cavalry sword in its leather scabbard was strapped to the near side of the saddle.

Waiting for a splash of moonlight, he slipped from his own saddle into the saddle of the lead horse without dismounting, and congratulated himself on the change, for as he could tell by its paces the led horse was an officer's charger. The saddle was easier, there was no heavy sword strapped to it, and there was a regulation cavalry revolver in the holster.

He unbuckled the holster-flap with some difficulty in the darkness, and drew the weapon out. Dropping the reins, he twirled the cylinder, and made sure that every chamber was fully loaded. Then he put it back again and left the flap open, so as to be handy in case of urgent need.

Jean, acting as guide, went first. With his dogs and his pedlar's cart, he had travelled every inch of the country roads and lanes in happier times, spending a day at this farm, a couple at that, and occasionally, it must be confessed, painting the nearest village a brilliant red in his moments of relaxation at the local inn.

Blake was riding second, Tinker bringing up the rear.

By common consent they rode in silence until they had regained the broad main road. This was wide enough for all three to ride abreast including the led horses.

In fact, it was so broad and so important a road that Blake began to get uneasy; moreover, it was what is locally known as "Paye." That is, paved with great blocks of stone, which were slippery in the drizzling rain, and on which the hoofs of the eight horses rang unpleasantly loudly. In fact, now that the wind had dropped, the noise must have been audible quite half a mile away to a listening ear.

Blake said nothing for the next mile or so, but sucked at the end of a damp, unlighted cigarette.

"I don't like this," he said at last to Jean, in a low voice. "We ought to leave the road and ride parallel with it through the fields. A German is an unimaginative brute when you get to the bottom of him, but he's dead nuts on roads, and his maps are excellent. If this isn't being guarded by patrols at short intervals, I'll eat my hat!

"It's too important for them to neglect. It's an ideal line for motor-lorries carrying supplies, shells, stores—anything you like. In my opinion we ought to take to the open."

Jean grunted, and flung out his left arm.

"The country yonder, monsieur, is a network of dikes— eighteen, twenty, thirty feet broad. We should be trapped in no time if we tried to cross them in the darkness, and to reach the cattle-bridges, which are few, we might have to go five miles round for every one we gained in the right direction. We must stick to the road, monsieur, believe me, there is no other way; at any rate, till dawn comes, and we can see where we are going."

He broke off to light his pipe, as Blake could tell by the sound of the scraping of a match.

191

"Don't do that, you fool!" he said hastily. On a night like this the flare of a match could be seen a mile away in this flat, billiard-table of a country, and, leaning across his spare horse, he grabbed the box from the man's hand and flung it away.

They hadn't gone another fifty yards when a hoarse challenge in German rang out:

"Halt! Who goes there?"

Blake bent low in the saddle, and could just discern the loom of a line of horses drawn up across the road. Jean's match had given the alarm.

"We've got to ride for it!" whispered Blake to the others. "Do as I do. We'll stampede the led horses straight into them first, and then try and break through in the confusion."

He slid the trooper's sword out of its scabbard, gave the led horse his head, and caught it a resounding blow with the flat of the blade across the quarters. The animal plunged, squealed, and dashed on ahead. The other led horses took fright, and, as Tinker and Jean released them, galloped after their companion.

There was a crash and a volley of oaths as the five riderless animals made a furious dash for the line of Uhlans, and everything was thrown into confusion.

"Now!" roared Blake. "Straight at 'em! It's pace that will save us if anything! Come on!"

He dug his heels into his charger's flanks sharply and shot ahead, guiding only with his knees, having dropped the reins so as to have both hands free.

In his right he held the trooper's long, straight cavalry sword, in his left the revolver.

The light was bad; everything was confusion. He fired twice at almost point-blank range, and heard the bullets hit with a dull thud. Then his horse blundered badly over some falling object, nearly unseating him; but he recovered in the nick of time, to catch a glimpse of a captain of Uhlans taking a

192

swinging back-handed cut at him. Stooping low, he evaded it, though the blade caught his horse a nasty cut on the rump.

The next moment his own point had found the German's throat, and he was through the line.

He heard Tinker yell out, and tried to swerve, but the pace was too great; and the next moment Tinker almost cannoned into him.

"Jean is down, and my horse is done for!" he gasped.

Blake tried to rein up and go back for Jean, and at that instant Tinker's horse staggered and fell. It was the safety of the paper they carried—involving the lives of hundreds and the peace of a whole neutral country—against the safety of one of themselves.

With a vague hope that Jean, knowing the country as he did, might yet escape in the general confusion, Blake leant down and plucked Tinker up by the arm.

"Your foot on mine, quick!" he cried. "Up you come! Hold me round the waist! That's it! We must ride for it!" And off they went clattering down the road, the trooper's sword dangling by a cord from his wrist.

Clatter, clatter, clatter! The hoof-beats rattled over the hard road. A watery moonlight was just sufficient to prevent them leaving the track and blundering into the deep ditch on either hand, which would have spelt disaster.

They crossed the steep rise of a narrow bridge, and dropped down on the far side. Then Blake drew rein and listened intently.

Far away behind them came the sound of pursuit. Some of the troopers had recovered their horses, and were in full chase.

Blake's mare, double burdened as she was, could scarcely hope to outpace them, though she was game enough to try, but she was badly handicapped, and the pursuit was gaining fast.

Blake, bending low, saw a gap in the hedge on his left, showing plain against a leaden sky, and eased the mare down preparatory to turning, for the light was very deceptive.

He took the ditch and the gap at a canter, with a warning cry to Tinker to hold tight. They cleared both easily, and then came a surprise.

The mare, on landing, took three strides, and dropped over an invisible bank into ice-cold water.

It wasn't deep—there wasn't more than four feet of water in the dark—but the bottom wall was slippery mud. She lost her footing, and decanted them neatly into the stream.

Blake, as he came up, remembered Jean's warning words about cross-country journeys. Still, there had been no help for it; and even as he emerged, spluttering and shivering, he heard the thunder of pursuit across the bridge.

He made a grab for the mare's bridle, and got her on to her feet. After which, with some coaxing, got her into the shadow of the steep bank down which they had fallen. He himself, and Tinker also, stood flat up against the bank with their backs to it. They were up to their waists in icy-cold water, but they scarcely dared breathe.

The thunder of pursuit was growing louder and louder; it rose to a clattering roar as the horses swept over the bridge, and Blake mentally calculated their chances.

There was one factor in the position which gave him a gleam of hope.

The Uhlan's horses for the most part were loaded up with all sorts of odds and ends—loot of all sorts, and pots and pans and kettles for cooking—which banged about and made a tremendous din as they rode. This row, combined with the clatter of the horses' hoofs on the paved way and the jingle of accoutrements, made a deafening row, which must effectually have prevented the riders from hearing whether there was anyone galloping ahead of them or not. The road was straight, so they took it for granted that the fugitives were still flying along it, and they swept past in pursuit, intent on capturing their quarry—all but two of them, that is, who seemed to have been delayed, and came riding along at a more sober pace some distance behind the others.

Blake could hear them talking as they rode; and then he suddenly caught his breath with a jerk. The pair had spotted the gap in the hedge, and they reined up opposite to it.

"They may have this way gone," said one. "If it was not as black as the pit we could see. This accursed country is such a mass of traps and pitfalls, one can't go anywhere at night, except along the roads."

One of the horses snorted, and Blake gripped the mare's nostrils, lest she should make a sound in answer.

"No," said the other, "not so. They cannot that way have gone, for I have seen the place in daylight. I even remember noticing the gap in the hedge.

"All along there, just over the bank, lies a canal thirty feet broad and more, and goodness knows how deep! It is for the barges, and on the far side is a towing-path for the horses. They could not have that way gone unless they had wings. Come on, we must catch the others up, or we shall get into trouble."

There was a sound of gurgling, as one of them took a long draught from a bottle, and smacked his lips; and then the pair reined their horses back on the road and cantered on again.

Blake heaved a sigh of relief.

"That was a narrow shave!" he whispered to Tinker. "But it was worth it to get that bit of news about the towing-path. If once we can gain that, we shall be able to go for miles without a break, along a fairly decent road, too. I know those towing-paths, with their interminable lines of poplars and bridges over smaller branch canals and streams at intervals. It will be safer than the road, and probably quite as direct."

He listened intently. There was no sound but the gurgling of the water about them. The pursuit had swept far ahead.

"We shall have to wade or swim for it," said Blake. "Come on, and look out for this infernal mud!"

They crossed, leading the mare with them. They lost bottom at one place and had to swim for it, but only for a few strokes, and then they were wading again, and could see the far bank loom up against the night sky ahead of them. This, however, presented a new difficulty.

It was a well-built bank, sloping sharply upwards, but the lower part, to well above high-water mark, was lined with big, smooth-dressed stones. They could have scrambled up themselves by using their fingers and toes in the crevices between the blocks, but to have attempted to get the mare up would have been hopeless; and they couldn't bring themselves to desert her in that helpless plight, so they waded along until they came to a little cross-cutting, where an ascent was possible by a muddy cattle-track, and so gained the path.

They were shivering with cold and half-frozen. Blake remembered having found a flask in the officer's saddle-bags, and from this they each took a long sip.

Then they had to decide on which way to take—whether to turn back or to go on in their original direction, for the towing-path ran parallel to the road.

"If we go back," said Blake, "we are just as likely to run into another patrol, and we shall be losing valuable time. I am for going forward. Ten to one those fellows will give up the pursuit before long, and will return this way along the road. We shall hear them if they do, and can slip by under cover of the bank, knowing that we have a clear path ahead of us."

"Right!" said Tinker. "Anything for a quiet life. I feel like a perambulating icicle!"

Blake nodded, and they strode along briskly, leading the mare, and keeping their ears open for any suspicious sounds.

They had gone, as nearly as they could guess, about three

miles when Blake caught sight of a light ahead of them round a bend. It evidently came from a house of some sort, for it was stationary, and there was another faint light above the first—too high for any canal barge lying at her moorings.

They approached cautiously, and then Blake took a sudden resolve.

"The mare might give us away," he said. "We must turn her loose; she'll be all right now. But we don't want to leave any tell-tale evidence behind."

He loosened the trooper's sword from his wrist and flung it far out into the stream.

Then they went through the saddle-bags.

The flask—a common affair, of glass—they kept. It was just like a hundred others of its kind. There was a prismatic compass, and a large-scale map of the district, which they would dearly like to have kept. But if they were stopped and searched such things, found on two ostensible peasants, would have been their death-warrant, so they went into the water after the sword. In the end the only thing they retained was the big revolver and a box of cartridges. Blake emptied the cartridges loose into his pocket, and flung away the box. Then he undid the girths, and sent the saddle after the other things with a splash. The last thing he did was to turn the mare round and pull the bridle over her head, so that it hung dangling loosely in front of her, in such a way that she couldn't move at any pace without tripping over it with her forefeet.

Then he gave her a farewell pat on the flank, and he and Tinker advanced cautiously towards the house.

As they came near they heard a creaking sound overhead, and, looking up, saw that it was caused by a signboard swinging dolefully on its rusty iron hinges. They had stumbled on one of the canal-side inns, which rely for their trade on the barge-skippers who are constantly coming and going.

The thought of an inn was more than welcome, but they dare not enter until they had explored the ground thoroughly. Tinker remained in the shadow, whilst Blake crept forward to the lower of the two lighted windows. It was latched partly open, and the curtains were undrawn.

Two men were seated at a table in front of a roaring fire.

There was a plentiful meal spread before them, and a third man, a typical Belgian innkeeper, waited on them. He evidently didn't relish the job, for every time he handed them a dish, or poured out wine, he scowled at them savagely behind their backs.

One of the men was tall—about Blake's own height and build. The other was shorter. Both were clean-shaven, and dressed in civilian clothes of a certain smartness of cut, and they ate and drank ravenously; but the most interesting point about them to Blake was, that so long as the innkeeper was in the room they spoke only in American, with an occasional mispronounced word in Flemish, when they gave an order to the innkeeper. Whenever he left the room, however, on some errand, they relapsed at once into fluent German, which was evidently their native tongue, and they discussed matters in rapid undertones, constantly referring to a map propped up against a wine-bottle in front of them.

Blake guessed their game at once, and made his plans quickly. A low whistle brought Tinker up to join him, and together they made their way round to the back of the house where the kitchens were. They knocked gently at the door, and the innkeeper flung it open. His wife was making an omelette over the stove.

He glanced at them, and, taking them for genuine peasants, he placed his fingers to his lips and jerked his thumb in the direction of the other room.

"Hist! Bosches!" he whispered. "Two of them!"

"They speak English with an accent when I am in the room, so that I may not understand; but the moment I go out and place my ear to the keyhole on the other side, they speak German, the swine, and I do not understand. They are spies, and their talk is all of supplies, and shipping large quantities of things from America, for the Bosches. I do not understand all, but that much I understand. Bah! I would put rat poison in their food if I dared!"[6]

Blake held out ten gold coins.

"We are British. I have been listening at the window, yonder, and I have heard. Take these coins, and leave the rest to us. There is a light in the upper room. Who is there—the room over the sitting-room?"

"It is theirs, and they waste my candles by leaving them to burn; but I dare say nothing."

"Good! Well, take the money, let us in, and keep out of the way till I call; then come quickly, and bring some stout rope with you."

"It shall be as the Herr Britisher orders," said the man. "Down that passage—the sitting-room door lies straight ahead."

Blake nodded, and he and Tinker crept down the passage in their stockinged feet. Blake had the heavy revolver in his hand, Tinker his automatic.

It must be confessed that they looked as bedraggled a pair of scarecrows as could well be imagined.

Blake opened the door, and they stepped into the room.

The two men poring over their map silently took no notice, thinking that it was the landlord returning. Blake moved behind one man, Tinker behind the other.

"Put 'em up!" said Blake cheerfully.

The two men startled, half-sprang from their chairs.

"Sit down!" ordered Blake sharply. "Or these will go off! That's better! Now you, Skeystein—or whatever your name is—

pass me your coat! No, don't touch anything in your pockets. Now throw your waistcoat down there—never mind about your watch. Shirt next. Now, off with your trousers, socks, and boots—quick! Chuck 'em all down there! Now stand over there with your face to the wall! Mosey, it's your turn now. Do as the other beauty did!"

In three minutes the men, barefooted and stripped to their underwear, stood facing the wall side by side, cursing, but helpless. Blake went to the passage door and whistled, and the innkeeper came in with a coil of rope. He grinned broadly when he saw his late guests. Blake drew the curtains tightly across the window and set to work roping the two up hand and foot, then he blindfolded them with napkins, and stuffed a gag into each of their mouths.

"Where?" he asked the innkeeper. "Help us carry 'em!"

The man grinned more broadly than ever.

"This way!" he said, and without more ado swung the taller man over his shoulders as though he were a dead sheep. Blake and Tinker carried the other.

He led the way down the passage, opened another door, and raised a heavy trap.

"The old store-room," he said, with a jerk of his thumb. "It is not used now, except by the rats in flood times."

"Down with them then!" said Blake cheerfully.

The man clambered down the ladder with his burden, relieved Blake and Tinker of theirs, and then came up again, dragging the ladder after him. He closed the trap, bolted it, and upset a litter of old rubbish and sacks and potatoes on top.

"Good!" said Blake, and held out another gold coin. "Now we want hot water to wash in, plenty of it, five minutes to change our clothes, and after that one of those omelettes, such as madame was making just now, and a bottle of your best wine."

"Good, monsieur!" said the man, and hurried away.

Blake and Tinker seized their victims' clothes, and went upstairs. In less than five minutes they were transformed. Clean clothes, of which they found abundance in the bag, scented soap, brilliantine, and a razor for Blake, worked wonders. It is true that Blake's coat was uncomfortably tight across the chest, but that was easily remedied, by leaving it unbuttoned. They searched the bags to make sure that there was nothing incriminating, locked them again, and went downstairs, where they found their meal just ready for them, and the wine warming before the fire.

The innkeeper stared at them, and burst into a guffaw of laughter. Blake looked round to see if there were any tell-tale cigars of the late occupants, and then drew the window curtains back as they had been before. So far as he knew, it might have been some prearranged signal.

"Now, listen," he said to their host, "and listen carefully, as you value your skin and property. Six hours—ten, perhaps would be safer—after we have gone, you will rescue your prisoners, with many expressions of regret and dismay. They never saw your face after we had collared them, their own were turned towards the wall. And they only heard you utter one short sentence—'this way'—which, in their dazed condition, might have been spoken by either myself or my friend, or any one of half a dozen other people, and for their own credit's sake they are sure to make out that they were overcome by at least twice that number.

"This is your story in brief, and you must stick to it like grim death, and mind you make no blunders.

"You were seized unexpectedly by some people—apparently peasants—who came in by the back way, begging. You had your suspicions that they were rogues, however, and tried to turn them out, upon which they promptly seized you, gagged you, and bound you to one of your own kitchen chairs. They did the same to madame, who was too terrified to cry out, and then, so far as you know, they proceeded to ransack the house whilst you were bound and helpless, and could give no warning to your guests.

"After hours of struggling, however, you managed to free yourself enough to get at your pocket-knife, and so hack yourself loose. Then you freed madame, and went in search of your guests, fully expecting to find them bound also. They had, however, vanished. You continued to search everywhere, and at last you have found them in the disused store-room. You follow me clearly?

"You at once release them, you take them to the kitchen, show them to overturned chairs, hacked pieces of rope on the floor, and possibly a broken door-latch. Madam is upstairs in bed, ill from shock. You are in a rage, but weak from exhaustion, and you might even drop a hint that you heard the men speak a few words in a language which you don't understand, but which you believe to have been English.

"That's clear enough, isn't it?"

The innkeeper grinned.

"It will be a droll farce to play," he said.

Blake nodded.

"Play it well, and it will not only save your skin, but you will probably get a reward as well. Now you'd better go and make all the arrangements whilst we finish our meal."

The innkeeper nodded and withdrew, and Blake and Tinker devoured their omelette, followed by bread and cheese.

"It is done," said the man, returning a few minutes later with some steaming coffee.

"Good!" said Blake. "Now go and see that everything is put straight in the room upstairs, and take away those clothes we were wearing. You can either keep them or destroy them, but they mustn't be seen by anyone until the affair has blown over. Put clean towels in the room, too. Off with you!"

"It shall be done, m'sieur," said the man, and hurried off again.

"Now," said Blake, lighting a cigarette, "the next step is to find out who we really are. They are sure to have all their papers in good order. Turn out your pockets—everything there is in 'em—and I'll do the same.

"Ah, here we are—passports! Humph! I thought as much. Max B. Schmidt—that's me. Otto Adler—that's you. Both of New York, American citizens, and the passports have been viewed both at Berlin and by the German commander at Brussels. Hallo! What's this? A cipher code! Humph! A fairly simple one—a telegraphic address to a New York agent rejoicing in the name of Eckstein, and some notes about the shipment of huge quantities of stores and provisions into German waters via the Cattgut and the Great Belt. Useful bit of information, that. A stock of money, some American notes as well, a cigar-case, two or three private letters, probably carried as an additional proof of identity in case of need, some keys and loose change, and that's about all. Well, with these vised passports we ought to be able to get along all right. You can't speak German, worse luck, but you can imitate an American twang to the life—remember that if we get pushed into a tight corner—and I can do the German end of the business for both of us.

"You've got our own papers safe enough, and they won't dare search us in the face of these passports."

Blake poured himself out another cup of coffee, and was in the act of drinking it, when he suddenly set down his cup again.

"Listen!" he said quietly. "I think the tight corner is coming to meet us. Keep cool and bluff hard; also keep your automatic and a handy pocket in case of emergencies, if things don't pan out all right. By Jove! That reminds me. I must get rid of that German cavalry revolver!"

He moved quickly to a window at the far end of the room that overlooked the canal, flung the revolver into it, and closed the window again, drawing the curtains.

He had barely done so when the innkeeper came rushing in.

"We are ruined!" he said hoarsely. "The Uhlans are coming, ten or a dozen of them!"

Blake nodded, and lit a cigar.

"I heard their horses a moment ago. Keep your head, and everything will be all right. How long have we been staying here?"

"Two days," said the man, reassured by Blake's coolness.

"Good! Now go and get another bottle or two of that excellent burgundy, and set it to warm. If I know anything about a Uhlan officer, it is that wine makes him talkative and prevents him asking too many awkward questions.

"They'll be here in a minute now. Don't be in too great a hurry to open the door—pretend to be sleepy and a bit fuddled, and see that the men have plenty of beer or schnapps. I shall give you an excellent character as a host. Off you get to the kitchen!"

The man grinned and withdrew.

"He'll do all right," said Blake, taking a long pull at his cigar. "Trust a Belgian peasant to do a bit of play-acting![7] You're looking a bit pasty about the gills, old man. Have another glass of that burgundy, and pull yourself together!"

Tinker gulped down his wine, and there came a clattering of hoofs on the cobblestones outside, raucous words of command, and a heavy pounding at the door.

"Cheer up, Otto!" chuckled Blake. "We're goin' to have a real am-using time!"

"Sure!" said Tinker, imitating a Yankee drawl. "I guess I'm beginning to feel good!"

The hammering at the door grew more violent, and a helmeted face showed for a moment at the uncurtained window.

Then there came voices in the passage, and the door was flung open as a captain of Uhlans strode in.

"Say, what the tarnation snakes—" began Blake, half rising; and then, as if recognising the presence of an officer, he drew himself up, and gave a stiff military salute in true Prussian fashion.

"Good-evening, Herr Capitan!" he said, in German. "To what do we owe this honour?"

The officer scowled at them suspiciously, but he instinctively returned the salute.

"Your papers!" he demanded gruffly.

Blake blew out a cloud of smoke.

"Certainly," said he, fumbling in his pockets. "You will find them all in order!"

He handed over his passport, and, turning to Tinker, said to him:

"Say, Otto, the officer wants to look at your blame passport. Tote it out right away. I guess these Germans have got passports on the brain these days! I reckon to have mine framed, and wear it as a chest-preserver!"

The officer glanced at the papers, and raised his eyebrows as he read the signatures of the visas.

"You are American citizens, I see," he said, speaking in fluent, if rather guttural, English.

"'The boy guessed right the very first time'," intoned Blake, using the words of an old comic opera song. "Yes, sir, we are American citizens sure enough, vouched for by your government, as you can see for yourself!"

The signatures had evidently made an impression on the officer's mind.

"Your business?" he asked, in a more civil tone.

"Is my own," snapped Blake, "and I'm not giving it away to any old thing that may be a spy dressed up in a captain's uniform!"

The officer dropped his hand to his sword.

Blake didn't move a muscle.

"Say, don't you try any of that funny business, sonny!" he said. "If you start in carving slices off me, I reckon you'll be getting into trouble with the boss who runs your department.

"If you just look at the signatures on that bit of paper again, you will see that there are some of your generals who consider us mighty precious. In fact, they'd rather break up a score or so of junior officers than get us scratched, and you'll be wise to remember it!"

The captain flushed and bit his lip. It was undoubtedly true that if he blundered he was likely to be stamped on first, and enquiries might or might not be made later.

"Your folk are mighty scary the way they bundle American citizens just now," continued Blake. "They're wanting all the sympathy they can get from us, and a good few other things as well. In fact, they're inclined to slop over a bit about it!"

"Your pardon, Herr Schmidt. I take it from the names that you and Herr Adler have connections in the Fatherland?"

"Sure," said Blake.

"Permit me to return you your papers. Truth to tell, there are two pestilential British spies at large. They've given us the slip so far, but my orders are to capture them at all costs. They have papers, you understand, of the first importance.

"You will pardon me, but I shall have to report your presence here, and must go through a perfectly formal enquiry—a mere matter of form."

"Fire right ahead! Say, here are the keys of our grip sacks, if you'd like one of your men to go through them."

He tossed a bunch of keys on the table as he spoke.

The officer took them up with a bow, and passed them to the sergeant behind him with a curt order.

"You have been here how long?"

"Round about a couple of days. We reckon to pull out tomorrow."

"Your destination?"

"Stiltz."

The officer looked surprised.

"I also go to Stiltz. It will give me pleasure to act as your escort as far."

"Right you are!" said Blake. "And now, look here! You're just itching to know our business, and I can't tell it you, that's flat; but I can give you a hint. I reckon there's some things your folk could do with a lot more of. There's copper—well, I guess the American mines are pretty good. There's pigs—Amurrica is the home of the hog, canned or otherwise. There's oil—what's wrong with the wells in little Pennsylvania?

"There's quite a lot of handy rations made in the States. Yes, sir, and there's considerable raw material lying around. Down South we grow cotton. We do a big trade in copra, and we own some fine big ships to take things across the Atlantic Ferry in. You can bet on that. We are business people—what's more, we've got the goods.

"What's wrong with a big private syndicate buying up those goods, and sending them in trade to a neutral country without asking too many questions about what the neutral country is going to do with them? I guess Holland, say, isn't at the opposite end of the earth to Belgium.

"I should surmise that whole heaps of things might be dumped down in a Dutch port, got into the wrong train, and slide over into Belgium by mistake; and if your folk—who seem to be running Belgium just now, all but one little corner—happen to confiscate those misguided trains, whose fault is it? Not ours!

We don't run the railroads this side, do we?

"There, sonny, I guess you know as much as is healthy for you. 'Nuff said!'"

"Herr Schmidt, I make you my apologies, and to the Herr Adler, too."

"Well, captain, what's wrong with a bottle of Burgundy? The barkeep here has got a first-class brand. There's a sample of it warming by the fire right now; and I guess, as you're cold after your ride, there will be nothing wrong with lacing it with some liqueur brandy. Otto, you tell the innkeeper to let us have a bottle of his best cognac and some clean glasses."

The captain beamed approval, and the liqueur was fetched. Blake poured him out a big goblet full of the mixture, and watched him gulp it down, and filled his glass again. His own glass he contrived to empty on the floor under the table, and Tinker was just going to do the same, when they were startled by the sound of a galloping horse.

Blake caught Tinker's eye, and dropped his hands significantly to his coat-pocket. New arrivals might complicate matters unpleasantly.

The captain drained his glass, and, going to the window, flung it open.

"Who goes there?" he shouted; and one of the men on guard at the door took up the challenge.

Blake and Tinker also peered out, and then suddenly a riderless horse came hurrying out of the darkness. It was the mare which they had turned adrift, and which in some way had contrived to break its bridle, and headed for the nearest human habitation in hopes of warmth and a feed. It slowed down into a trot, as the sentry ran out and caught it. The captain and the others also went out.

"Thunder!" cried the captain, as soon as he got a clear view of the animal. "That's Karl Elteir's mare. I should know her anywhere. He's lieutenant of B troop. See the metal-work on the bridle; and here's the regimental brand mark. How the deuce does the mare come here in this state?"

"I guess she must have decanted your lieutenant into a ditch somewhere," drawled Blake. "Girths must have snapped; saddle's clean gone, irons and all; bridle's busted. I guess there's been an ill-forsaken smash."

"Ach, so!" said the captain. "Karl was always heavy with his hands. And the mare has a vicious temper. I know her. She has thrown him before now. He was not a good horse-master. But, all the same, this alters affairs. I must push on to Stiltz at once. Does that suit your convenience, Herr Schmidt?"

"Sure," said Blake. "But I reckon you'd better finish the bottle first. And I guess we can't walk all the way—with your permission, I'll ride Von Elteir's mare. A bit of sacking for a saddle and a rope-bridle will fix me. And I guess one of your men can lend Otto here a mount?"

"We'll leave our 'grips' right here in charge of the landlord, and look for them on the way back. I don't reckon to be detained more than twenty-four hours in Stiltz, anyway. And we Amurrricans can get around this old globe comfortably with a toothbrush and a celluloid collar; we're used to it. I'll just pay my bill, and then I'm ready."

He walked down the passage to the kitchen, purposely leaving the door open; but as soon as he got to the back of the house, where the innkeeper was, he laid his finger on his lips as a sign for caution.

"Keep an eye on your two prisoners," he whispered. "We ride with the German officer because we must, to avoid suspicion. Also, he goes our way, and it will be easier for us." Then he added in a loud voice, as he handed over some coins: "I reckon that squares our account and a bit over. We'll call back for the luggage to-morrow, or maybe the day after."

The man winked knowingly.

"It shall be as the Herr wishes," he said; "and I'll keep all his belongings very safely until he requires them," he added, with a grin.

"Good for you, sonny," said Blake, and returned to the main room.

The troop horses had been brought round, and the captain, rather befuddled, was waiting for them.

A rickety old saddle had been found for the mare, and a forage horse was ready for Tinker—alias Otto Adler—and they set out through the darkness for Stiltz.

It was a dull, wearisome ride. The roads were bad and slippery, the night was pitch-dark, and more than once they lost their way altogether, and went wandering down accommodation roads which led to nowhere in particular, or ended up at a gate and a ploughed field. It was at one such halt that Tinker suggested to Blake, in a whisper, that they should do a bolt, and ride for it. But the latter negatived the idea altogether.

"We've got to get to Stiltz somehow," he whispered back, "and we can get there best with these fellows to look after us. Besides, that officer man isn't quite such a fool as he looks. My mare is fast enough to beat anything they've got; but that old cow of a thing you're riding couldn't stay a couple of furlongs without breaking something. And he knows it. He picked it out on purpose.

"You lie low, old man, and we'll get through to Van Zyl all right."

They rode on steadily through the night, and about eleven they reached their destination.

The captain made straight for an inn named the Three Crowns, billeted his men in the stables and hayloft, and ordered rooms for himself and his two "American" friends. Incidentally, he posted a couple of sentries at the door, with orders that they were to be relieved every two hours.

The little frontier town was very busy, and in spite of the lateness of the hour all of the cafés remained open, and were ablaze with light.

Pleading fatigue after their ride, Blake and Tinker elected to go straight to their room. The officer, too, was yawning and drowsy, and professed himself ready for bed, his room being next to theirs. The partition dividing the two was only thin matchboarding, and very soon they had the satisfaction of hearing him snore as only a German can.

"That's good enough for us," whispered Blake, sitting on the edge of the bed. "Give me the paper—quick! I'm off to try and find Van Zyl. The Lion d'Or is only a hundred yards or so away. I spotted it as we came by here. I shall go out by the window, to avoid giving the sentries pain. You must keep the door locked while I am gone, and snore like a grampus if there's any disturbance. Stand by to give me a hand in when I come back. I may be in a hurry."

"Right-ho!" said Tinker, and handed over the paper.

Blake took it, raised the window gently, and dropped out. It was only a short drop—six foot or so—and there was soft ground to land on. This was lucky, for there was still a light burning in the captain's room, and the stables where the men were quartered were only just across the yard, and he could hear some of the horses moving restlessly in their strange quarters.

He skipped round through the big archway leading out of the yard, and glimpsed the sentries standing by the main door. They were drowsy, and obviously wearied of their job. Neither of them so much as glanced in his direction, and in a flash he was round the corner and out of sight.

He had taken his bearings well, and a sharp couple of minutes' walk brought him to the Lion d'Or.

He did not dare ask for Van Zyl openly, for there were several German officers in the cafe; so he ordered himself a cup of coffee, and made a pretence of reading an evening paper.

Presently he noticed a big, weather-beaten man eyeing him curiously, and a trifle furtively, and after a little while the man got up and moved to Blake's table, with a murmured grunt of apology, as he took his seat and ordered a glass of schnapps.

He sipped this slowly, and Blake continued to make a pretence of reading his paper, until, without a word, the big Dutchman's hand slid out across the marble-topped table, and when it was withdrawn there lay on the table a piece of paper identical with one Blake had seen before, with the lower left-hand corner missing. At the same time the Dutchman's eyelids fluttered perceptively, and with a jerk of his thumb he indicated the German officers at the next table.

Blake nodded, took up the piece of paper, rolled it into a spill, which he held to the candle-flame, and lit his cigarette with it.

"You are from Antwerp?" said the captain, in fair English. "Is it not? A description of you was sent on to me by a friend." With a stub of pencil he scrawled his name on the table, and presently rubbed it out again with his forefinger. "There are spies—spies everywhere," he said, in low tones; and once more he indicated the Germans at the next table. One of them was watching them keenly from time to time.

Blake, with a quick movement of his hand, slipped the precious document between the pages of the paper and yawned.

"You would care to read the paper?" he said in German. "It is dull. There is no news." And he slid the paper with the document concealed in it across the table under the very nose of the watching German.

Van Zyl took it composedly, with a grunt of thanks, and fumbled for a pair of all-removed glasses, which he perched on his nose, preparatory to reading. He turned over the pages, gave one swift glance at the document under cover of them, and pressed Blake's foot under the table.

Then, after reading for a minute or two, he cursed the light volubly, folded up the paper, document and all, put it in his pocket, and, with a curt good-night, strolled out by a private door.

Blake finished his coffee leisurely, then he, too, got up, and went out by the main door leading onto the street, very conscious that the German officer was watching his every movement.

He made his way back to the Three Crowns, had to wait for a while as the sentries were just being changed, and then slipped in through the archway, and gave Tinker the signal agreed upon.

The latter was waiting in readiness, and in two minutes Blake was back in his room again, and the German officer next door was snoring, more like a hog than ever.

"Well?" asked Tinker, in a whisper.

"All serene!" said Blake. "The place is simply riddled with spies; but Van Zyl is as sharp as they make them, though he does look like a Boer farmer who has been to sea by mistake. His appearance is a treat. Guileless-looking sort of johnnie until you happen to notice his jaw, and then you see the man's true self. Oh, he's a hard nut to crack, and as cool as a cucumber with it all!

"Now it's me for bed. We'll pull out of here early in the morning. We've done all we guaranteed to do, and you can trust Van Zyl to do the rest!"

Blake fancied that he had slept about two minutes by the clock, when he was awakened by a tremendous uproar, and discovered that dawn had already broken, for a grey light was filtering through the window-blinds.

Thunderous knocks were being rained on the front door. Hoarse German voices were shouting, and the captain, newly aroused, was swearing like one of his own troopers as he struggled into his boots.

Blake pulled aside the blind, and peered out. Tinker did the same, and both gave low whistle of surprise.

"Looks as if our number was up, old thing," said Blake, "for there are the genuine articles. In other words, Messrs Max B. Schmidt, which is me, and Otto Adler, which is you.

"They must have got out somehow, and now the fat's on the fire with a vengeance. We were fools not to have brought their baggage along with us, only I was afraid of making things look too suspicious.

"They must have learnt which way our party had gone, and as soon as they get five minutes with that pig-headed captain man, they can prove us to be frauds using fake passports.

"That means a convenient wall and a firing-party. We can't get away by the yard, it's just swarming with those infernal troopers, and, as we know, there are sentries at the front.

"We can't even put up a decent bluff, for it's ten to one Schmidt & Co. will have half a dozen people ready to identify them as the genuine thing, even though we have got their passports. Better slip into some things as quickly as we can, and stand by for trouble. Thank goodness the paper is safe anyway. They can search us till they are blue in the face, and not find a trace of it. You destroyed those photographs, by the way?"

"Burnt 'em!" said Tinker laconically. "It was the safest way!"

"Good egg!" said Blake. "Better hurry up and dress. Personally I've a great objection to being shot in a pair of stolen pyjamas, and it's snowing outside, too!"

They dressed hurriedly, and had just finished when there came the dull thud of a rifle-butt on the panelling of the door. The frail woodwork splintered to pieces, and another blow splintered a second panel.

"Stand back, you British spies!" roared a voice. "We've got

you cornered like rats in a trap. Cover them, some of you men, and one of you open the door!"

A couple of Mauser rifles came peeking through one broken panel, an arm came through the other, fumbled for the lock, found it, and turned the key.

Sexton Blake lit a cigarette, and the door was flung open.

The officer charged in with a drawn sabre in his hand, followed by three of his men, and Schmidt and Adler.

"That's them!" shrieked Adler. Being a small-built man, he was naturally the more excited of the two.

"Look at them, the dirty British dogs! Why, they've even got on the clothes they stole from us. I'll tell you what they did. They made us strip, took our things away and our papers, and then they roped us up and pushed us into a dark cellar to starve, for all they cared! But we found an old rusty knife which had been left there and forgotten, and, after a lot of trouble, we managed to work our way loose. Then we broke a way out. They had stolen our passports and our papers, but luckily they had left us a change of clothes, so we were able to follow them up."

Blake flicked the ash off his cigarette.

"This seems rather idiotic talk, Herr Capitain," he said quietly. "Who are these people, and what's all the trouble about?"

"Your passport!" demanded the captain gruffly.

"Certainly!" said Blake, and produced it, though with an inward feeling that the game was up, for Tinker's German would have betrayed him in a single syllable, and the officer was full of suspicion. In fact, he seemed to recognise that Tinker was the weak link in the chain, for he turned and questioned him sharply in German. Tinker gurgled inarticulately, and the officer laughed harshly.

"British pig-swine!" he said. "Firing-party of six men!" he ordered. "We'll soon show how we Germans treat spies!"

"One moment!" said Blake genially. "How do you propose to prove that we are spies? We are British, certainly; in fact, we are rather proud of it, if you want to know the truth; but we haven't the slightest intention of being murdered to please the whim of a drunken, irresponsible, under officer like you! We demand to be searched for any incriminating documents or papers, and if you find any, to be tried by court-martial in due form. You're getting above yourself, my man!"

The captain snarled with rage, and made a savage lunge at Blake with his sabre. The latter dodged, snatched up a light walking-stick, parried a second lunge, and drove the ferrule home full in the German's teeth.

"That is to teach you manners," he said, as the man went reeling back, spitting out blood and teeth.

The three troopers sprang forward, but Blake and Tinker met them with levelled automatics, and they sprang back again with equal alacrity. They were rather raw recruits, and they didn't like the look of things at all.

Schmidt and Adler were more agile even than the recruits. They made a spring for the door, and vanished into safety down the passage, from the far end of which they yelled frantic abuse.

Blake snatched up the passport which the captain had let fall.

"We must risk a dash for it, old man," he whispered. "Follow me, and keep close. I don't think they'll fire on us without orders."

Still with their automatics ready for immediate use, they made straight for the door with a rush, and it turned out very much as Blake had anticipated.

The captain was too busy spitting out teeth to give the requisite orders, and the men fingered their rifles uncertainly.

One, a sergeant, an older man than the rest, made a tentative grab at Blake's shoulder, and was met with a left-hander on the jaw, which fairly lifted him off his feet, and the next moment the two were racing down the passage.

They passed the astonished sentries at the door, and before the latter could even challenge or collect their wits, the pair were far down the street, and out of sight. But they knew their escape was only momentary. With the town swarming with German soldiers, the search would be taken up quickly and thoroughly, and in a small place like that it was clearly impossible to obtain anything like an effective disguise.

They hurried along down back streets and alleys, and finally chanced upon an old, tumble-down empty house, which promised at least a temporary shelter in which they could have a rest up, and discuss their plans.

Van Zyl might have helped them, but they dare not seek him out for fear of betraying the fact that he was in any way connected with them, and possibly upsetting all his plans. There was no chance of reaching the open country, for the two gates of the old town were sure to be already guarded. Also, they had had to come away without headgear of any kind, which in itself would at once lay them open to suspicion if they tried to pass the sentries!

Blake philosophically lit a cigarette, and sat down with his back to the wall.

"We've got into the trap right enough," he said. "But how to get out beats me. That fat-headed captain must be feeling pretty vicious," he added, with a grim laugh, "and so must Schmidt and Adler."

Tinker grinned dolefully.

"You bet!" he said. "Listen to that."

Through the broken window came the tramp, tramp of soldiers' feet and harsh words of command.

"One of the search-parties," said Blake. "They'll have dozens of them out by now."

The men were evidently going methodically from house to house, with the true German thoroughness.

"The thing is," said Blake, "if they come here shall we put up a fight for it, or shall we surrender and demand to be taken before the senior officer in the place? I think on the whole that that would be the wisest."

"It might give us a chance, anyhow," agreed Tinker.

"Ah, here they come!"

Footsteps clumped through the broken doorway and began to ascend the stairs.

"Got them!" cried a voice. "Here they are—and we get the fifty marks reward, Karl!"

Two men dashed into the room with fixed bayonets, but a young lieutenant, a pleasant-faced-looking fellow, thrust them aside. He looked first at Blake, then at Tinker, and returned his sword to its scabbard with a smart click. Then he clapped his heels together and bowed stiffly.

"Gentlemen, I beg to inform you that you are my prisoners!" he said.

Blake returned the bow.

"We surrender to you, Herr Lieutenant," said Blake "and although armed, I call you to witness that we made no resistance."

He handed over his automatic, and signed to Tinker to do the same.

"But we surrender on conditions," Blake continued. "First that you accept our parole not to try and escape so long as we are in your charge."

"Granted."

"Thank you! Secondly, that you take us at once before the senior officer in command, so that we can explain matters to him."

"Again granted, sir."

"Very good; then we are ready to accompany you at once."

They stepped forward, and the lieutenant waved back the men who had stepped forward to seize them.

"These gentlemen are on parole!" he said sharply. "Fall in behind. If you will kindly follow me, sir, you and your friend," he added to Blake. And the little procession formed up and marched down the stairs into the snow-covered street.

"So far so good!" said Blake. "We've fallen into good hands, at any rate. I hope our luck will hold."

But it was destined not to. They had barely gone fifty yards when they ran slap into their friend the captain, who, with a guard of ten men, had been searching the houses farther down the street.

At the sight of them he gave a shout of triumph.

"Well done!" he cried. "You can turn over your prisoners to me, Lieutenant Muller."

"But they have given me their parole, my captain, and I have passed my word to take them to the commandant. They surrendered of their own accord on those conditions."

"Their parole! Bah! No one but a fool would take the word of a British spy. I'll show you how to deal with them. Here you, sergeant, tie those men's hands behind them and set them up against the wall there. A firing-party of six load with ball, distance ten paces!"

The lieutenant turned livid with anger.

"It cannot be done. I have passed my word of honour!" he cried.

"A fig for your word of honour!" was the brutal retort.

Muller took a step forward and half drew his sword.

"You shall pay me for that!" he said.

"Consider yourself under arrest!" roared the captain. "I will break you for that—attempting to draw your sword on your superior officer, and hindering him in his duties. That will mean degradation to the ranks and two years in a fortress for you. Sergeant, take the lieutenant's sword."

"Never!" said Muller, and, placing it, scabbard and all, across his knee, he snapped it in two and flung the pieces down in the snow.

Then he gravely saluted Blake and Tinker.

"I have done my best," he said bitterly. "I am shamed!"

Blake nodded.

"It is no fault of yours that you happen to be the fellow-countryman of a thing like that, lieutenant. Good-bye!"

They were placed together against the wall, and the firing-party lined up.

"So-long, old man!" said Blake. "Keep a stiff upper-lip. Don't let the beasts think they can scare us!"

"When I drop my sword-point, you will fire!" said the captain, moving to one side.

The next minute he was sent staggering half across the road, and a stentorian voice bellowed, "Halt, there!"

It was Captain Van Zyl!

"What is the meaning of this?" he growled. "I am burgomaster of this town, and if these men, whoever they are, have committed any offence, it is for me to deal with them!"

"They are British spies, travelling with a stolen passport, and they have insulted me, a Prussian officer. Both offences are punishable by death under the German military code."

"I would remind you, Captain," said Van Zyl, "that you are not in Germany, but in Holland, and that you Germans are very particular in keeping on good terms with us Dutchmen. These men may or may not be British spies. In any case, it is for me to deal with them, and whilst I am looking into the matter they will be my prisoners, and I shall see that a full report of this matter and your behaviour goes straight to the commandant. He will deal with you as he thinks fit.

"Now," he added to Blake, "are you British?"

"I am."

"Travelling with a passport not your own."

"Yes."

"Produce it."

Blake did so.

"Humph! You are both my prisoners under arrest. Will you come quietly, or shall I call the Civic Guard?"

"We will come with you. We are unarmed."

"Good! I trust your word. As for you, sir," he went on to the German, "march your men off at once, and don't dare to try and forcibly enter another house in the town. You shall hear more of this, and you will be held responsible for any damage done up to date. By what I have heard, the bill will be a heavy one!"

The officer scowled and bit his lip, but Van Zyl spoke with authority, and there was nothing for it but to obey, and he marched his men away.

"Pouf!" said Van Zyl. "So much talking makes a man thirsty. That was a near thing. But word was brought me of the row at the hotel, and so I came at once. Now let us go and have a glass of schnapps. After which I shall take you to the lock-up." He winked prodigiously. "But you shall not be alone. You shall have a roast chicken and a bottle of Burgundy for company, and as soon as it is dark—Well, there are more doors to the lock-up than one, and to-night I make a journey to the coast in my 'hog-cart.' If you happen to be in the fore-cabin when I start, is that my fault? Pouf! No, not at all. How am I to tell—eh?"

So Blake and Tinker were solemnly marched to the lock-up after Van Zyl had quenched his thirst—equally solemnly locked in—in the presence of half a company of German soldiers, who appeared casually from nowhere, and Van Zyl rolled off on his lawful occasions.

The "lock-up," the only substitute for a genuine prison in that usually well-ordered little town, was a small, square, stone building about sixteen feet by sixteen, with two bunk beds, a table spotlessly clean, and four or five rush-bottomed chairs.

The single window was heavily grated with iron, and the door was about as solid as the door of a cathedral, with steel knobs all over it, and a ponderous lock which would have taxed a strong man to carry.

"Looks as if we were here for keeps," said Tinker gloomily. "I do hope, guv'nor, Van Zyl won't forget that chicken. I feel as if I could do with about a turkey and a half."

"You always were a greedy young pig," said Blake. "What are you grumbling at? We've got comfortable quarters enough, even if they have forgotten the steam heating and the electric light, and they don't charge us anything."

A rattling at the door interrupted them, and someone was evidently trying the lock.

Tinker peered out of the window as far as he could.

"All the German soldiers have gone, vamoosed," he said, "but there's someone whom I can't see monkeying with the door."

Blake smiled grimly.

"I don't want to see. I know," he said. "It's our old friend the captain. Van Zyl gave him a bad scare when he had us stuck up against the wall, and has threatened to report him. Don't you see that we should prove very awkward witnesses against him in the case of an inquiry? I'll bet you what you like that he has dismissed his men on purpose. He knows we are unarmed, whilst he has both his sword and a revolver of some sort. Dead men tell no tales, and it would be most convenient for him if our mouths were closed for good and all. By the sound he's using a bit of wire to pick the lock. To put it perfectly bluntly, he means murder, neither more nor less, if he can bring it off.

"That looks a pretty hefty sort of a chair. Now listen to me! Collar the chair and stand behind the door, which swings inwards. The moment he crosses the threshold do your best to brain him or knock him endways. It ought to be easy. I shall stand here in full view, behind the table, and about half a second before he fires I shall drop flat.

"Look out! Here he comes! Don't make a boss shot."

Tinker darted off with his chair and crouched behind the door. They could hear the wire click-clicking in the lock, and then the door burst open unexpectedly. The captain, his face inflamed with rage, rushed in. He saw only Blake, and dashed straight at him. Tinker rushed, but missed the man by inches, for the chair was not only heavy but cumbersome, and the blow fell short.

The German fired once and a second time, and Blake dodged. And then, before he could pull the trigger again, Blake had dived under the table and got him by the ankle. With a quick jerk he had the man off his balance and on his back, the pair of them rolling close-locked on the floor.

Tinker, furious at having made a bungle of things, darted forward again, brandishing his chair.

"Get out, you young idiot!" panted Blake. "You are just as likely to brain me as you are him, and I've got him anyway. My meat, sonny. Run away and play!"

Slowly and carefully, but surely, Blake shifted his grip. The German was a powerful, beefy man, but he lacked all sense of intuition of what the next move was going to be, and, above all, he lacked initiative.

He was a cheap bully at heart, accustomed to dealing with men who daren't for their lives answer him back, and now he found himself up against something he couldn't understand. Inch by inch Blake's steel-like grip crept from forearm to wrist. There was a momentary tension, and then, as the grip got in to fine work, paralysing the motor nerve centre, the arm began to curve inwards helplessly.

The man's forefinger was still on the trigger, and the pressure of Blake's weight was remorseless, increasing more and more till the revolver muzzle was close-up to his temple.

Then suddenly Blake released his grip altogether, and the nerve reaction did its work. The trigger finger squeezed automatically, and the sears had been filed. The explosion seemed to shake the room, and when the sound had died away there was only half a face left to the dead man.

Blake rose slowly, looking rather grey.

"It was beastly, but it had to be done," he said. "I would have avoided it if I could, but there was no other way. And the worst of it is they—his men, I mean—must have known that he came in here and has never come out again. We shall have them making inquiries inside of ten minutes."

"Yes," said Tinker, "and I always did hate the sight of a rope. They'll try and make horrible examples of us by hanging us to one of those beastly poplar-trees. I know I shan't look my best on a poplar. Give me an apricot or plum-tree against a sunlit wall, and I might manage. They don't grow more than about eight feet high, and, anyway, you could always eat the fruit."

Blake strode to the door, which had been left ajar, and peered out. It was already growing dusk, and heavy snow was falling silently; but the square, at the end of which the guard-house stood, was empty and deserted. A little way off on either hand were the tall, grim houses, with storm shutters carefully closed, only a chink of orange-coloured light here and there, and the snow already gathering thickly on the steep, slanting roofs and gables.

"Let's slip out and make a bolt for it while we can," said Tinker. "It's our best chance."

"And be tracked in the snow in a few minutes. Listen! There

224

are German soldiers in that cabaret opposite at this moment. The one with the door partly open. I can hear them talking. No, sonny, that wouldn't do at all. We couldn't go to the place where Van Zyl is staying, and we don't know where his boat lies. We must just wait till he comes, as we said we would, and trust in him and our luck. But in the meantime we can take precautions."

He slid his arm through the opening of the door as he spoke, grabbed for the piece of bent wire, and, having got hold of it, slammed the door to again and set to work on the great, ponderous lock.

"If he could unlock it from the outside, I can certainly lock it again from the inside," said Blake, fumbling about in the dusk, "and I shall feel a jolly sight safer when I have. You remember that Van Zyl spoke of a second entrance known only to himself. We must have a look round for that presently.

"Ah! Listen! I told you they wouldn't be long."

There came the tramp, tramp, tramp of heavy footfalls muffled by the snow, and a thunderous knock at the door.

"Are you there, my captain?" called a voice.

Blake and Tinker kept perfectly still, and there was a sound of gruff muttering from the men outside.

"Are you there, my captain?" called the voice again. "Donner und blitzen, if someone doesn't answer we will break in!"

There was more muttering, and then bang came a rifle-butt against the heavy door, followed by another and another.

Blake picked up the dead man's sword and revolver and measured the height of the window grating with his eye.

"Three shots left in the chambers," he said softly. "I don't think they'll gain much by monkeying with that door. If they try volley firing through the panels, lie flat and as close to the wall as possible. The window is our weak point. They can't get in, but they could pot us through that like rats in a trap, if they had the sense to mount one man on another man's shoulders. Let's hope that they haven't. If they were only to look through they'd see their captain's body, and then I doubt if even old Van Zyl could save us. Thank goodness it's pretty dark now!"

"Listen to the beauties! They're making enough row to rouse the whole town."

"Hello! What the deuce is that?"

A faint scraping noise had caught his quick ear in spite of the din outside, and he wheeled sharply, peering through the gloom in the direction of the sound, sword and revolver both ready for action.

One of the big flagstones of the flooring was slowly rising upward, evidently on a well-oiled hinge, disclosing a square opening, through which emerged the head and shoulders of Van Zyl, carrying a storm-lantern in one hand and a basket covered with a spotless white napkin in the other.

"Pouf!" he grunted. "I told you there were more ways in here than one." And then, as he heard the din of the battering on the door, he stopped short.

"Name of a thousand fiends, what's that?" he said, as he continued to emerge like a seal from an icehole.

Blake said nothing, but he plucked off his coat and flung it round the storm-lantern, lest the light should be seen from the outside.

Then very cautiously he raised one little corner of the coat so that a ray of light fell on the floor, and pointed to the dead man.

Van Zyl blew out his cheeks and made a noise like an outsized grampus.

He was a difficult man to astonish, and phlegmatic by nature, but this time he certainly did show surprise.

"The captain!" he said, in a gruff whisper.

Blake nodded.

"And those are his men out there kicking up all that shindy," he whispered back. "They saw him come in, or at least they knew he was coming in, with the amiable intention of murdering us, and they're puzzled all to pieces why he hasn't come out again. Some of them must have been keeping an eye on the place from the inn across the square."

"Pick him up, you two," he said under his breath. "He must not be found here. Follow me! I go first with the lantern. The way is easy."

They did as he bade them, and he himself lowered the trap behind them before uncovering the lantern and handing Blake back his coat.

The sound of muffled battering still reached them faintly.

"So!" said Van Zyl, and slipped two heavy iron bars on the underside of the trap back into place.

They found themselves in a stone-lined tunnel-like passage, which sloped gradually downwards for a little way and then became level.

Van Zyl led the way with the lantern, which threw fantastic shadows. Blake and Tinker followed with their gruesome burden.

They must have gone all of two hundred yards before Van Zyl pointed upwards and showed them a similar trap overhead.

"To the cellars of a house I own," he said. "By that way I came." And he swung on again down the passage.

"Much good cognac and wines of France used to find their way along here in old times. Some to my cellars"—he winked—"and some was stored beneath the prison-house. That was droll, was it not?" He gave a deep chuckle, and strode on.

Another fifty yards brought them a whiff of fresh, cold air, laden with the tang of salt seaweed, and the floor underfoot became damp and slippery.

Van Zyl produced a ponderous-looking key, unlocked a heavy wooden door, and pointed downwards at a glimmer of sluggish water.

He was not a sentimentalist.

"In with him!" he ordered. "Pooh! He will not be found for days, never fear, and then ten or fifteen miles down the river, for when they opened the sluices there is a strong stream here."

His advice was certainly sound, and to have hesitated would have been to risk Van Zyl's own safety. So they lowered the body into the stream. The man had been a bully, and would have been a murderer if he could, so their regrets were not of a lasting order.

Van Zyl locked the door from the outside behind them, and they found themselves standing on a narrow ledge. A rough ladder, built into the wall for the convenience of the fishermen at low-tide, was within easy armstretch on their left, and up this Van Zyl led the way with the activity of a lamplighter, and they found themselves on the top of the quay.

Fifty yards along this Van Zyl's hogaast lay, moored alongside. He clambered down to her by a similar ladder. She was a fine boat, of about twenty tons, though so well devised that in light weather she could be managed single-handed. She had a fine roomy cabin, with plenty of head room, and on the table of this their host set down the lantern and the basket of provisions, to which he had clung persistently throughout.

"Clothes first," he said; and, going to a locker, produced two suits of typical Dutch Fishermen's things, baggy trousers and all. Their own things he did into bundles as they took them off, weighted them with lumps of iron ballast, and hove them over the side into midstream.

Then he looked at his transformed guests, and broke into a guffaw of laughter.

"There is a German patrol five miles downstream," he said, suddenly becoming grave and businesslike once more. "You must not be seen. After that all is well. But till then I sail the boat myself. Take the basket and the wine and go to the fore-cabin. No one shall come there. When it is safe I will call you. Here are cigars to smoke. Off you go, and then I get under way."

They went to the cabin, and Van Zyl secured the door on them. Afterwards, whilst they ate, they could hear him clumping about overhead, and the creaking of blocks and gear. Then there came the gurgling lap and ripple of moving water against the vessel's outer skin, and a hoarse shout of farewell from Van Zyl to someone on the quayside.

Sure enough, as Van Zyl had warned them, after going about five miles they came to a lock, and sail had to be got off the vessel.

There was much shouting and yelling as she warped alongside, and then more tramping overhead and voices speaking in German.

Van Zyl, however, was evidently prepared for emergencies, for they heard him bellowing to his visitors to come down, then there was a clinking of glasses and a pungent smell of cigar-smoke.

Van Zyl knew how to handle his guests and avoid awkward questions. Once when he was asked what cargo he was carrying he burst into a roar of laughter and replied, "British prisoners-of-war," and, of course, was naturally disbelieved.

Finally the Germans took themselves off, Van Zyl calling after them that he was going to pull out at dawn. He gave them about twenty minutes' grace, however, and then slipped his mooring-ropes and slid off silently into the darkness, satisfied that the combined effects of Schwepps and a warm fire would prevent a second intrusion that night.

When they had left the lock half a mile and more behind them he called to Blake and Tinker that it was all clear, and that they could come on deck with safety.

They found him swathed in oilskins, smoking a particularly

villainous black cigar, a thick muffler round his neck, and a copper kettle sizzling on a small stove beside him, into which he occasionally dropped green coffee-beans from some mysterious recess of his numerous pockets.

He steered apparently entirely by instinct, for compass he had none, and in the pitch-black darkness it was impossible to make out even the loom of the long rows of trees on either side of the canal-like stretch they were in.

He had both lee-boards up, his little canvas gaff was partly dropped, and in confidence he told them that he steered his course almost entirely by sound. Long years of training had enabled him, even on the darkest and thickest of nights, to distinguish between the sounds of five foot of water and over and, say, three or four. The flat bottom of his boat—she drew under two foot—acted for him as a sort of submarine telephone, and only once—in early days—had he run her ashore or alongside the dyke bank without meaning to. The ensuing disaster, involving the purchase of a new Oregan pine-pole mast and gear, a gashed head, and a carpenter's big bill, had taught him caution and the knack of skilful handling.

"In five hours we reach Huis, you understand. That is on the coast, and there are ten, twelve, thirty of your tramp-steamers, as you call them, who have been carrying cargo. Five miles out you will find a guard of your destroyer peoples just beyond the territorial limit.

"Oh, they are very careful, your people! But they are watchful—watchful as a cat at a mousehole."

He chuckled again.

"Twice last week they got a German submarine. How do I know? Pouf! It was not in the papers—no, not at all! But I have a nephew fishing, you understand, for herrings, and he sells some of his catch to your destroyers. As he sailed back he noticed two little calm pools of oil on the sea not a mile apart—little still pools of oily water. Yet there was what you British call a nasty lop of sea on.

"That meant two of their submarines gone. Pouf!

"At Huis I sail you out beyond the limit. I have a permit. Then one of your destroyers picks you up, and away you go. I know things! I—"

Blake nodded.

"We owe you a great deal, Captain Van Zyl. Our lives to start with. Do me one more favour, and you will find our Government is not ungrateful."

He stooped down to the light of the stove and scribbled a message on the back of an old torn envelope.

"Shipment unadvisable at present," it ran. "Coast too carefully watched."

It was addressed to Eckstein, New York. The address was in code—a code taken from Adler's private papers.

Seven hours later the hogaast was bumping gingerly, with rope fenders out, against the side of a long, lean destroyer, whose youthful commander was extremely annoyed until he had had five minutes' brief and lurid conversation with Blake under the shelter of the forebridge, with its murderous little gun on top.

"Can do!" he said, with a laugh. "Jimmy—I mean, Sir James, happens to be my avuncular relative, and Van Zyl is a pal of ours. My dear chap, we'll run you over in time to catch the Harwich mail."

He ran up an iron ladder, barked out a few rapid orders, and then came down again in a hurry.

"So-long, Van Zyl, old man—unless you'd like a run over to London to see the picture-palaces and get some decent grub! Lor'! What wouldn't I give for a devilled bone and a pate de Schwalof at the club! Canned horse and biscuits may be all right in their way, but one can have too much of a good thing."

"I come some other time," said Van Zyl.

"Right-ho! Get a move on, then, because we're in a hurry. I can whack her up to thirty-four-and-a-bit knots now under oil fuel and forced draught."

Van Zyl ponderously shook hands with them all, refused a glass of mess port, and clambered back on to his own deck.

"So-long, uncle!" yelled the commander. "See you again soon. This is our busy day."

The long, lean hull glided away, gathering speed as she went, whilst a signalman struggled frantically with a mass of bunting, sending messages to sister ships—some of them strictly unofficial and pointedly insulting.

At half-past seven that night she decanted Blake and Tinker at Harwich, backed away, and slid off into the North Sea again on her lawful occupation.

Blake managed to secure a couple of overcoats at a slopshop near the docks to cover their Dutch clothes, and they caught the train, with exactly one minute and a half to spare.

Sir James sat at his writing-table in his room near Whitehall. His face was more haggard and lined than before, and a silver clock, at which he glanced anxiously from time to time, stood just beneath the green-shaded reading-lamp.

There were papers before him—small, neat bundles of official documents—but they lay unread and unheeded. His mind was far away from them and their contents, and quite unconsciously he drew idle scrawls on the blotting-pad in front of him, and then glanced at the clock again.

There was a whir of the telephone-buzzer on the table at his elbow, and he started nervously. He was overstrained by long extra hours of work and lack of a proper amount of sleep. He took up the receiver.

"What is it?" he said testily.

"Two gentlemen to see you, sir. Important business, they say."

Sir James swore softly under his breath. He had been pestered day and night for months by requests for interviews from people on important business.

About one percent of them really had any business at all, the rest were mostly touts for contracts, or looking for a soft job with good pay and nothing to do. Still, he felt bound to see them all, in case he should miss the man with the real business.

"Very well, show them up," he said reluctantly, and turned back to his aimless scribbling. Then he took a blank telegraph-form, wrote an address on it, and glanced at the clock once more. He hesitated for a moment, and then dashed off a brief message.

There came a tap at the door.

"Come in!"

The door swung open, and Blake and Tinker came in, both in immaculate evening-dress.

"Good-evening, Sir James!" said Blake.

"Good heavens!" said Sir James, starting up. "I had given you up for lost! See!" He pointed with a quivering forefinger. "I had just written out the telegram for your successor, and ordered him to report for duty early to-morrow. Ten days was the time-limit you mentioned. It is now over—a quarter-past twelve. I know your punctual ways. Can you blame me if I fancied you had failed?"

Blake glanced at his wrist-watch, walked to the window, and threw it open.

"We have not failed," he said quietly. "Listen!"

Big Ben was just striking the hour of midnight.

"It is your clock that has failed; in fact, we have arrived in the nick of time—with a couple of minutes or so to spare.

"I'll tell you what made us run it so fine. Your Antwerp agent—there is no need to mention names—was murdered a minute or two before we reached him. He was in a state of collapse, but retained strength to gasp out a word or two before the end. So we took the paper on to Stiltz. I haven't the receipt for it, for the simple reason that I was obliged to light a cigarette with it under the eyes of a German officer. But you can take my word for it that it is now in the right hands.

"Incidentally, we were travelling with false passports, which we had annexed, to put it mildly, from some German-Americans who were ordering and arranging for big consignments of foodstuffs and material for Germany via Holland."

Sir James looked up sharply.

"Schmidt and Adler!" he snapped.

"Precisely! Well, I took the liberty of wiring to their people— Ecksteins, of New York—in their name and private code, cancelling the whole deal, as too risky and unsafe a proposition."

Sir James chuckled.

"That's great!" he said. "We've been trying to lay those fellows by the heels for months, I don't mind telling you in confidence.

"Look here, Mr. Blake, there's still that C.B. at my disposal, if you feel like changing your mind."

"I'll accept it on one condition," said Blake, smiling.

"And that is?"

"That you allow me to request you pass it on to your nephew, because without him we should never have got here by now."

"My nephew?"

"Yes. He ran us across in his destroyer."

"Good Lor'! The young rascal! Well, if you really wish it, Mr. Blake, I'll see what can be done. It is more than generous of you to suggest it. In any case, I personally shall send him a good fat cheque. The young rascal is an extravagant young dog, and always hard up."

"Thank you!" said Blake. "He deserves it; for without him we certainly couldn't have been here in the nick of time. Good-night!

I feel that I could do with about forty-eight hours' solid sleep.

"I suppose," he added, smiling, "we needn't leave by the coal-cellar, or whatever it was, this time?"

Sir James pressed a bell.

"My car shall take you home, and, I trust, deliver you safely in the nick of time. Good-night and good luck!"

THE END

Notes

3. Originally "pig-eating German," which indicates how petty the language could be in war-time. It's extraordinary how much focus was placed in these war stories on the fact that Germans ate sausages, as if by doing so they somehow demonstrated a level of barbaric inferiority.

4. "—those pig-swine" excised.

5. Uhlans were German lance-carrying cavalry units. They were already outdated at the start of the war and were disbanded by the end of it.

6. One further instance of "the swine" and two instances of "the pigs" have been excised from the innkeeper's discourse. While it's understandable that the author, Cecil Hayter, disliked Germans during the Great War, his contempt appears to have run away from him while writing this scene, making it rather distasteful to modern sensibilities.

7. A sentence that manages to insult both Belgians and Jews has been excised.

PRIVATE TINKER—A.S.C.

A SUSTAINED BARRAGE of thunder rumbled and crashed, marking the acme of the storm. Sexton Blake looked across the room but his eyes were focused beyond the window and into an unfathomable distance.

In that thunder, I wondered, is he hearing the artillery, has his mind gone back to that terrible conflict, to those hideous years of relentless carnage?

"For Tinker," I said, "it was a different story. He joined the Army."

Blake blinked and turned his attention back to the binder on his lap. He flipped the plastic sleeve to see which issue the next one contained.

"He did," he confirmed. "Though under false pretences. He was young. Boys of his age were chomping at the bit to join the fray. They had no conception of the wholesale slaughter occurring at the Front. No one understood that the Great War wasn't simply a clash of nations, it was also a collision of two very different time periods. You had pennant-carrying cavalrymen galloping with lances straight into machine-gun fire; sword-waving infantrymen charging at tanks; it was a bloodbath."

"Well-reflected in this account," I said. "Tinker killed a lot of Germans. Or was the writer, William Murray Graydon, exaggerating?"

"Tinker did his duty." Blake paused, then continued. "It changed him. I don't know how well that's reflected in the published stories, but Tinker went to war a boy and came back a man." He gave a slight shrug. "Mind you, it altered everything. Do you notice how, before the conflict, I had a great many cases involving cheated heirs, stolen heirlooms, missing aristocrats, and so forth—how so many of my clients came from the gentry—but how all that began to dwindle after the war, and even more so after the second one? There were colossal shifts in British society and they are all right here—" he held up the binder, "in these stories. That is why they are important. Yet all these years after their publication, they are still regarded by the intelligentsia as cheap throwaway fiction, unworthy of study. It's a missed opportunity. They are 'Ground Zero' history. They were written in the midst of it by—and for—ordinary people. There's no academic distance here. Also, somewhere in these so-called 'adventure yarns,' there's an explanation for what happened next; for what was unleashed in Britain after the Great War ended, and as a consequence of it."

I asked, "To what are you referring?"

He didn't respond.

PRIVATE TINKER—A.S.C.

by William Murray Graydon
UNION JACK issue 589 (1915)

PART ONE

THE FIRST CHAPTER

Tinker's Bad Luck

AT THE SOUND of footsteps on the stairs Pedro raised his massive head from the rug, and vigorously thumped the floor with his tail; and Tinker, who was curled in the depths of a lounge-chair, sat up by a languid effort, and tossed aside the newspaper he had been reading. The door was opened, and Sexton Blake entered the big, cheerful sitting-room which could have told many thrilling tales and betrayed many a weighty secret, had walls but ears and tongues.

There was on the detective's clean-cut features a strained, harassed look which had of late become almost a fixture. For days past, in this time of national peril from the horde of Germans who were within London's gates, he had been zealously assisting the shrewd brains of Scotland Yard, working on behalf of his country, and neglecting his individual interests. Having nodded to the lad, and spoken a kindly word to the bloodhound, he pulled a bell-cord that communicated with the basement, and then dropped heavily into a chair.

"I didn't expect you before to-night," said Tinker. "Have you had any luck?"

"Yes, good luck and bad," Blake replied. "The clue that I mentioned this morning led us to a house on Highgate Hill, where we discovered the two unregistered aliens. One succeeded in making his escape, most unfortunately; but we caught the other, and found carrier-pigeons and a wireless apparatus on the premises. So there can be no doubt of the man's guilt."

"What will be done with him, guv'nor?"

"I don't know. He ought to be quietly shot at daybreak by a file of soldiers, and in all probability he will be. That is the proper way to deal with spies in time of war."

"They have shot some of them, I have heard. I wish they could all be caught."

"That is a big task, Tinker. But I must stick to it. There is a fresh trail to be followed to-morrow, and I may have need of you and Pedro."

"Right you are," assented Tinker.

Mrs. Bardell, the portly landlady, came into the room with a laden tray, and put the tea things on the table. She was in a bad temper because the milkman's assistant, whom she adored, had been persuaded to take the King's shilling. And when she had complained of that, and grumbled at the increased price of provisions, she shook her fist at an inoffensive bust of the immortal Vidocq which graced a pedestal.[8]

"I wish that was the Kaiser, alive and in the flesh," she declared. "Wouldn't I pinch 'is nose for 'im! Oh, these wicked Germans, and the Alleys, and the whole blessed lot of 'em! A setting at it, and blowing one another to bits with bombs and shells and suchlike, as if they was the Kilkenny cats and dogs![9] What I can't understand about it, as I was saying to my friend Jemima Primp, which is cook at the next 'ouse but one, is why the Powers don't intervene and stop the war."

Blake laughed, and the lad could not repress a smile, moody though he was.

242

"Why don't they?" fairly shrieked Mrs. Bardell. "Why don't they do what the papers were always saying they were likely to do, now they've got the chance? It's disgraceful their looking coolly on while millions of soldiers are rushing into arms, and falling in 'eaps on the gory field of massage!"

With that the landlady departed, viciously slamming the door behind her.

"A queer woman, Tinker!" murmured Sexton Blake.

Tinker nodded, and gazed absently at the bloodhound, who was squatted by the tea-table. The slanting rays of the September sun were shining into the room. Down in Baker Street the flags of various nations, British and French, Russian and Belgian, were fluttering in the breeze. On taxi-cabs and motor-'buses, and displayed in shops, were posters printed in red letters, calling on the people to take up arms for their King and country, and join Kitchener's force. The tap of a drum rose above the throbbing of the traffic, and it sent the lad hurrying to the window.

It was a Scottish regiment approaching. It marched past, and was followed shortly afterwards by a long train of the Royal Field Artillery. A score of guns rumbled by, with mounted offices here and there, and khaki-clad soldiers riding stiffly on the draught-horses, and others perched on the carriages with their arms folded across their chests. Tinker cheered with the spectators on the pavement, and when he returned to the table his cheeks were flushed and his eyes were bright.

A FEW DAYS had elapsed, and Sexton Blake and Tinker were sitting in a taxi-cab that was progressing by fits and starts through the sloppy, crowded thoroughfares of the City. It had been raining all of the morning, and the afternoon was damp and dismal. The weather mattered nothing to Blake and the lad, however. They were going down to Essex to make inquiries concerning a man who was suspected of being an unregistered alien of a dangerous type, as they were keen on their quest. It was a consolation to both to feel that they were serving their country as well, in a way, as if they had been under arms at the front.

"I wonder if the fellow really is Wertheim?" said Tinker.

"I have no doubt, Tinker, since the description fits," the detective replied. "I knew that he had been in hiding, and I believe he has been run to earth."

Having arrived at Liverpool Street, and bought their tickets, they plunged into a mass of humanity that seemed to be moving in all directions; and as they were jostling through, towards the gates, Sexton Blake saw a familiar face approaching him.

"Hallo, Grant!" he said, accosting a young naval officer who had his arm in a sling. "What are you doing here?"

"I have just come from Harwich," replied Captain Grant, of the cruiser Centipede, with a smile that lighted up his thin and haggard face.

"You have been in hospital there, I suppose?"

"No, I haven't been so bad as that. I was put ashore from my ship this morning, on special service."

"I was sorry to hear that you had been wounded. That was a fine set-to you had with the enemy the other day."

"It was a costly one for them, Blake, and a bitter pill to swallow after all their bragging. We shall be at them again before long, I hope. I am going back as soon as—as I have—"

The officer's voice faltered. An ashen pallor was mounting to his cheeks, and he suddenly swayed against Blake.

"What's wrong?" Blake explained.

"It is nothing much," gasped Captain Grant. "I am not as strong as I thought I was. My arm hasn't entirely healed yet, and there is a splinter from a shell in my body."

"You are ill! I shall have to look after you."

"No, no, Blake, don't let me detain you. Never mind about me. I'll be all right in a moment."

"I don't think you will be."

The naval officer's remonstrances were unheeded. Sexton Blake and Tinker led him, almost a limp weight in their grasp, to a waiting-room that was deserted, and put him on a couch. The detective hastened to the bar, and returned with a small glass of brandy, and when Captain Grant had swallowed this a tinge of colour ebbed back into his face, and he was able to sit up.

"Thanks!" he murmured. "I am better now."

"You don't look it," Blake answered. "You need rest, and I will send you home at once. Your wife lives at the same address in South Kensington, I believe?"

"Yes, that's right. But I can't go home until I have transacted my business."

"You will have to go at once, Grant. You are not fit for anything."

"I am afraid I am not," the young officer assented, as he sank back on the couch. "This is most annoying. Perhaps you will do me a kindness. I have a despatch of some importance, from the commander of the fleet, which must be promptly delivered at the Admiralty. Will you take it there, and tell them that I am ill?"

"I am sorry," the detective replied, "but I am going down to Essex on an urgent matter, and I have only ten minutes in which to catch the train. I can help you out of your difficulty, however. Tinker will take the despatch for you."

"Can I trust it to him, Blake?"

"Yes, as readily as to me. He will deliver it safely at the Admiralty, you may be sure."

"Very well. Here it is."

Captain Grant drew from his breast pocket a sealed envelope, and gave it to Sexton Blake, who handed it to the lad.

"Take the best care of this," he said earnestly. "Remember that you are on Government service. When you have delivered the despatch you can go home. I shall probably return in the morning, or possibly late to-night."

It was a disappointment to Tinker that he was not to accompany his master, but he concealed his feelings.

"Right you are, guv'nor," he said. "You can rely on me."

He slipped the envelope into his pocket and hurried off. As he made his way towards the station exit he was followed by a man who had been peering furtively through the waiting-room window, and had seen the despatch change hands. But there was not the slightest suspicion of evil in the lad's mind. It had not occurred to him, or to Blake either, that German spies might have been prowling about at Liverpool Street on the chance of learning something of advantage. Tinker stepped into a taxi-cab, and gave the address to the chauffeur; and as he was driven away the individual who had been shadowing him entered a motor-car that had been waiting for him, and whispered a few words of instruction to a comrade who was at the wheel.

The dull, grey day was drawing to a close, and it was already so dark, though the time was only six o'clock, that lamps were beginning to twinkle here and there. The lad leaned back in the seat, and gazed moodily from the window at the hurrying crowds of people.

"I had rather be going down to Essex," he reflected. "I shall miss the fun if the guv'nor arrests that fellow Wertheim. But it can't be helped."

Owing to the heavy traffic in the main thoroughfares at this hour, the chauffeur avoided Fleet Street and the Strand, holding a course by Queen Victoria Street to Blackfriars Bridge, and thence along the Embankment, where a thin mist from the river hung in the air. The pursuing motor-car, which had its hood up, was not far behind. The driver of it waited until half of the stretch of the Temple Gardens had been passed, and the road was comparatively free of traffic; and then, by a twist of the wheel, he sent his vehicle against the rear of the taxi-cab with just sufficient force to cause it to swerve, and collide with one of the street-refuges. The cab was checked with a jerk, pitching the chauffeur onto the tram-line, and hurling Tinker violently from his seat.

"Confound it!" he muttered. "Some clumsy fool has run into us!"

The motor-car had not sustained any damage. It had pulled up a couple of yards ahead, and a lean, clean-shaved man had jumped out of it. He darted to the taxi-cab, and as the lad opened the door and was about to emerge, a staggering blow was dealt him. He reeled back, and the next instant his assailant was inside and on top of him, busy with both hands.

"Help! Help!" Tinker called hoarsely.

Another blow half dazed him, and his struggles relaxed. He did not lose consciousness. As he offered a feeble resistance he felt his coat being ripped open, and the sealed envelope being wrenched from his pocket. The daring man had achieved his object. He sprang from the cab and dashed back and into the motor-car, which started at once. And it was gliding swiftly away, melting into the murky gloom, when the bruised and dishevelled lad scrambled out of the damaged vehicle, and gazed about him in bewilderment.

"Stop them!" he shouted, as he realised what had happened. "Stop that car! I have been robbed!"

It was a futile appeal. Nobody had even observed the number of the motor-car, which had now vanished in the mist. The whole affair had occurred in almost less time than it takes to tell. The lad swayed against a lamp-post, pressing his hand to his throbbing head. A clamour was ringing and swelling in his ears. Constables hastened from here and there to the scene of the accident. The chauffeur was dragged unconscious from under the wheels of a tramcar, and from other cars, which had stopped by the refuge, swarmed men, women and children. They gathered around Tinker, and annoyed him with absurd questions. One of the policemen sent for an ambulance, and another, having pushed his way into the crowd, glanced at the lad, and recognised him.

"Hello, youngster!" he exclaimed. "You're Mr. Sexton Blake's assistant, aren't you?"

"That's right!" Tinker dully assented.

"And what's the trouble? Didn't I hear you shouting that you had been robbed?"

"Yes, I have been. The guv'nor sent me with a paper to be delivered in Whitehall, and I must have been followed by some scoundrel in a motor-car. He ran into my cab, and attacked me before I could get out, and stole the paper from me!"

"Would you know him if you were to see him again, my boy?"

"No; I didn't get a glimpse of his face."

"Was the paper of any great value?"

"My word, I should think so! I was taking it to the—"

The lad broke off, loth to say more in the presence of the curious spectators. An automobile that was now passing misfired with a report like a gun and some waggish person cried that a Zeppelin had dropped a bomb, with the result that the crowd scattered in panic and confusion. And while they were straggling back Tinker briefly explained matters to the constable, who shook his head gravely.

"A government despatch, eh?" he murmured. "That's bad."

"Bad isn't the word for it," declared the lad. "There may be a lot of harm done."

"I dare say it was a German spy who robbed you, judging from what you told me."

"I'm sure it was. The scoundrel must have seen the naval officer arrive at Liverpool Street, and heard him talking to my guv'nor. There is no chance of the despatch being recovered, I suppose?"

"Not the ghost of a one, I'm afraid, since there isn't any clue," the constable replied. "But it wasn't your fault that you were robbed. Mr. Blake won't blame you."

"Won't he, though?" the lad said dismally. "You don't know him."

"Well, I'm sorry for you. All I can do is to report the affair."

"But it must be kept quiet. Don't let the news leak out to the public."

"That will be all right, my boy. Don't you worry. I'll make a private report to my inspector."

The ambulance had now appeared. With a nod the constable turned away to assist his mates with the chauffeur, who had meanwhile come to his senses, a broken leg being the extent of his injury. Tinker waited for a few seconds, and then he slouched across the road, and melted into the gloom of the falling night.

"A nice scrape I've got myself into!" he muttered, as he walked along the pavement towards Waterloo Bridge. "What will the guv'nor have to say about it?"

THE SECOND CHAPTER

Tinker Meets an Old Friend—and Has a Wild Idea.

WHAT WOULD SEXTON Blake say? Again and again, as the lad strolled aimlessly on, the question recurred to him. Now that he had recovered from the rough handling he had received, and his mind was quite clear, a full sense of his position dawned upon him. It was not his fault that he had been robbed, yet had it been he could hardly have felt the loss more keenly.

Experience had taught him what to expect. Fair in his judgement though Blake was, he was at times inclined to be a little too exacting.

"I'll catch it hot!" Tinker reflected. "He will say that I ought to have looked behind me to see if I was being followed, and that I should have put the envelope in a safer pocket. I daren't face him. What the deuce am I to do?"

He was loth to go home. As for going to the Admiralty, to confess that he had lost the despatch that had been entrusted to him, not for a moment did he contemplate braving the wrath of the Sea Lords. He was in the mood to exaggerate the situation. The fault was not his, and a flash of temper from his master would probably have been followed by an apology. But he could not be sure of that. The shadow of disgrace hung heavy on him, and in all London that night there was no person more wretched than he.

"What am I to do?" he repeated.

There was good news from the front. The placards posted on the Embankment side of Charing Cross District Station, announcing the retreat of the enemy and the vigorous pursuit of the allies, caught Tinker's eye in passing. He saw more of them at Westminster Bridge, and in Victoria Street, to which he made his way with no purpose whatever, later official news, referring to a list of British casualties, was bellowed in his ears by a ragged urchin.

"What gallant fellows they are!" he said to himself, half aloud. "Dying in a foreign land by hundreds, for the sake of their country! I ought to be out there, too, sharing the risks. It is my duty to go. Every man who can bear arms is needed for—"

The lad paused and stood still, gazing into vacancy. He was in the grip of the war-fever; a wild desire flamed in his heart.

"I'll enlist!" he reflected. "By Jove, I will! Why shouldn't I? Yes, I will fight for my country, and perhaps come back covered with glory."

Tinker's resolve was made. He walked briskly on for a few yards, his eyes sparkling, and stopped again as a chilling thought occurred to him. Sexton Blake would have to be reckoned with. It was certain that he would make inquiries at the recruiting-stations, and would visit the places where new recruits were temporarily kept, in the provinces as well as in London, in quest of his assistant, who could not expect to be sent to the front at once.

"It's no use," the lad sighed. "The guv'nor would be sure to find me, and he might exert his influence to prevent me from being sent abroad. I know he wants me to help him in this new alien rounding-up scheme. He does not want me to enlist, and he'll guess that's what I've done."

His elation was gone. The shadow was heavy on his mind again. He would have to go home and face Blake's anger and stick to the old treadmill. But as he was standing at the edge of the pavement, reluctant to bend his steps towards Baker Street, a hand clapped him on the shoulder, and he turned to see a familiar face.

"Hello, Tinker!"

The speaker, who was of the same height and build as himself, was a young man of twenty-six, slim and fair and clean-shaved.

"Hello, Rokeby!" Tinker replied. "How are things going with you?"

"Not as well as they might be," Jack Rokeby replied. "I hope they are better with you. What are you doing here?"

"Just knocking about, that's all. I shouldn't have expected to see you. I thought you had gone to the front."

"I meant to go. There is no chance of it, though, worse luck. But I am afraid you are in trouble. You look as if you hadn't a friend in the world."

"That's the way I feel. I'm in a rotten mood."

"What's wrong old chap?"

"Everything is, Jack."

"Tell me about it, and I may be able to help you."

"No, not now. I am going home."

"Come with me. I want to have a chat with you. I live close by, near St. John's Square."

Tinker demurred, but his friend grasped him firmly by the arm and drew him along. Having walked for a short distance, and turned into a quiet and gloomy street, they entered a large building, and ascended a stone staircase to the second-floor. A door was unlocked and opened, and the lad stumbled through into darkness. Jack Rokeby switched on the electric-light, revealing a narrow hall hung with pictures.

"This is my flat," he said. "It isn't a bad sort of place. I would like you to meet my wife, but unfortunately she is not here. The fact is that—that—"

His voice faltered. He led the way into an apartment off the hall and switched on another light, which illuminated a sitting-room that was comfortably furnished but in a state of neglect. A big gate-table, smeared with dust and littered with all sorts of odds and ends, showed the lack of a woman's presence. Tinker dropped into a basket-chair and glanced around him. His friend passed him a box of cigarettes and began to fill a pipe, and when he had put a match to it, he sat down opposite to the lad and looked at him kindly through a cloud of smoke.

"Now tell me your trouble," he bade. "What is it?"

Little urging was needed to open Tinker's lips. He was in the mood now to confide in somebody who would sympathise with him, and in a gloomy voice he told of the theft of the precious despatch, and of his dread of Blake's anger, and of his desire to enlist.

"But it wouldn't do any good," he went on. "The guv'nor would soon be on my track."

"Yes, I dare say he would," Jack Rokeby assented. "I am sorry for you; but you had better give up the idea. Go home and make a clean breast of it. Mr. Blake won't blame you."

"I am sure he will," the lad replied. "And I am keen on going to the front."

"So am I; but it can't be done. We all have our troubles, and I have a lot more to bear than you have."

"I shouldn't have thought so, Jack."

"Ah, you don't know. It is like this with me. As I had been in the Middlesex Regiment, and could count on being sent off to join the British force in the field, I put in an application to the War Office. I heard from them several days ago. I got a letter informing me that I had been attached to the Army Transport

Service, and telling me that I was to report myself to-morrow to the commanding-officer at Avonmouth Docks. I drew the money to which I was entitled and bought my kit. And now I can't go. I shall have to back out and refund the money."

"How is that? Why can't you go?"

"Because of my wife, Tinker."

"She don't want you to leave her, I suppose," said the lad.

"It is worse than that," Jack Rokeby answered, in a husky tone. "I'll tell you all about it. We were married three months ago, and for a time we were the happiest couple in the world. Then Lilian was taken ill, and she didn't get any better. She seemed to be fading away, and finally I sent her down to Penzance to her aunt, hoping that the Cornish air would do her good. That was two weeks ago, and yesterday I heard from the physician who had been attending her that she had an incurable complaint, and that she could not live for more than a month or so. That is why I am not going to the front. How could I, when Lilian is dying? If I were to leave her, it would be for ever. I—I should never again—"

The young man's voice choked. He leaned forward and buried his face in his hands.

"I know how you must feel," Tinker said softly. "I am awfully sorry for you."

"I am sure you are," his friend replied. "Thanks, old chap."

"Doctors aren't always right. Your wife may recover," said Tinker hopefully.

"No, there isn't a chance of it. I am going to lose her, and I must be with her until the end. It is bitterly hard, for she is the dearest, sweetest girl. I can't tell you how much I love her."

There was a hushed silence in the room, where still seemed to linger the fragrance of the young wife who was doomed to an early grave. A lump rose in the lad's throat, for he was deeply, sincerely affected by what he had been told. Tears trickled from between Jack Rokeby's fingers. He brushed them away and lifted his haggard features, twitching with emotion.

"I am awfully sorry," Tinker repeated. "It is a hard thing to bear, I know."

"It is breaking my heart," the young man answered hoarsely. "You understand now, and I don't want to talk about it any more. I am going down to Cornwall to-morrow, instead of to Avonmouth."

"You must stay with your wife, of course," said the lad. "Your first duty is to her. I wish I could take your place in the Army," he added, as a vague idea occurred to him.

"I wish you could, old chap. It will be a fine berth."

"Have you written to the War Office to tell them that you must withdraw?"

"Not yet. I shall write to-night."

"Would there be anybody at Avonmouth Docks with whom you are acquainted, Jack?"

"No, I should think not."

"Suppose you were to go to the front. Would you be likely to meet with any of your old comrades of the Middlesex Regiment?"

"I might, but there would be very little chance of it. What are you driving at, by the way?"

"Can't you guess?" exclaimed Tinker, his face flushing as he spoke. "I told you that I wished I could take your place, and I mean to do it, if you will let me."

"Nonsense!" cried Jack Rokeby. "You can't be serious!"

"Certainly I am. I was never more in earnest in my life. You will go to Cornwall to stay with your wife. And I will go to Avonmouth in your name. But I won't be there long. I shall soon be at the front."

"My dear chap, the thing is utterly impossible."

"Nothing of the sort, Jack. It is perfectly simple. You have admitted that nobody at Avonmouth will know me from you, and that I am not likely to meet any Middlesex men abroad. And if I did they wouldn't suspect me, not unless they were to hear me called by your name."

"It is madness, Tinker, for you to think of—"

"Let me finish. As for the rest, I have served in the Terriers, and I should be able to do what was required of me. And your uniform will fit me, as I am of the same height and build as you. So there you are. Won't it be easy?"

The lad was full of his project, brimming over with enthusiasm. Jack Rokeby's face was grave and troubled. He rose from his chair, and paced to and fro, biting on the stem of his pipe.

"I wish you would give up this wild idea," he said.

"Don't ask me to," begged Tinker. "It is too good to be missed, such a splendid opportunity. You can't deny, after what you have said, that it will be easy to carry it through."

"That is true enough. You might serve through the war, or be killed and buried, without the deception being discovered. On the other hand, you might get me into the worst kind of a scrape with the War Office."

"I won't, old chap. I swear I won't. You sit tight in Cornwall, and trust to me. I'll see to it that there is no exposure."

"It is too much to expect of me, Tinker, even for a friend."

"Don't refuse, Jack. Please don't."

"I really must. That's all there is about it."

"But think how much it will mean to me. I am ashamed to walk the streets in these days, when everybody is enlisting. I want to fight for Britain, and show the guv'nor what I can do. He will be angry with me about the stolen despatch, but when I come back with honours—"

The lad paused, breathless with excitement. He jumped up, and put his hand on his friend's arm. And so earnestly did he plead, persevering in spite of denials, that at length Jack Rokeby was reluctantly won over.

"Very well," he said. "I'll have to agree, I suppose. You may be sorry, though, and so may I. But I'll risk it."

"There won't be any risk," declared Tinker. "Thanks so much, old chap. You're a brick."

"I am a fool for yielding. We won't quarrel, however. My kit is in that cupboard yonder, and there are my papers on the table, in that large envelope. I have filled them in."

"Then there is nothing more to be settled between us, Jack?"

"No, I believe not. You can spend the night with me. In the morning I will travel down to Penzance to stay with my wife, and you will go to Avonmouth Docks and report to the commanding officer."

"Right you are," assented the lad.

"But aren't you behaving very cruelly towards Mr. Blake?" asked Jack Rokeby. "I know how much he cares for you. I am sure that your disappearance will be a terrible blow to him."

"He will miss me, of course."

"You had better change your mind before it is too late."

"No, old chap, I can't. I've had enough of skulking at home while others are fighting. It is the front for me."

Tinker's voice trembled slightly. There had risen before his eyes a vision of the lonely rooms in Baker Street, and Sexton Blake sitting there in grief and anxiety. His purpose wavered, but only for a moment. Stronger than the affection he had for his master was the desire to serve his country, to bear arms against the German foes who had boasted of a triumphal march into London.

"The guv'nor will have to do without me for a time," he said. "But I won't keep him in suspense, Jack. I'll drop him a few lines now."

And with that he sat down to the table, reached for a pen and paper, and began to write.

THE THIRD CHAPTER

Sexton Blake Discovers Rokeby's Secret.

FOR SOME DAYS the shadow had been lurking in the house in Baker Street; a shadow that could not be driven away, or dimmed, by the brightest rays of sunshine. It could be felt, but not seen. Mrs. Bardell had gone about her duties listlessly, with an unwonted expression of melancholy on her florid face; and at every ring of the bell, Pedro, the big bloodhound, had pricked up his ears, and listened expectantly for a familiar step or a familiar voice. They missed their young master, and of Sexton Blake they had seen very little. His sorrow was deeper than theirs, but less obvious.

He had been devoting his time to a single task. Having made close inquiries at the London recruiting offices, and visited the places where the new recruits were being trained, he had taking taken an admirable likeness of Tinker to a photographer, and had procured a large number of copies of it. These he had circulated amongst the officers in charge of the provincial recruiting stations, and of the depots that had been established for the young soldiers. But it had been labour wasted. Not the slightest success had rewarded his efforts. He had waited day by day, and in vain, for tidings of the missing lad. He would not have been angry with him in regards to the lost despatch. It had not been recovered, but no harm had been done by the theft, since the information which had been obtained by the spy could not have been of the slightest value to the Germans.

Meanwhile, during the period of suspense, the strain had been telling on Blake. His step was less springy than it had been, and there were dark lines beneath his eyes when he emerged from his bedchamber one morning. Having caressed Pedro, he sat down to the breakfast-table, and with fresh hopes gave his attention to the mass of correspondence that was heaped by his plate. Rapidly and nervously, while the vague hope dwindled, he tore open envelope after envelope and glanced at the contents.

He tossed the last one aside and leaned back in his chair, shaking his head sadly.

"Nothing," he murmured. "Still nothing. Not the faintest clue. Tinker cannot be in England. Had he failed in his purpose he would have come home. By some means or other—I cannot imagine how—he must have contrived to get to the front. Well, it can't be helped. I must do without him as best I can."

He had no appetite. A pain gnawed incessantly at his heart, and he pictured the lad under the fire of the German guns, and lying dead or wounded on the field of battle, as he sipped his coffee and nibbled at his toast. Mrs. Bardell, on coming in to clear the table, found her master at his desk; and she left him there, scarcely aware of her entrance and departure, reading once more the letter which Tinker had written to him from Jack Rokeby's flat. Every word had a pathetic meaning for him, and there were fragments of sentences that stabbed like a knife-thrust:

"I am sure you will be angry—so it is the only thing to do, as you will blame me for losing the dispatch—will miss you as much as you will miss me—sorry to disobey you, but you won't think the less of me for—forgive me, dear guv'nor, and try hard to—I hope to come safely back some day, but if I don't, if you never hear of me again, you will know that I died bravely, for the honour of my—"

Blake put the letter back and shut and locked the desk, then sank down in a chair, and sat there for some minutes, with the bloodhound's head resting on his knee. When at length he rose there was not a trace of emotion on his features, though the inward pain had not been stifled. He descended the stairs, took his hat and stick from the stand in the hall, and passed out of the house as an empty taxi-cab was approaching. He stopped it, and got in.

"The Horse Guards Parade," he said to the chauffeur.

Sexton Blake had found a new sphere for his patriotic zeal. For the past two or three days, during the rush to enlist which had followed a slight loss of ground by the Allied armies, he had been assisting the recruiting-officer at the principal station. And he was going there now to scrutinise the applicants, lest some alien, with a fluent knowledge of the British tongue, should seek to take the King's shilling for a sinister purpose.

ALL SORTS AND conditions of men, belonging to all phases of life, had presented themselves that morning at the recruiting-officer's marquee on the Horse Guards Parade. Poor and prosperous, shabby and well dressed, wasters with the right stuff in them, and industrious clerks and artisans, and the languid swells who had realised that they could be better employed than by gaping from the bow-windows of West End clubs—all had shown a keen desire to be at arms for their country. They had filed in a steady procession under Blake's shrewd and discerning eyes, and had for the most part, with very few exceptions, been passed on to the doctor and the swearing-in magistrate.

Between twelve and one o'clock there was a brief lull, and

then a fresh applicant stepped into the booth, and advanced to the sergeant's desk. He did not look at Sexton Blake, but the latter shot a searching glance at him, and knitted his brows in surprise and perplexity. The applicant was a young man, well under thirty, of slim build, with fair hair and a light moustache. He wore a band of black crepe around his arm, and on his face was such an expression of deep-seated, heart-breaking grief as the detective had rarely seen before.

"I wish to enlist, sir," he said, "if there is any likelihood of my being sent abroad at an early date. I don't want to be kept at home to guard bridges and railway stations."

"I can't guarantee anything," the recruiting-officer replied, "but it would be to your advantage if you have been in the Service."

"Yes I have been," stated the applicant, after a brief hesitation. "I am a trained soldier."

"Then it probably won't be long until you are sent to the front. They need trained men there."

"Very well. I will take the chances."

The young man was gazing straight before him, and was apparently unaware of the presence of Blake, who then stood off to one side. Having reached for a sheet of blue paper, the sergeant picked up a pen, and dipped it in ink.

"I will have your name and age first," he said. "What are they?"

"My name is John Davis," the applicant replied, "and I am little more than twenty-six years of age."

"Where were you born?"

"In London, in the parish of Hampstead."

"Any trade or profession?"

"No; since I left the regiment I used to belong to I have been living on my income, which is something under six hundred a year."

"Are you married?"

"I have been," was the faltering answer, "but—but I have recently lost my wife. She is dead."

"I see," murmured the officer. "What corps do you want to join? Have you any preference?"

"No, it doesn't matter," the young man replied. "Only so I get to the front, where there will be a chance of fighting."

The sergeant nodded. While he had been putting the questions he had been writing the answers on the sheet of blue paper, which he now blotted, and handed to the new recruit.

"There you are," he said. "You will now report yourself at the office at Scotland Yard, to be examined by the doctor. And if you are passed by him you will be sent upstairs to be sworn in by a magistrate. That is all. I have finished with you."

The initial formality was over. The young man turned on his heel, and with his gaze still fixed ahead of him, without looking towards the detective, he left the marquee. And he had no more than disappeared when Sexton Blake rose and hastened after him. He had to walk fast for a number of yards.

"Rokeby!" he called, in a low tone.

The new recruit pretended not to have heard. He strode on, increasing his pace.

"Stop, Rokeby!" the detective called again. "I want to speak with you!"

The young man paused and swung round. He was obviously confused and frightened.

"I think you have made a mistake," he said.

"I think not," Blake replied. "You have grown a moustache since I last saw you, but it has not altered you very much."

"I—I have always had a moustache."

"You had none several months ago. I am sure that you are a friend of Tinker's, and that your name is Rokeby."

The young man, who was indeed Jack Rokeby, flushed to his

263

temples. He had a strong reason, other than the false statement he had just made to the recruiting-officer, for being desirous of avoiding an interview with the detective. But he had been cornered, and he knew that further denials would be useless.

"You are quite right," he said. "I must admit that. I saw you in the marquee, but I did not suppose that you had recognised me."

"Your identity was obvious," Sexton Blake answered drily.

"Don't betray me, please. I did no wrong in giving a false name."

"I am not so certain of that. It calls for an explanation, at all events."

"There was nothing wrong about it," Jack Rokeby persisted, in a dogged tone. "I want to get to the front, and as long as I do my duty out there how can it matter what name I go by?"

"I have been under the impression that you went to the front some weeks ago. I understood, from what Tinker told me, that you had applied to the War Office, and that they had given you a commission, or a billet of some kind, because you had been in the Middlesex Regiment."

"Yes, that is true. I did have an appointment, and I was ordered abroad. I fully intended to go. But my wife was so ill that I could not leave her. She has since died, down in Cornwall, and—and—"

The young man's voice faltered and choked, and his eyes filled with tears. His distress moved Blake, whose cold expression relaxed. He stepped closer to him, and put a hand on his shoulder.

"I am sorry for you," he said—"very sorry. Come along with me! We will have luncheon together, and a friendly chat."

"But I must go to the medical officer at Scotland Yard," Jack Rokeby demurred.

"You can go there afterwards. Come along!"

"Will you promise not to betray me to the recruiting-sergeant, Mr. Blake?"

"I can't promise anything now. I will tell you later."

"Very well. I don't mind having something to eat with you. I can't see what there is for us to talk about, though."

Sexton Blake knew, but he judged it best to drop the subject for the present. Having passed out to Whitehall, the two walked up to a modest restaurant near Trafalgar Square, where they found a quiet corner table in a room that was far from crowded. A small glass of sherry whetted the young man's appetite, and some champagne that followed, in the course of the meal, slightly loosed his tongue. He was not communicative in regard to himself, however. It was not until he had finished and had lighted a cigarette that he was led to speak of the illness and death of his wife.

"You can understand what that was to me," he continued, striving hard to retain his control. "I don't believe any man ever loved a girl as I loved Lilian. She was charming in every way. She appealed to all my senses. I don't think I fully realised that that I was going to lose her until she was dead, until I heard the sods falling on her coffin. Then something seemed to break inside me. I suffered acutely for a time, and next came a feeling of numbness, and after that a sort of resignation. But I had lost all interest in life. There was nothing worth living for. That is why I am going to the front, in the hope that a bullet may soon find its way to my heart. On the day when I left Penzance I put a wreath of flowers on Lilian's grave, and before the winter snow has fallen on them I trust I shall be with her, and if there is another world where the spirits of true lovers are—are—"

Jack Rokeby gulped down a sob, and looked at the detective through a veil of unshed tears.

"That's my story," he murmured. "That explains everything."

"You have my deepest sympathy," Blake replied. "It must be hard to lose a beloved wife—bitterly hard."

"It has broken my heart."

"Time heals all wounds, Rokeby, and brings consolation."

"It won't to me, sir. I am sure of that."

There was an interval of silence, while the young man toyed with a liqueur glass, and stared into vacancy. Sexton Blake bit the end off a cigar, and touched a match to it. He had been not a little moved by the pathetic story he had heard, but he did not propose to let sympathy for his companion divert him from the object with which he had invited him to luncheon. It was his duty, he felt, to probe the matter to the bottom.

"Either way," he said quietly, "you have not explained everything."

"I think I have," Jack Rokeby answered.

"No; there is one point in regard to which I am rather curious."

"And what is that, sir?"

"Why did you give a false name to the recruiting officer?"

There was silence again for a few seconds. The simple question, which could not be evaded, had taken the young man by surprise. He could not hide his confusion. He hesitated, at a loss for words.

"Why did you do it?" the detective sharply asked.

"I—I don't know," Jack Rokeby stammered.

"You don't know? Come, you can't expect me to believe that. You must have had some motive for the deception."

"I had no motive in particular."

"You must have had, Rokeby. There can be no doubt of it. Have you committed any crime that leads you to fear arrest? Is there any person from whom you are anxious to conceal your whereabouts?"

"No, nothing of the sort."

"Is there any other reason that would account for your being afraid to fight for your country under your real name?"

"None whatever, sir. It—it was a mere whim that—"

"Don't lie to me. I ask you again why you gave a false name to the sergeant. Will you answer me?"

"You have had my answer. I can't tell you anything more. I shall have to leave you now, if you will excuse me."

As the young man spoke he rose from his chair, but Blake leaned over the table and forced him down. A light had dawned suddenly on his mind, a conviction that thrilled him to the heart. He believed that he had hit on the solution of the mystery.

"You have let somebody else take your place," he declared, "and go to the front in your name, and with your papers."

"What has put such an idea into your head?" faltered Jack Rokeby.

"Don't deny it. Own up to the truth."

"I suppose I will have to, Mr. Blake. There is somebody in the British Expeditionary Force in my name."

"And that person is my boy, Tinker?"

"Yes, it—it is."

"I thought so, Rokeby."

Sexton Blake leaned back in his chair, his features twitching. The memory of his futile search, of the anxious days and nights he had spent, had roused his indignation. He looked angrily at the young man, who was a picture of guilt and fear now that his secret had been dragged from him. He was ready to confess, and he did so in a low, tremulous voice, taking the blame on himself.

"I have no excuses to offer," he went on. "I should not have yielded, I know."

"Tinker must have pressed you very hard," said the detective.

"Yes, he did," Jack Rokeby admitted. "He was in trouble,

and I was sorry for him. He was afraid to go home because he had been robbed of the despatch."

"I should not have blamed him for that."

"So I told him. It was no use, though. He dreaded your anger, for one thing, and he was very keen on enlisting. He was determined to get to the front, and he begged me to let him take my place."

"By now, I suppose, he is somewhere in France with the Army Transport Corps."

"I have no doubt that he is. I have not heard from him since he left London for Avonmouth Docks."

"I presume that work the work in which he is engaged," said Blake, "will not be as dangerous as ordinary soldiering?"

"Not nearly, I should imagine," the young man answered. "He will be in charge of the supplies that are sent to the soldiers at the front."

"But transport trains are liable to be cut off by the enemy."

"That might happen, of course."

The detective nodded, and puffed at his cigar, blowing a cloud of smoke that masked his thoughtful, worried features. His anger had been appeased, and it was sorrow he felt now.

"I have been having a bad time of it," he said, after a pause. "I have been searching for Tinker high and low, making enquiries everywhere. You probably know how dear he is to me, Rokeby, so you can realise how desolate and lonely my chambers in Baker Street are without him."

"I am sure they are," Jack Rokeby assented. "I am more than sorry for you. I did a wrong thing, and I wish with all my heart that I had not."

"You thought it was for the best, no doubt."

"I did, Mr. Blake. I hope you will forgive me."

"Yes, I will. What has been done can't be undone, and I won't harbour any ill-feeling. As for Tinker, he will have to stay where he is, at least for the present."

"And what about my enlistment?" asked the young man. "I have told you how anxious I am to get to the front. It was impossible for me to go under my own name, so I was compelled to—"

"I will keep your secret, under the circumstances," Blake interrupted. "It can do no harm, as the motive for the deception was a good one. Go off to the war, and fight for your country. But don't seek to end your existence. Remember that your wife would have wished you to live. Think of her and keep up your courage."

"I will try, sir," was the low reply. "Really I will."

The waiter had brought the bill. Blake paid it, and then he and Jack Rokeby left the restaurant, and separated a few moments later in Whitehall. The young man went off to Scotland Yard to pass the medical officer; and Sexton Blake slowly retraced his steps across the Horse Guards Parade. Deeply attached to Tinker though he was, there was in his mind now a very slight tinge of resentment.

"The boy should not have kept me in suspense," he reflected. "He has made his bed, and I will let him lie on it."

THE FOURTH CHAPTER

Sexton Blake Consents to Go to the Front.

BLAKE WAS NOT used to a sedentary life, and the long hours in the booth on the Horse Guards Parade, seated at a desk, tired him more than active work could have done. He was glad to leave off at six o'clock. Having walked home, and let himself into the house, he met Mrs. Bardell in the hall, and was informed by her that visitors were waiting for him. He mounted the stairs, and entered his consulting-room, to find there two persons. The one was a gentleman of middle-age, tall and slim, with iron-grey hair and a military moustache; the other was a lady of perhaps thirty, simply but expensively dressed, with a very lovely face on which sorrow had stamped its mark.

Sir Francis Leeson, an influential official of the War Office, rose from his chair.

"Ah, here you are!" he said, as he shook hands with the detective.

"I am sorry to have kept you waiting," Blake replied.

"We have not had a long wait," Sir Francis answered. "We were told that you would probably be back soon after six. But let me introduce you to Mrs. Chumleigh, the wife of Colonel Chumleigh, of the Guards. It is on her behalf that I have called."

"I am very glad to make Mr. Blake's acquaintance," murmured the lady. "I have heard so much of him."

The detective bowed to her, and sat down on a couch. He looked expectantly at the Government official, who twisted his moustache, and glanced at his fair companion.

"Mrs. Chumleigh is in trouble," he said. "She has appealed to me, and I have concluded that you are the person to help her. It would be best, however, if she were to tell you the story herself."

"If it is in my power to assist her," Sexton Blake replied, "I will be glad to do so."

Mrs. Chumleigh lifted her veil with a daintily-gloved hand, disclosing to view a face that was even more beautiful than the detective had judged it to be.

"I will be as brief and clear as I can, Mr. Blake," she said, in a low, sweet voice. "It is not a very easy story to tell. I have been married for seven years, and up to a comparatively recent period there was no prospect of our having any children. Meanwhile, as I had a small fortune in my own right, my husband had made a will that was to a large extent in favour of his brother, who is in modest circumstances. It was the proper thing for him to do, and I fully approved of it.

"Two months ago I had a child—a little boy," she continued to explain. "My husband was delighted, and he at once announced his intention of making a new will, and bequeathing the bulk of his estate to his male heir. He wrote to his solicitor, directing him to draw one up, and giving him full instructions. I got him to write without delay, as I knew him to be a careless and thoughtless man where business interests were concerned. But, unfortunately, that new will was not signed. It must have been forgotten by my husband, who went abroad in a hurry, at short notice, soon after war was declared against Germany, and when his little son was only four or five days old."

Mrs. Chumleigh paused again, and her features twitched painfully, as if at the memory of her parting from the gallant soldier who had obeyed the call of duty.

"Though I was worried by my husband's neglect," she went on, "I did not then attach any great importance to it. My only income was nearly two thousand a year, and I managed to leave it all to my child. But an unexpected disaster happened. My fortune proved to have been badly invested. I learned recently, within the last week, that owing to the failure of several companies, I had lost three-fourths of my money, beyond all hope of recovery. It was a hard blow to me, naturally, because of the existing state of affairs. I did not know what to do at first. I consulted my friends, and on the advice of one of them I went to the War Office to-day, and had an interview with Sir Francis Leeson, who suggested that I should—"

"I was anxious to be of assistance," Sir Francis broke in, addressing the detective. "I did not see my way clear, however, to take any official action in the matter. So I have brought the lady to you, and I trust that you will go to the front on her behalf, find her husband, and have him put his name to the unsigned will in the presence of witnesses."

"That step is hardly necessary," said Blake. "I presume that the will in favour of the brother has been destroyed, and therefore, even should the new will remain unsigned, the greater part of Colonel Chumleigh's estate would, in the event of his death, pass by law to his wife and child."

"But the former will still exists," replied Sir Francis.

"Yes, that is the trouble," declared Mrs. Chumleigh. "The signed will is in the hands of the solicitor, Mr. Levenham, of Gray's Inn. And he has firmly refused to destroy it, since he had no instructions to do so."

"Ah, I see!" murmured the detective. "That puts a different complexion on the matter."

"It means everything," Mrs Chumleigh told him. "If my husband were to be killed before he had signed the new will, his brother would inherit most of the property, and my child have only seven or eight hundred a year instead of as many in thousands."

"Yes, I understand that. It is very unfortunate."

"It must not be. My husband intended otherwise. You can imagine how worried I am, how it preys on my mind."

"It is a case for you, Blake," said Sir Francis. "There is no reason why you should not take it. The War Office will give you every facility for getting to the front, and for going where you like. And it will not be difficult for you to find Colonel Chumleigh. He is with his regiment, and he has distinguished himself in several actions."

"He might make a new will out there, and send it home," the detective suggested.

"Yes, if he was aware of the situation. But it would be much easier for you to find him than it would be for a letter of instructions to reach him."

"I daresay you are right, Leeson."

There was silence for a few seconds, while Sexton Blake stared into vacancy. He was not keen on leaving London, where he had work to do.

Seeing that he was in doubt, Mrs. Chumleigh leaned towards him with outstretched arms.

"Please, please, Mr. Blake," she begged earnestly. "It will be such a kindness to me. And you will be doing a great service to my child. It is for his sake, for the sake of the little one who may be poor instead of rich when he grows up, that I implore you to find my husband, and have him put his name to the unsigned will. Oh, don't refuse. Surely you won't. Go at once, else it may be too late. It is with dread, with a sickening fear in my heart, that I pick up the newspaper each morning, and read the casualty-list. My dear Arthur is in the fighting-line, and he is so brave, so impetuous, that he must have risked his life again and again. You know what peril he is in, how gallantly the British officers have been leading their men into battle, under the terrible fire of the German guns. I may hear at any day that—that he has been—"

Mrs. Chumleigh's voice faltered and choked. She was overcome by emotion, and the tears that now streamed down her cheeks, the look of anguish on her lovely face, so deeply stirred Sexton Blake's sympathy, that he felt as if he could go to the end of the world for her. He rose and stepped over to her, and gently rested his hand on her quivering shoulder.

"Don't cry," he said. "It hurts me. I will do what you wish, and I will do it gladly."

"Oh, thank you!" was the fervent reply. "Thank you so much! How good you are!"

The pressure of two ruby lips on his fingers, and a smile that flashed through tears, like sunshine on an April shower, more than rewarded the detective for the sacrifice he had consented to make.

"I thought you would go," said Sir Francis Leeson, with a twinkle in his eye. "Beauty in distress always appealed to you, Blake. And now to discuss the details," he added. "They can soon be settled between us. No time should be wasted, as you are aware."

Sexton Blake was to meet Mrs. Chumleigh at eleven o'clock on the following morning at the solicitor's office in Gray's Inn, and take possession of the unsigned will. He was to proceed from there to the War Office, and receive from Sir Francis Leeson such official documents as he would require for freedom of movement at the front. He was then to start on his journey by the first boat or cruiser that should be available. All this having been arranged, Sir Francis and Mrs. Chumleigh took their departure. And when Blake had heard the lower door swing behind them, he dropped into his big chair, and filled and lit a pipe, and fell into a reverie. Visions grew amidst the blue reek of smoke that drifted around him. He was thinking of Tinker with mingled feelings.

"I may run across the lad out there," he reflected. "I hope I shall. Where ever he may be, whatever he may be doing, I am very sure that he is serving his country as well and nobly as any man in the field. I can't forget his behaviour of a month or two ago, when we were both under fire."

PART TWO

THE FIRST CHAPTER

Lorry v. Uhlans.

TAP! TAP! TAP!

Three men in khaki, one armed with a sword and a revolver, and the others with rifles, were standing by the big motor-lorry in the glare from the sun that was shining in the cloudless, blue sky of France. Two of the men were privates, Smith and Carter by name, and the third was a young officer, scarcely more than twenty years of age, with a handsome, boyish face that had acquired a measure of dignity during the past week or so.

When at home, off duty, Tommie Drake had been a typical nut, a bit of a swanker—a frequenter of West End restaurants, and a lounger in the bay-windows of a Piccadilly club. But Lieutenant Drake, of the Army Transport Corps, on active service, was a vastly different person. He had the right stuff in him, as the future was to prove. And it already had been, and was to be, the same with hundreds of other officers who had never before had any experience of actual fighting.

Tap! tap! tap!

There had been a procession of eight of the motor-lorries, all of them commandeered in London by the Government. They had been brought by boat to Havre, and up the Seine to Rouen, whence they had set forth on the previous evening, bound for the far front with supplies for the British Expeditionary Force. This morning something had gone wrong with one of them on a lonely road, and the others had gone ahead. On the disabled vehicle the inscription "Salmon's Brewery, Pimlico," was painted in large letters. The young officer glanced at it, and sighed. He passed a hand across his dry lips.

"Makes me feel thirsty and homesick every time I read it," he murmured. "I wouldn't mind so much if it was 'Whiteley's' or 'Peter Robinson,' or something of that sort. But a brewery! That's the limit."

For an hour the tapping had been going on at intervals. It now ceased, and a few seconds later there crawled from beneath the lorry a flushed and perspiring youth with several tools in his hand, and grease and dust on his uniform—and on his face as well. It is doubtful if Sexton Blake could have recognised him.

"It is all right, sir," he said, as he rose to his feet. "I've fixed things."

"Are you sure you have?" asked Lieutenant Drake.

"Yes, sir, I am," replied Tinker, otherwise known as Private Jack Rokeby. "I saw at first what was wrong, and knew I could repair it. It was only a matter of time."

"By Jove, you are a clever chap! Where did you pick it up?"

"From my guv'nor, sir, he taught me to be handy at all sorts of things."

"You were lucky to have such a guv'nor. He is still living, I hope?"

"Yes, sir, he is alive."

"What is he, Rokeby?"

"He—he is a—"

The lad paused, loth to give a truthful answer to the question. A wave of colour had tinged his cheeks, but it was not observed by Lieutenant Drake, who had on a sudden impulse taken a map from his pocket. He glanced at it, and tapped it with his finger.

"Here is where we are, at this spot," he said, the subject of Tinker's guv'nor already forgotten. "My instructions are clear, and we should get to the front by evening. And now to be off. We mustn't lose any more time."

The young officer mounted to the seat, and Tinker climbed up beside him and grasped the wheel, while the two other privates settled themselves comfortably at the back, on the tarpaulin that was stretched over the supplies. The motor-lorry throbbed and rattled, and moved ahead with increasing speed.

"A jolly fine day, isn't it?" murmured Lieutenant Drake. "What a pity there should be a war!"

Tinker did not reply. There had gripped him again, as had more than once been the case since his departure from Paddington several weeks ago, a feeling of homesickness. As he steered the big vehicle, sending it along the smooth, white road, mental pictures rose before his eyes—Sexton Blake sitting with bowed head in his favourite chair at Baker Street, Pedro stretched on the rug by the fireplace, and Mrs. Bardell fretting and fussing in the kitchen.

"I shouldn't have run away like that," thought the lad, with a lump in his throat. "It must be awfully rough for the guv'nor."

But vain were his regrets. What had been done could not be undone. He was a sworn soldier, pledged by solemn oath to serve his King and country, and not if he had wished could he have gone back to the master he had deserted. As for the deception he had been guilty of, that also caused him some qualms now and again. Worthy though his motive had been, it was unpleasant to remember that he had attained it by fraud, and to feel that an unforeseen mischance might lead to his exposure.

His spirits rose presently, and he took an interest in his surroundings. For hour after hour, swiftly and steadily, the lorry rumbled on through the fair, wooded land of France. In villages and at wayside cottages, people rushed to their doors and cheered the British uniforms. For many miles there was little or nothing to suggest the great war, since the enemy had not advanced into this region. Only the uncut corn and the absence of rustic labourers from the fields hinted at the black shadow which had killed industry and torn fathers and sons from their homes.

Towards the close of the day, however, as the sun was dipping to the horizon, ominous signs were to be observed. Here were the charred ruins of a farmhouse, and there the ashes of a hayrick; here a dead horse, and there the body of a peasant who had been shot. In a deserted village that was passed two more peasants lay dead.

"This must be the work of Uhlans," said Tinker.

"Yes, no doubt," the young officer assented. "Small parties of them have ranged round from the German lines."

"They're a cruel lot, sir, them 'Oolans," remarked Private Smith, who, like the lad, had been to the front before. "They don't spare anybody or anything."

Another ruined farmhouse was seen, and yet another. From beyond the range of hills on the left, miles distant, floated a dull, booming sound.

"That's artillery-fire," said Tinker, in a puzzled tone.

"It is, and no mistake," declared Private Carter. "But it strikes me we shouldn't be hearing it from that direction."

Lieutenant Drake looked uneasy. He produced his map again, and when he had studied it for a few moments, and gazed about him, an expression of dismay crept over his face.

"By Jove, we've done it!" he said. "We have blundered somehow or other."

"I hope not, sir," Tinker replied.

"Yes, I am sure we have. We are going wrong. We must have

been bearing towards a flank of the enemy's lines. It was my fault, Rokeby. I told you where and when to turn."

"Can you put me right, sir?"

"Not at once, I am afraid. We must wait until we get to a signpost. That will give me my bearings, with the aid of the map, and I shall then be able to—"

The clatter of hoofs swelling above the noise of the vehicle stifled the sentence on the young officer's lips. All glanced back, and beheld with consternation a troop of cavalry, to the number of a score, who had just emerged by a cross-road from a wooded ravine. Their gleaming helmets and lances, and their bluish-grey uniforms, left no doubt as to what they were.

"'Oolans!" exclaimed Private Smith. "By ginger, that's what they are!"

"Yes, a patrol of them," said Lieutenant Drake, as calmly as if he had been speaking to a body of Territorials, "and only a quarter of a mile behind us. We must give them the slip, Rokeby, and save our transport stuff. Keep straight ahead."

"Right you are, sir," Tinker answered. "I don't think we need worry about them. We are sure to shake them off, unless we have a breakdown."

He increased the speed of the lorry, and for a couple of miles it gained very slowly on the pursuing Uhlans, in spite of their strenuous efforts. Then a rugged, undulating stretch of road was encountered, and, as the heavy vehicle could not travel like a motor-car, and the horses of the German troopers were comparatively fresh, it was now their turn to gain. They thundered on and on, drawing nearer and nearer, until they were less than an eighth of a mile in the rear.

"This is getting a bit too thick, sir," said Tinker, as he looked over his shoulder. "They are overhauling us."

"Can't we go any faster?" asked the young officer.

"No, sir, not on such rough ground."

"Well, Rokeby, I'll be hanged if we surrender. We'll put up a fight, though we haven't a chance against such odds."

As the intervening space dwindled the race grew more exciting. The Uhlans began to fire their revolvers, and while bullets whistled dangerously close to Lieutenant Drake and his companions, and trees and hedges flew by in a dizzy blur, Smith and Carter discharged their rifles, taking steady aim at the enemy. A trooper reeled and fell. Two more saddles were emptied, and now there were three riderless steeds galloping amongst the others.

"We are nearly through with this stretch, sir," said Tinker. "I'll show you in a minute how we can go."

A little farther on the rugged road lost itself in a main highway that was broad and smooth, and here the lad increased the speed of the lorry to such an extent that the pursuers at once lost ground. For a mile the big vehicle thundered recklessly along, gradually gaining; and it had left the Uhlans a good half mile behind when a screaming, hissing sound was heard, and a shell dropped fifty yards ahead, in a field to the left. There was a tremendous explosion. A luckless cow was wiped out of existence, blown to bits, and a crater was torn in the ground.

"There is a battery yonder!" cried the young officer, pointing to a wreath of grey vapour on the crest of a hill that was a couple of miles away.

"They've as good as got our range, sir," said Private Smith. "They must have discovered us through glasses."

He was right. The German gunners had the range, and they were aware that it was a unit of a British transport-column they were firing at. The situation was extremely critical, but Lieutenant Drake and his companions pretended to make light of the danger, though they expected to be blown up at any minute.

The Uhlans were still holding doggedly to the chase. For another mile the motor-lorry dashed on, while shells burst on both sides of it, in front, and at the rear, sprinkling the occupants with dust. An abandoned village, partly in ruins, slid by in a blur. Beyond it was a stone bridge spanning a river that was two or three hundred yards in width, and on the farther side of the stream the continuation of the road wound amongst wooded hills.

"We'll be safe if we can get over there, sir," declared Tinker. "I'll let her rip," he added, as he increased the speed a little.

The vehicle slid out on the bridge, and ran half-way across. Then a shell dropped close in front of it, and the explosion that followed demolished a whole arch of the structure, leaving a yawning chasm. There was the crash of falling masonry, and a shower of metal splinters. Tinker was grazed by a fragment, which skimmed over his shoulder and hit Private Smith, who was instantly killed.

"By heavens, we are lost!" gasped the young officer.

THE SECOND CHAPTER

A Narrow Escape.

THERE WAS NO chance of averting the disaster. For a second or two, with horror in his eyes, the lad clung to the wheel; and as the lorry plunged into the ragged-edged gap he leapt wildly to one side, and shouted to Lieutenant Drake to do the same. So great was the speed of the vehicle that it turned a somersault, and fell bottom-up, pinning Private Carter beneath it.

For a short space Tinker's senses were in a dizzy whirl. He kicked and floundered in the cool water that had closed over him, and when at length he got a footing and rose above the surface, submerged to the waist, the mangled corpse of Private Smith had drifted past him, and the young officer was nowhere to be seen.

"My word, am I the only one left?" muttered the lad.

At that instant Lieutenant Drake's head bobbed up, within a yard or two. He too, had jumped, and had escaped without serious injury; but he was half-dazed from the shock, and in such pain that he could not stand. Tinker waded to him and grasped him by the arm as he was about to sink.

"Come, I'll help you," he bade. "There are only the two of us now."

"Only two?" panted the young officer.

"Yes, that's right," the lad replied. "Smith was killed, and poor Carter has been crushed under the lorry. Come along, before they fire at us again. We must get over to the woods."

"It's no use, Rokeby. I hit my knee on a boulder, and it has crippled me."

"Then you'll have to get on my back, sir. I'll carry you."

"No, don't worry about me. Save yourself, while you have the chance."

"I'll be hanged if I will, sir. I'm not going to leave you. Come, be quick."

"Very well, then," assented Lieutenant Drake. "You're a good sort, Rokeby, and I won't forget this."

As he spoke he threw his arms around the neck of the lad, who took hold of his ankles, and set forth on his perilous and difficult task. Fortunately the river was shallow, and he did not once get out of his depth. But there was imminent danger from the shells, which were still falling in the vicinity. At frequent intervals they dropped and burst, now striking and shattering the bridge, and now tossing up cascades of water. Tinker paid no heed to them. He waded on with his burden as fast as he could, across the stream, fighting against exhaustion. A shell exploded near to him, and the concussion hurled him off his feet. He scrambled up, spluttering and dripping, and took a fresh hold of the young officer's legs.

"It isn't much farther, sir," he gasped.

"Put me down, we shall both be killed," urged Lieutenant Drake. "Look after yourself."

"If I were to desert you, sir," was the plucky answer, "I should be ashamed to wear this uniform any longer."

By strenuous exertions Tinker kept his footing. His head was swimming, and his heart was pounding against his ribs; but he set his teeth hard, and splashed slowly on and on, while the deadly missiles burst to right and left of him. At last he safely reached the goal. He waded out of the river on to a narrow margin of sand and pebbles, and staggered deep in to the fringe of green cover at the base of the hills. Lieutenant Drake slid from the lad's back, and both fell sprawling on the grass, in the purple shade of the trees.

"I—I've done it, sir!" panted Tinker. "And now we'll have to rest a bit."

"By Jove, you're a hero!" vowed the young subaltern. "That's what you are, Rokeby, and no mistake."

They were too exhausted to talk. For some minutes they lay there in silence, while the lad recovered his strength, and Lieutenant Drake's knee, which had only been slightly bruised, ceased to pain him. They had lost the motor-lorry with its supplies for the troops, and their two comrades had been killed. But they accepted these disasters as a matter of course, as they had already become hardened to the gruesome side of war. They felt that they had done their duty, and their sole thought now was to get on to the front, and report at the headquarters of the Service Corps.

No shells were bursting. The German guns on the distant ridge had been muzzled, and the rippling of the stream was all that could be heard. Tinker presently rose from the grass and assisted his companion to his feet.

"We had better be moving, sir, if you are able," he said. "How is your knee?"

"It doesn't hurt," the young officer replied. "It is a bit stiff, but I can walk."

"Do you know which way to go?"

"I am afraid I don't, Rokeby. I have only a general idea of my bearings. We'll have to trust to luck to—"

"Hark, sir. What's that?"

"It sounds like hoofs. Those confounded Uhlans again, I'll bet."

A muffled noise was swelling in the direction from which Lieutenant Drake and the lad had come, and when they had crept to the edge of the cover and peered out, they saw on the opposite bank of the river the party of Prussian cavalry who had pursued them. They were riding down the slope, to one side of the ruined bridge, with the evident intention of fording the stream. The young subaltern drew his revolver from its holster and examined it.

"Those fellows are coming over to search for us," he said. "We must repulse them if we can."

"Right you are, sir," Tinker replied, as he unslung the rifle that was strapped to his back. "My word, we'll give it to them hot!"

The spirit of war was rioting in their blood, and they were naturally keen on avenging their slain comrades. They watched the Uhlans as they approached through the shallow water, and let them get half-way across; and then, from the shelter of the thickets, they opened a raking fire. The officer in command of the patrol was the first to drop, hit in the chest.

"I bagged him, sir," exclaimed the lad, as pleased as if he had brought down a rocketer in a pheasant-covert.

Two more troopers reeled from their saddles, a third and a fourth. Riderless horses were plunging, and bodies were drifting on the current. The Germans still spurred forward, falling fast, until the fusillade was too much for their courage. They swung their steeds around, and, in panic and confusion, with yells of rage, they rode back as quickly as they could.

"That's done it," said Tinker, as he fired a parting shot and emptied another saddle. "It's funny how one gets used to killing men, isn't it?"

"By Jove, it is," Lieutenant Drake replied. "I don't mind a bit. We'll be off now," he added. "Come along, Rokeby."

They turned away, and mounted the hill behind them, reaching the top of it as the sun was touching the horizon.

Though they were pretty sure that they were going in the direction of the British lines, they were still in a part of the country that was occupied by the enemy; for, in the course of an hour they saw from open ground, as they pressed on by the fading light, two distant patrols of Uhlans, and a marching body of German infantry.

"It would be hard luck if we were to be captured," said the young subaltern, in a gloomy tone.

"My word, it would be," Tinker answered. "There would be no more fighting for us, sir. We should be kept prisoners until the war was over."

The dusk of evening that was now shrouding them, and the chill, autumn air, depressed their spirits. They were traversing a wooded plateau, and presently they observed a winding footpath, which they followed for a quarter of a mile. It led them to a solitary cottage, in which a candle was burning; and there they found, huddled in a big chair, a grey-bearded old peasant, bent and toothless. They told him that they were English, and his stolid, wrinkled face brightened a little. He had heard of the gallant soldiers who had crossed the Channel to fight with the French. His wife was dead, he stated, and his only son had joined the colours.

"You are welcome, messieurs," he went on. "There is food in the closet, and a bottle of red wine. And you can sleep under my roof, if you wish."

"It is kind of you," Lieutenant Drake replied. "We are hungry and thirsty, and tired as well. But you can give us some directions, perhaps. How far are we from the village of Sarly?"

"It is a distance of twenty miles," mumbled the old man.

"And how do we get there?"

"There is a road yonder, at the bottom of the hill. If you will follow it to the left, monsieur, it will take you straight to Sarly. You cannot miss it."

The young officer nodded, and turned to Tinker.

"That's all right," he said in a tone of relief. "Sarly is on our way to the front, and close to the lines of the Allies. But we will spend the night here, Rokeby," he added. "We both need sleep and rest."

There was plenty for them to eat and drink. They joined the old Frenchman at supper, and listened to him while he chatted about his soldier son; and when he had retired to bed, in an adjoining room, they stretched themselves on the floor, and were soon wrapped in heavy slumber.

THE THIRD CHAPTER

A Daring Capture—and a Successful Escape.

TINKER AND HIS companion awoke to find the sun above the horizon, and streaming through the window. They rose, and glanced into the other room, where the old peasant was still asleep. There was food on the table, left from the evening meal, and they were about to sit down when a throbbing, grinding noise floated to their ears, from no great distance. It sounded familiar, and as they were listening to it, and looking at each other in perplexity, it ceased abruptly.

"I believe that was a big motor-vehicle of some kind," said Lieutenant Drake.

"I am sure it was," the lad assented, "and it has stopped not far off."

"Yes, yonder on the road."

"It may belong to a British or French transport-column, sir."

"Let us see, Rokeby. Come along. I would rather go without anything to eat than miss a chance of getting a lift to the front. We can take something with us, though."

Each thrust some bread and cheese into his pocket, and placed a couple of silver coins on the table, in payment for the hospitality they had received. Then they stole quietly from the cottage, and hastened through the woods, traversing a footpath which brought them very shortly to the crest of a steep hill. They paused here, and gazed down. Below them, running along the base of the hill, was one of the broad, white roads of France. A little to one side was a small, square building that was obviously an inn, since a signboard projected from it. And in front of the building, unattended, was a large motor-omnibus. The young subaltern took a pair of binoculars from their case, and put them to his eyes.

"No good," he declared. "That 'bus is from Berlin. It has the names of several of the streets on it."

"Then it must be carrying supplies to the German troops under Von Kluck," said Tinker.

"Yes, it is packed to the roof. And the soldiers in charge of it are no doubt having their breakfast at the inn."

"It is a fine chance for us, sir."

"The chance for us? What do you mean?"

"I have been thinking that we might steal the 'bus," replied the lad, "and drive it to the British lines in place of the one we lost."

"By Jove, that's an inspiration!" exclaimed Lieutenant Drake. "You have a clever head."

"Thank you, sir."

"But it is a tough problem, Rokeby. It is ten to one that we will both be shot if we try to carry off the 'bus."

"I am willing to risk it, sir, if you are."

"I am more than willing," said the young officer. "I shouldn't dream of missing such an opportunity. Won't our Tommies be pleased if we bring them a load of German sausages and beer? The worst of it is, though, that the 'bus will have to be turned the other way. The front of it is to the right, and Sarly lies to the—" He broke off, and began to descend the hill. "We will settle the details as we go down, Rokeby," he added. "I have an idea how the game can be played."

Talking as they went, they made their way to the bottom of the wooded slope by the path they had followed from the cottage, and emerged from the green cover within a dozen yards of the inn. For a few seconds they listened to boisterous voices, and the clatter of knives and forks; and then, with unfaltering courage, they glided forward.

"Be quick, Rokeby!" bade the plucky young subaltern, as they separated. "If they do for me tell them how it happened."

"I will, sir," Tinker replied.

With that he darted straight to the motor-'bus, and in a trice he was on the seat of it, clutching the wheel. He started the engine, and as the big vehicle rattled and moved, swerving across the road, the noise was heard inside of the inn, where five German soldiers and a corporal were at breakfast. Jumping up from the table, in alarm and bewilderment, they rushed to the open door, and stopped short. For outside, with his revolver in his hand and levelled, was the slim, khaki-clad figure of Lieutenant Drake.

"Get back, you vermin!" he cried.

At the same instant he fired, and at the first shot the corporal screeched like a stuck pig, and pitched to the floor with a bullet between his ribs. Crack!—crack, crack!—crack! Three more of the soldiers went down, one dead and the others wounded. During the brief interval that had elapsed Tinker had turned the motor-'bus around, in the direction of Sarly; and now, having disposed of four of the enemy, the young officer took to his heels, and clambered to the seat of the vehicle by the side of his companion.

"Hurrah! Here we go!" exclaimed the lad.

As the 'bus lumbered on, with increasing speed, the uninjured German dashed out of the inn, bellowing with fury. He threw his rifle to his shoulder, and fired several shots. But excitement spoilt his aim, and the bullets flew wide of the mark.

"Good-bye, Fritz!" shouted Lieutenant Drake, as he looked back and waved his hand. "Give my regards to Kaiser Bill!"

"And mine, too," chimed in Tinker. "Tell him we'll see him in Berlin one of these days."

Success had crowned the daring venture, and the young Britishers were in high spirits as they drove on in the bright sunshine, along the broad, smooth road which they had been told would lead to the lines of the Allies. In all likelihood they would have to pass through a zone of danger, but the thought of that did not trouble them now.

"The country ahead seems to be clear of the enemy," said the young officer, as he looked through his binoculars. "It won't be long, I imagine, until we meet some of our fellows. And then we will have to be jolly careful, or we may be shot."

"That's right," Tinker replied. "They will take us for Germans in disguise. Only hope they give us a chance to explain matters," he added, "instead of shooting first."

For some miles they traversed a region of deserted farms and cottages, many of them damaged by shell and flame. Then peril beset them, their uniforms betraying the fact that they were British. They were chased by two parties of Uhlans in succession, and twice fired at from the cover of wooded hills. But they ran the gauntlet unscathed, and left behind them the marauding bands of Germans. The morning wore by, and towards noon they were stopped by a patrol of French cavalry, who pointed their rifles at them. The story that they told, however, was readily believed by the officer in command.

"It is well," he said. "You can pass. On to Berlin, messieurs!" he added, with a laugh, pointing to the names on the vehicle.

Tinker and his companion enjoyed the joke, and repeated it more than once, as they thundered on their way. Again and again the motor-'bus, labelled "Friedrich-strasse" and "Rixdorf" was halted for a short time, and permitted to continue its journey.

"On to Berlin! On to Berlin!"

Jean Grapaud shouted the words in French, and Tommy Atkins bawled them with a Cockney accent. Laughter and jests rang loudly. It was an amusing incident, a ray of sunshine splitting the black cloud of war.

"On to Berlin!"

The cry rolled like a wave. Khaki uniforms grew more and more frequent, and at length, the motor-'bus having entered the British lines, Tinker brought it to a stop at a signal from an elderly officer, with a grey moustache, who just emerged from a cottage over which the Union Jack was floating. His horse, held by a military-servant, was waiting for him. He screwed a monocle into his eye, and stared at the two dusty, dishevelled figures on the driving-seat of the vehicle.

"What the deuce?" he ejaculated. "The Friedrich-strasse! So are you going to Berlin, eh?"

"We don't expect to get so far as that, sir," replied Lieutenant Drake. "At least, for the present. We belong to the Service Corps, and we are looking for Colonel Melton. I am to report to him."

"I am Colonel Melton," said the officer. "And you?"

"My name is Drake, sir."

"Ay, yes, you were in charge of a motor-lorry that has been reported missing. What happened to it?"

"Something went wrong with it, sir, and after we had got it repaired, it fell through a bridge that had been blown up by a shell."

"And what do you mean by waltzing into the lines with such a thing as this? Where did you get it?"

"We captured it from the Germans, and brought it with us instead of the lorry. I think it is packed with supplies."

"You captured it from the Germans?" Colonel Melton echoed in amazement. "The two of you?"

"That's right, sir," the young subaltern answered. "There were four of us when we left Rouen, but two of my men were killed."

He and Tinker had meanwhile descended from the 'bus. In simple, modest language they told the whole story to the colonel, who learned with increasing interest of the race with the Uhlans, and the plunge into the river, and the fight at the inn. He might not have believed the narrative, but for visible proof of it.

"That was fine!" he exclaimed. "You have done splendidly! By Jove, you fellows are made of the right stuff! I will give you some other kind of work to do next. There will be heavy fighting to-morrow, and you shall assist at the field-hospitals, or in transporting the wounded to the nearest point on the railway-line. I will not forget to mention you in my report to—"

He paused, his eyes glistening with admiration, and stepped to the rear-end of the motor-'bus. He opened the door, and nodded with satisfaction as he glanced within.

"Well done," he said. "Sausages, cold beer, pickles, and so forth. This will be a welcome change in rations. You had better have something to eat now," he added. "Go into the cottage and my orderly will attend to you. I will see you again."

With that Colonel Melton swung to the back of his horse, and rode away. And Tinker and the young officer entered the little dwelling, greatly pleased by the praise that had been bestowed upon them. They had safely reached the front, and they could count on being plunged into the thick of events, which was what they keenly desired.

"You are a jolly good sort, Rokeby," declared Lieutenant Drake, "and I hope we shall see a lot of each other."

THE FOURTH CHAPTER

Sexton Blake at the Front—Wounded!

ON THE FOLLOWING day, as Colonel Melton had predicted, heavy fighting began. During the morning the enemy fell back, and made a dogged stand on fresh ground; and the battle was still raging when, about the middle of the afternoon, Sexton Blake penetrated the rear of the British lines on a bicycle which he had purchased at Boulogne, and brought with him by rail.

He was going into danger, but that knowledge merely acted as a spur to his resolve, since the person for whom he had come to search must also be in peril. He was aware that Colonel Chumleigh was somewhere ahead of him, and he was determined to make every effort to find him, and that as soon as possible.

"If only I am not too late!" he reflected. "The list of casualties must have been piling up."

Now and again, as he advanced, he gave a thought to Tinker and wondered if he were dead or alive. He had with him the unsigned will, and also the documents that Sir Francis Leeson had given to him. These he was compelled to show frequently, as he made progress towards the front; and on one of these occasions, while his credentials were being examined, he observed the German motor-'bus, and heard the story that attached to it. His informant, however, was unable to tell him the names of the two young heroes.

"I did know, sir," he stated, "but I've forgotten. One was an officer and the other a private."

The tale had interested the detective, and it occurred to him, as he mounted his bicycle, that Tinker would have done the same in similar circumstances.

"Perhaps it was the lad," he said to himself. "He is with the Service Corps."

Nearer and nearer, louder and louder, rang the thunder of the artillery and the bursting of shells. Once in a while there could be seen, far-off, a red flash streaking the cloud of great vapour that masked the horizon. More and more frequent grew the signs of the battle, in all their ghastly reality. Here was a field-hospital, showing glimpses of surgeons with their sleeves rolled up; there wounded men hobbling to the rear, grumbling at their ill-luck. Here Red Cross bearers carrying motionless forms, and there a group of sullen prisoners under escort. To the right and left reinforcements were pressing forward—batteries of guns, regiments of infantry, and cavalry with fluttering pennons. And yet the actual fighting was still at a distance of several miles.

Sexton Blake went on and on, stopping to make inquiries, and now halted by a sharp word of command. And at length, soon after he had passed a chateau that was the headquarters of the staff, he dismounted from his machine on a knoll of high ground, and saluted a small party of officers who had checked their steeds here, and were holding an earnest discussion. One of them was General Trench, and he stared in surprise at the detective, with whom he was acquainted. Sexton Blake smiled, and again raised his hand to his cap.

"Good afternoon, sir," he said. "I am sorry to intrude on you at such a time."

"My dear Blake!" exclaimed the Chief of Staff. "How did you get here?"

"I have come on a matter of private business," the detective replied.

"And they allowed you to get so far as this? I cannot understand by what means you—"

"I have documents from Sir Francis Leeson, of the War Office."

"Indeed?" murmured General Trench. "Your business is official, then?"

"No, not exactly," Blake answered. "I am in search of Colonel Chumleigh of the Guards."

As he spoke he produced his papers, and while the general was looking over them he briefly and clearly explained the situation to him.

"I was told that I should have to obtain your consent," he concluded, "before I could get to the actual front."

"I can't give it to you," said General Trench, in a curt tone. "Colonel Chumleigh is close to the firing-line with his regiment. It is impossible for you to reach him, however. The risk would be too great."

"I am not in the least afraid," vowed the detective.

"I don't doubt that. It is a question of my duty. You should not be where you are now. As for going farther, that is not to be thought of."

"But the matter is urgent, sir. The more so because Colonel Chumleigh is in danger. It would be a serious thing for his child if he were to be killed before he had signed the will."

"It won't do, Blake. Really, it won't. You must go back and wait for a safer opportunity."

"I may never get one. You know that. I have been sent out here by the colonel's wife. Have pity on her, general, and grant my request."

"I ought not to. Your life is of more value than the will."

"Don't refuse, sir. You have the authority, and I am willing to take the chances."

Blake persisted, and in the end he prevailed on the commander, who reluctantly took a notebook from his pocket. He scribbled a few words on a leaf, and tore it out.

"Here you are," he said, with a shrug of the shoulders. "This will pass you anywhere. But I shall blame myself if you don't come back alive."

The detective thanked him, and leapt astride of his bicycle, and a moment later he was forgotten by General Trench, who was gazing through his glasses, and talking to his staff officers. Sexton Blake pedalled along as fast as he could. A mile slid behind him, and yet another, while the roar of the battle swelled louder in his ears. More than once he had to show the slip of paper that had been given to him, and that magic talisman sent him forward without question. He rode through a village from which the enemy had been driven that very morning, and here was evidence of desperate fighting at close quarters. Cottages were riddled with holes, and pools of blood had clotted on the grey cobblestones. Dead bodies, and helmets and weapons were scattered about in the winding street.

Just beyond the village the detective burst a tyre. He abandoned the useless machine, standing it against a hedge; and when he had walked for a short distance, and called in vain to a motor-scout who whizzed by him, he inquired for the Guards of a wounded soldier. Following the instructions that he received, he branched off to the left of the road, and traversed open ground that mounted to a belt of woods. The noise was now deafening, and the smell of powder was in his nostrils. Having entered the green cover, and gone for eight hundred yards or so, he was so near to the actual conflict that he found himself to be under fire.

"By Jove, this is getting warm!" he reflected. "But I must find

Colonel Chumleigh. I may never get another opportunity. I am afraid I am too late, as it is. The Guards have probably been engaged in the course of the day."

A purple haze, borne on the wind, had clouded the sun. The roar of the big guns had ceased, and there was an incessant rattling and spluttering of musketry. Bullets were flying overhead, whining and twanging, humming like bees. Leaves and twigs were falling, lopped off as if by a pruning-knife. A white furrow suddenly appeared on the brown trunk of a tree, and a leaden pellet hit a stone that was within a yard of Sexton Blake. He hastened on amongst the thickets, while the fire grew hotter and hotter, until at last he emerged from the woods on the edge of a plateau, and beheld so thrilling, terrifying a scene that he could scarcely believe it to be real.

He was at the very front now, and exposed to view. Above him drifted a reek of smoke. Not far beyond him the British troops were working machine-guns from their trenches, and solid masses of German infantry, in blue-grey uniforms, who were advancing to the attack, were being mowed down by the raking hail of lead. Off to one side, sheltered by a ridge, a squadron of Lancers were riding at a trot, in a blaze of cherry and gold and green, their guides leading the way.

Blake felt as if it was all a ghastly nightmare. Bullets whistled past his ears, and spat viciously at his feet, flinging up dust. Voices shouted to him, but he heard nothing. He stopped, plunged blindly on, and stopped again.

"By heavens, what an inferno!" he muttered. "I can't do it. To go any farther would be sheer, stark madness. I'll have to turn back, and try to get to shelter before—"

At that instant he was hit. A burning, stabbing twinge shot through him, and his senses whirled into oblivion as he was dashed violently to the ground. And there he lay motionless, like a huddled corpse, while the spitting fire of the machine-guns slackened, and the Lancers charged like a hurricane into the decimated ranks of the enemy, and steeped their pointed weapons in a bath of crimson.

THE FIFTH CHAPTER

A Dramatic Meeting—Bad News for Blake.

THE THUNDER OF the battle had ebbed to silence, and the night had fallen when Sexton Blake recovered consciousness. He had been picked up at sunset, and carried to a field-hospital at the rear. He was weak and dizzy, and he felt as if his limbs had been pounded with hammers. He was lying on a cot, under a blanket, with a bandage across his breast. He glanced around the big tent.

"This is strange," he thought. "I must be ill."

His mind was almost a blank at first. He observed the other patients, and the surgeons and Red Cross nurses moving to and fro, and the deal table littered with instruments and drugs. Presently the cloud passed from his brain, and he had just remembered his plunge into the hail of bullets, and the sharp pain that had bowled him over, when his wandering eyes rested on a slim, khaki-clad youth who was approaching him. He stared incredulously for a moment.

"Tinker!" he gasped. "Tinker!"

Blake raised himself on his elbow, then dropped back with a bitter little laugh. He was under a delusion, of course.

It could not be the lad who was coming towards him. His senses swam again for an interval of a few seconds, during which he imagined that he could feel the touch of a cool hand on his brow, and listened, as one might listen in a dream, to the sound of a familiar voice. The cloud passed. He looked up with a clear intellect, and now he knew that he had not been dreaming.

"Tinker!" he murmured. "So it is really you!"

"Yes, guv'nor," the lad replied. "I'm here right enough, in the flesh. But don't excite yourself. You have had a bad time of it, and you mustn't talk much."

Sexton Blake did not want to talk yet. There would be plenty of chances afterwards. He was content now to lie still and silent, with a bronzed hand resting on his own, and gaze into the face of the boy who was so dear to him; the boy to whom his thoughts had turned constantly, by day and night, at home and abroad, since they had been wrenched apart.

"Will you forgive me?" Tinker presently asked, in a low tone.

"Forgive you?" echoed Blake. "Yes, how can I help it? But—but you treated me very cruelly."

"I know I did, and I am sorry for it, in a way. There was a lot of misunderstanding on both sides. I was afraid you would be angry about the despatch, for one thing."

"I should not have been, my boy. It wasn't your fault that you were robbed."

"Well, it can't be helped. Here I am, serving my country, as I wished to do. It is fine, guv'nor. My word, I've been in some warm corners! By the way, you must be careful how you talk, and so must I, or I shall get into trouble. No one suspects who I am."

"But I know," said Blake, a grim smile twitching his mouth. "I shall have to call you Rokeby, I suppose, when there is anybody near."

"That's right," the lad answered, flushing hotly as he spoke. "How did you tumble to the game? Have you seen Jack?"

"Yes, I met him in London, and got the truth out of him. He has enlisted in an assumed name, since he dared not use his own, and he will probably be sent to the front before long. A nice mess you have made of it."

"I did wrong, I know. I was tempted. That is my only excuse. Don't be angry, guv'nor. And please don't force me to go back with you."

"It is not likely that I could take you back if I wanted to. For the present matters must remain as they are. If the deception were to be disclosed the results might be serious for you and for your friend."

"But you came out here to search for me, didn't you?" asked Tinker.

"No, I did not," Sexton Blake replied. "I came to the front on professional business, on behalf of a client. You shall hear all about it. Tell me first where I was hit. I feel as if there wasn't much wrong with me."

"There isn't, guv'nor, thank goodness! A German bullet struck you in the chest, and passed clean through the silver cigar-case I gave you last Christmas, and stuck in the muscles between your ribs. It was the shock that bowled you over. One of the surgeons dug the bullet out, and you will be on your feet in a day or so, as fit as ever."

"Did you find me, Tinker?"

"No; you were picked up by the Red Cross men. I was on duty here, and it gave me a fright when they brought you into the hospital. I believed at first that you were dead, and the thought that I might never have a chance to ask you to forgive me made me feel as if—as if—"

A lump rose in the lad's throat, and choked his voice. He turned his face to hide the tears that had filled his eyes.

"You—you know," he faltered.

"Yes, I know," Blake whispered tenderly.

For a little time they were silent. Then the detective told the story of Colonel Chumleigh's unsigned will, and when he had finished, Tinker modestly described the thrilling adventures that he had passed through since his departure from Rouen with the convoy of supplies. Sexton Blake looked at him in admiration.

"So you are one of the heroic fellows they told me about," he said. "I saw the German motor-'bus, and heard the story of its capture."

"It was dead easy," the lad declared. "Lieutenant Drake had all of the risk. My word, he did pepper the Germans."

"You are quite happy out here, I suppose," murmured Blake, with a sigh.

"More than happy. I have been in the thick of things, and I am not a bit afraid. I should hate to chuck it and go home."

"I could not take you back with me, much as I should like to. It would be a difficult matter to obtain your discharge."

"Don't try, guv'nor. It would make me look like a coward. I wish we could be together, though."

"That is impossible, my boy. I shall have to return when I have found Mrs. Chumleigh's husband, and got his signature to the will. I hope he is safe. He was somewhere at the front to-day."

"I don't know anything of him. All I can tell you is that a part of the Guards made a gallant attack on the—"

Tinker paused abruptly. He jumped up from the camp-stool on which he was sitting, and lifted his hand to his cap. General Trench had entered the big tent a few moments before, and now, after a brief conversation with a surgeon, he was coming straight to the detective's cot.

"Ah, here you are, Blake!" he said. "I warned you, but you wouldn't listen to me."

"I took the risk," Sexton Blake answered. "I insisted on going to the front, and I have only myself to blame."

"Well, I am glad it is no worse. They tell me that you are not seriously injured. You will have to stay in bed for several days, though."

"I sha'n't mind that, sir, if you will be so kind as to send Colonel Chumleigh to me."

"It is impossible. I am sorry to say that—"

"He has not been killed, I hope," the detective interrupted.

"No, it is not so bad as that," General Trench replied. "He is reported as missing."

"Ah, what a pity!"

"Yes, I am very sorry. The Guards swept into the German infantry last evening, cut them to ribbons, and rode back without any losses. They left Colonel Chumleigh behind them, however. He was seen to fall from his horse. But as he was not picked up afterwards, when our troops occupied the ground, it is certain that he was carried off the field by the enemy."

"He must be a prisoner, then!"

"I have no doubts that he is, Blake."

"And he has probably been wounded."

"If so it was a slight wound, else the Germans would have left him for our Red Cross men. At all events, you will have to abandon your purpose for the present."

The general nodded, promised to call again, and passed on to another bed. Tinker stiffly saluted, and sat down.

"What are you going to do about it, guv'nor?" he enquired.

"I don't know," answered Blake, who was keenly disappointed by the bad tidings. "This is most unfortunate. I think I shall remain at the front for a time, on the slim chance that the colonel may contrive to escape. But there is little or no likelihood of that. I am afraid he will remain a prisoner until the end of the war."

One of the surgeons now stepped forward, and, after taking Blake's temperature, he forbade further conversation. He gave a sleeping-draught to the detective, and sent Tinker away to assist the ambulance-bearers who were bringing in more wounded.

THE SIXTH CHAPTER

A Thrilling Flight—Brought Down.

"Hello, Rokeby! Hello, there!"

The lusty hail, ringing from one side, floated to Tinker's ears above the "chug-chug" of the motor-bicycle on which he was spinning along a road that was on the flank of the British lines.

"I say, Rokeby! Come here!"

The lad dismounted from his machine, and put it against a tree; and then, having squeezed through a gap in a hedge, he hastened across a field towards a small aeroplane by which half a dozen khaki-clad figures were standing. Five of them were privates, and the sixth, the lad recognised as he drew near, was Lieutenant Drake.

"I thought that was you, Rokeby," he said. "I haven't seen you for two or three days. What have you been doing?"

"Hospital work and despatch carrying," Tinker replied.

"Well, I've got a job that is more to my taste. I used to be a flyer at Hendon, so they have given me this aeroplane. It belongs to a member of the Royal Flying Corps who was killed the other day with his mate."

"You are in luck, sir. I envy you."

"I am going to make a reconnaissance over the enemy's lines. Would you like to come with me?"

"My word, wouldn't I? But dare you take me?"

"Yes, if you have nothing else to do."

"I haven't, sir. I have just delivered a despatch at the rear, and I'm off duty."

"That's all right, then. I will be ready shortly. But there will be some risk about it."

"I sha'n't mind that," vowed the lad.

"You may change your tune when Archibald pops at us," laughed Lieutenant Drake. "That is the name our chaps have given to one of the special guns that the Germans have ready for air-craft. I had a taste of him when I was up yesterday, and it was jolly unpleasant, I can tell you. Archibald is no joke."

"Were you in danger, sir?"

"Yes, for a time. But wait and see, Rokeby."

Tinker's eyes glistened. He had the greatest admiration for the plucky men of the Royal Flying Corps, and he was elated by the opportunity that had now been offered to him. He was not in the least afraid, though he knew that there would be considerable risk. The young officer examined the machine, and gave some instructions to his companions, then turned to the lad.

"By the way," he said, "what about that chap you were so chummy with in the field-hospital the night you and I were working there together? How is he getting on?"

"Finely," Tinker answered, his cheeks flushing as he spoke. "He will be discharged to-morrow."

"Somebody told me that he was Sexton Blake, the famous detective. I wonder if it is true?"

"Yes, that's quite right."

"How the deuce did you happen to know him, Rokeby?"

"He—he is a friend of my guv'nor," was the faltering reply.

"Oh, I see," murmured Lieutenant Drake, not noticing the lad's confusion. "Your guv'nor must be a pretty big pot, I should imagine. Come, jump up," he added. "We are ready to start now."

He mounted to the seat, Tinker following him, and they adjusted the straps. The engine was set in motion, as the aeroplane, released by the soldiers, slid along the ground, and rose from it as gracefully as a bird. It was a neat little machine, designed for scouting, with a speed capacity of more than ninety miles an hour. Up and up it went, soaring into the blue sky.

"I'm the pilot," said the young officer, "and you are the observer."

"I am afraid I am not much good at that," Tinker answered.

"You needn't be. I'll keep my eyes open and watch for any new position that the enemy may have taken."

"How far are we going, sir?"

"I don't know, Rokeby. It will depend on circumstances."

The lad was too interested to talk. It was not his first flight, by any means, but it was the first chance he had had of viewing the field of war from a flying-machine. He looked down enraptured, thrilled to the heart, without a trace of giddiness. There was no fighting to-day. The armies were resting after a prolonged struggle. The British lines were passed over, and then came the German lines, with glimpses of white tents, and moving figures, and batteries of guns. Here was a village, and there a farmhouse. The aeroplane swept steadily on for nine or ten miles, until at length it ran into a bank of clouds that muffled it like a grey blanket.

"My word, how cold it is!" said Tinker. "Not much fun about this."

"We have had enough of it," Lieutenant Drake replied, as he glanced at the instrument-board. "We will turn back now."

"You seem to be worried, sir. Nothing wrong, is there?"

"We are rather too low for safety. That's all, Rokeby."

"Then why not go higher?"

"Because we might lose our bearings amongst the clouds. We'll have to drop a little, and chance it."

The course of the machine was reversed, and presently it emerged at a lower altitude from the rolling vapours. And soon afterwards, when it had gone for two or three hundred yards, there was a muffled roar, followed by a spluttering report.

"They are firing at us!" exclaimed the lad, as he saw a puff of white smoke beneath him.

"That's Archibald," declared Lieutenant Drake. "I know the sound of him. They must have shifted the iron devil to a new position."

"They haven't got the range, sir, luckily for us."

"They may get it yet. That first shot was only a feeler."

A regular bombardment had begun. Other pieces of artillery of the same type as the familiar Archibald were belching forth shrapnel, which are shells that scatter around bullets when they explode. The young flying-men were in imminent peril, for the German gunners fired at them with better aim, and more rapidly, as they strove to mount out of harm's way. Shells burst close below them, and off to the right and left, spurting a rain of lead.

"By Jove, this is getting a bit hot!" said Tinker. "Look at the bullet-holes in the planes!"

"That was a narrow escape for me!" gasped the young officer, as the instrument-board dissolved in fragments. "Confound those chaps! They are learning to shoot! Don't be frightened, though."

"I'm not, sir. I'm afraid it is all up with us, though. They can't keep on missing, at this rate."

"We'll give them the slip, Rokeby. See if we don't."

The fusillade increased, and the shells kept pace with the

rising aeroplane, as many as eight of them exploding around it at one time. The pellets that they scattered hummed like angry bees. One of the instruments was struck and shattered, and finally, when a safe height had almost been reached, a bullet perforated the tank, and the petrol gushed out in a cascade.

"That's done it!" cried Lieutenant Drake. "They've crippled us!"

"What are we to do?" asked the lad, in a tone of dismay.

"There is only one thing for it. We shall have to go down."

"Into the midst of the Germans, sir?"

"Perhaps not, Rokeby. There is no hope of our getting clear of the enemy's lines, but we can travel for some distance yet, and we may be able to land at some spot where we will have a chance to escape."

The guns had been left behind, and they were silent now. The aeroplane slid on, at a rapid pace, while it gradually descended. It fluttered and dipped, swerved this way and that, like a wounded bird that can scarcely keep on the wing. At length a brisk, crackling noise was heard.

"They are German infantry," said Tinker, as he looked down. "They are firing from the trenches."

"That's all right," Lieutenant Drake replied, in a tone of contempt. "They can't hit us with their rifles."

At least a thousand shots were fired, and without effect. The volleying slackened, and ceased, and presently Tinker, who was still gazing into space, announced that the country immediately in front appeared to be free of the enemy.

"I hope it is," said the young officer, "for we can't go much farther. Only so we don't have a smash."

"There is a field ahead, beyond those woods," the lad answered. "Can you land there?"

"I think so. I'll have a try!"

"I doubt if you can do it, sir."

"I'll bet you I can, Rokeby. It will be out of the frying-pan into the fire, though, for I can see Uhlans on that hill a mile in front. We are still well within the German lines."

It was a gloomy prospect. Tinker watched with keen anxiety, and his companion set his teeth hard as he clung to the steering-wheel. The exhausted aeroplane glided on and on, with erratic movements, and it seemed at first that it must come to grief against the belt of timber. But it skimmed over the tops of the trees, dipped lower and lower, and at length fluttered lightly to earth in the middle of a field of trampled, uncut corn. The passengers loosed their straps and climbed down, and they had no more than done so when a company of German infantry burst from the strip of woods to the rear, where they had been hidden.

"By heavens, look at that!" exclaimed the lad. "Nearly a hundred of them! We must run for it!"

"Hold on!" bade Lieutenant Drake. "Let's give them a dose of lead first!"

Both were armed with revolvers. They aimed and fired, discharging a rapid volley that dropped three of the enemy; and then they swung round, and took to their heels, running as fast as they could towards another and larger tract of woods that was a couple of hundred yards beyond them. A hail of bullets whistled by them, but they were not touched. They dashed on through the tangled grain, with the clamour of the pursuing soldiers ringing in their ears, and dived safely into the green cover, where they bore to one side. For half a mile they continued their flight, winding amongst trees and undergrowth; and then they stopped, breathless and exhausted, and crawled into a thick copse of bushes. They were safe for the present. They lay here in concealment for nearly an hour, hearing occasionally the shouting of the Germans who were searching for them at a distance. And when all was quiet they crept from hiding and rose on their cramped limbs. The sun was low on the horizon, and the air was turning chill.

"Hard luck, isn't it?" muttered the young officer.

"It is the sort of thing one must expect, sir," replied Tinker. "That doesn't make it any easier, though. What a pity we had to abandon the aeroplane!"

"I am glad it is no worse. We have our freedom, and we may be able to get back to our own lines."

"I am afraid there isn't much chance of it, sir. The enemy will be on the alert for us."

"And we will be on the alert for them, Rokeby. I have a general sense of my bearings, and the darkness will be to our advantage. I believe we can slip through."

"I hope so. My guv'nor will be awfully worried if I don't get back to-night."

"Your guv'nor will be worried? What the deuce do you mean?"

"I—I was thinking of something else," stammered the lad.

"I thought you didn't know what you were talking about," said Lieutenant Drake, laughing as he spoke. "Come along!" he added. "We go this way."

It was a miserable ending to their daring flight. They set off with lagging steps, in low spirits, depressed by the fear that they would fall into the hands of the Germans, and be held in captivity until the war should be over. They knew that they were in a trap from which it would be extremely difficult to escape.

THE SEVENTH CHAPTER

The End of the Supply Chain.

THE YOUNG OFFICER may have had his bearings at the start, but he did not have them long. When night fell he and Tinker were still wandering in the woods, which were of much greater extent than they had supposed them to be, and it was not until a couple of hours later that they emerged on the edge of a grassy embankment, below which was a railway line. This signified nothing to them. They were utterly at fault. They might have been guided by the moon or by stars, but there was no moon, and the sky was overcast with heavy clouds.

"Where now, sir?" asked the lad.

"I'll be hanged if I know!" replied Lieutenant Drake, shrugging his shoulders. "We are tied up in a knot."

"It strikes me we have got to the rear of the enemy's position."

"I shouldn't wonder if we had. But what's that, Rokeby? Do you hear?"

"Yes, sir. It sounds like a train."

Tinker was right. There was a rumbling noise in the distance, and presently there appeared to the left, from round a curve, a glaring ball of fire. The fugitives stepped back into deep shadow, and watched the train as it rolled slowly by them. Two German soldiers were driving the engine. Next to that were a dozen trucks, loaded high above their tops, and covered with tarpaulins, and then came a dozen more trucks, with an armed soldier perched on the top of each. The last one stopped opposite to Lieutenant Drake and his companion, and they were on the point of retreating into the woods again, when a most daring scheme occurred to Tinker.

"It must be a convoy of supplies for the troops," he said.

"That's what it is, of course," the young officer assented. "I wish we could destroy the stuff, as compensation for our lost aeroplane."

"That's just what I've been thinking of doing, sir."

"The two of us? Don't be stupid, Rokeby."

"I am in earnest. It can be done, and without much risk."

"I should like to know how."

"I will tell you, sir."

And in a few words the lad explained what he had in mind to Lieutenant Drake, who listened with keen interest.

"My word, that's a ripping idea!" he declared. "You deserve a commission for suggesting it. What a blow it will be! There won't be much risk, as you say, and we can escape afterwards by jumping off."

"Shall we do it, then?" asked Tinker.

"Rather! I shouldn't dream of missing such a chance. But will we have time, Rokeby?"

"We won't if we stand here talking. Come along, sir! We must be jolly quick about it."

Rapidly and noiselessly they followed the verge of the embankment, keeping to the shadow of the front of the train. Then they crept down the slope, and darted along the line to the engine. The driver and stoker were armed with rifles, but they got no chance to use them. As the one made a grab for his weapon Tinker's revolver cracked at him, and he pitched forwards to the ground like a log, with a bullet in his heart. The next instant the other man fell dead, shot by Lieutenant Drake, who dragged the quivering body from the footplate, and swung up himself. The lad at once mounted to his side, and snatched the throttle. And when he had thrown it partly open, putting on considerable pressure of steam, he bade his companion take it.

"Keep your hand on it," he said. "That's all, sir. I'll do the rest—it won't take me long."

"Be careful," urged the young officer. "Don't let those other chaps pot you."

The engine had jumped like a thing of life, and was gathering speed with every second. The daring feat had been accomplished in almost less time than it takes to tell, and the soldiers on the trucks at the rear had not yet recovered from the surprise caused by the revolver shots, and by the sudden start as Tinker climbed over the coal tender and down to the narrow platform of the truck that was next to it. Having raised the tarpaulin, and disclosed to view a number of wooden cases that were packed in layers of straw, he whipped a matchbox from his pocket. In a trice he had scraped a vesta and ignited the straw. And then, chuckling with delight, he hastily clambered back over the tender and rejoined his companion on the footplate.

"All right, sir!" he exclaimed. "I've done it, and you'll see some fireworks that will beat the Crystal Palace show. And now to raise the wind," he added, as he seized the throttle and opened it wide. "Here goes for rush and tear, risk or no risk!"

The lad's shrewd calculations were verified. As the speed increased so did the fleet, humming rush of air, and the flames, fanned by this furious draft, spread with amazing celerity, leaping from truck to truck, and devouring the contents as if they had been in a furnace. Slanting tongues of fire writhed high in the air, sending up columns of smoke spangled with sparks, and above the strident roaring could be faintly heard the horrified clamour of the German soldiers as the scorching wave of heat compelled them to jump for their lives. They plunged right and left from the trucks, to be killed or maimed. It was not likely that a single one could have escaped uninjured.

"My word, you have done it!" declared Lieutenant Drake. "It's grand, Rokeby! What a clever head you've got!"

"Thank you, sir!" Tinker replied. "It wasn't a bad idea, was it?"

"But where are we going to?"

"I don't know any more than you do. We'll slow up presently and slip off, before we run into danger."

It was grand indeed, the spectacle of the laden goods waggons blazing to destruction amidst a crimson glare that made the surrounding country as light as day. On and on thundered the engine, rocking and swaying on the metals, with the train flaming behind it like the tale of a gigantic meteor. For a couple of miles woods and fields flashed by in a dizzy blur, and at length, as a curve was rounded, an encampment of German infantry appeared on open ground to one side.

"Duck your head, sir!" cried the lad.

The soldiers shouted, and ran to and fro, and discharged their rifles. But not a bullet touched the daring young Britishers. They safely passed the zone of peril, and travelled on like the wind for another mile, shut in by woods again.

"We have had about enough of this," said Lieutenant Drake. "Don't you think so? Suppose we—"

His voice was drowned by a tremendous explosion that shook the earth, and nearly flung the engine off the metals. There was a blinding, dazzling glare. Trees and boulders were rent asunder, and a shower of debris pattered like hailstones.

"What the deuce was that?" gasped the young officer. "By Jove, only half of the train is left!"

"There must have been ammunition in one or two of the trucks at the back," Tinker replied. "That would account for the explosion. It's a jolly good thing for us that it wasn't at the front, else we should have been blown to bits."

As he spoke he reversed the throttle, and when the speed had decreased to something like twelve miles an hour he and his companion swung down from the footplate. They hurried up an embankment at the side of the line, and stood there while the charred and blazing trucks rattled by them, and then, none the worse for their thrilling adventure, they dived into a plantation, and were shrouded in the black shadow of the foliage.

"Good business, sir, wasn't it?" said the lad, when they had threaded the timber for three or four minutes. "We must have destroyed a big lot of supplies and ammunition. It may be a serious matter for the Germans."

"I imagine that it will be," Lieutenant Drake replied. "And what's more, the runaway train may cause a disaster before the steam is exhausted. I wish we had thought of heaping the furnace with coal."

He had barely spoken when there was heard, at a distance of several miles, a heavy, thunderous crash. The young officer's prediction had already been verified. The train had come to grief in its mad dash, and it could hardly be doubted that it had collided with and wrecked another train, perhaps one filled with fresh soldiers for the front.

"There's been a smash!" exclaimed Tinker. "Another whack at the enemy. My word, if they catch us after all we've done! I can imagine what the Berlin newspapers will say. Panic and destruction caused by two desperate villains from General French's contemptible little army! The Kaiser tears up another British uniform! More reserves to be mobilised at once! The bath-chair brigade to be called to the colours, and a kindergarten battalion to be formed!"

Thus he rattled on, in jesting vein, while his companion walked silently by his side. Lieutenant Drake had fallen into low spirits, and the lad presently shared his despondency. It was not a cheerful prospect for them. They had not the remotest idea in which direction they were going. That they were well within the German lines was a certainty, and there was little or no likelihood of their being able to elude capture and get back to their own lines.

"There isn't so much risk by night," the young subaltern said at length, "but it will be different in the morning. We'll be caught then."

"Not if we hide through the day," Tinker answered. "That's what we shall have to do."

It took them an hour to traverse the woods, and when they emerged from them it was at the edge of a wide, straight road. Bearing aimlessly to the left, they soon came to an open gateway and saw beyond it the vague shape of a large building that was obviously a chateau from its towers. Hunger, and the need of rest, bade them venture up the winding drive to the dwelling, which was dark and silent. They found the door lying flat, battered from lock and hinges, and when they had stepped over it Lieutenant Drake struck a match and led the way into a reception-room, where he perceived a candle on a table and set it alight. The luxurious apartment was in a state of disorder— and worse. No little damage had been wantonly done. Couches had been ripped open with swords, antique cabinets had been smashed, and paintings had been torn from the walls and trampled under heel.

"The Huns have been here," said the lad, in a tone of disgust.

"Rather!" his companion assented. "They must have been looking for hidden valuables."

"I don't suppose any more of them will come—at least, not to-night. Shall we have a rest, sir?"

"Yes, we may as well. We will be as safe here as anywhere for an hour or so. But what about something to eat, Rokeby?"

"That's what I've been thinking of. Perhaps we can find something."

"We'll see. Come along!"

The search was fruitless. What food had been left behind by the occupants of the chateau had been devoured by the Germans, as was shown by a table in the kitchen that was littered with dishes and bottles. Having scoured the lower part of the premises, without finding even a crust of bread, Tinker and the young officer mounted to the next floor, and here discovered a bed-chamber that had been scarcely molested by the vandals. The big, four-poster bed, with its clean, white coverlet, invited to repose.

"I can't resist that," said Lieutenant Drake. "It reminds me of home."

Tinker grinningly agreed, and a few moments later Drake was sleeping soundly, with the lad snoring by his side.

THE EIGHTH CHAPTER

The Escape from the Chateau.

THE DRUMMING PATTER of rain against the windows, and the gurgle of water pouring from a spout, awoke Tinker in the early dawn of the morning. For a little time he lay in drowsy contentment, and he was on the point of dropping off to sleep again when he heard a crackling noise and a sound of voices. The young officer was also awake now, and listening.

"I believe there are Germans below," he whispered, as he raised his head from the pillow.

"There must be," the lad replied. "Only hope they don't come up here."

"They are pretty sure to come, Rokeby. We had better clear out at once."

"If we can, sir. It will have to be by the back of the house."

From the sounds, the invaders were in the reception-room, which was at the front of the chateau, and directly under the bed chamber. Tinker and his companion noiselessly rose from the bed, in which they had slept fully dressed, and as quietly they stole from the room. They took it for granted that there was a rear staircase, and, doubtless, there was one. But their efforts to find it were of no avail, probably because they encountered one or two locked doors which they dared not try to break open. They wandered from room to room, from corridor to corridor; and in the end, fearing that they were in a tight trap, they retraced their steps to the front-stairs. They stood here in hesitation for a minute, listening to confused voices below.

"Come, here goes for it," bade Lieutenant Drake, in a low tone. "If they get a glimpse of us we will make a dash."

As stealthily as cats, with their nerves on edge, they descended the staircase to the hall, and stopped there. To their left, within a couple of yards, was the open doorway of the reception-room; and almost immediately opposite to them on the other side was a deep alcove, partially screened by a drapery, in which was a figure in armour.

"It is all right, sir," Tinker murmured. "We won't have to to go by them. I don't think there is anybody at the back. We can escape that way, and—"

He paused abruptly. A sentinel, with a rifle on his shoulder, had just strolled into view at the open front of the hall, on the terrace beyond the shattered door. At once, on the impulse of the moment, the young subaltern grasped the lad by the arm, and whipped him quickly over to the alcove and into it.

"By Jove, that was a narrow squeak!" he said under his breath, as he stretched the drapery to its full length. "I thought it was all up with us, Rokeby."

They had not been perceived by the sentry. They were now in a safe shelter, hidden from observation; and when they had recovered from their brief fright they peered from a crevice of the curtain, and found that they could see distinctly into the reception-room across from them. It was a pathetic and interesting sight that they beheld. At the rear of the large apartment, huddled in a group, were nearly a score of wretched-looking prisoners, in wet and muddy uniforms. All were French soldiers with one exception, and that was an elderly officer in khaki, with an iron-grey moustache, who was clearly a Britisher. His bearing was haughty and defiant, but there was an expression of melancholy on his bronzed features. Five Germans, wearing cloaks and helmets, were in charge of the captives. One of them was blowing at a fire that had been started in the grate, and another was breaking a chair for fuel. The other three were standing together, talking and joking as they leaned on their rifles, and puffed at porcelain pipes with long, curved stems.

"Poor fellows!" breathed Tinker. "How sad they look!"

"I don't wonder," Lieutenant Drake whispered, "since they are going to be kept in confinement somewhere in Germany until the end of the war."

"That British officer is a colonel, isn't he?"

"Yes, and I know his name. He is Colonel Chumleigh of the Guards."

"Chumleigh? Is—is he really?"

"That's right. He was reported missing the other day."

"It was supposed that he had been killed," said the lad.

"He couldn't have been," Lieutenant Drake replied. "I know him right enough, Rokeby. He has been wounded, though," he added, as the officer pushed his cap back from his brow with a weary gesture, and disclosed a bandage that was tied around his head.

A humming, throbbing noise was now heard. A motor-vehicle of some kind had turned in at the gate of the chateau, and presently a handsome car slid up the drive and stopped. From the alcove Tinker and the young subaltern could see it clearly. It contained two German officers, one of whom remained in the car, while the other sprang from it and entered the house. He paused on the threshold of the reception-room, and took in the scene at a glance.

327

"Ah, Keller, you here?" he said in surprise, addressing a sergeant who was in charge of the soldiers within. "I thought your battalion was at Antwerp."

"We were detached from it, some of us," the man answered, lifting his hand in salute. "We have been guarding prisoners, and we are taking this lot south. It was raining so hard that we stopped here for breakfast."

"Have you seen or heard anything of those two British ruffians who are at large in this part of the country?"

"I have not, Captain Roth. What have they done?"

"They have been raising the very devil, and if they should be caught they are to be shot at once. They were brought down in an aeroplane last evening, but they made their escape unhurt; and subsequently they set fire to a train loaded with ammunition and supplies, and started it on a dash to destruction. Part of it was blown up by the explosion of the ammunition, and the engine and the other trucks ran into a troop-train and caused much loss of life. Major Vierke and I are searching for these mad Britishers, whose footprints were traced in this direction from the railway-line."

"We have seen nothing of them," said the sergeant.

"I thought they might have taken shelter here," Captain Roth replied. "They can't be far off, at all events."

"They are not in the chateau. I had a look about."

"Well, you must assist me. Leave two of your men with the prisoners, and bring the other two along. The major and I will accompany you, and we will scour the woods for the ruffians, who are probably lying asleep somewhere in the thickets."

"Very good, herr-captain."

The order was promptly obeyed. Sergeant Keller and two of his four men departed from the dwelling with Captain Roth. The officer who had been waiting in the car joined them, and they all set off towards the plantation that was at the rear of the chateau.

Lieutenant Drake and the lad had overheard the conversation, and while listening to it Tinker had been thinking of the interesting fact that he had learned. He was very anxious to rescue the captive colonel, and yet he was loth to confide in his companion, lest by some slip of the tongue he should draw suspicion on himself, and perhaps be forced to admit the imposture of which he had been guilty. A daring idea occurred to him now, however, when the little party of Germans had disappeared around the corner of the house. And he also felt that he could offer a truthful explanation which would satisfy the young subaltern.

"Do you remember speaking to me of Sexton Blake, the detective?" he enquired.

"Yes," Lieutenant Drake answered. "What of it?"

"I mentioned him," said the lad, "because he came to the front for the purpose of finding Colonel Chumleigh. He wants him to sign an important paper of some kind about money."

"That's rather curious. How do you know?"

"Mr. Blake told me, when he was in hospital. And there's the colonel within a few yards of us."

"He might be in Berlin for all the chance the detective will have of getting his signature to the paper."

"But we may be able to set him free, sir, and the others as well."

"What the deuce is in your head now, Rokeby?"

"I'll tell you, sir. Why not tackle those two guards and polish them off? It will be quite easy. The Frenchies can look after themselves then, and you and I will bolt in the motor-car with Colonel Chumleigh."

"By Jove, that's fine. I'm with you."

"And if we put on their cloaks and helmets we can pass for Germans, which will help us to get through to our lines."

"Better still, Rokeby. We'll do it, risk or no risk. You ought to be a detective yourself, with the clever brain you've got."

This chance remark brought a smile to Tinker's lips. He and the young officer held a brief discussion, and then, steeling their hearts for the ruthless deed that was justified by the grim necessities of war, they whipped out from the alcove with drawn revolvers, and dashed across the hall and into the reception-room.

"Mein himmel, the mad Britishers!" gasped one of the German soldiers. "They are armed, Fritz! Be quick, or they will—"

The lad's weapon cracked at him, and the ball struck him in the throat, silencing him forever. He pitched to the floor gurgling horribly; and, as the other German threw his rifle to his shoulder, and aimed at Lieutenant Drake, the latter shot him through the heart, and he fell dead on the body of his comrade. It had to be done. A soldier's trade is to kill.

"You are free, my good fellows," the young subaltern said to the startled French prisoners. "See to yourselves. I wish you luck. You will come with us, sir," he added, turning to Colonel Chumleigh. "We are going to escape in the car."

The French soldiers, exulting in their liberty, hastened from the room and fled to the rear. Tinker and Lieutenant Drake snatched the cloaks and helmets from the dead Germans and put them on; then ran out of the chateau at the front, followed by the colonel. He sprang into the big car with the young subaltern, and, when Tinker had started the engine he leapt to the driving-seat, and clutched the wheel.

"Hurrah, we're off!" he exclaimed.

The vehicle swung round and rattled down the gravelled drive to the open gateway, where, at random, the lad swerved it to the left. A straight, smooth road stretched ahead, entirely deserted as far as the eye could reach. From the woods behind the dwelling, at a considerable distance, floated the faint, shouting voices of Captain Roth and his companions, who had heard the pistol-shots. The rain had ceased, but the sky was overcast with heavy clouds. Though the sun was probably above the horizon by now there was no visible glimmer of it that might have served to guide the fugitives.

"We want to go towards our lines, sir," Tinker said to the colonel. "Do you know the direction?"

"No, I don't," the elderly officer replied. "I have no idea of my bearings."

"Neither have I," observed Lieutenant Drake. "We'll have to trust to luck."

The lad remained silent. He did not intend to speak one word to the rescued prisoner, as yet, concerning the errand that had brought Sexton Blake to the front. He sent the car swiftly on, while the young subaltern related to Colonel Chumleigh, in simple and modest language, the whole story of what he and Private Rokeby had done since their descent in the aeroplane. It amazed the colonel, and caused him some anxiety.

"It will go hard with both of you if you are caught," he said when the narrative had been finished.

THE NINTH CHAPTER

The End of the Car.

THE WOUND THAT Colonel Chumleigh had received was of a trifling nature, and it had nearly healed. As he had expected to be imprisoned in Germany until the end of the war, the first sensations of freedom were as stimulating to him as a draught of champagne. But his elation did not last long. His spirits soon sank again, and the apprehensions that he felt were shared by his companions. With Lieutenant Drake and the lad disguised as Germans, and the colonel in the role of their prisoner, they mighty elude suspicion for an indefinite period, no matter whom they might meet. But it was remotely possible that they would be allowed to pass out of the German lines under such circumstances. Moreover, there was the practical certainty that the field-telegraph would flash messages far and wide giving a description of them, and bidding a watch be kept.

Presently, however, they had one difficulty the less to contend with. Colonel Chumleigh had made a careful study of a map of the area of war, and when several miles had been covered he got his bearings accurately from a signpost, and bade Tinker turn into a road to the right, stating that it would lead through the enemy's lines at a point no great distance from the front of the Allies.

"A bold dash may carry us out," he continued. "I would face any risk rather than be caught."

"It will have to be soon, sir, or not at all," the young subaltern replied. "That German officer will know that we have stolen his car, and he will see that the dead soldiers have been robbed of their cloaks and helmets."

The next couple of hours were fraught with thrills and excitement. The faint roar of artillery could be heard in different directions, and bodies of troops were in motion. The fugitives met a force of Uhlans, who spurred right and left to let them go by. They saluted a convoy of wounded crawling to the rear, and passed a regiment of Bavarians and one of Westphalians. But no attention was paid to them. They held to their course unmolested, clinging to the hope of ultimate freedom, until the middle of the morning; and then, swinging round a curve, they found themselves within a hundred yards or so of a railway station that was occupied by a detachment of Wurtemburg infantry.

Owing to the noise of a train that had just left the station, the approach of the motor-car had not been heard. As soon as it appeared an officer ran into the road waving his sword, and some of the soldiers hastily shut the gate that protected the level crossing.

"That's done it!" exclaimed Tinker. "They know who we are. They have had a message!"

"Don't stop!" bade Lieutenant Drake. "Let her rip! full steam ahead, Rokeby!"

The lad set his teeth, and bent low, his hands glued to the wheel, and his eyes measuring the chances. There was a fleet, dizzy rush, a chorus of shouts, the crack of a rifle. A convulsive leap saved the officer from being pulverised, and the next instant there was a crash that rent the gate to splinters, and hurled fragments of wood and metal in the air. The car did not capsize, nor was it crippled by the impact. It swerved a trifle, but Tinker kept control of it, and sent it scudding over the line up a hilly road beyond. In the rear the rifles spluttered, and a hail of lead was poured after the daring fugitives, not one of whom was so much as grazed by a bullet. They safely topped the rising ground, and dipped down into a valley that was clear of Germans. By reckless, dare-devil courage, at imminent peril of their lives, they had broken from the trap that had been set for them.

"A nasty smack in the eye for the Huns!" chuckled Lieutenant Drake.

"That was well done, my brave fellow!" Colonel Chumleigh said to the lad. "I shall bear you in mind."

"Thank you, sir," replied Tinker. "But we are not out of the woods yet," he added to himself, "and it is about a thousand to one that we don't get out at all."

The valley was left behind. The big car topped another crest of high ground and sped down a slope which led to an arched bridge, shaped like the back of a camel, that spanned a deep, swift little river which was some hundreds of yards in width.

"There are wooded hills over yonder," said the colonel. "Perhaps it would be better for us to take shelter there, instead of—"

"More trouble, sir!" Lieutenant Drake interrupted.

There was a blaze of silver across the bridge, and above the hump of it there rose to view a wall of plunging hoofs and tilted lances, helmets, and grey cloaks, and bronzed faces.

"My word, they're Uhlans!" said Tinker.

"There will be no getting through them," said Colonel Chumleigh. "We shall have to—"

"Hold tight, sir!" the lad broke in.

And as he spoke he gave the wheel a twist, and drove slant-wise down a grassy embankment that was at one side of the road. At the bottom of it was a hedge. The car tore a gap in this, and a few seconds later it was rattling along a narrow stretch of hard soil and gravel, with the reedy margin of the river on the left, and on the right a field of uncut corn that had been levelled by the wind.

"Go it, Rokeby!" urged the young subaltern.

The Uhlans had checked their steeds on the bridge, and drawn the revolvers that they carried. They opened fire, and the fugitives heard the whistling of lead, like angry hornets buzzing at their ears, as they went jolting and swaying on for a short distance. They kept ducking their heads, expecting every instant to be hit. Crack!—crack, crack!—crack, crack! A bullet punctured a tyre, and there was a muffled explosion.

"We are done for now!" exclaimed Tinker.

The car jumped, and skidded to the left. It lunged off the hard track, and in the twinkling of an eye it had turned half over amongst the reeds, and pitched the occupants into the water, which was fortunately shallow. In a trice they were on their feet, submerged to the knees.

"Look!" cried the lad. "There's a chance for us!"

Within a dozen yards, as luck would have it, was a small boat that was tied to a stump, and contained a pair of oars. Tinker and his companions waded to it as fast as they could, and scrambled in. They were still exposed to the fusillade from the bridge. Lieutenant Drake snapped the mooring-rope by a jerk, and the lad, dropping to the middle seat, hastily shipped the oars, and bent to them lustily. A bullet split the blade of one, but by then the little craft had gained some impetus, and was gliding towards the middle of the deep and rapid stream.

"Lie down!" bade the young officer. "Be quick!"

Tinker let go of the other oar, and threw himself flat on

the bottom of the boat. Lieutenant Drake did the same, and the colonel was about to follow their example when he felt a burning twinge of pain. He reeled, and tumbled limply on top of his companions.

"Have they hit you, sir?" asked the lad.

There was no reply. For a few moments the shouts of the Uhlans mingled with the crackling of their revolvers. Bullets chipped splinters from the drifting craft, and spat viciously on the surface of the water, tossing up tiny jets of spray. And then, of a sudden, the firing ceased entirely. The swift current had swept the boat around a curve of the river, and a fringe of trees and bushes that lined the one shore concealed it from the view of the Germans on the bridge. The fugitives were safe for the present, floating on towards wooded hills that dropped to both banks of the stream. Rain had begun to pour again, and a grey mist was darkening the air. Tinker and the young subaltern had not been even scratched but Colonel Chumleigh lay motionless, with closed eyes, bleeding from a wound in the shoulder.

PART THREE

THE FIRST CHAPTER

In Pursuit of the Train.

A MOTOR-OMNIBUS FROM London, which had been commandeered for transport purposes, stopped on a road that was at the rear of the British lines along the battlefield of the Aisne.

"Here you are, my lad," said the driver of the vehicle to a companion who was seated at his side. "This is the place you want."

A sturdy youth, in a khaki uniform that was torn and soiled, descended slowly and stiffly to the ground. The omnibus rumbled on its way, and as the youth stepped towards a mess-tent, which had been pitched a little to one side of the road, two men emerged from it, smoking cigars. One was Sexton Blake, and the other was a friend of his, Major Wilson by name. At the sight of the slim figure in khaki a glad, joyous light leapt to the detective's eyes. The word "Tinker" was on the tip of his tongue, but he promptly repressed it, and by a hard effort he concealed his emotion as he hastened to meet the lad, and gripped his hand.

"Rokeby!" he exclaimed in a tremulous voice. "This is a surprise! How are you?"

"All right, sir," quietly replied Tinker, who was as deeply moved, and was under as severe a strain.

They looked straight at each other for a moment, in silence that was more eloquent than speech. The officer had joined them, and caution was necessary.

"I thought it was all over with you," said Sexton Blake. "You and Lieutenant Drake have been given up for lost. Has he too escaped?"

"Yes, sir, he has," the lad answered. "He has gone to report himself. We have had more than one narrow squeak. We have been amongst the Germans, but we got away from them in the end, and we brought Colonel Chumleigh out of the Guards with us. We found him a prisoner at a French chateau."

"And you rescued him?" Blake cried eagerly. "That is good news!"

"Where is he now?" asked Major Wilson.

"He is in a field-hospital at the village of Santenay, about twenty miles from here," Tinker replied.

"Is he wounded or ill?"

"He is wounded, sir, but not very seriously. A bullet hit him in the shoulder."

"You and Lieutenant Drake appear to have had some interesting experiences. Let me hear the whole story."

Tinker told it, and as modestly as he could, yet with a sparkling in his eyes that marked the elation he could not entirely conceal. He began the narrative with the descent of the crippled aeroplane within the enemy's lines, and carried it on, describing the burning of the supply-train, and the adventure at the chateau, and the crash through the railway barrier, to the point when he and his companions had escaped in the boat, under a hot fire from the Uhlans on the bridge after the capsizing of their car.

"Colonel Chumleigh was the only one of us who was hit,"

he continued. "We soon drifted round a curve of the river, and then we were safe. The current was swift and we floated on for miles and miles, and came in the evening to the lines of the Allies near Santenay. Meanwhile, we had bandaged the colonel's wound as best we could. He was taken to a field hospital, and he was resting easy when we saw him there this morning. We walked back along the lines part of the way, until we fell in with a motor-'bus that gave us a lift. Lieutenant Drake left me, and I came on to find Mr. Blake. I made inquiries for you, sir," he added, addressing the detective, "and I was sent here. I thought you would be glad to know that Colonel Chumleigh had been rescued."

The lad paused, and stood at attention. Sexton Blake and the officer had listened quietly to the thrilling tale, and when it was finished their faces were glowing with admiration. They had heard of the destruction of the German supply-train. A report of it had reached the Allies.

"That was fine work," was Major Wilson's comment. "You are a credit to Britain, my brave fellow. Such deeds ought to live in history. Don't you think so, Blake?"

The detective nodded. He dared not trust himself to speak. So intense was his pride, so deeply had his emotions been stirred that he was strongly tempted to disclose the fact that this young hero was his own boy, the assistant that he had trained from childhood. But he checked the impulse, which might have led to unpleasant consequences. Tinker guessed what was passing in his master's mind, and a lump welled up in his throat.

"Yes, you have done splendidly," declared the major.

"Thank you, sir!" the lad murmured.

He made no move to depart, foreseeing what was likely to result from the information he had brought. And he was not to be disappointed. Major Wilson turned to Blake, of whose errand to the front he had full knowledge.

"I am heartily glad that you will have an opportunity of transacting your business with the colonel," he said. "No doubt you would like to go to him at once."

"Yes, I should," Sexton Blake replied. "The sooner the better, for they are fighting near Santenay, and the place may be occupied by the enemy."

"Very well. I will lend you my car."

"That is kind of you, Wilson. I will accept the offer."

"Do you know the way?"

"I can find it, of course. Perhaps it would save time, though, if this young fellow were to—"

"He shall accompany you, Blake, as a guide. There will be no trouble about that. Take him along, by all means."

The car was in a shed in the vicinity of the mess-tent, and in the space of a few minutes Tinker and the detective were on their way to the distant village, there to get Colonel Chumleigh's signature to the will. Major Wilson waved his hand as they slid past him. They were together again, and they could talk as freely as they chose.

"My brave boy!" Blake said softly.

Their feelings were at first too deep for many words. For a time they sat in silence, Tinker at the wheel, while they traversed the rear of the vast battle-line; and when at length they had drifted into a flow of conversation they were careful to avoid one subject, each judging that it had better be let alone. For what was to be gained by discussing it? There was now every prospect that the detective's mission would soon be accomplished, and he would then have to return to London. But he could not take Tinker with him, much as he would need his services at home; nor, on the other hand, would the lad have been willing to go. He was enjoying a soldier's life, despite its perils and hardships. The only thing that worried him was the position he was in, the deception by which he had gained his heart's desire. And that was preying also on Sexton Blake's mind.

"It is a rather ugly affair," he reflected, "and I am afraid that one of these days there will be an exposure which may have serious consequences. It may come about through the real Rokeby, who is probably somewhere at the front in his assumed name. By holding my tongue I have been an accomplice in the double deception. I wish I had put a stop to it all when I learned the truth from young Rokeby."

They were fighting at various points along the Aisne. The booming of great guns floated from miles distant, and now and again the faint rattle of musketry was heard. Signs of the conflict grew more and more frequent as Blake and the lad drew near to their destination. There were German prisoners in the market-place of Santenay, and a battery of artillery was moving out to action. Yonder on the hills clouds of smoke were rolling, bluish-grey against the green and brown of the foliage. A staff-officer went galloping towards the front, and a motor-cyclist pedalled furiously to the rear.

"We'll soon be there," said Tinker. "Only another mile to go yet, guv'nor."

The car glided through the village, bore to the left, and stopped by a field-hospital that had been pitched at the side of the road, in a meadow. A man in khaki, bronzed and bearded, emerged from the big tent, and stared in surprise.

"My word, if it isn't Blake!" he exclaimed.

"Blake it is," replied the detective, with a smile. "How are you, doctor? I hope you haven't many patients."

"Not a great many at present. But I had no idea that you were in this part of the world. Have you come to pay me a friendly visit?"

"No, Crofton, I have come on business."

Surgeon-Major Crofton, of the Army Medical Corps, was not acquainted with Tinker, but he had known Blake for some years. He offered him a thin, flexible hand that was stained with drugs, and shook his head in answer to a question that the detective put to him.

"You are too late," he said. "Colonel Chumleigh has departed."

"He is not dead?" Sexton Blake cried in dismay.

"Not a bit of it," declared Dr. Crofton. "He isn't going to die. I extracted the bullet from his shoulder, the wound is as clean as a whistle."

"And he has been discharged already?"

"No, I have shipped him north. I'll tell you how it happened. The Germans gained some ground this morning, and threw half a dozen shells into Santenay. There was a probability of their advancing farther, and shelling my field-hospital. I received word that a train was at the station a couple of miles in the rear, under orders to leave for Rouen; so I sent as many of my patients as could be moved over to it, on ambulances, and Colonel Chumleigh was one of the number. It is just as well that I did so, for the enemy are still dangerously close. I hope they will be driven back. I have a score of wounded here who are in a critical condition, and cannot be shifted."

The surgeon-major paused, and glanced at the lad.

"By the way," he added, "I observe that you have with you one of the plucky chaps who rescued the colonel from the Germans, and brought him to me last evening. They told me a thrilling story."

"Yes, they had some lively adventures," Blake assented. "It was from Rokeby here that I got the information about the colonel. He knew that I had come from London to find him. I want him to attach his signature to an important document."

"I am sorry you have missed him."

"So am I, Crofton."

"What will you do about it?"

"I shall have to go after him, I suppose, if the train has left."

"It has, Blake. It started something like half an hour ago."

There was a short interval of silence. The detective was disappointed, but not much concerned. He could easily reach Rouen that night, and get Colonel Chumleigh's name to the paper. Tinker, in anticipation of a further journey, over-looked the car, and refilled the petrol-tank. From out of the tent floated the sickly smell of iodoform, and within could be seen motionless figures swathed in bandages, and nurses and attendants wearing the badge of the Red Cross. Cannon were roaring and rumbling in the distance. A battalion of infantry swung by, marching at a brisk pace.

"I won't detain you any longer," said Sexton Blake. "I shall follow the colonel."

"I don't believe you will have to go as far as Rouen," replied Dr. Crofton.

"Why not?"

"For a couple of reasons. In the first place, the train will travel at a fairly slow rate of speed, and it will make several stops. And the distance is considerably shorter by road then it is by the railway-line."

"I see your meaning, Crofton."

"It is simple enough. Wait a moment, and I will show you a—"

The surgeon-major broke off, and disappeared within the hospital. He came out with a small map in his hand, and when he had unfolded it he traced a line on it with a blue pencil.

"Here you are," he said. "This is the road that you will take. You can't miss it. And here is the village of Malmon, where your road crosses the railway-line. You should be able to get there ahead of the train, before nightfall, and have it stopped. You can have the map."

"Thanks very much," Blake replied. "I will do what you have suggested."

"But I must warn you that you may run into danger."

"How is that? Is there a likelihood of encountering any of the enemy?"

"Yes, patrols of Uhlans have been reported to the north. They are venturesome people, those chaps."

"Well, the risk won't deter me," said Sexton Blake. "I'll chance it. Good-bye, Crofton, and thanks again for your information. We'll be off now, Rokeby," he added, as he mounted to the seat and sat down by the lad. "You can drive as fast as you like."

"Right you are, sir," said Tinker. "It won't be my fault if we don't intercept the train."

And with that he sent the car rattling forward. It rolled on with increasing speed, and Dr. Crofton and the field-hospital soon faded from view. It was late in the afternoon and the sun was sinking in a cloudless sky. Blake took the map from his pocket, and studied it, comparing the highway with the railway-line.

"The major is quite right," he said. "It should be a simple matter for us to intercept the train."

"If we don't have an accident," replied the lad, "or run into a patrol of Germans."

The country was quiet and lonely. The red arm of Mars had swept over it, leaving blackened, shell-riddled ruins where had been farmhouses and cottages.

For a couple of hours the big car rushed steadily on, at a rate of speed that would have been dangerous had there been any traffic. A village was passed, but it was not the one that had been mentioned. There had been fighting here, and the inhabitants had all fled.

"We can't have much farther to go," said the detective, when he had glanced at the map again. "A mile or so, I should judge."

"Perhaps that is Malmon yonder," suggested Tinker, pointing to a cluster of roofs that had just appeared, rising from foliage, on the farther side of a wide valley. "Do you think so?"

"I am pretty sure that it is, my boy."

"Well, we'll be there in another five minutes."

The car had topped the brow of a hill, and was running down a long slope. It reached the bottom, and when it had glided on for half a mile, with deep woods to the right and left, the lad half-started from his seat, and almost lost his grip of the steering-wheel.

"Look, guv'nor, look!" he gasped.

"Uhlans, by Jove!" exclaimed Sexton Blake.

THE SECOND CHAPTER

The Bomb on the Line.

EIGHT OR NINE grey-cloaked figures, wearing spiked helmets, emerged from the leafy cover to one side, within a distance of twenty yards. Several of them were carrying a thick log, which they threw down directly across the road, and the others promptly levelled revolvers at the travellers, who had no alternative but to stop and surrender. Tinker checked the car close to the obstruction, and he and the detective got out, and were surrounded by the Germans, who were highly pleased by their capture. The officer in command, a brutal-looking fellow, could not speak or read English. He searched Blake, and took his papers from him, but returned them after a brief scrutiny.

"What are you doing here?" he demanded, in his own tongue.

"I am in France on private business, which has no connection with the war," Sexton Blake answered. "I am a civilian and non-combatant, and I claim the right to pass on unmolested."

"But you are with a soldier."

"Yes, he is my guide. I am on my way to Rouen, herr-captain."

"You are probably a spy, my fine fellow. I am inclined to doubt your tale."

"I am nothing of the sort. I have told you the truth, as my papers will prove."

"I can't read them," the officer replied. "I shall have to detain you on suspicion, and if you have lied to me you will be shot."

Blake's protests were of no avail. He was not much alarmed, as far as his safety was concerned; but it was exasperating to him to be caught at such a time, when he was so near to accomplishing the task that had brought him from England to the front. And he was terribly afraid, moreover, that the lad might encounter somebody who would identify him as one of the two daring soldiers who had destroyed the supply-train, and outwitted the Germans at the chateau. And the same fear was in Tinker's mind. He knew that if he were to be discovered summary death would be his fate.

"Yes, I shall have to detain you," the officer repeated. "Don't argue with me."

The day had now drawn to a close, and the rim of the sun was touching the horizon. The log was removed, and the motor-car was pushed in amongst the trees and thickets, presumably so that they should not attract the attention of any French or British soldiers who might come by. The Uhlans then penetrated the woods, taking their reluctant prisoners with them; and when they had gone for two or three hundred yards they reached an open glade where more troopers were waiting for them, to the number of a score.

Apparently they had been lurking here for a considerable time, and keeping a watch on the road. The horses were tethered in a group, cropping the short grass, and scattered about on the ground were the remains of a meal, and a dozen empty champagne bottles that had doubtless been looted from some dwelling.

The captives were greeted with jeers and laughter, to which they paid no heed. The detective fortunately had no fire-arms, else he might have been shot at once. He was searched again, but was not robbed of his papers. As he was gazing around him he was surprised to see a familiar face, and he was himself recognised at the same moment. A plump little Uhlan, with flaxen hair and moustache, stepped up to him. He clapped him on the arm, and grinned.

"Ah, it is Herr Blake!" he cried, "and the boy Tinker too!"

"So this is how we meet again, Mittleback!" the detective said quietly. "Do you like soldiering better than waiting?"

"Much better. I kill the English now, not feed them."

"But you miss the tips, don't you?"

Hans Mittleback, formerly a waiter at the Corona Restaurant in London, showed his teeth in appreciation of the joke.

"I want to get to Rouen on important business," Sexton Blake continued. "Can't you have me set free? You can vouch for it that I am not a spy."

"No, no, herr," the German replied, shaking his head. "I will do nothing. You gave me good tips at the Corona, and I bear you no ill-will; but it is well that you should remain a prisoner until the war is over. And the boy, too."

"Where will we be sent to?"

"I don't know. Our colonel will decide. We are on patrol duty, and we are waiting here for the arrival of a train. We have learnt that it is coming, and we have laid a trap for it."

"A trap?" exclaimed the detective. "What do you mean? From what direction is this train coming?"

"It is running from your lines to Rouen," Mittleback said. "The railway line is over yonder. We have put a bomb on it, and as the train is passing it will be blown up."

"By heavens, how dastardly!"

"All is fair in war, Herr Blake."

"Have you any idea how near the train is?"

"It should come very soon. We are listening for the explosion."

The colour had ebbed from Tinker's cheeks, and there was

a gleam of horror in Sexton Blake's eyes as he turned to the Uhlan officer.

"I have some knowledge of this train," he said hurriedly. "You are not aware, I imagine, that it is carrying a number of wounded soldiers to the hospital at Rouen?"

"It makes no difference," the officer replied, in a sneering tone. "They are enemies, and that is enough."

"But it will be cold-blooded murder if you kill them, and contrary to the rules of war. They are under the protection of the Red Cross."

"It is no affair of yours, herr. Be careful how you talk."

"By heavens, do you really intend to destroy those poor, wounded men? It will be infamous! You can't be so cruel! Have the explosive removed at once, I implore you in the name of humanity! There may be still an opportunity of—"

"Hold your tongue, you British dog!" the German interrupted, with an oath. "I won't warn you again. Another word, and I'll shoot you!"

The appeal had failed. The officer was not to be moved from his ruthless resolve. Blake's brain was in a whirl. What could he do? He was in a desperate mood, ready to face any risk, and it was the same with the lad. They exchanged meaning glances, and each read in the other's half-veiled eyes a message that was as plain as words could have been.

The chances were favourable for a dash for freedom. Their wrists had not been bound, nor were they closely hemmed in by the Uhlans. For a few seconds they hesitated, their features betraying no sign of their purpose; and then, with one accord, they sprang across the glade, and dived into the woods in the direction that had been indicated to them by Hans Mittleback.

"Do your best, my boy, and stick to me," urged Blake. "We must save the train if we can! There may yet be time. I pray Heaven there is!"

THE THIRD CHAPTER

The Will is Signed.

THE GERMANS WERE taken completely by surprise. It was so sudden, so unexpected, that not a man of them stirred until Blake and Tinker had vanished in the leafy cover. They then gave chase, led by the officer, some snatching their lances, while others drew their revolvers. They could not have used their horses to advantage, so on foot they scurried through the dense, tangled plantation, with lusty hue and cry that rang in the ears of the fugitives, and spurred them to strenuous efforts.

Pistol-shots, fired blindly, cut twigs from the boughs over their heads. They ran as fast as they could, and when they had gone for half a mile the clamour was fading behind them. And soon it had ceased entirely. They were shrouded in silence.

"We've given them the slip," panted the lad. "They must have abandoned the pursuit."

"No; don't deceive yourself," Sexton Blake replied. "They have turned back to get their horses, and they will ride round by the road."

"It may be a considerable distance, guv'nor."

"It is not a question of that, my boy. I think we shall reach the line before we can be interrupted. But we may be too late to save the train."

For another half-mile they traversed the sombre woods, now and again slackening speed to regain their breath. It was rough going. They floundered amongst thickets and boulders, and caught their feet in trailing vines. At length streaks of pale light shone ahead of them out of the purple shadow, and shortly afterwards they emerged from the cover, and stopped. They were on the verge of a low, grassy embankment, and at the bottom of it was the railway line, in a shallow cutting. In both directions it was visible, as straight as an arrow for some hundreds of yards. The sun had just dipped beneath the horizon, there was a golden glow in the sky. All was quiet.

"I don't hear anything of the train," said Tinker.

"No, thank Heaven," Blake replied. "It can't be very close."

"And now to find the explosive. I wonder where it is?"

"It is somewhere about here, I should judge. We mustn't waste a moment, my boy."

"In which direction shall we look?" asked the lad, as they darted down the embankment. "That is the question."

"We will separate," said Blake. "You go one way, and I'll go the other. That will be better than to—" He paused, as a shrill, shuddering whistle was heard to the left. "The train!" he added sharply. "It is approaching! Come, come, be quick!"

Was the instrument of death to the left or to the right? Would there be time to discover and remove it, or would the wounded soldiers meet with a terrible disaster? It may be imagined what harrowing suspense Tinker and the detective felt, what ghastly visions filled their minds as they took to their heels and ran in the direction from which the whistle had floated to their ears. They had forgotten the Uhlans. With increasing anxiety they hastened along the line, scanning the metals in quest of the bomb, while nearer and nearer, louder and louder, came the muffled grinding of wheels. They were still searching, straining their eyes ahead, when the engine appeared in view around a curve that was at a distance of a quarter of a mile.

"There it is!" exclaimed the lad.

"We must stop it if we can," declared Blake. "Let us try to attract the driver's attention."

They dashed on, frantically waving their caps, and shouting in their excitement, though their voices could not be heard. The train continued to approach rapidly, until it was within a hundred yards of them, and close to a road that crossed the cutting on a level with it.

"The driver knows that there is something wrong," cried Tinker. "He is pulling the throttle. It is all right."

"Yes, thank Heaven!" replied Blake. "The disaster will be averted. The bomb must have been placed in the other direction, beyond the point where we started to—"

The sentence was stifled on his lips by a tremendous explosion. There was a lurid blaze, and a sulphurous cloud shot up, hurling fragments of metal high in the air. The engine, its wheels and stack blown off, was lifted from the metals and thrown on its side, followed by the tender. The foremost carriage also turned over, but the rest, after a succession of violent jolts, remained on the line.

"Too late!" gasped the detective, as the smoke lifted and revealed the tragic scene. "Too late, my boy!"

"What a shame!" Tinker said hoarsely. "And just when we were sure it wouldn't happen!"

Fortunately, however, the bloodthirsty intentions of the Germans had fallen far short of what they had anticipated. The bomb may have been defective, for one thing, and probably its effects had been lessened by the fact that the brakes had been applied before the explosion occurred. At all events, no great harm had been done. The driver and stoker had lost their lives, having been crushed under the engine. But the occupants of the capsized carriage, and of the others as well, escaped with a severe shaking.

The disaster had taken place just where the road crossed the line. Sexton Blake and the lad hurried forward, and their anxiety was relieved soon after they had reached the spot, though they could not as yet be certain that there had not been more than the two deaths. They promptly lent assistance, working with those who had flocked from the train, doing their share with civilian passengers, and Red Cross nurses, and a young surgeon who had been in charge of the patients. There was a busy scene for a time and groans were heard, and piteous appeals for help, as the wounded soldiers were lifted tenderly from the overturned carriage and made as comfortable as possible.

"It might have been much worse," said Sexton Blake. "These poor fellows have got off lightly. But I am afraid the shock will be bad for their wounds."

"If only Colonel Chumleigh has not been hurt!" replied the lad. "He must be here somewhere, for I have looked in the other carriages."

"He is in this one, then."

"I will know him as soon I see him, guv'nor."

"So shall I, my boy. I was introduced to him at his club several years ago. He may not remember me, however."

He was the last to be brought out. There was no mistaking the colonel, with his handsome features and grey moustache. He was conscious, and very pale, suffering from the bullet-wound in his shoulder. But the bandages had not slipped from it, nor had he sustained any other injuries. Two nurses drew him through the door of one of the compartments, and put him in the care of Blake and the lad, who helped him to the side of the line, and seated him there on the grass. The detective got some brandy for him from the surgeon, and the stimulant eased his pain and steadied his shaken nerves. His face brightened, and he smiled as he recognised the young soldier.

"Ah, so we have met again!" he said. "You are one of the brave fellows who rescued me from the Germans at the chateau, and brought me to the field-hospital at Santenay. And surely I know you, too," he added, glancing at the lad's companion. "Yes, I recall you now. You are Sexton Blake. We met at my club."

"That is quite right," Blake assented. "And I have been searching for you, curiously enough. I came from London purposely to find you."

"To find me?" Colonel Chumleigh exclaimed. "How is that?"

"At the instigation of your wife, and on behalf of your child."

"I don't understand, Mr. Blake."

"The explanation is simple. You went to the front, leaving with your solicitor, unsigned, the recent will in favour of your infant son. And you also left in his possession the previous will, by which your brother would succeed to a large part of your estate. The solicitor had not the power to destroy it, so you can account for your wife's anxiety when she learned what the situation was. She was naturally afraid that her child might be deprived of its inheritance."

"I see," said the colonel. "I have been very careless. It was stupid of me to leave matters in such a state. My wife has more business sense than I have, by far. I am heartily glad that my wife sent you to seek for me."

"It was through the War Office," Blake replied. "They gave me the necessary permission, and I reached the front on the very day when you were captured by the Germans."

"You have brought the will with you, I suppose?"

"Yes; I have it in my pocket. I got it from your solicitor."

"Then I will sign it at once. The sooner the better, for my wound is rather serious, and there is no telling what will happen."

"You will be wise not to delay, sir, for there is a patrol of the enemy in the neighbourhood. We were captured by them, and we made our escape, after learning that they had planned to wreck the train by putting a bomb on the line."

The will was produced, and a fountain-pen was handed to Colonel Chumleigh. He rested the document on his knee, and when he had attached his signature to it Sexton Blake and the lad wrote their names as witnesses. The inheritance had been secured for the child, whatever might betide. The mission that had brought the detective from England had been accomplished at last, and now, just as the signed will had been returned to him, a sound of clattering hoofs swelled on the air.

"My word, look!" cried Tinker. "This is bad for us!"

"Very bad, I am afraid," said Blake.

A shadow crept into his eyes as he spoke. The patrol of Uhlans were approaching along the road, riding at a gallop straight towards the wrecked train, their helmets and lances glittering in the sunset glow that still lingered.

THE FOURTH CHAPTER

Tinker Loses his Uniform.

GENERAL ALARM WAS caused by the discovery. It was a threatening and complicated situation. There were no weapons amongst the wounded soldiers, nor had the nurses or the civilians any arms. They were not supposed to have any, under the circumstances; yet, despite the fact that the Red Cross flag was conspicuously shown on the carriages of the train, they had every reason to fear that brutal acts would be committed by these dreaded troopers, who bore a worse reputation than any branch of the Kaiser's army.

As for Sexton Blake and the lad, their position was more than critical, and they knew it. As they had escaped from the enemy, and attempted to frustrate their bloodthirsty designs, they could not doubt that death would be their fate if they should be recaptured. They glanced at each other, their faces betraying the apprehensions that they felt.

"It will go hard with us," said Tinker, "if they find us here."

"You had better both take to flight, since you have incurred the anger of the Germans," urged Colonel Chumleigh. "It is your duty to do so, Mr. Blake. You owe it to me. Remember that you have my will, and that it is of the greatest importance. If you were to be robbed of it I might never have an opportunity of signing another one."

This was a logical argument, and it put the detective in a quandary. During the brief conversation the Uhlans had been drawing nearer, and when they had got to within less than three hundred yards, and Sexton Blake was still trying to make up his mind what to do, a most unexpected and welcome diversion occurred. Out from the woods, by a cross-roads, galloped a little column of British Lancers. And in a trice they had wheeled half round, and were charging at the enemy, who were slightly inferior to them in numbers.

"Hurrah!" exclaimed Tinker. "By Jove, that's done it!"

It was, indeed, a most fortunate interposition. In the presence of all of the passengers, who watched eagerly, there was a short and desperate fight. For a few moments Lancers and Uhlans were mixed together in a seething, shouting mass, while hoofs clashed, and lance was shivered against lance, and pistol-shots rang in rapid succession. Saddles were emptied, and riderless steeds dashed to and fro.

"They're off!" cried Blake. "There they go!"

"Yes, our gallant fellows have the best of it," declared the colonel. "That was fine work."

The struggle was at an end. The enemy were in flight, retreating as they had come, and leaving a third of their number dead on the ground. The Lancers had also suffered losses, but not nearly so many. The greater part of them gave chase to the panic-stricken Uhlans, and the remainder, to the number of half a dozen, spurred in the opposite direction. They rode on to the railway-line, and dismounted from their horses by the train. They were greeted with hearty cheers, and when the applause had died away one of the troopers stepped towards Tinker, and said loudly:

"Hallo, Rokeby! I didn't know you had been wounded."

"I'm not," the lad replied, supposing that the speaker knew him.

"I didn't mean you," was the answer. "I was talking to somebody else."

Tinker looked in surprise at the Lancer, and then, as he turned round, the situation flashed upon him. Close behind him, with his arm in a sling, stood the real Jack Rokeby. He had been amongst the wounded on the train, and it was to him that the words had been addressed by an acquaintance. That he had not been observed by Blake or his young assistant was because he had been careful to avoid them. The youths flushed, and tried in vain to hide their confusion.

"Yes, old chap, the game is up," Jack Rokeby assented. "We'll have to face the music."

"I don't think I have made a mistake," said the Lancer. "You chaps needn't look so queer, even if you are both named Rokeby. What's the matter with you?"

Double exposure was inevitable, and the detective, who, to some extent, had a guilty conscience, dreaded it more than did the culprits.

There was a puzzled expression on Colonel Chumleigh's features. He could see that there was something wrong, and his interest and curiosity had been roused.

"What does it all mean, Mr. Blake?" he said. "I believe you can tell me. I have known this plucky soldier as Private Rokeby, of the Transport Service? Is not that his name?"

"No, it is not," Blake replied. "He is my boy Tinker."

"Your boy?"

"Yes, that's right. The young rascal got into the army by a daring stratagem, and the other youth, with whom I am acquainted, has also been masquerading under a false name."

"They have both been guilty of deception? This is a serious business."

"I will admit that it is, colonel. But there is something to be said in favour of each of them."

A ray of light had dawned on the detective's perplexity. Being aware that Colonel Chumleigh had a great deal of influence, and that he was a personal friend of the commander-in-chief, he felt that he might be able to persuade him to straighten out the tangle in such a way that there would not be any unpleasant consequences or public exposure. So he briefly told the whole story, making clear the circumstances under which Tinker had got into the army and Jack Rokeby had enlisted in a false name.

"I should regard it as a great favour," he concluded, "if you would use your efforts on behalf of these young soldiers."

The narrative had stirred the colonel's sympathies. He tried to assume a stern expression, but he could not. There was a kindly look in his eyes, and a smile on his lips.

"You are right," he said. "There are mitigating facts."

"I hoped you would think so," Sexton Blake replied.

"Will you accept my judgement?"

"Yes, with pleasure."

"Very well. There will be no difficulty. When the real Rokeby has recovered I will see that he goes into the Transport Corps, where he belongs in the place of this other youth who has stolen his name. As for your boy, I authorise you to take him home and keep him there. He is too young, and too reckless, to throw his life away out here at the front."

"But—but I don't want to—" Tinker began to protest.

"There is no but about it," Blake cut in. "You are going to shed your uniform, and come home with me."

He spoke in a cold, curt tone, and the lad had to submit, knowing that appeal would be futile.

A TELEGRAPH MESSAGE sent from the village of Malmon brought another train that night, and the passengers of the wrecked train were carried on to Rouen, where the wounded soldiers were transferred to a hospital. Several days later, when Colonel Chumleigh was quite out of danger, Sexton Blake and Tinker returned to London; and the detective took the first opportunity of calling on Mrs. Chumleigh, and relieving her anxiety by giving her the signed will.

Blake was very glad to have the lad at home again, but Tinker, though he felt that he had got out of an ugly scrape more lightly than he deserved, would have preferred to be back in the thick of the fighting, amidst the hissing bullets and the bursting shells.

THE END

Notes

8. Eugène François Vidocq, a former French criminal who became the founder of the Sûreté Nationale and the head of the first known private detective agency. He is generally regarded as the world's first private detective.

9. "Kilkenny cat" is a now little-used reference to anyone who fights with tenacious ferocity. The origins of the term are unclear.

BAKER STREET, LONDON

Outside, the storm was passing and occasional glimmers of sunlight came and went, making the droplets on the window glint like diamonds.

Sexton Blake had finished reading and was gazing through the mesh of the fireguard at the flames behind it, seemingly lost in a plethora of memories. I took the opportunity to scrutinise his face and hands and was intrigued by their lack of scars. Recently, I'd read five stories in a row in which he'd been shot in the shoulder. No normal human being could take that amount of punishment and still have full use of his arms. So either the accounts were highly fictionalised or Sexton Blake was not a normal human being. His very presence in the chair opposite me made the latter the most probable truth.

I quietly repeated the question I'd asked earlier. "To what were you referring? What was unleashed by the First World War?"

He drew in a sharp breath, adjusted his posture, clicked open his silver case, and took another cigarette from it.

Yes, there was that, too: a man who'd smoked his way through countless physically gruelling adventures yet who appeared to function perfectly well without assistance from an oxygen tank.

I thought, *One day, Sexton Blake, I shall have the truth of you.*

He lit his cigarette, drew on it, expelled a cloud, and said, "From out of the Great War came the master crooks: Zenith the Albino, Waldo the Wonder Man, Count Ivor Carlac, Professor Kew, the Council of Eleven, many others."

Suddenly, unexpectedly, he stood.

I scrambled to my feet.

He handed me the binder.

"But of them," he said. "We shall speak tomorrow."

Abruptly, the first interview had ended.

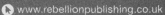

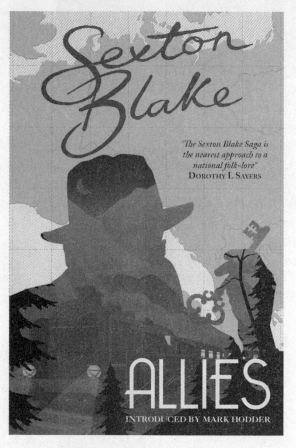
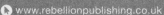